Indian Lake In November

Indian Lake In November

Ted J. McGoron

Writers Club Press
San Jose New York Lincoln Shanghai

Indian Lake In November

All Rights Reserved © 2001 by Ted J. McGoron

No part of this book may be reproduced or transmitted in any form or by any means, graphic, electronic, or mechanical, including photocopying, recording, taping, or by any information storage retrieval system, without the permission in writing from the publisher.

Writers Club Press
an imprint of iUniverse, Inc.

For information address:
iUniverse, Inc.
5220 S. 16th St., Suite 200
Lincoln, NE 68512
www.iuniverse.com

ISBN: 0-595-19525-3

Printed in the United States of America

This book is dedicated to the McGorons and all the other descendants of Gor, the great Celtic warrior, both those in Ireland and those elsewhere. Most of them I have never known and will never know. The name has evolved in so many ways that it would be almost impossible to trace them all. It is a shame for they must have so many lovely tales to tell. May they all be blessed.

Acknowledgements

I would like to acknowledge the help I got from my wife Mary and Several of my children, Katherine "Casey" Nastold, Paula "Dixie" Hix, and Francis Xavier McGoron, in editing this composition. Not only did they unearth some of those "little" mistakes in grammar and spelling that so often elude an author, but they even called to my attention several places where something could be said better. I appreciate their help more than they know.

The portrait of the author on the back cover is a colored pencil drawing by his wife, Mary Catherine Westerkamp McGoron.

Chronology

THE FAMILIES

The children of Pat (1870-1938) & Mary (1878-1965) O'Maury
Aloysius (1900)
John (1903)
Eileen (1904)

The children of Max(1865-1920) & Heidi (1875-1935) Hoect
Alex (1900)
Wendell (1902)
Kate (1904)
Fred (1905)
Paul (1907)

**John O'Maury & Kate Hoect married in 1924
These Are Their Children And Grandchildren**

Jack (1929) married Marilyn (1930) in 1956

Norman (1930) ordained in 1956

Aloysius (1932) married Pam (1934) in 1962
Dennis (1964)
Robert (1965)
Clint (1966)

Polly(1937) married John Comstock (1936) in 1957
Joan (1962)

Elleen (1935) married Dan Frankl (1933) in 1956
Libby (1957) married George Ryan (1953) in 1979
Ginny (1981)
Pat (1982)

Danny (1959) married Helen in (1960)
Millie (1961) married Harry "Whitie" Scott (1961) in 1983

Bill (1934) married Jill (1930) in 1952
Billy (1953) married Ann (1951) in 1975
Billy (1976)
Sandy (1978)
Fritz (1980)

Fritz (1934) & Ginny (1931)
Tammy (1953)

Carrie (1939) professed in 1959

Introduction

Indian Lake is real, a somewhat wide but very shallow man-made body of water in West Central Ohio. Russells Point is real too, a little town that snuggles securely next to the lake. Nevertheless the people who live in or around Russels Point today will be surprised to learn about the people who lived there before them and the things that went on there, at least those about which (and about whom) they will in fact never hear unless someday they read this book.

Many of the other places referred to in the book, in addition to Russells Point, are also real, but not many of the things that happen in the book are. And, although this book is not about places but about people, of the characters directly involved in the story none of them is real either.

Now this is not to say, of course, that I have never met any people anything like the characters in this book, only that, except for a very few, the characters who walk back and forth across its pages cannot be directly identified by name anywhere on God's real earth. On the other hand though, they are usually conglomerations of several people whom I have indeed actually at least met.

Most writers, one way or another, will write about things actually done by people they have really known or known of, even though the characters in their works whom they "enlist" to perform those actions are not necessarily real individuals, unless, of course, the composition the author is producing is historical. But this book is not meant to be a historical work.

John for instance is not someone I have ever met, nor someone I ever heard about. In fact although I probably possess some of his personal characteristics, both good and bad, I don't think he is someone I would have the determination or the charity to be very much like.

And Patrick is a legitimate representative of a particular class of men, but of a very different one than John. Product of a time and social atmosphere when the mores of society were defined all in blacks and whites, it was easier for him to recognize the standards he felt he should meet than it was for John, although in fairness we must admit it may have been in some ways more difficult for Patrick to adopt those standards as his own because he was allowed such little leeway by other members of the world in which he lived.

I must admit I sometimes envy Patrick because in his society it was so much easier for everyone to know specifically what one should do and what one should not do. The problem was usually in finding the will to do that which one decided was moral. Alas, although I sound as though I really knew him, Patrick too exists only in the pages of my book.

When I was young men such as Patrick did not seem as rare as they do now and I met more than a few, men who had learned from their elders what and how they would be expected to contribute to the world and what, as well, they might reasonably expect to receive from the world in return. And when they tried very hard to do what they understood was their duty, only to realize that the rules of the game of life which seemed so obvious to them did not somehow seem so apparent to everyone else with whom they interacted, they often became frustrated. However, like Job, they did not resort to blaming their ill fortunes on God and from then on proceeding to ignore the rules in retaliation. Call it stubbornness if you will, or naivete if you prefer, they generally continued without swerving from that path which they perceived would require the least amount of explanation at such time when they knew they would be asked by the Creator to justify their actions. Men such as them I admired (and admire) very much. And I regret that I had not the will or the strength to emulate them very faithfully.

One final point; it would surprise me if no one has observed by now that in the preceding paragraphs in which I have described some characteristics of the champions of my work I use only masculine pronouns, and further that no one has objected to this on the grounds of chauvinism. To those who do I insist by way of explanation that this should not be accepted as proof that I do not think women hold to the same ideals I have attributed to the men I mention, for they do, sometimes to a greater extent than the males actually. It is only that the roles in life of most of the stalwart women of my experience have been identified by them as positions supportive of someone else, rather than leading. The fact that, knowing full well they were extremely capable of leading, they were still willing to accept lesser positions because they understood it is what was expected of them, makes them all the more heroic in my mind. I have known many heroic women in my own life who, with the men, died believing they had done nothing at all more than what they perceived as having been assigned to them as their proper roles by a just God. What this book provides is a window through which we may watch some of them as they absorb the cuts and bruises of life with proper acknowledgement on their part of those cuts and bruises, but without becoming obsessed. It is always the good things which the Lord provides that they seem to remember the longest.

If the characters in this book are modeled from some of the beautiful men and women it has been my privilege to meet, to respect, and to love and learn from, I pray that I have had the inspiration, and blind fortune, to do the same thing for myself.

WHERE THEY CAME FROM

(The Mah of Oor legend)

At night, covered by a heavy animal skin, Oor would lie near the back of the little ship in the moonlight that broke through the rigging onto the deck. Everyone else except those who stood watch would be asleep, but sleep was something he could not risk. He was a chieftain of his small tribe and master of the tiny ship, but he was well aware that although the members of his crew all feared him when he was on his guard, and had solemnly pledged their allegiance, there were those who would not shed a tear if someone slew him and threw him overboard, because then they could openly contend with each other to take his place.

He surveyed the deck before him through half-closed eyelids. By his side was his giant sword which, it was said, could cut through a tree his two hands could not fit round. Within his easy reach was the circular shield which bore the elephant sign he had adopted. It was not a picture of an elephant but merely a symbol. Actually he knew no one who was able to draw a picture of an elephant nor anyone who had even seen one. But he had talked to someone who had talked to someone else who said he had seen one and, not knowing what was truth and what was myth when he heard a description of the animal, Oor had decided the elephant was the only creature he would want to use to symbolize himself both in peace and in war.

He had been told that every other beast feared the adult male elephant, that even the lion would slink away from his presence and the fierce tiger always gave wide berth to the elephant, who was able to uproot trees and dislodge gigantic rocks with his trunk and his tusks.

And the organ he used in mating was so large that it caused the females to trumpet in pain. And yet they sometimes traveled miles to seek him out because they longed for his attention.

Mah, son of Oor, rose and to bring himself awake poured on his head water dipped up from the ocean in a wooden pot attached to a rope. He went and reported to his father and, standing together, they urinated over the railing in the rear of the deck. Then they went to the front of the ship.

As always the men who had stood watch throughout the night were relieved and a new watch took their places. Everyone was given a ration of dried meat, bread, and water and while they ate the helmsman who was going off duty reported to Oor who then issued the orders for the next watch. After that Oor felt safe enough to sleep for a few hours with Mah standing nearby.

Seventeen year old Mah was nearly ready to take Oor's place as chieftain. With long flaxen hair and dark brooding eyes he was an inch taller and nearly as strong as his father. His shoulders were wide and his arms and legs thick as tree branches. But son and father knew that the young man could not take Oor's place without first fighting with some of the others. It mattered not whether Oor was killed or that he merely stepped down. Mah would be forced to prove himself by fighting one or more challengers. And he would have to kill or be killed. Mah looked forward to this but did not want it to happen for a long time because he loved his father and did not want anyone to take his place. But he dreamed.

Sometimes at night, when they sailed before the wind, he would stand at the bow of the ship and listen to the water beat against its keel below. Looking at the moon he would remind himself that the god who watched over all of them had come from that moon. It was, he believed, that very same all-powerful god who had told them Oor should guide this band and Mah would never consider doing anything to thwart the will of the god even if he didn't love his father. But at times, just the same, he could imagine himself in charge, and it felt good. He would carry the biggest sword. He would have the biggest piece of meat when they made a kill. And if they captured women he it would be who would get the healthiest looking one. It was a pleasure to contemplate.

They had been traveling for a long time. They and others had decided in council that their Viking land of rocky coastal areas and fjords was not capable of sustaining them, so they had begun building ships capable of carrying raiding parties to other lands in search of booty and, in some cases, areas which could be settled.

Oor had heard some of the returning warriors talk of places from which they had taken goods of all kinds, places with strange names such as Innismurray and Inisbofin, and he and some of the men from his tribe had decided to go back there themselves and see what they could find. If they found only goods they could take home they would do that. If they found hospitable land they would come back with their families and settle it. They were adventurers. But they were also fighting men, afraid of no one on the earth.

On the morning that the lookout reported seeing land the crew spent hours looking for a suitable place to go ashore. They intended to send a small band to look for fresh water and horses, and anything else worth taking. When the group set off Oor stayed behind but allowed Mah to go with them. The landing party took a small boat and rowed as close as possible to the stony beach and then waded the rest of the way, pulling the boat with them. They dragged it into the trees and then separated into two groups to scout the area and report back.

Mah and the three men who went with him walked several miles before they found anything worth their attention. It was a fence as tall as a man, made of logs and forming a large enclosure in a clearing. When they crept closer and peered through the logs they could see a trio of rude huts built of branches and mud. They saw no humans but at one end of the enclosure they saw two horses grazing on sparse vegetation.

Because of his father Mah was considered by the others as being in command, but Mah asked for everyone's opinion before making the decision to walk to the other side of the log fence, where there appeared to be a gate, and go inside and steal the horses. This they did as quietly as they could. The crude gate was made of more logs tied in place with vines. Mah severed the vines easily with Oor's sword which his father had allowed him to take with him as a sign of Mah's authority. When the vines parted and the logs fell away two of the men ran quickly into the enclosure and jumped up onto the backs of the horses. The logs had made a loud sound as they fell and suddenly a man ran from one of the huts to see what had happened, but he was unarmed. As soon as he saw that someone was stealing the horses he turned around and started back to the hut, probably for a weapon. But Mah overtook him in a few steps and, with his father's sword, cut off the man's head.

The two raiders on horseback rode the animals outside the enclosure and waited while Mah and the other man on foot made a quick survey of the primitive buildings.

As Mah entered one of them he was alarmed by the sound of a swift movement. He jumped quickly back into the doorway he had just come through and a sword blade just missed the side of his face and struck the door frame. Before his attacker could recover Mah threw his body against the blade, wrapped one arm around the other's shoulders and with the other arm raised his father's sword over his head. But then he stopped. The person in his arm was a woman. Mah could feel her breasts against his chest as he pressed her close to prevent her from freeing her sword.

She was nearly as tall as Mah and she looked directly into his face with hate filled eyes. She pulled one arm free and knocked his helmet from his head and clutched his hair, pulling it back as far as she could. Mah dropped his sword and squeezed her hand until she was forced to let go of his hair. He seized her sword, yanked it from between them, and threw it against the wall behind her. Then he picked her up and put her across his shoulder and went outside stooping on the way to pick up his helmet and put it back on his head.

The woman tried mightily to dislodge herself but Mah was much too strong. He took her out of the enclosure the same way they had come in.

He dropped her to the ground near where he and his companions had come through the fence, rolled her over on her stomach and put his foot on her back to hold her down. Then he took a piece of the vine which had held the gate of logs in place and tied her hands behind her. He put her back on his shoulder and held her with one hand, carrying the great sword of his father in the other hand, and ran off to follow the other three who had already disappeared into the trees.

The two men who were mounted had gone nearly half the way back to the water when they came upon a party of more than a half dozen men on foot apparently returning to the enclosure from which Mah's raiding party had taken the horses. Both groups saw each other at about the same time and the returning party, recognizing their horses, realized what had happened. With a great cry they started to run in pursuit of the mounted raiders. The raider who had been running along behind caught up with the men on horseback and leaped up behind one of them. Because they were outnumbered they began to run the horses toward the ocean. Mah was far enough behind his companions that the local men did not see him as they ran off in pursuit of their horses. He pulled the woman from his shoulder and put his hand over her mouth to keep her from calling out. Then he followed at a distance waiting for an opportunity to join his comrades. It never came.

The other four men from the ship were waiting by their boat as the three on horseback approached. They jumped in when they saw the others coming near and pulled out a few yards from land. As soon as they got near the shore the men on the horses jumped off, chased the horses away, and swiftly waded out to the waiting boat.

Most of the pursuing hunters went off to catch their horses while a few quickly shot some arrows toward the men in the boat, now rowing swiftly toward the ship. The arrows were shot too quickly and aimed too poorly to hit anything and fell harmlessly into the water. Soon the raiding party was on board the ship which was making ready to put out farther to sea. Oor noticed that Mah was not with them but, not knowing how many natives were on the shore nor how they were equipped, he could not wait. The story the returning members of the raiding party told led him to believe that his son was dead. He would not allow himself to mourn for his son until the ship was safely far away from the shore though he resolved to kill all of the men who had left Mah to die. That could wait however until they had returned to their homeland.

Mah did not know he would never see his father again but he realized that now he was all alone. He went farther inland as swiftly as he could until he could safely allow his captive to call out if she wanted to. He put her down but she did not do anything except look at him sullenly. Surely she must have been fearful for her life but she hardly showed it. Actually as she examined the sturdy warrior closely her eyes seemed to show some admiration even though it was still mixed with hate.

Mah was hungry. It was the middle of the afternoon and he had not eaten since early in the morning. Even more than that he was thirsty. He and the others had carried bags of water with them but they had drunk all of it before they had found the log enclosure.

Mah asked the woman where they could find food and water but she seemed not to understand his words at all. Finally he resorted to sign language by pointing to his mouth and making chewing and swallowing motions. The woman seemed to understand him this time but remained silent with a sneering look on her face. It was apparent that she did not intend to help her captor in any way. Mah then threw her to the ground on her back and put one foot on her stomach. With one hand he raised the great sword, now his own, as though he was about to cut off her head. She must have been sure he meant to follow through because she shouted something and began making eating motions of her own. Mah rolled her over and pulled her up on her feet by her hair. He gave her a slight shove to indicate that he expected her to lead him but he held onto her hands, still bound behind her back. Slowly she started off.

After a very short time she stopped and when he stopped also she turned around and looked at him as though she was about to say something. He watched as she pointed first to her stomach and then in the direction of her groin. He soon realized that she wanted to relieve herself. He decided that the faint path which she apparently followed was used often enough that they should avoid defiling it. He took her by the shoulder and steered her into the brush off to the side where he stuck his sword into the ground. Then he raised the bottom of the woman's tunic above her waist in front of her and held it so she could squat backward slightly against a tree and urinate on the ground. When she was finished he turned his back toward her but, continuing to hold her hands with one of his hands behind him, he also urinated. When he was finished he picked up his sword and pushed her back toward the path. Then he continued following her. Eventually they came to a place where a shallow stream ran swiftly over gravel. He helped her to kneel and put his hand under her collar so that she could drink from the stream without falling into the water. When she was finished he had her sit on the ground and he drank while holding onto her ankle. When he was finished he filled the water bag made of skin which he still carried fastened to his belt. Then he helped her up.

Soon they came upon a grove of trees which bore ripe fruit. Mah untied the woman's hands and retied them around one of the trees. He climbed the one which had fruit at the lowest level and was able to knock some of it to the ground. Then he untied one of her hands and they both ate.

When they were finished eating Mah pulled the side of her tunic up and through her belt to form a sort of pouch so that he could put several more pieces of the fruit into the fold to carry with them.

They went for many miles. Mah knew that somewhere there must have been more people from the settlement they had raided because there were no other women either in the enclosure or with the hunting party. Surely, he reasoned, there must have been more females off somewhere and once the entire group was back together some of them would set out after Mah to recover the woman he had taken. He wanted to be as far from them then as possible.

Before it started to get dark he noticed the woman seemed to be tiring and he began looking for someplace they could stop for the night. Having no idea what kind of wild animals they might encounter he would like to have found a cave but the kind of landscape he saw did not look like the kind of terrain likely to provide many caves. Finally he settled for a little knoll which was concave on one side. It would provide them with some shelter from the elements and allow him to protect his back to a degree.

Mah and the woman each ate another piece of fruit and by the time they were finished it had become quite dark. He made her sit on the ground and put her legs around a sapling, tying her ankles on the other side so that it would have been difficult for her to free herself. Then he lay down close by against the side of the knoll and went to sleep. He was exhausted.

When he woke several hours had passed. The temperature had dropped considerably and he was uncomfortably cool. He got up to check on the woman and make sure she was still tied. She was wide awake and when he bent down to feel her bounds he noticed that she was shivering and, so it sounded, sobbing in the dark. Reminding himself that she had done nothing to him except in retaliation for having been taken prisoner he began to feel sorry for her. He had never intended for her to be hurt but he didn't want to release her either because any information he hoped to get about where he was and where he could find food he knew would have to come from her. Besides she was the only living person with whom he had any association. She may not have been a friend in any sense of the word, but there was no other person in that strange land whom he could even recognize. He made what he knew was possibly a dangerous decision. He untied her ankles and carried her nearer to the knoll. Then he removed his outer garment, which was made of fur. Underneath it he wore a short tunic of linen. He lay down next to her and pulled her close to him and then spread his fur garment over the two of them. In a little while he could feel that she had stopped trembling and soon was asleep. Then he too drifted off. When he awoke again her head was on his shoulder and one arm was flung over his chest. He did not move but let her sleep a while longer.

Eventually she opened her eyes but at first did not move. Then she looked up and in the morning light could see that he also was awake. Slowly she sat up and stretched. He watched her warily but she did not seem eager to run away. Nevertheless he was afraid to relax. Finally she said, "Marah", and pointed to herself.

He pointed to his chest and said, "Mah. Mah of Oor."

She answered, "Mah of Oor?" at which he nodded his head in approval.

She seemed happy to know his name. She said it, "Mah of Oor," several times. Then she pointed to her mouth and pointed toward the trees. Assuming that she wanted to show him where they could find something to eat he nodded his head again. They both stood and he put his fur cloak back on. She held her hands in front of her so he could tie them but he shook his head, wondering if he was making a mistake but wanting to make friends with her. He knew in order to do that he would have to learn to trust her.

She led him a little way along the footpath again and then left it and walked through the brush. Soon they came to the stream again but now it was a bit deeper and ran more slowly. She went very close to the edge and by pointing indicated that he should look. He did and he was able to see many large fish swimming about in the clear water.

It was tantalizing to see them swimming so close. He was sure they would be good to eat but he had no idea how he could catch them. Marah did though. First she gathered some grass and then she had him take off all his clothes. She took his inner tunic and let him put the outer garment back on. Then she used the grass to close off the arms and neck of the tunic. She found two short sticks with which to hold the bottom open and put the whole thing into the water several feet from the edge of the pool, facing into the slight current. Then they sat down in the weeds to wait. Twice fish swam into the trap but both times when she tried to pull it out the fish escaped. After the second time he laughed at her. But she seemed hurt and he stopped laughing immediately. The third time she stood very still in the water behind the trap and when she saw a fish swim into it she was able to pull it out with the fish still flopping around inside. She put it on the shore and tried again. After little more than an hour they had three fish. With his sword Mah cut a branch from a small bush and stuck it through their gills so they could be kept in the water while he and Marah built a fire using a piece of flint she carried in a little pouch around her neck. Then they cooked the fish and ate them.

For several weeks they continued to eat fruit and fish and Mah learned to communicate with Marah, mostly in her tongue. The weather was getting colder and Mah knew they would have to find someplace to stay for the winter.

It was nearly a month before Marah was able to persuade Mah that they should go back to where her people lived. She told him she could convince the leaders in her tribe to let the two of them stay there because they needed a warrior like Mah to help them defend themselves. Mah was still not sure he could trust her but he had come to be somewhat fond of her and he decided to take the risk.

It took several days for them to get back to the clearing and the log enclosure from which Mah had kidnapped Marah. When they got close she had him wait while she went on by herself to talk to the elders of the little village. Mah did not want to let her go but he could think of no other way to make sure he could safely enter the enclosure. And he wanted to be able to trust the woman for whom he had developed much affection. After she left he moved away from where she had last seen him and climbed into a tree so that he could watch her when she came back without being seen himself.

Mah waited a long time very nearly deciding to jump to the ground and retreat in safety. But eventually the woman returned. She was not alone but Mah noted she had only one person with her. He watched them quietly as they returned to the place where Mah and Marah had parted. She looked around and seemed disappointed but not surprised that Mah was not there. She looked up into the nearby trees but could not see him.

It appeared to Mah that the only weapon the man had was a short dagger stuck in his belt. Mah was still leery but he knew he must take a chance on the two of them being honest. He dropped to the ground and called out. They approached him slowly, the man appearing very cautious. As he came near he kept his hand on his dagger. Mah almost laughed out loud at the notion of the man thinking he and his dagger could overcome Mah and his father's sword. But then Mah remembered that some men could throw such a dagger a great distance with lethal force. He realized he had had a careless thought and resolved not to do it again.

As the other two came closer Marah approached Mah and stood between the two men. It seemed to Mah that she was trying to form a sort of neutral area with her body. First she pointed to Mah and said his name, "Mah'Oor." Then she pointed to the other man and said, "Luden."

The two men at first did nothing, each apparently trying to assess the other. Finally Luden raised his hand in a gesture that Mah took to be a greeting, and he did the same thing.

Marah, continuing to stand between them, told Mah that he was welcome in the enclosure. Apparently the others were willing to forget that he had beheaded one of them, helped to steal their horses, and kidnapped Marah. Perhaps it was because he had brought her back and she assured them he would be willing to help them defend themselves. They were obviously much less warlike than Mah and his companions.

After many minutes of evaluating each other, with some posturing, both men seemed willing to proceed, but warily. Mah had the most to gain since he had nowhere else to go, but he realized the others were probably very much frightened by the sudden attack. They must have heard of other raiding parties and feared they were not prepared to defend themselves. They hoped Mah could help them.

Eventually Mah followed the other two into the enclosure keeping his hand on his sword hilt as they walked.

Inside Mah noticed what looked like a newly dug grave and assumed it was for the man he had killed. To him it looked as though every person who lived in the little village was in the center of the compound watching him, most with rather sullen expressions on their faces, but all with curiosity. Luden, who must have held some authority, and Marah, led him to the last hut and stood aside indicating that he was to enter. But he pointed to Luden and gestured to show that he wanted the other man to enter first. Luden shrugged his shoulders and went into the grass thatched hut. Then Mah followed him, still with his hand on his sword. Marah came closely behind him.

Once inside Luden explained to Mah, with Marah interpreting as well as she could, that the structure they were in would be where Mah would sleep, along with several other men. This would only be temporary until another small building, which they would begin working on the following day, was finished. He would be required to work with the other members of the community but most of all he would be expected to help them ward off any further attacks. They did not seem to have any idea that he had been the leader of the raiding party. And they also must have thought that he had deserted the group rather than that he had been left on the beach. Mah did not try to correct them.

Mah was given some animal skins with which to make a bed on the dirt floor. He deposited them far in the back and against the wall. When they went back outside some of the women were cooking food for their supper and he was invited to eat with them. It was the first meat he and Marah had eaten for months. He tried to show them how grateful he was.

It was already late in the year when Mah agreed to remain with the small community, mostly because he knew the weather would soon be bitterly cold and he and Marah had no shelter. Besides that he had no way to catch much food.

He was obviously the best fighting man of the group but by no means the only one. To train and lead the others he set up a system that much followed the way it was done in his country. He was determined to do the best he could. From the beginning though he made it clear that if anyone from his old Viking village came back he would not fight against members of his own family. He was particularly afraid that a younger brother of his might return and he did not want to have to kill him.

Over the months that followed he made friends with some of the people of the community even though many of them remained distrustful of him. And he and Marah became closer during the period. She helped him learn to communicate with the others and he adopted many of their customs.

Mah came to learn that they were followers of a religious belief that had been brought from far off. One day Marah took him on an all-day journey to a community of monks who lived in solitude in tiny huts. The two of them were allowed to stay there for several days in separate huts of their own. One of the monks spent a good bit of time explaining the main tenets of the group's creed to Mah. He learned that the God they worshiped did not merely come from the moon Mah had watched from the bow of his father's little ship, but had created it. Mah determined that serving such an obviously powerful God would be a very wise thing to do. Eventually he allowed himself to be baptized in the little stream he and Marah had fished in and became what would be known as a Catholic Christian. After that the people in the community in which he and Marah lived accepted him much more easily as one of them. And finally he and Marah were married in a ceremony performed by one of the monks.

It was an accepted custom for the man to present the father of the bride something valuable in exchange for his daughter's hand. Mah had nothing which was of sufficient value except the sword his father had given him. So he gave that to Marah's father. The old man gave him a smaller weapon so that Mah would still be able to protect his new bride.

Nearly a year later Marah gave birth to a boy. After that Mah decided the three of them should leave and travel southwest in an attempt to find at least a little warmer climate. In nearly two years of travel they finally found themselves close to the west coast. And there they settled.

The family grew through generations in the county of Clare below Galway Bay, some leaving and some men returning with wives. The most famous of the family was a warrior known as Cladder Mah'Oor, or

Cladder of Mah The Son Of Oor. And his descendants were called "the Mah'oories", or the sons of Mah of Oor. This soon became the "people of the Mauries". And eventually this name too was changed to what it was at the time when, after the potato famine in the late nineteenth century, a dark haired Terrence Krag O'Maury decided to try to find his fortune in the new world where the streets were said to be paved with gold.

Chapter I

There is something in the autumn air, even on a warm day, that feels different. Watch the little honeybee. All summer he bumbled along as though looking for honey was a game. But when the honeysuckle vine is sere and withered, when the gladiola bed has been dug up, when nothing is left but the roses and a few cosmos blooms his search for nectar becomes frantic.

From The Last House On The Left, by Kelvin Roods.

* * *

The End Of Summer 1987

While Elleen and Libby finished getting the cabin ready to close up for the winter Mr. O'Maury sat on the porch in the autumn sun that slanted in under the roof. It was actually rather warm. Even so he wore his old baseball cap, but only because he was sensitive about his thinning hair—although he would never admit that.

Four or five grackles fought over a crust of stale bread the old man had thrown over the railing. Perhaps they recognized him because one of them came up and stood on the top step as if waiting for another handout. But, when nothing materialized, after a while it flew away, and finally so did the others. One could feel in the air that there was very little time to waste waiting for things that might not happen. It was time to be off.

Mr. O'Maury would have preferred to remove his old gray sweater but he knew that he wasn't allowed to and, furthermore, that he would probably get in trouble if he did. He had heard Elleen give young Ginny instructions to keep an eye on her great grandfather, and tell them if he didn't stay bundled up. And he knew the little girl would do it, partly because she was a little tattle-tale, but also, he knew, partly because she loved him and was concerned for his well-being.

Little Pat was probably in on it too. The boy came out and sat on the very spot from where the grackle had flown off a few moments before. He peered out across the lake, perhaps trying to see what it was his great grandfather was watching, but not able to because what the old man was seeing was no longer on the lake. Actually the old man's eyesight was still very good, but even so he could see much better into the past than he could in the present. And he could see hardly at all into the future.

Now he scarcely took note of the three small boats which trolled slowly back and forth in what was left of the morning's mist. But when he sat erect, as he nearly always did, and squinted his eyes against the sun which was burning the mist away, he could see a much younger John O'Maury, without the neat white beard he wore now, out on the lake swimming, fishing, skiing—why Kate had even teased him into flying out there on one of those fool hang gliders. He smiled, remembering.

The boy said, "What are you looking at, Bin?" Years ago, when Libby had begun to talk, unable to say "grandpa", she had called him "Bindah", and the name had stuck. Thereafter all the grandchildren and later the great grandchildren had referred to him as "Bindah" or, just as often, merely "Bin".

Mr. O'Maury looked at the boy and his smile widened. For a five year old he was a mite short, but his little legs were stocky looking as though he did a lot of running, which his great grandfather knew he did. His blond curls were trimmed close and he had wide blue eyes. "From Kate's side", thought Mr. O'Maury. His gaze returned to the invisible spirits out on the water. To his great grandson he said, slowly and with a touch of melancholy, "I was just watching out on the lake."

He lit his pipe and the fragrant blue smoke drifted through the trellis covered with morning-glory vines which had already stopped blooming but had not yet started to turn brown. In the nearly still air the smoke drifted across the yard and onto the porch next door, but no one noticed.

The Stanbergs had closed up their cottage the week before. In fact everyone else on the bottom end of Pokey Lane had been gone at least a week. Pat moved a bit closer to the old man's knee and peered out toward the far shore. The smell of the smoke from Bin's pipe and the feel of the blue denim trousers, much older than the boy, gave him a comfortable feeling because he associated those things with good times, both at the cabin and at home in town.

Inside Libby dried the last cup and put it upside down on the shelf. When she closed the cabinet door her mother wiped a few drops of water from the top of the counter.

"There," she said, "I guess that about does it."

Young Ginny handed her towel to her grandmother, then turned to her mother for approval. Libby didn't disappoint her. "You were a big help, sweetheart," she told her as she gave her a quick hug. "It would have taken us a lot longer without you." Ginny smiled in smug satisfaction. "Pat's too little to help, isn't he?" she suggested.

"He helped," Libby told her. "He swept the porch. Now he is keeping Bindah company." She turned toward her mother who had sat down on a stool to lean an elbow on the counter. "We can leave now if you want to, mom," she said.

Elleen gestured with her head toward the porch. "You know," she said, "pop won't want to go. He never does."

"I know," Libby agreed. "He really likes this place, doesn't he?"

"What you mean is he likes his memories of this place," corrected her mother. Then, thoughtfully, she added, "So do I."

"Mom, don't you think we all do?" Libby touched her mother's hand in a quick gesture. "We can go out and sit on the porch for a while. We'll have to leave before lunch time though because there isn't anything left to eat."

"Good," Libby's mother said. "That will give us an excuse." She stood up and took one last look around the spacious kitchen. As usual she was both eager and reluctant to leave; eager because of all the things she had to do at home, things she had ignored all summer. The reluctance was caused by that familiar feeling that when they left the leaving would mark the end of another chapter in her life. "How many more chapters in the book are there?" she wondered.

Libby recognized the look on her mother's face. She knew Elleen was taking mental inventory of people and things which had passed through that particular kitchen and all the others too. "We've been coming here a long time, haven't we?" she said. "And I guess grandpa was just a little boy the first time he came into this cabin."

"Oh no!" Elleen smiled, eager to talk about old memories. "I think he was about seventeen years old or so the first time his family came to Indian Lake. And then it was not to this cabin, it was to one they rented. And you know this isn't even the first one the family owned. Libby, think how long ago that was and how things have changed."

* * *

Summer 1919

"Johnny, close that screen door, dear," Mary directed as she set the table. "That's a good boy. You would think for the ten dollars we're paying to rent this place for a week the least they could do would be to fix the spring on the screen door."

John got up from the table—he had been waiting for something to eat for about an hour and did not want anything to distract his mother when she seemed so nearly ready to serve supper—and pulled the screen door shut, hooking it to keep it from swinging open again, and sat back down. He put his elbows on the table, his chin in his hands, and watched his mother with anticipation. This did not go unnoticed by her.

"Patience," she said with a twinkle in her eyes. As she passed behind him she patted him on the head, observing how his dark hair hung down over his forehead the way his father's did. In many ways he was like the older man, taller, but with the same broad shoulders, big ears, and, she smiled, big appetite.

It was a warm day and they were in what was both kitchen and dining room. Mary had been cooking Friday dinner on the kerosene stove which made it even warmer. John sat at the table in his trousers and undershirt even though he realized it was not proper for a gentleman to sit at the table in semi-nudity. In spite of the heat his mother, he noticed, had kept her dress buttoned all the way up; and she was doing all the work. There were two other rooms in the cabin. One held the big bed where John's parents would sleep; the other was the living room. When it was time to retire it would double as a bedroom for Eileen, John's younger sister. John would sleep on the screened in porch and so would Aloysius if he ever got there. Aloysius, who would begin his second year at the University of Dayton in the fall, was supposed to have a ride as far as Lima with another student who was from a wealthy Toledo family.

John's brother had said he would have no trouble finding a ride to the lake from Lima, but one could never be certain what Aloysius would do.

Eileen, who had been sitting in the living room doing her fingernails, came through the wide doorway into the kitchen and sat across from John. Her small face, wreathed in tiny black perspiration soaked curls, was pink from the heat. "God, it's hot in here," she complained.

Mary stopped what she was doing and frowned at her daughter. "Young lady, you say 'God' when you are praying—no other time. You're lucky your father didn't hear you." Eileen said nothing and bowed her head in apparent repentance. But she smiled at her brother who quickly looked away as though he hadn't noticed. Mary finished setting the table, including a place for Aloysius.

"Where is papa?" asked John.

"He was wiping the dust off the car." Mary dried her hands on her apron before adding, "He is probably finished by now. Why don't one of you go out and tell him we are ready to eat?"

John stood up quickly and went to the side window opening onto the yard which ran along the side of the cabin. His father, standing next to the Packard with a dust cloth in his huge hand was still dressed in his good clothes. He had managed to call on a few customers along the way up from Cincinnati. Now his coat was off, however, and his shirtsleeves were rolled up above his elbows. His tie was pulled down and his stiff collar unbuttoned. His black derby was pushed back revealing a forehead that seemed to get a little higher every year. He looked up when he heard his son at the window.

"Well, now," he told John as he gestured toward the gleaming vehicle, "I'd say that is a bit better."

"I would have done that for you, papa, if you had waited a little while," John said through the window screen.

"Yes, shouldn't I have known that, son?" It was a mild reproach from the father. "But it needed to be done right away. The dust from the road will ruin the paint if you wait too long to get it off."

"You're right, papa," John agreed. "Next time I'll do it right away. I promise." Pat's smile was skeptical.

"Anyway," added John, "momma says come in and eat."

Pat retrieved his coat from inside the car and came around to the porch while John unlatched the screen door for him.

"The spring seems to be missing," said Pat as he came in, locking the door behind him. He went to the bedroom and removed his tie and his shirt, leaving them on the bed with his hat and his coat. Then he thought better of that and hung the coat, the tie, and the hat in the closet. In the kitchen he found a bowl and a pitcher of water which he used to wash his hands and face. When he had finished he poured the water he had used into the sink. Drying his hands on a towel he turned toward the table where the others waited.

"Would Mrs. O'Maury mind if I were to eat in my undershirt?" he asked.

"If you want to set a bad example for your children, you go right ahead," Mary answered.

"In that case I will," he returned, winking at Eileen. "I've got to balance the overabundance of good example they get from their sainted mother."

"I do the best I can," she said, an air of impatience in her voice. "While I was in here making your lordship's supper you were out there wasting time on that machine of yours."

Pat had been teasing but the tone of Mary's voice warned him that she did not appreciate it. Slowly the smile faded from his face. He carefully folded the towel he had been using to dry his hands and face and hung it over the back of his chair. He did not want to pursue the matter.

But Mary would not let it drop. "When he might have been fixing the door he was outside playing with his new toy and ruining his clothes that I try my best to keep clean for him."

Pat could remain quiet no longer. "A toy is it then?" he said deliberately, his tone a mixture of indignation and frustration. As usual he was taken off guard by her peevishness and did not know how to handle it. He could not understand how two people, both of whom worked so hard and made such an effort to do their best for each other all the time, could ever find themselves at odds over anything that seemed so trivial. Yet they did and it always seemed to begin the same way. He would be in a good mood and try to tease his wife. She either would not understand that he was joking with her or would refuse to be amused by it. Soon they would be arguing.

Eileen hoped they would not begin shouting at each other and wind up not speaking. John felt that perhaps the whole thing was his fault. If only he had gone out and cleaned the car as soon as they had arrived Pat could have come inside and kept his wife company, maybe even helped her.

"A toy is it then?" Pat repeated, his voice rising slightly but still controlled. "Might I remind the lady of the house that it was that same toy that brought her to this very cabin. And also it is that very same toy that I use in my work. Would you be wanting me to give that up, I might ask?"

"Well now," Mary challenged, hands on hips and her grey eyes flashing, "would Mr. high and mighty like to get himself a regular job and spend his time at home with his family? Oh no he wouldn't, because then he would have no excuse to flit around the country talking with the young girls and such. And would I be asking him to? I wouldn't dare."

"Mrs. O'Maury, now you are close to going too far. By all the Saint Mary's, how can you say what you are saying in front of your children? You know I spend my time talking to those who might be my customers. And can you tell me how many young girls that might be—who might own a store, indeed the kind of store that would have use for the big items I sell to my customers? Can you tell me how many young girls that might be? You know that would be none at all. Now enough of this nonsense. We are ready to eat. If you want to continue this discussion you and I can do it later."

His eyes had turned to black smoldering coals, and his fists were clenched in frustration. He sat down abruptly and, bowing his head, said grace quietly for himself. The others also bowed their heads and waited for him to finish. Mary, as usual, knew when to stop. Quickly she turned to the stove to get the fish she had been frying. But every short rigid motion of her arms, her legs, and her whole body conveyed reluctant submission—and she meant it that way. Mary O'Maury was a very good actress.

They would eat in relative silence, speaking only about the weather and other topics which could cause no controversy. After supper Eileen and John would wash the dishes without being asked. Pat would take them for a ride later to find an ice house. They would buy a block of ice for the ice box and make arrangements for regular delivery while Pat was gone.

Later on, when they went to bed, Pat would make love to his wife and, because they had quarreled, would be less gentle than usual. It would be as though he was trying to assert himself, proving his dominance. She knew this would happen and she looked forward to it with as much anticipation as she had on her wedding night.

And Pat knew what she was thinking. He knew because it always ended in the same way. It was a ritual that they both went through without really understanding why. The result was always the same and in the process he sometimes found out things about her that she could not tell him any other way.

In any event they could not talk about it because the admission of the thoughts and desires they would be forced to make would destroy the images they needed to keep, both of themselves and of each other.

The only thing that changed what was to happen on that particular night was that Aloysius arrived. But, in the end, all that did was make it happen later. In the morning Mary would be, once more, the absolutely dutiful wife and extremely happy for it. She would be that way for at least a month.

They had just returned from picking up the ice when Aloysius and his friend pulled into the driveway. Pat still wore his derby but neither coat nor tie, and his collar was open. John, both eager to show that he could take care of the ice as easily as his father and also anxious to please, had jumped out of the car before the others. With the tongs he had taken the ice off the rear bumper and carried it up onto the porch. He put the ice on the floor so that he could latch the door behind him before he carried it to the kitchen to place in the ice box when he heard the Oakland Roadster turn into the lane. He had never seen the car or even heard that particular six cylinder roar before but he knew it had to mean his older brother, Aloysius, had arrived. He forgot the chunk of ice on the porch floor and ran back outside just in time to see the sporty little coupe pull into the driveway behind the Packard with his mother still in it, sliding to a stop in the loose gravel.

Aloysius reached through the open window on the passenger side and, unlatching his door, leaped to the ground. His shirt collar was buttoned but he wore no tie. In fact he was dressed much like his father except that in place of the older man's derby Aloysius wore a cloth cap. Conscious of his image, he made sure it was tilted slightly to one side before he ran up and hugged his mother as she stepped from the Packard.

"Hi, mama," he said, and he kissed her on her cheek. "Are you glad to see me?"

Pat had stepped from the Packard on the other side and had been standing with his arms folded watching John take the ice inside when the Oakland had turned into the driveway. Upon hearing the sound of the tires sliding in the gravel he turned, startled, and then, realizing that it was Aloysius, pushed his hat back off his brow and shook his head slowly.

Pat was very proud of his oldest son but he often found himself wondering when the young man would grow up. Well perhaps it wasn't so much growing up as it was acting like the grownups that Pat knew and expected his children to emulate.

Aloysius let go of his mother before she had a chance to answer him and turned to Pat. "How have you been, papa?" he asked.

"Fine as usual," the father answered drily. Then he added, "Aloysius, might I be asking if all of your friends drive that way?"

Aloysius, of course, ignored the question. Rather dramatically he struck himself on the forehead, as though he suddenly had remembered something very important. "Rod's still in the car," he said. "I completely forgot about him."

While Aloysius was greeting his parents the driver of the sporty roadster had remained behind the wheel, apparently more interested in observing the scene before him than in becoming part of it, at least for the time being. His eyes shifted from his friend's parents to the younger brother and eventually to Aloysius' younger sister, Eileen. At that point he could have been seen to become more interested.

Eileen had left the Packard from the seat behind her father and had begun walking toward the rear of the cottage when she too was stopped by the sound of the smaller car. She sensed, just as John had, that the noise signalled the arrival of her brother, Aloysius, and she turned around to watch as the coupe skidded into the driveway.

Eileen was not beautiful. True, her long black hair, tied as it was now, loosely with one narrow white ribbon, was striking, but her eyebrows were too dark and thick, and her nose was much too small for her to be considered more than just pretty. Nevertheless the fading light of evening blurred her features and emphasized their contrast with her fair, nearly milk-white skin. Furthermore Eileen had been walking away from the others when she was stopped by the sound of the car. Turning and standing with her feet demurely together, holding her hat in front of her slim waist with both hands and smiling eagerly in anticipation of the greeting she expected from her brother, she appeared shy and, perhaps to a stranger, vulnerable. She looked very much the young girl. And yet it was easy to see she would inherit her mother's large bosom. There was no doubt she would soon be every bit a woman.

Aloysius opened the door on the driver's side of the Oakland and grasped his companion's sleeve pulling him gently but firmly out of the car. "Hey, everyone," he said, "This is a friend of mine, Rodman Schultz." To Rod he said, pointing one by one to the members of his family, "This is my mother. This is father. And this is my kid brother, John (punching him lightly on the bicep) and my little sister, Eileen." As he said the last he walked over and hugged her.

The other young college student greeted Mary O'Maury politely, shook hands with Pat and John, and then smiled and said, "Hi," to Eileen.

"Rod was going on to Toledo," went on Aloysius, "but I was trying to get him to stick around for a while."

When Aloysius said this Mary's first thought, of course, was about where the young man might sleep. She was particularly conscious of the sleeping arrangements because the cottage had no inside plumbing. If anyone felt compelled to find relief during the night it probably meant using the facility in the backyard. Since the cottage had only one door this would require passing by the bed of whomever might be sleeping on the porch. Such an arrangement involving a young man and her daughter was unacceptable to Mary. Yet she could not put even the possibility of such a situation into words. Instead she asked, "Won't your parents wonder where you are, Mr. Schultz?"

"Not for a couple days, Mrs. O'Maury," he assured her. "They're out of town and won't be back until the middle of next week, so I guess I'm free as a bird sort of. But listen I don't want to put you people out. I'm sure you weren't expecting company."

Perhaps the young man had realized what Mary was thinking and what she had been reluctant to say. Ordinarily that would not have made much difference to him for Rodman had become rather spoiled by his family's wealth and he didn't usually pay a great deal of attention to how other people felt about what he did. But this was different. For one thing he liked Aloysius, not a lot, but more than most of the other men with whom he was forced to associate at the university. Aloysius was one of the people he sought out. Realizing long ago that he would never be more than an average student he had made it a habit to cultivate people who were scholars and who might also be willing to help him. Aloysius was one of those. But to say that Rodman's friendship with Aloysius was only based on what he could gain from it would not be completely accurate; there was more to it than that. As a matter of fact he enjoyed the young Irishman's company, so much so that he had once asked his father if there was not some way they could enhance the economic prospects of the O'Maury family to the point that no one would be embarrassed were he to elect to associate with Aloysius away from school. Nothing had come of it.

Rodman Schultz had offered Aloysius a ride to Lima because it was only a little out of his way. But once they were that far he had decided to continue on to the lake because, since his own family would not be at home when he arrived in Toledo anyway, he had no reason to be in a hurry. But he had intended to go on from there and not waste any time with his friend's family. At least that had been his intention before he had seen Eileen. Now he wasn't sure what he wanted to do.

Rodman's feelings in regard to Eileen had nothing to do with romance, of course. She represented no more than the possibility of an interesting interlude, at least more interesting than anything he thought might happen to him in Toledo.

Nor would it be fair to say that Rodman intended anything particularly immoral. He merely wanted to impress her, to attract her, to get her interested in him in a personal way. Of course, if this led to something more than holding hands he would not object.

Rod felt sure she was too young and inexperienced to resist him if he could get her alone and turn on his college man charm. But he knew he would have to be careful. He realized that it would be necessary for him to disguise his intentions for a while at least and to take his time, even though he was not usually patient in his relations with girls.

To Aloysius, Rodman said, "Maybe I would like to stick around for a day or two and see what the lake is like. But I wouldn't think of intruding on your family. There must be some place in town where I could find a sleeping room. And if your folks wouldn't mind maybe you could stay in town with me. I'll promise to have you back first thing in the morning."

Aloysius looked first at his mother. He knew she would not be enthusiastic about him not sleeping under the same roof as the rest of his family. Even more would she object to him spending the night—perhaps several nights—not only away from the guidance of both family and school, but also with one of those "college men", none of whom she trusted very much. It, of course, would not occur to her that Aloysius was a college man too. When he looked at her, waiting to see what she would say, she only lifted her eyebrows and said nothing.

Rodman instinctively realized that Mrs. O'Maury would likely not approve of what he had suggested and, because he had suggested it, probably not approve of him either. But he understood the relationship between all the members of the family and particularly between Aloysius and his younger brother. There was a way, he knew, to make what he had suggested sound innocent even to their mother. That was to invite the brother also.

"I was going to ask John if he would like to go with us too. Al talks about his brother so much of the time I thought they would probably both enjoy it. And we can tell him all about college life so he won't be so surprised when he gets there next year." He winked at Aloysius and, smiling, added, "But naturally we won't tell him everything, will we?"

And Aloysius, going along with the act, answered, "No, we can't do that can we? He isn't old enough yet."

Rodman was playing a game, trying to prove that he could manipulate some of these people, first the son and later on—he hoped—the daughter. But he would only be able to prove it to himself. He knew that if they, especially the mother, realized that he was challenging them, playing a game in a way, he wouldn't stand a chance.

Pat had said nothing so far because he hadn't decided whether or not he approved of what the Schultz boy had suggested. Without realizing it he was waiting for his wife to say she agreed or did not agree before he made up his mind, at which point he would feel that whatever she said was what he had wanted all along. Actually he might have asked her except for the fact that she had not said anything to him at all since before supper and hadn't given any indication that she was at all ready to forget that they had argued.

John suddenly made a sharp cry and ran for the porch. He remembered the ice still sitting where he had left it on the floor.

"What's wrong, Johnny?" called his father, wondering if the boy had perhaps become ill.

But Mary knew. "There's a mop behind the kitchen door," she called after him. Then, to Aloysius more than to his friend she added, "Maybe the two of you had better take him with you. He has been looking forward to seeing you all week. I'm hoping after you and he have caught up on all the things you have to talk about he will be able to pay a little attention to what else is going on around him."

Then Pat said, agreeably, "If you are sure you can squeeze him in that little roadster it will probably do him good. But I want no running around in the machine. There's a tourist home in town near the drugstore. It has a good reputation. If you can get a room there it will be the best place to stay." He took a small wad of bills from his pocket, selected one and gave it to Aloysius. "Here," he told his son, "this is for the room. You can come back here to eat in the morning."

"Say," Rodman protested, "you don't need to do that. I invited Al and his brother. I sure wouldn't mind a real breakfast in the morning, though."

Pat hesitated for the briefest of moments as though trying to think of something to say to Rodman. He felt it should be unnecessary for him to explain to the young man that what he said and did concerning his family's conduct and activities was never open to discussion. In the end he said nothing in response to Rodman's remark, merely ignoring it.

He patted his son on the shoulder in a mixture of affection and dismissal. To both of the young men he said, "If John is finished putting the ice in the box you had better be off to town. Your mother will expect you here in the morning."

Then, to Aloysius, he added, "Morning, you know, is before noon."

Aloysius laughed. "Yes papa," he agreed. Then as Pat went inside to make sure that John had indeed put the ice in the box, Aloysius moved over to where his mother stood. She had been watching Rodman Schultz quietly, wondering what he was really thinking. Perhaps he was just lonely, she thought, with time on his hands, looking for some innocent entertainment with his friend, Aloysius. But in her mother's heart she was not convinced. Something about the young man from Toledo seemed too shrewd and calculating for Mary to be comfortable with, or for her to feel satisfied that the relationship between him and her sons was one she should encourage. On the other hand she had confidence in Aloysius. She did not expect him to do anything foolish. Then, in her mind, she smilingly amended that to 'anything very foolish' as Aloysius kissed her on the cheek and promised that they would be back long before noon.

Sometime later, after the boys had left and Eileen had gone to bed, Pat, sitting on the edge of their bed while he took off his shoes, paused for a moment as though trying to decide something. Finally he asked, "Mary did you think your son and his friend had been drinking?"

Mary, already washed and in her nightgown, stood in the small space between the foot of the bed and the dresser, brushing her long hair. She did not stop, giving the impression that she gave the question he had asked very little consideration. Finally she decided to answer him. "No, I do not. Why do you ask? Do you think they were drinking?" She said it with impatience in her voice and went on brushing her hair.

Pat had removed one shoe and put it on the floor beneath the bed. He took off the other one and put it beside the first before he slowly replied. "I always think when you have two college boys together and away from school, and away from family too, that they will probably think of drinking." Pat had taken off his trousers and hung them over the bed's footboard. Standing in only his underdrawers he put his hand on his wife's shoulder. "I am not so old that I can't remember what goes through a young man's mind," he told her.

She pushed his hand away before she went on with her brushing. "The boys are so much different today. It seems that they try so to find ways to prove they don't need to conform," she said, but then added quickly, "Thank the lord Aloysius isn't like that."

Pat considered what she had said before replying, "Well I hope he is not." Then he got into bed and waited for his wife.

Rodman drove past the tourist home and continued on to the town limits. He remembered having seen a row of small cabins on their way in earlier. He felt, and rightly so, that they would have much more privacy in a cabin than in a tourist home under the same roof with the owners. He drove on only a mile or so and there it was. The wooden sign, lit on both sides by what appeared to be carbide lanterns, said "Wilson's," and underneath, "Travelers welcome."

Rodman pulled into the driveway and stopped. There were four or five other cars parked before the small cabins, but no people to be seen.

"Well my friends, what do you think? Should we give it a try?" he asked the other two.

John said, "I think papa wanted us to stay in the tourist home in town."

"I think so too," agreed Aloysius.

"I think he was just making a suggestion," Rodman insisted. "After all why should he care where we stay as long as we get back there in the morning?"

Both of the O'Maury boys knew the answer to that but neither of them wanted to say so. They looked at each other but both said nothing. Aloysius made a gesture, a sort of a shrug, that to Rodman indicated agreement. He opened his door and jumped to the ground. "Why don't you two wait here while I see if we can get a room."

After a few minutes he came back, chuckling to himself, obviously pleased with what he had done. He leaned in the open window of the Oakland. "What an absolute ass," he said to the other two.

"What do you mean by that?" asked Aloysius. "What happened? Did you get a cabin or not?"

"Oh yeah," Rodman assured him, "we got the place okay. All it took was a little extra folding money. But first the creep asked me if I had a woman with me. Then when I told him we were three men he asked me if we were, you know, strange or anything and if there would be any fooling around. I felt like punching him."

John heard what Rodman said and, understanding what he meant by it, did not feel very pleased. He had been eager to spend the night with his brother and his friend, not because of Rodman, of course, but because of Aloysius. John did more than look up to his brother; he idolized him. The standards which he hoped someday to meet were being able to run as fast as Aloysius, or being able jump as high, to swim as far, to dive as deep, to eat as much corned beef and cabbage, to drink as much lemonade, to sing as loudly in church—in this regard quality was not necessarily an issue— and to know as much about the important things in life. These were, for instance, things such as what the snazziest looking car on the road was in any given year, as well as the fastest one, what the most popular dance was—even though Aloysius didn't necessarily know how to do it—and also the names of important people such as the current most popular movie stars, the baseball player with the best batting average—and the one with the best ERA, and the country's vice president (even Eileen knew who the president was). John's father was a very important and definitive source of principle but John's brother knew what was going on.

Lately though, John had sometimes wondered. He still loved and admired Aloysius very much but he had begun to harbor the suspicion that his brother could possibly (in rare circumstances) be wrong (about some items).

There were other things. Aloysius had always represented a size norm, being so much bigger than John. But now he had stopped growing and although he was very tall, nearly six feet in fact, John was nearly that and still growing. Also John knew, because he had heard some of his aunts and older female cousins say so to his mother, that his brother was good looking. At least partly because of this he had always wanted to look like Aloysius. He knew he never would, though. Aloysius had inherited the soft brown hair and grey eyes of their mother while John and his sister favored Pat. Both had nearly black hair and dark green eyes. And John had already been forced to begin shaving every week just to look presentable, while Aloysius had taken nearly two months just to grow a moustache.

They went to their cabin and spent a few minutes inspecting. Finally they all sat, Aloysius and John on the only two chairs and Rodman on the large bed, half sitting and half lying down.

Finally Rodman said to Aloysius, "Well old buddy, are you ready for a drink?"

John saw Aloysius, before answering, look at him as though wondering what John would say. A strange feeling came over him, as though something very important was happening; and in fact he knew what it was. At that very moment he realized that what he was and what he would be would no longer depend on what someone else thought. From then on he would be John Francis O'Maury, a complete person on his own, and not Aloysius O'Maury's younger brother. Oh he knew he would still learn things from Aloysius as well as a lot of other people, including his parents. But when he saw that his brother was waiting to see what John thought before he answered Rodman, John became an adult. His relationship with everyone would never again be the same.

He had suspected that the other two young men would have something alcoholic to drink, for the same reason his father expected they had already been drinking. They were college men, and they had to both prove a point and live up to expectations. Since it was illegal John did not approve of drinking on principle but, on the other hand, he had never seen anyone cause trouble because he was drinking and, therefore, did not think it was something always wrong. In any event he decided to go along with the other two.

"What about me," he said, "I could use a drink too if you've got enough."

"You're a regular sport," Rodman said, then turning to his fellow collegian added, "Isn't he?, and "But of course he'd have to be, with the kind of brother he has."

Both O'Maury boys wondered what Rodman meant by what he had said. Was he, Aloysius thought, implying that Aloysius was becoming too well known for his drinking and partying?

John, on the other hand, unconsciously reluctant to change the way he had always thought of his brother, wondered if Rodman was chiding the other young man for his usual attitude toward partying, which John would have expected to be rather conservative.

As a matter of fact neither of them was correct. Rodman was merely indulging in what the young people referred to as kidding around. Both would probably remember what he had said long after he himself had forgotten.

Only Rodman had brought any luggage, the two O'Maury men having brought their change of clothes and toilet articles in a convenient paper bag. Rodman put his large suitcase on the bed and opened it. From under his shirts, where he had secreted it, he withdrew a pint sized bottle of clear liquid and held it up for inspection.

"What is it?" asked John.

"Only the absolutely best bathtub gin you ever drank in your life," answered Rodman.

"It will probably be the first bathtub gin he has ever drunk," said Aloysius, grinning at his brother with a mixture of teasing and affection.

"Actually," John admitted honestly, "I've never had any gin at all. I've had some wine. And I drank some beer that papa made once. What does gin taste like?"

Although he would not admit it John was, in fact, more than a little apprehensive. He was fully aware that drinking certain impurities associated with illegal alcoholic concoctions often caused sickness which sometimes crippled and blinded. He knew it was something to be wary of.

Aloysius realized that John had asked about the taste but was, no doubt, more interested in whether or not it would be safe to consume the liquid Rodman was carefully measuring into drinking glasses for each of them.

To reassure John he told him, "It doesn't really taste like anything you have ever had before probably. But in case you're wondering about how safe it is you don't have to worry. We got the best grain alcohol from some of the pharmacy students we know. They get it from the drug store. We mixed it ourselves with water and juniper berry juice. It really is first class gin." Then he added with a grin, "And don't worry about the bath tub. Where we live nobody ever uses it for anything but making gin."

John accepted the glass held out to him by Rodman. Both Rodman and Aloysius, with apparent pleasure, took big swallows from their own glasses. "Go ahead and try it," encouraged Rodman.

John did finally. He took a very small sip at first. It tasted slightly sweet and bitter at the same time. It really was not too bad. He took a bigger drink. This time he felt the bite of the alcohol in his throat as he swallowed.

"Well how was it?" asked Aloysius.

For a few seconds, but only for a few seconds, John was not able to talk. Then his voice returned. "Not bad," he answered. "It's very strong though, isn't it?"

"Well," Rodman told him, "the alcohol was more than a hundred proof, but we cut it with water. It's probably not more than eighty now. How about some more?"

John held out his glass. "A little," he said, "I'm not finished with what you gave me yet."

As they drank a feeling of exhilaration came over John, not unpleasant but a little alarming. Although he had never been drunk before he knew that if he drank another glass of their homemade gin he would be, and he thought he would rather not. On the other hand he didn't want to do anything that would make him appear either too young to have a good time or old enough but disagreeable. Besides he really didn't want to do anything that would reflect badly on his brother.

He would have liked very much to pour out what was left in his glass, but there was nothing in the room to pour it into. Besides the double bed and a cot which was not yet unfolded the furnishings consisted of the two chairs, an ancient chest of drawers, and a table. On the table were the pitcher of water and the bowl in which they would wash.

John decided that would have to do. He nursed his drink as long as he could, the other two apparently not noticing how it seemed to last. Finally he stood up and stretched. "This stuff is making me sleepy," he announced. "You know I'm not as used to it as you two are."

"Yeah," answered Aloysius with just a bit of a slur in his speech, "it can creep up on you. You got to be careful."

"I'm going outside for a minute," John told them. He carefully put his glass down next to the washbowl and headed for the door.

"We know where you're going," sang Rodman inanely.

When John came back his brother and the other young man were telling each other stories about their friends and teachers at school and laughing (giggling actually) and they paid no attention to John as he prepared for bed. He thought to himself that they were really pretty good fellows, just not quite grown up. That thought actually ran through his head and then he chuckled to himself as the implication of it in relation to him, the younger brother, struck him.

While they were not watching John poured what was left of his drink into the washbasin. At home in Cincinnati they of course had indoor plumbing and John had at first found the lack of it at their lake cabin uncomfortable but not unacceptable. He knew it was much worse for the women in the family and they had not complained (as a matter of fact his sister had a few times, but not to him) so he felt neither should he.

He took off his shirt and his undershirt and hung them on a hook on the wall. Then he poured water onto the gin. He wondered whether or not gin was good for the skin, then wondered why he was wondering about it in the first place since he did not intend to make a habit of washing his face in gin.

Eventually they did all decide to retire, John and Al in the double bed and Rodman on the cot. The last thing John thought about was whether or not other people said the same kind of prayers before they went to sleep as the members of his family did.

*   *   *

The next day the three of them went back to the cabin on the lake for breakfast. By the time they got there Pat had already left to make a few calls and Eileen was not yet up, so Mary was able to pamper her sons and, of course, Mr. Schultz. She fixed them biscuits with bacon and eggs, which they ate with apparent relish even though Aloysius and Rodman most likely would have preferred something lighter. But the meal agreed with them and after they had finished the two older young men went off in Rodman's car to get gas and then to look at the lake. John was invited to go with them but said he had some letters to write and would join them later. After they left he put paper and pencils in a box and went out with it under his arm. He crossed the road and at a very leisurely pace began walking in the direction of the lake shore.

Eileen had gone into the bedroom vacated earlier by her parents as soon as she heard the young men coming back. Now as soon as she heard John go out the door she put on a robe and went out to use the outhouse.

"I thought they would never leave," she grumped to her mother as she passed her on the porch.

Mary smiled at the girl in amusement but she really did sympathize with her. She herself had grown up in a house with no inside plumbing but that had been some time ago and she had since become used to a bathroom indoors. She was sensitive and uncomfortable using the outhouse and she was painfully aware that her city bred daughter must like it even less. She resolved that if they came back to the lake next year she would insist that they find a cottage with running water and a bathroom.

When Eileen came back in she took a kettle of hot water into the bedroom so that she could wash before she put on her clothes. Once she felt reasonably clean and was dressed she was more cheerful. She ate what was left of the breakfast her mother had prepared for her brothers and Rodman and afterwards offered to do all the dishes. Mary, however, insisted that they do them together, she washing and the girl drying. Mary enjoyed doing things, even chores, with her daughter. Eileen appeared to most people to be rather shy, but those who knew her well recognized what others saw in her as shyness rather as a strong tendency to observe quietly and with a genuine interest what others were doing around her. When she felt the need to respond she generally demonstrated that she was both articulate and witty. She most often said what she thought but usually with a great deal of tact. On the other hand if anyone was imprudent enough to bait her she generally responded sharply enough to discourage further teasing. She had inherited her mother's quick tongue and Mary knew it and was proud of it. She saw no point in raising a daughter whom others would be encouraged to take advantage of. Just being a female would provide enough opportunity for that without the extra burden of a retiring character.

Because of all this Eileen was very popular with girls her age and even older, but not equally popular with young men. Like some other young women her age Eileen accepted as a challenge the brashness with which the typical young man tried to hide his lack of confidence and responded in kind. This was usually devastating to the young men and they did not often tease her again. As a matter of fact even those males with enough brains and backbone to verbally joust with her didn't enjoy it. It was so out of character for a female to respond to their bantering with anything but a giggle that it threw them off guard and made them feel uncomfortable, and they didn't like it. Eileen's mother knew this and was not unhappy that it was so. She was fully cognizant of her own place in life as a woman; in fact she was proud of the fact that what she was required to do she did well. Nevertheless she wanted everyone to know that what she did she did because it was her job and not because she was incapable of doing anything else. She was as sure as she could be that, given the opportunity, she could run any organization—even govern the country—as well as any man. She hoped her daughter would acquire the same confidence in herself.

When the dishes were done Eileen sat on the screened porch for a while watching the lake through the trees on the other side of the road. Mary took off the apron she had been wearing all morning but she wasn't ready to rest yet. It was time to begin planning lunch and dinner.

"I wonder what Louise is doing," Eileen said after a long period of silence. She and Louise Bentsen had been best friends ever since either of them could remember.

Mary was paging through a cookbook, trying to match recipes with the ingredients she had brought along. She didn't look up nor did she answer Eileen immediately. But she had heard her. Finally she closed the book. "Oh," she said, "I suppose she is sitting at home wondering what you are doing too."

"Probably," Eileen answered without much enthusiasm.

"Don't tell me you're bored already," admonished the girl's mother. "Goodness, we've not even been here one day yet."

Eileen sighed dramatically while gazing steadily out the window but when she noticed that her mother's interest had shifted to something else she stood up and moved toward the door. "I think I'll take a walk," she said, putting as much despair as she possibly could into her voice. "Maybe I'll see something interesting."

Actually she was less unhappy than she acted but she knew that if she appeared to her parents to be enjoying this outing less than they were but not really complaining it might work out to her advantage. Experience told her she must take care not to overdo it though.

It was beginning to look as though it might rain. Out over the lake dark clouds covered up the blue sky and gave the water a muddy gray cast. Now and then the breeze stiffened and blew the lines up against the boats of the few fishermen still out. Finally, one by one they realized it was not a good day for fishing and soon the lake surface was deserted.

Eileen left the door open because the spring was still broken. Mary got up to fasten it and standing in the doorway told her daughter that, since it looked so much like rain, not to go very far. She smiled as she watched her walk down the gravel driveway fully aware that the girl's sad face and mien were at least partly for Mary's benefit, but she intended to humor her, at least for a while.

Eileen turned left and started slowly, somewhat aimlessly, down the road, apparently with no particular destination in mind. Just then the Oakland roadster came from the other direction, stopping long enough for the two riders to wave at the girl, and turned into the drive. She looked back and acknowledged their presence, but little more, then continued on her way.

Mary, realizing that Eileen's counterfeit depression was only an indication of the 'little girl' still in her, smiled to herself as she turned away from the doorway. She was happy really that all her children had not yet irrevocably reached adulthood and were not, therefore, beyond mothering. They have time, she considered with pleasure, lots of time to grow up. She picked up her cookbook again. Her last thought concerning Eileen was the speculation that the girl would find John and point out to him that it looked like rain and that perhaps he should start back. Mary relaxed in her feeling of domestic security.

Perhaps Mary would have felt at least a small measure of apprehension had she been standing next to Eileen as the Oakland turned into the driveway and if she had intercepted the looks that passed between the girl and Rodman Schultz.

Their eyes had met, if only for the briefest fraction of a second, before Eileen had turned and walked on. The encounter had been short and, at least to the girl, meaningless. Nonetheless Rodman, perceptive as he was, had noted that she had looked for him rather than her brother, and to Rodman that was significant. It meant that she was looking for something different, something new. Perhaps she was bored, he speculated. And, if that was the case, he reasoned further, she would be vulnerable to a smooth talking college man, which was what he considered himself.

If Eileen was impressed with the young man from Toledo she failed to show it. The fact is she hardly thought about him at all, either positively or negatively. She had been taught that girls her age were too young to think seriously about men. This she heard from the nuns at school as well as from her parents at home, and she believed it. Still sometimes, like now, she could not help wondering what it would be like when finally she was old enough.

Eileen sauntered aimlessly down the road that ran in front of the summer cottages on one side and along the lake on the other. She cast a tentative look in the direction in which her brother had disappeared, thinking that she might try to find him. But when she saw no sign of where he had gone she decided to continue on in the direction she had started. Surely, she thought, there would be someone or something down that road different enough to be interesting, perhaps a girl her age, or maybe a young child. Even a puppy or a kitten would do. She walked on without a backward glance.

Eileen rounded the bend and found, to her disappointment, nothing but more of the same, narrow driveways leading back to cabins similar to the one being used by her family, shielded from the traffic by shrubbery. But she kept on even though the air had become heavy and still, certainly signalling a storm. Then, just as she was about to turn back, she found another road forking to her left away from the lake. It went off abruptly, fitting narrowly between two trees whose branches reached almost to the ground, and was nearly hidden. Because it was paved Eileen decided it was not just another driveway, but that it might be a private street. She decided to at least see where it went before going back. As she turned into the new road a few big drops of rain began to fall, but they did not come through the trees and she didn't notice.

Eventually, some time later, the rain came like a spring storm. Heralded by broken spears of lightning and great explosions of thunder, it came in a sudden torrent of water and noise punctuated by bright flashes of light and rolling sound, until the storm moved off growling and grumbling because it had to leave so soon after it had just settled in.

Later the rumbling resonance receded slowly, rolling and echoing back and forth across the lake, leaving only the steady stream of water pouring down from the clouds torn open by the fierceness of the storm. It hurtled to the ground scrubbing the air as it came, the air that had started to feel close and sticky but now began to feel cool, and smell clean and fresh.

When the storm first started Rodman and Aloysius had been standing on the porch by a screened window, watching the water flood the drive and the gutterless road, when John burst from the trees by the lake, carrying the sodden box of writing material and running as though pursued.

When Aloysius saw his brother he unlatched the screen door so that John could fling himself through the doorway, nearly out of breath, and stand there in a pool of water which he was creating on the floor.

"For the Lord's sake," Mary exclaimed as she came out onto the porch to see what had caused the commotion. When she saw it was John, his dark hair plastered down over his forehead and water dripping from all over his body the concern of a mother was overcome by her innate sense of humor.

At first, holding her hand in front of her mouth, she was able to nearly control her laughter; but finally she gave up. "Oh Johnny," she gasped, "you look terrible, but you look so funny too."

The young man did not appreciate that. He stood there, the puddle around his feet growing bigger and his eyes, almost hidden by his wet hair, glancing from mother to brother, seeking at least a modicum of sympathy, but finding absolutely none. In fact his brother too began to chuckle and at length to point at the younger man and howl with merriment.

"Gee whiz, thanks a lot," John muttered mournfully to both of them. "It sure is a good thing I don't need any help 'cause I wouldn't get it from either of you." Then he added, "Do I really look that funny?"

At that Aloysius nearly exploded with laughter but was able to choke it back, "I've never seen anything funnier in my life." And then he did something that John would always remember as characteristic of his older brother. He grabbed John, rain soaked clothes and all, in a close hug, so that his own shirt was soon nearly as wet as John's.

"Hey," said John, "watch it. You're gonna get youself all wet too."

And Aloysius, still smiling but no longer laughing answered, "So what, little brother? It's all in the family anyway. Come on, let's go in mom's bedroom and I'll help get you out of those things. Then if mom will make you a cup of tea maybe Rod can find something to put in it to warm you up faster."

Mary acted as if she hadn't heard the last of that. She picked up two towels from the table where she had been folding some laundry earlier. "Here," she directed, "take these with you. I'll heat the water."

In the meantime Rodman, who had apparently missed the humor in what had been going on waited until Mary was busy at the stove then hurried out to the car to retrieve what was left of his supply of gin. He came back in and gave it to Aloysius, then returned to his watch by the door.

Mary, to no one in particular, mused, "I wonder if Eileen is out in this." Rodman heard the remark and began, himself, to wonder about her, probably caught in the rain and disoriented. It had slackened considerably but was still coming down too hard to walk in. Suddenly he made a decision.

At that very moment the Packard turned into the drive and stopped in a crunch of gravel. Pat got out and hurried inside. Immediately he noticed the look of anxiety on his wife's face and noticing that Eileen was not there surmised that she was the cause of it.

"Where is your daughter?" he asked Mary.

"I don't know," was Mary's worried answer. "She went out for a walk more than an hour ago and is not back. And it is storming."

"Well, I can see that," he said with a hint of irritation in his voice. Then he added resignedly, "I guess I had better go out and see if I can find her." He put the papers he had been carrying in his hand on the table and started out.

"Wait," said Aloysius. "I think I'll go with you. I can help you look." Pat did not answer but nodded, which Aloysius correctly took to indicate agreement. Together the two went out and as the rain started to come down harder the Packard backed out of the drive and started in the same direction Eileen had taken.

Rodman had said nothing, but he had heard the mother's words and, more importantly, the apprehension in the mother's voice. He knew that Mary was worried about Eileen getting wet and perhaps getting sick because of it. But he also thought he heard something else, perhaps the worry that Eileen, knowing a storm was coming, would look for shelter and somehow be put in some compromising situation. He knew because it was the sort of thing mothers always worried about. He made a decision. He stood up and started toward the door.

"Eileen seems like a smart girl," he said, "and I agree she will probably be back before this gets worse. But just in case she got too far away before she decided to turn back I'm going out too. If two of us are looking it won't take as long."

Rodman was fairly certain Mary would have reservations about him looking for the girl because he might find her before her father did. In that case she would find herself alone with him in his car and Mary would not like that. On the other hand she could hardly tell him not to go. If she did she would have to say why and Rodman knew she would not be able to say what she really was thinking, nor would she have time to think of anything else reasonable. She might even have suggested that John go with him but he did not give her the chance to do that. He hurried out into the still light rain before either of the others could say anything, and soon he was in the roadster and backing out onto the road.

Pat and Aloysius had gone several miles before deciding that they had gone farther than Eileen could have walked. Then they had started back but on the way had turned into the second of two crossroads they had noticed. Eileen might have turned off on either one of them to explore.

That was when the rain had started to come down in wind driven sheets so that one could not even see the lake through the occasional break in the trees. Flowers and some shrubbery had been flattened by the violence of the wind and the water. It had grown very dark but now and then the lightning illuminated the road and prepared Pat and Aloysius for the tremendous claps of thunder that came after it. At one time the sound followed the lightning so closely that they were sure something nearby had been hit. The possibility of course allowed for considerable speculation, but neither of them put his thoughts into words. They both realized though that the rain was making it hard to see and that they were not likely to accomplish anything. Finally Aloysius suggested that they go back to the cabin to see if perhaps Eileen had already returned. Pat agreed and carefully turned the car around to start back.

While Pat and Aloysius had been exploring the farthest of the two crossroads Rodman had passed it and therefore had not seen them. He too went a considerable distance before deciding he had gone too far and turning around. As the fury of the storm increased and reduced his ability to see to almost none at all he felt that the prudent thing to do was to stop until there was a break. He reasoned correctly that if he had come upon Eileen walking in the road he might very easily have run into her. He did not bother to pull into the ditch because he wasn't sure where it was and he doubted there would be any other traffic for a while anyway. He merely stopped and left the motor running and the lights on.

After several more minutes of violence the storm began to subside. The rain decreased enough for Rodman to roll down his window and let in some cool clear air. On either side of the road the branches dripped water like laundry that had been hung up without being wrung out very well. If Rodman had looked closely enough at the trees next to his roadster he would have seen a small spider repairing his web. The little fellow had been smart enough to build it under a very large leaf and it had been relatively untouched by the storm, only a few anchoring strands having been pulled loose by the force of the wind. Industriously he secured them and settled down to wait for some unwary insect to drop in for dinner. Light was returning too and once again Rodman could see farther than a few feet past the hood of his car. He decided to continue his search.

As he drove slowly along Rodman tried to peer into the trees on both sides of the roadway and that is probably how he noticed the side road onto which Eileen had turned when he had not noticed it the first time and the others in fact had not noticed it at all. It left the main road at an angle and turning onto it required a sharp turn. He was very satisfied with himself and his expectations were somewhat higher as he drove on. The buildings there were different, more like small houses than vacation cabins. They stood farther back from the side of the road and some of them had open front porches with roofs. It was on one of these, on a house on the right side of the road, that Rodman saw Eileen, standing next to a somewhat older woman. The two of them were talking rather casually and smiling, but it could be observed that Eileen seemed concerned as she continually glanced up and down the road.

Rodman stopped at the end of the walk that ran from the porch steps and reaching over the seat next to him rolled down the window on the passenger side.

"Eileen," he called to her, "are you ready to leave?"

Eileen's companion seemed much more relieved to see Rodman than Eileen did. She waved toward the car as though it might have been someone she knew. Then she turned to Eileen.

"There they are," she told her, "just like you said they would be."

Eileen was surprised. She had expected to see the Packard and now she peered into the Oakland hoping to see her brother sitting there but knowing that Rodman was alone. She knew she should be glad that someone had come for her and she should show it, but she did not know how to do this while at the same time making it clear that she was not necessarily glad that it was Rodman. On the other hand she did not want to appear rude. After all it was, she thought, nice of him to come.

Eileen's friend was Sharon Deener. She and her husband, Art, were from Toronto. In the little more than an hour that had elapsed since Eileen had run up on her porch to escape the downpour, and the two had talked, she had become interested in the girl. Not more than ten years older than Eileen she recognized in her an innocence, a naivete, that had once been her own. She hoped that the sweetness she perceived in Eileen, people had once been able to see in her. Now she noted Eileen's confusion and also realized that the driver of the car was neither Eileen's father nor one of her brothers, but she drew the wrong conclusion.

Well," she remarked conspiratorially, "is this young man your friend? He certainly has a nice machine."

Eileen was now more confused than ever. "Oh no," she said. "He's not my friend. I mean he's a friend but he's not really my friend. He's my brother's friend." Then she added, "Well, he's a friend of my family, too."

Sharon laughed and put her arm around Eileen. "I'm not sure I understand completely. But I think I do. I think you'd better say something to him, though. He is probably worried about you."

"I think maybe I'd better go," Eileen told her new acquaintance." She started to remove a sweater that she wore around her shoulders. "Here is your sweater. Thank you for letting me wear it."

"Why don't you keep it on?" Sharon suggested. "It still feels a bit cool to me. You can bring it back in a day or two when you have time. I'm hoping that will give you an excuse to come back and visit."

"You really wouldn't mind if I did?" Eileen asked.

This time Sharon hugged her rather warmly. "Actually, young lady, I insist," she assured her.

Eileen started down the two steps to the walk then turned around. "I'll be back," she promised. Then she walked slowly down the walk and got into the car. "Hi, Mr. Schultz," she said.

Rodman had at first thought that perhaps Eileen was not going to let him take her back to the cabin. He also felt that he understood why and, assuming that the lady on the porch knew why too, he was somewhat embarrassed. Because of that when she finally got into his car he was relieved. Besides relief though Rodman felt something more. If he had been satisfied with himself earlier now he felt almost triumphant. He was not quite sure how he had triumphed, only that he had planned something and that it had worked out the way he had planned it. And actually beyond getting Eileen alone in his car he had planned nothing. He would just see what happened.

Rodman did not consider himself particularly attractive to women. He did not think of himself as handsome and he knew that the girls did not refer to him as 'cute', which was the adjective in vogue. As a matter of fact he wasn't sure he wanted to be considered cute. In his mind the word carried a connotation of one's being a bit immature, perhaps even a bit amateurish, and being called that would not be considered a compliment by Rodman Schultz. He liked to think of himself as being able to get what he wanted by planning and, sometimes, by making it obvious that he had access to more money than most other college students did.

Rodman was very much attracted to Eileen and he wasn't sure why. To be sure she was good looking, but he knew a lot of better looking girls both at home and at school. She had not been particularly friendly toward him but that did not usually influence him one way or the other. Perhaps it was that whether or not he liked Eileen did not seem to matter to her. It seemed to him that all the girls he knew wanted to be liked. They wanted to be the ones who decided with whom they would go out. As a matter of fact he knew that this was a bit of acting on their part too. He knew that most girls worried about being asked out and would accept a date with almost anyone who was not completely obnoxious, even though they all had preferences. He also knew, from talking to many women, young and old, that girls thought a lot about being kissed and about being made love to, especially those who were still virgins. This, he also knew, could be taken advantage of. But, for some reason, he did not think this applied to the girl who sat next to him. And for some reason he could not understand he wanted this girl to respect him. He did not want her to think he was trying to do anything wrong. At first he had intended to do what he usually did with girls he had just met. He never tried to talk them into anything. What he did was try to engage each one of them in a personal relationship and then take advantage of whatever happened. That sounded rather innocuous he knew, and he also knew it would sound so to Eileen. Reluctantly he turned the car around and slowly started back.

It took only a moment to get back on the road which would run past the O'Maury cabin. Rodman stopped the roadster for a moment before leaving the little side road.

"This was hard to see in the rain," he said to Eileen. "That is why Al and your father missed it, I guess. They were looking for you too. Everyone was worried about you."

"I know," she answered softly without looking at him. "I caused everyone a lot of trouble, didn't I? And I appreciate your coming out to look for me. I really do." She tried to sound grateful, of course, but it came out rather weakly. Rodman smiled to himself. She was trying to be nice but she really didn't care what he thought. Suddenly he wanted to tell her that he too had been worried about her, that he cared for her safety, but had the feeling that it would sound contrived and that she wouldn't believe him anyway. Actually he wasn't sure he believed it. He started the car moving again.

Say! Where are we going?" She had suddenly noticed that they seemed to be proceeding in the wrong direction.

Rodman chuckled. "Be patient," he told her. "This road is too narrow to turn around in and the shoulder is so wet I'm afraid to get too close to the edge. I'm going to drive on a bit to see if it gets any wider. "Look," he assured her, "I'll get you home in no time. Don't worry."

Eileen tried to look as though she was at ease, in fact she tried to tell herself there was no reason not to be.

"I'm not worried." she asserted. "I know we'll get back and I'm only a little damp."

He said, "We can roll up the windows now and it will be warmer in here."

Eileen knew very well that she should insist Rodman turn the car around and return to the cottage. As a matter of fact she wanted him to because she knew it was what should be expected of her. Nevertheless she kept her eyes on the water soaked shrubbery that slowly wound past her window. When they came to a paved driveway Rodman turned the roadster around and started back the way they had come.

Eventually the narrow lane on which they had been traveling turned back to the main road. Rodman hesitated at the intersection. He wanted to turn away from the direction which would take them back to the security of the girl's family but, since he could think of no excuse for doing so without stating his real reason, he was sure the girl would be alarmed and would object.

Eileen had never before been alone with a young man who was not a relative. From her mother and from the nuns at school she had learned that, to allow herself to remain in such a situation was to risk some danger. The danger, however, was somewhat vague although Eileen knew that it involved sex somehow. In any event she realized that she should be, if not frightened, at least apprehensive; but she was not. At the very most she was uneasy, but the unease was caused mostly by the feeling that she might be asked to do something she had never done before and would not know how to respond. She was afraid of being embarrassed.

By now the sun had begun to set. A giant ball of orange flame, it colored the patches of cloud decorating the sky and laid a path of deep gold across the water. Rodman's car passed an open spot in the trees on the lake side and suddenly he could see the spectacular picture that was being painted by nature. He was so stunned that he uttered, "Wow!" and at the same time stopped the roadster again.

Feeling the car stop and hearing Rodman's exclamation, Eileen at first thought something was wrong but as she turned her head to see what it was she saw the sun and she too was overcome by the sight. Without thinking she said, "Oh", making it sound like a sigh.

A little farther on was another roadway that turned toward the lake. Rodman, seeing it, started forward again and turned there, driving on as if drawn by the light, stopping finally in full view of the water and the sun, and turned off the motor. There they remained, not speaking, glowing in the wonderful light that made everything the same color.

Rodman recovered first, turning and slipping his arm behind Eileen who sat erect staring out the front window, her eyes wide and a slight smile on her lips. She did not move or change her expression until the sun had all but disappeared and the lane it made over the water had turned to deep crimson. Then she relaxed, murmuring softly almost to herself, "That was so beautiful," and leaned back into the seat. When she felt Rodman's arm against her shoulder she recoiled, but only slightly and only for a moment. She felt that this was what she had wanted to happen, but it was only a feeling. There was no great new knowledge of life or sudden understanding of good or evil, just the feeling that something was about to happen that would be different from anything that had ever happened to her before. But still she did not know what to do. She turned her face toward Rodman and waited; and he kissed her, at first gently, but then more warmly. He put his other hand on her shoulder and pulled it slowly around so that they faced each other.

Eileen had never been kissed like that before. Not knowing what she was expected to do she kept her hands folded in her lap and did not respond. Still she did not pull away from Rodman and although she kept her lips closed they were warm and soft. Her heart was beating rapidly and a strange feeling was spreading over her body. She wanted something else to happen to her and although she did not know what it was she felt that it would somehow change her, would make her psychologically different, perhaps even wiser.

Rodman could sense both the excitement and the apprehension in her, even though he mistakenly assumed the latter to be caused by moral principle rather than embarrassment related to her lack of experience.

Rodman felt the girl becoming more pliant and the passion within him grew. Slowly the hand he had on her shoulder slid down to her breast. He could feel that there were several layers of cloth between his hand and her body but, in spite of that, he could feel her nipple which had become erect. He squeezed softly, reveling in the fullness and firmness under his searching fingers. She made a sound, half sigh and half moan, and raised her hand. She meant to push him away but when she put her hand on his her resolve weakened and she left it there.

Rodman's mouth was still on hers. He moved his head in a gentle motion, trying to coax her into opening her lips. Little by little he was overcoming the last vestige of her reluctance. She was becoming more and more relaxed, slowly leaning backwards so that she seemed to be sliding under him when suddenly something happened that he would never be able to explain even though he would think about it many times. The realization of the girl's openness, her trustfulness, her innocence, her real goodness were thrust on him. It was as though he were trying to seduce his sister, or perhaps his daughter. The passion drained out of him as though someone had opened a tap.

Now it was nearly dark. He drew back and sat erect. Her eyes, which had been closed the whole time, opened and she too sat up, moving away from him toward the door.

He could faintly see her face, a pale oval framed by her dark hair. He put out his hand and touched her cheek, cool and soft in the darkness. He felt more than saw how beautiful she was. "I'm sorry," he said quietly, "sorry for what I almost did." She said nothing. She sat with her hands in her lap and waited. She did not know what had happened to her but, whatever it was, she knew it would never ever happen again.

Rodman started the engine and switched on the lights before turning the car around and driving back to the main road.

Aloysius and John would have dashed back out to look for their younger sister except that neither of them had any idea where to begin the search. Aloysius, at least partly because he knew the young man in question, could not make up his mind whether he would feel better if they knew Rodman had found Eileen or not. John sat with his father at the table, already set for dinner. Pat gripped a mug of steaming tea which he stirred distractedly now and then, but did not drink.

Aloysius stood next to his mother who stared through the screen into the gloom outside. No one spoke.

From up the road a car approached slowly, only its headlights visible. John and his father heard it and glanced toward the door to see what the other two made of it. The car stopped by the drive, a door slammed, and the car drove on, its rear light passing slowly out of sight into the night.

Eileen walked deliberately toward the door, her feet crunching in the gravel. Aloysius unhooked the screen door and she came in. Everyone watched her closely but no one said anything.

Eileen acted surprised to see them. She stopped and said, "Is something wrong?"

"We were going to ask you the same thing," John said.

Aloysius tried to see out through the screen. "Was that Rodman?" he asked.

"Yes," she answered.

Aloysius studied her face. She looked rather too undisturbed for it to be natural. "Why did he leave?" he asked her.

"Oh," she told him absently, "he said he thought he had worn out his welcome and he thought he'd start home. Say isn't dinner ready? I'm almost starved."

"Just a minute, young lady," her mother ordered. "I want to know where you have been and why it took so long for you to get back."

"Oh, mother," Eileen answered impatiently. She seemed angry at the questions and about to say something short. Then, once again she said, "Oh, mother." But this time she looked at Mary as she said it with a look in her eyes that was almost pleading.

But Mary was not ready to let her go yet. "Did anything happen?"

"What do you mean?"

Mary suddenly backed down. She dropped her eyes. "Well all right," she said. "Let's eat. I am sure your father is starving too."

The others, actually uneasy with Mary's questions, were glad to begin preparing to eat. As they turned away, though, Eileen took her mother's hand and murmured, so low that only Mary could hear, "Mama, nothing happened, nothing at all." And Mary thought the girl sounded just a little disappointed.

Chapter II

That's what they were going to do, just like they did every Friday night, sit on Ray's porch and drink a jug of beer and talk about the weather, and baseball, and maybe politics. Trouble was neither of them had a dollar for the beer. So Ray said, "Well, I guess it'll have to be ice water." And Mac said, "After the first one or two I can't usually tell the difference anyway." They both laughed.

From Our Depression, by Evan Oel.

✷ ✷ ✷

1921

It was sometime past midnight but the day had not yet decided whether it was still Friday or had quietly turned into Saturday. Nothing else moved on McMillan Street but the bicycle as it turned into the dark convent driveway and stopped in front of the main entrance. The steady crunch the tires made in the gravel sounded too loud and when it stopped the quiet dropped back like a black velvet cloak. The driver jumped off, kicked down the parking stand and took an envelope from his saddlebag. He struck a match and checked the address before rapping on the massive door three times with the great brass knocker. Nothing changed. The huge brooding edifice remained dark and silent, no light showing anywhere. After a few minutes the messenger knocked again, this time slowly and deliberately, and even louder. Then he stepped back and watched the windows for any sign of life. He was ready to knock a third time when finally he saw a light. It was obviously carried for it moved steadily along from window to window until it disappeared on the other side of the entrance.

When the door at last opened the messenger saw that the light shown from a candle in the hand of a nun. She was short and her black habit covered her from the top of her head to her feet so that, besides her hands, he could see nothing of her but her wrinkled face. With one hand she shielded the candle from the draft, but it flickered and danced, casting eerie shadows on the wall behind her.

"God bless you," she said. "Can I help you?"

"Western Union," he announced. "I have a telegram for a Sister Theodosia. If you're Sister Theodosia you need to sign for it."

She answered, "Sister Theodosia is our Mother Superior. I am Sister Philomena. Would it be all right if I sign her name?"

"Just sign your own name, lady," the messenger told her, taking a stub of a pencil and a receipt book from his pocket and thrusting them toward the little doorkeeper. Not knowing what to do with the candle she held it out to him.

"Can you hold this please?" she asked.

He took the light, standing close so that she could see where she was to sign the page. When she was finished and they had both retrieved their property she thanked him, once again blessed him, and started to close the door.

"Hey lady," he said loudly, "we usually get a tip for this."

"My goodness," she said thoughtfully. "Then she added, "If you could wait for a minute I will be right back."

She closed the door, leaving him alone in the scant illumination that trickled through the trees from the street light. He waited several minutes, deciding eventually that she was not coming back, when suddenly the door was reopened. The little nun stood there with a tray. On it were the candle, now in a holder, a cup of coffee, and a large pastry roll on a saucer.

"I am not permitted to have money of my own," she explained. "And everyone else is sleeping. I got this from the kitchen. I hope it will do. The coffee has milk and sugar in it because I forgot to ask how you like it."

The messenger, somewhat older than most but nevertheless still a young man, took the cup and the saucer from the tray, too surprised either to protest or to thank the old nun who smiled sweetly at him and once again said, "God bless you." Then she added, "When you are finished just leave the dishes on the step." And with that she was gone. The door closed with a quiet click and once again the messenger was alone. He drank the coffee, which was very strong but not much more than lukewarm, in a few gulps. Then, very carefully, he put the cup in the saucer and put both of them on the top step. Then he rode off, steering the bicycle with one hand and eating the roll with the other. It was delicious.

If the messenger had had the temerity to lift the skirt of the diminutive doorkeeper he might have noticed she had had time to put on neither stockings nor shoes. Now her bare feet made soft patting sounds on the tile floor as she walked through the dining hall to return the tray to the kitchen. She moved rather quickly because the floor was cold.

When the tray was back where it belonged she left the dining hall and walked toward the stairs which would lead to the nuns' sleeping quarters. But on the way she passed the chapel and decided to make a brief visit there. Inside she genuflected, then sat down in the last pew, putting her feet on the kneeler, up off the cold floor.

The old nun folded her arms, pushing each hand into the sleeve on the opposite arm, and, leaning back in the near darkness, closed her eyes. She loved to sit in the chapel like that, alone with her God and her memories. To her it was the essence of peace but it was not often she had the opportunity to enjoy it.

Eventually she remembered the telegram and retrieved it from the deep pocket in her skirt. She stood up and genuflected, crossing herself with holy water at the door on her way out.

At the mother superior's door she knocked twice softly and almost immediately heard a voice from the other side.

"Yes, what is it?"

"Philomena, mother. I have a telegram for you."

"A telegram?"

There was a rustling noise, then silence. Then the door opened.

"A telegram?" wondered Theodosia aloud again. "Let me see whom it is from." She took the envelope which the older nun held out and tore it open neatly with her thumbnail. She took a paper from inside and unfolded it, holding it under the gaslight in the hall so that she could read.

"Dear Lord," she gasped as the message became clear. "Aloysius O'Maury is dead."

In the deep gloom of the hallway the two women stared at each other, their eyes wide in shock, as they understood the implications of the news. The scene had an unrealness about it, as if it were only an illustration out of a story book. In the darkness that masked everything in the hallway the one element that persisted and connected what was happening with the normal world of the two motionless nuns was the steady hiss of the gaslight. Sister Philomena finally broke the tableau and spoke softly.

"Poor Eileen. How did he die?"

Sister Theodosia held the paper up to the light again but she didn't really need to. The terse message was already written indelibly in her memory. "It was an auto accident."

"Oh my!" Sister Philomena, her mind suddenly filled with visions of flaming wreckage and twisted metal, pressed her knuckles against her mouth. "How will you tell her?"

The younger nun stared at her companion for a time. Then she drew a long resolute breath. "I'll tell her now. She should know." She put her hand on Sister Philomena'a shoulder. "You had better go back to your bed and get some rest. I'll need your help in the morning. Besides it is cold in this hall."

"Yes," the little nun answered. She pressed her skirt back against her knees and looked down. "And I don't have any shoes on."

"Philomena!" Sister Theodosia scolded. "Do you want to catch your death? Go on now." Gently she turned the other woman around and nudged her in the direction of her room.

The superior remained motionless for a few minutes, deep in thought, then, having decided what to say, walked slowly down the hall, stopping at the second to the last door. She rapped twice and waited. Shortly the door opened a few inches and Eileen O'Maury peered out through the crack. When she saw who had knocked on the door she opened it all the way and stood there in a long nightgown, her young face pale and apprehensive in the dim light.

"Mother," she said, "what is it? Is something wrong?"

"Put on your robe and come down to the chapel," was all Sister Theodosia said before she turned and began to walk away.

"But what have I done?" the girl called softly, apparently thinking she was being punished. The nun stopped and turned around. Although she did not smile her voice was kind. "It is nothing you have done. Now hurry." She turned once again and disappeared into the shadows on her way down the stairs.

Sister Theodosia had a problem that concerned her relations with the other nuns, particularly the very young ones. She found it necessary to make a constant effort to keep from getting too close to them.

She had a sister, Karen, nearly twelve years her junior and in the four years which had passed between the younger girl's birth and the older one's entrance into the convent they had become very close. The older girl, then Marilyn Hightower, had developed a feeling for her baby sister that bordered on maternal. When she left home she became very homesick, as most novices do. She missed her mother and father very much but it was her little sister that she thought of the most at night when the lights had been turned out and she had finished her night prayers; when, just before she drifted off to sleep, she allowed her mind to wander to another time.

In the years that followed the child had grown up, making friends and associations of her own. But Sister Theodosia had maintained the memory of the little one whom she had held on her lap and treated like her own living doll, and she secretly longed to be able to do it again.

In the beginning it had been most painful, the thought of her baby sister growing up without her. But the young girl had indeed grown up and had graduated from Our Lady Of The Woods College in Illinois. She had worked for a while and saved her money, enough to attend graduate school at Indiana State University, earning a masters degree in English. During a workshop at the Indiana College Karen had met a young writer by the name of Willa Cather who was establishing a reputation, and had begun corresponding with her. Eventually they had become good friends, with Miss Cather encouraging the younger girl to try to write.

Sister Theodosia had a hard time trying to understand her feelings toward her baby sister. Unfortunately she hardly ever saw her younger sister who now lived in a different city. She saw Karen often enough to realize that the younger woman had become an adult. And yet when she thought of Karen the recurring image that filled her mind was of herself lovingly kissing and hugging the little girl. And in her mind it was so much of what she missed that she longed to do it. But the longing she felt had to be directed toward something or someone else. This turned out to be the young girls who came to the convent and were in her care. She could hardly keep from holding them close and kissing them on the lips, much as she had often done with her baby sister; but she never did. In fact she went to great length to keep the younger women at arms length, partly because she was not sure how to interpret her feelings. As a matter of fact the urge was so strong sometimes that she wondered if she was not, well, as they used to say on the South Lebanon farm where she was raised, "queer".

The idea shamed her, so much in fact that she went to great lengths to avoid physical contact with the other nuns, especially the young ones; and she most carefully avoided accidentally touching any nun's breast. In fact so preoccupied was she with this fear that she touched her own bosom only when she bathed, and then only as long as was necessary.

Why she felt this way, seeming to doubt her own femininity, she really did not know. Although she had had only one sexual encounter with a male in her entire life her reaction had been completely normal.

She would never forget that afternoon. Tom was a young seminarian from St. Gregory's in Cincinnati. He worked summers on the Hightower farm to raise money for his tuition. She had happened upon Tom while he was cleaning stalls in the barn, or perhaps she had been there first and he had come in. It had been so long ago she could not recall precisely the events which led up to what had happened. But what had followed she would never be able to erase from her memory. However it had come about they had found themselves together and otherwise alone on a warm afternoon in August. He had no shirt on and the muscles that rippled beneath his bare sun-bronzed skin showed the effect of his summer occupation. She wore a dress with a long skirt, as was the custom then. But, because of the temperature, she wore very little beneath the dress and it clung damply and revealingly to her young body.

The two were good friends. If either had been asked he or she would have described their relationship as that of brother and sister and, before that afternoon, that would have been a fairly accurate picture.

They began, as usual, by teasing each other about one thing or another—often it was about how much they ate, both being more gourmand than gourmet. The teasing then turned to throwing straw at one another, the verbal chaff turning to chaff more irritating which stuck to their hair and their clothes, and they laughed at each other. Then she took a dipper of water from a pail near the door and doused him with it. He started after her and she, cornered, tried to climb the ladder to the hay mow upstairs, but he was too close. He grabbed her ankle, something he ordinarily would not have thought of doing under any circumstance, and pulled her back. She let go of the ladder and fell back upon him. They began to wrestle on the straw covered floor and soon she was lying partly beneath him, his hands on her wrists, holding her arms above her head so that she was unable to pull her skirt down. It had crept up nearly to her hips and as they lay there catching their breath he found himself looking at the slender beauty of her legs and realizing how close he was to this wonderfully developing young girl's body.

He kissed her gently. Then he released her arms and kissed her with the passion he had begun to feel, and soon they were kissing each other with a heat neither had suspected in the other.

He shifted his weight so that he was supported by one elbow and began fondling her breast timidly with his free hand. She closed her eyes, feeling a warmness she had never known before. Soon, realizing that she was responding to him, he put his hand beneath her dress and began fumbling with her loose fitting underpants.

He was so clumsy that she realized he was as much a novice at what he was trying to do as she was so she tried to arch her back to make it easier for him to remove her underclothes and soon she felt her pants begin to slide down her legs.

The voice from outside was loud and impatient, as though the owner had been calling for some time. "Tom," it said again, "where in the dickens are you, boy?"

The young man jumped to his feet. "Oh, my God! It's my father, come to pick me up. I wonder how long he's been out there. What if he came in here?"

She too jumped to her feet. She avoided looking at him while she pulled her pants back where they belonged. Then she tried to brush away the hay that stuck damply to her skirt.

He could not look at her either, so embarrassed was he. He said nothing but hurried out into the bright sunlight and began talking to his father.

Marilyn did not follow him. She did not move until she had heard the engine in the father's car roar, echoing the impatience of the driver, then slow as the gears were shifted, and finally fade into the distance. Then she walked to the open door and peered outside. The yard was empty except for a few chickens scratching in the gravel, and one guinea hen.

The guineas usually announced visitors, she reflected, wondering why this one had ignored Tom's father and the noise the car had certainly made. She tried to imagine what might have happened if the man had come into the barn and surprised them. Then, further, she wondered what might have happened if he had not arrived just then. There was no doubt in her mind that she would have had intercourse with Tom. She was glad, perhaps relieved, that it had not happened. But she knew in her heart that she would not have tried to prevent it.

For a long time she stood in the shadow of the doorway and gazed at the dust that slowly settled behind the car that had left. She had a feeling of heartache, as though a romance of long duration had just ended. A tear squeezed from the corner of one eye and rolled slowly down her cheek. She waited until her father began driving the cows in the side door of the barn for milking before she left, making sure he didn't see her.

She had never again been close to Tom. She had seen him often during the rest of the summer, but both of them had taken great pains to avoid a confrontation.

That was the last summer Tom had worked at the farm, but it would have made no difference anyway for that autumn she had joined the postulants in the convent.

There were only three lights in the chapel and they were all on the other side of the communion rail. Next to the tabernacle was the red lamp that signalled the presence of the Blessed Sacrament and in front of the statue of St. Joseph by the altar on the Epistle side was another red lamp. On the gospel side, a statue of the Blessed Virgin stood. The lady peered yearningly toward heaven, a slight smile on her face, her arms spread in an age old gesture which suggested her desire to gather the entire human race to her bosom. The candle before her altar burned steadily and cast its light through blue glass.

The three vigil lights in their colored jars cast only faint illumination in the front of the chapel and could barely be seen from the pews in the rear. Nevertheless, when Eileen entered the little chapel and crossed herself with holy water she had no trouble finding the mother superior, a dark shadow kneeling in the last pew.

Sister Theodosia heard the girl come in. "Here," she said, sliding over in the pew to make room for her. When Eileen sat the nun took one of the younger woman's hands in both of hers.

"You must be strong," she said, and immediately Eileen thought, "It must be papa. He is dead. Or maybe it is mama."

Sister Theodosia went on. "There is no easy way to say this. Your brother Aloysius is dead, killed in a car wreck. Oh, my child I am so sorry. I have a telegram from your father."

Eileen gasped. "Aloysius! No, not Aloysius. It couldn't be. Oh, sister, it couldn't be Aloysius."

The grief in the girl's voice so affected the older woman that she had to pause for a moment before going on. "Oh, my dear," she said, "it is so difficult to accept the death of someone so young, so difficult. I know. But would it help even a little if you try to remember that now he is with God in Heaven?"

But the girl's answer was a tremendous sob. Sister Theodosia put her arm around Eileen and put the younger woman's head on her breast. For several minutes they sat there without saying anything, the only sound being Eileen's sobbing. Finally Eileen said, between sobs, "Can I go to them? My mother will need me."

The superior answered her slowly. "I know your family's burden would be lessened if you could be with them now. But it would not be taken away. Eileen you know what the rules of our order are. You can go if you want to. But you would not be permitted to return. You will have to decide if that is what you want."

Eileen, her hands clutching the back of the pew in front of her, leaned forward so that her forehead rested on her hands. Her long thick hair, which soon would be cut short, cascaded from her postulant's cap and hid the sides of her face. She had stopped weeping. After a while she rose and walked slowly to the front of the chapel where she knelt before the blue light at the Virgin's altar. The steadily burning candle hardly illuminated the pure white figure that stood above the tabernacle. The girl peered intently into the shadows, staring at the face, hoping for some sign, a smile, or the blinking of an eye perhaps, something that might help her decide what to do. But she saw nothing. Alas, it was only a statue.

Then suddenly she felt a warmness, a complete sensation of peace and total serenity. It was as though someone she trusted had rested his hand on her shoulder. A feeling of joy and love flooded her heart and she felt so close to God that she thought she would never want to leave the chapel. Then, just as quickly as it had come, the feeling was gone, but the memory remained and she had the knowledge that she would be able to recall it sometimes, but only by absolute abandonment of herself to her Creator and her Saviour. Now tears of happiness coursed gently down her cheeks and fell onto the marble communion rail.

In the rear of the chapel Sister Theodosia knelt and fingered her rosary beads. She prayed for guidance for herself, for patience, for spiritual strength and, most of all, for the Lord's help for Eileen. She knew that the girl was torn between her love and devotion to her family and her loyalty to her vocation. The superior was certain that Eileen belonged in the convent but she was not as certain that Eileen knew it yet.

In the shadows the nun thought she saw the young girl stand up and she too stood, waiting for her by the door, waiting to learn whether Eileen would leave or stay. But Eileen never came.

Sister Theodosia strained her eyes trying to cut through the darkness in the chapel. She was sure Eileen no longer knelt before the altar. But then where had she gone?

The nun began to walk toward the front of the chapel, slowly, and silently, so that she would not disturb Eileen if the girl still knelt in prayer. When Sister reached the first pew, though, she saw no one. The thought that she was all alone in the chapel brought an eerie sensation and suddenly her scalp began to tingle. But, as she turned toward the rear of the chapel, intending to leave, she noticed a darker shadow lying on the front pew and she realized that it was the girl.

Relieved and smiling to herself, amused at her somewhat juvenile reaction, sister started to speak to Eileen but before she did she realized that the young woman was asleep. It brought back memories of another young postulant many years ago, terribly homesick, who would lie in her bed in the darkness, her knees pulled up to her chest, and sob until she drifted off to sleep. She had never mentioned it to anyone, not even her mother when she came to visit. Eileen too had pulled her legs up in a fetal position and in the pale light from the Virgin's lamp Sister Philomena could see Eileen's robe had fallen away from her body and her leg was bare. Sister Theodosia entered the second pew and looked down on the shadowy form. The nun could see the outline of white flesh against the darkness of the pew but not the soft hair which would cover it, since the women in the convent did not find it necessary to shave their legs. White and lovely in the shadows it curved delicately out of the hem of her gown, exposed from her thigh to her slim ankle. Deliberately Sister Theodosia reached out and, taking the hem of Eileen's robe in her hand, covered the girl's leg, being very careful not to touch her skin. She knew that Eileen would not be leaving the convent. The mother Superior then leaned back and continued praying her rosary. She remained there until dawn.

*   *   *

Earlier in the day John had left the campus as soon as his last exam was over. Actually he rather liked going to college but he could not wait to return home whenever his schedule permitted. Aloysius, who was now ending his third year, did not seem nearly as eager to join his family as his younger brother, although once with them he always appeared happy to be there. As usual he was somewhat indefinite as to when they could expect him, but John was sure they would see him before bedtime.

Pat was late but he had been late before, always because of his work. John thought of his father as completely dependable. He could not imagine Pat doing anything unexpected or showing any kind of weakness. John felt his father would always be a source of strength to the rest of the family.

Actually Pat's tardiness was more of an excuse than a reason for Mary to be upset, but for the fourth time she went to the door and looked out to see if he was coming. John had noticed her irritation and, knowing how she would enjoy having something legitimate to complain to her husband about, would have been amused had he not been, as usual, getting hungry. He too went to the door and he put his arm around his mother's shoulder. "Come on, mom," he urged, "don't worry about dad. He's not very late and he's probably turning into the lane right now."

Mary indicated her impatience and annoyance by sniffing

indignantly, but just then the Packard pulled into the driveway. Pat opened his door and got out, setting his hat at a rather jaunty angle and casting a look of cautious defiance at the cottage. He hesitated only slightly before coming around the dust covered front of the car and starting to walk toward the front door. As he did so another car, a light Buick coupe, pulled slowly past, then backed up and stopped on the side of the road. The driver did not turn the engine off. He called out his window to Pat, "Is this the place where the O'Maury folks are staying?"

Pat, recognizing neither the car nor the driver, had stopped to see who it might be and was immediately apprehensive. He started toward the car saying, "I am Pat O'Maury." When the man who had called him got out of the little car Pat noticed he was wearing a uniform and a badge, but no gun. His apprehension increased and at once he thought of Aloysius.

The man said, "Mr. O'Maury I'm Constable Buckler. I'd like to ask you if you have a son named Aloysius."

From inside the cottage Mary and John heard the first exchange and saw the two men approach each other. As they began to talk Mary noticed her husband seemed to flinch, almost as though he had been struck. The man in uniform put out his hand as if to offer support but withdrew it as Pat seemed to regain control of himself. They spoke for a few more minutes before the officer removed his wide brimmed hat in what the two inside recognized as a gesture of sympathy. He said something else to Pat who then seemed to nod his head.

Finally the officer, still holding his hat, returned to his car, backed into the driveway, and slowly drove off the way he had come. Pat turned toward the cottage, his face drawn and ashen, and tears already beginning to run down his cheeks.

Mary could wait no longer. She burst from the building. "It is Aloysius," she cried, "isn't it?"

"Yes, yes," sobbed Pat, his wide shoulders shaking in anguish. "Oh my poor Mary, our Aloysius is dead." With that his body seemed to lose volume like a balloon with the air escaping. John was surprised to see his father's head bowed and his shoulders sagging. Pat's arms hung limply at his sides and he seemed unable to find the strength to proceed.

Mary put her hand on her husbands's arm. Gently she pressed him toward the step in front of the door. "Come on, my dear," she urged, "let's go inside. I'll fix you a cup of tea and you'll feel better. Then we can talk."

Pat allowed himself to be almost led into the cottage where he sat down heavily at the table. Mary took his hat from his head and put it next to the plate in front of him as he sat, staring without seeing, his cheeks wet with his tears. To John she said, "Get your father a cup of strong tea. I'm afraid he has some bad news for us and he will need it."

The kettle was already boiling so John had only to take a thick mug from the cabinet, shake a generous amount of tea into it from a paper bag, then fill it with hot water. He realized he should have used a strainer because the tea leaves floated in the liquid, making it impossible to drink. Mary noticed what he had done. "Get another cup," she directed, "and pour it through a strainer."

When John put the cup of clear tea in front of his father Mary picked it up and tasted it. To Pat she said, "It will be cool enough to drink in a minute. Do you want to tell us what the policeman said about Aloysius?"

Pat drew a deep agonizing sigh, then took a handkerchief from his pocket and used it to wipe his face. With swollen and reddened eyes he looked first at Mary and then at John who had sat down across from him and waited in shocked silence.

Pat said, in a voice so low they could hardly hear him, "Aloysius is dead. He was killed in a car accident near Dayton." Then he looked once more at his wife and added, "Oh, my Mary, what are we to do?"

Mary patted him on his hand. "Pat," she said, "drink your tea. Then you can decide what we are to do." When he did not say anything she went on. "First we will have to eat. I know you will not be hungry but we have a long night before us and we will all need our strength. Besides we still have John and I have never known him to go long without eating." She smiled grimly at her son when she said this. He realized that she was trying to communicate to him her love and her acknowledgement that he too needed her help and reassurance. Suddenly John understood that she had always been closer to him than to his older brother, only slightly, but closer. It made him both happy and sad at the same time.

He also realized that, regardless of her relative feeling for the two of them, she very much loved Aloysius, and she must now be in utter anguish. None the less she contained her grief and provided stability to him and her husband. It was a side of her that John had never seen before. Quietly she put the supper which she had been preparing on the table and poured tea for herself and John.

John tried to eat in deference to his mother, but he only nibbled at his food, Mary pretending not to notice, absently stirred her tea, now and then taking a small sip. "John," she asked, "have you not been driving your father's car now and then?"

He looked at his father cautiously before answering but Pat appeared not to have heard the question. Finally John answered, "Sometimes, but only in the driveway."

"Well do you think you could drive it into town? We will have to send a telegram to the convent and I don't think your father should go back out now."

"Yes, mama, I can drive the car. What should the telegram say?"

So Mary found pencil and paper and composed a short message to Eileen's mother superior, relating what little they knew, promising to provide more information later, and signing it for Patrick T. O'Maury. She went outside with John, kissing him on the cheek before he climbed into the Packard. "Be careful," she whispered, "you are all we have now."

A single tear escaped from the corner of her eye. John saw her wipe it away with the back of her hand and try to smile, but the effort was too much. Her voice trembled as she whispered, "I wish so much Eileen was here. But I wouldn't want her to know how much we miss her. This will be hard enough on her as it is."

John gave her a quick hug. "I will be back as soon as I can, mama," he promised and jumped into the car.

John was back in less than twenty minutes. He pulled into the driveway very carefully, turned off the engine and got out of the car. It was the first time he had ever driven anywhere except back and forth in the family driveway. He was exhilarated by the experience and at the same time he was relieved to have returned without damaging his father's car. As he walked around the front, toward the cottage door, he patted the fender with what appeared to be affection.

John's parents sat at the table in darkness except for the light from above the stove. With his right hand Pat was eating soup from a bowl Mary had placed in front of him. With his left hand he covered both of his wife's. When John came in Pat put his spoon down and looked up. To John it seemed that he had regained his composure.

Pat said, "It didn't take you long, son."

"The nearest telegraph station is in Wapakoneta," John explained, "but I didn't have to go all the way. One of the troopers had to deliver something there. He said he would take it for me." Then he added, "They knew all about the accident." Actually they had told him some details that he thought his parents did not know, but he decided it was not yet the time to tell them.

Mary said, "I forgot to give you some money. Did you have enough?"

"The trooper said he didn't know how much it would be and that he would straighten it out with us in the morning. He said he was coming over anyway to see if we needed any help. He has a sister in a convent, too."

Pat said, "I thank you, John, for helping me and your mother. We will be needing a lot of help. It is a comfort to know we can depend on you."

John sat down across from his father. He was glad Pat seemed to have recovered and he realized how much he really depended on his father, how uneasy he had felt when the older man had appeared even slightly out of control.

One of the troopers had showed him a report on his brother's accident which had mentioned the possibility that drinking was involved. It had emphasized that it was only a possibility though and John was sure that drinking had nothing to do with it. What disturbed him was that the driver of the car, who had also been killed, had been a young housewife from Dayton. No explanation had been given for the two of them being together. Some years later John would try to find out exactly what had led up to the accident, but he would never find out. For the present he decided that there would be no advantage in telling his parents what he had learned. He knew they would eventually see the same report he had seen.

They sat and talked for some time, about Aloysius, and about Eileen, and about the things they had done together, the good times and the bad times. Finally Mary said they should all go to bed and try to get some sleep because they would certainly be taxed the next day. John told them to go on to bed and that he would put away the dinner things, most of which had been untouched, and clean up the kitchen. Mary gratefully agreed.

When John was finished he quietly went outside and walked around to the backyard. He had intended to use the outhouse but then he remembered that Aloysius, in a sort of mild revolt against convention had made a point of relieving himself at night behind the building rather than inside it. John, smiling to himself, did the same.

There was an old stump in the corner of the yard, more than a foot in diameter but scarcely more than a foot high. The two brothers had sometimes sat on the ground and used the stump as a surface on which to play cards. John remembered and, walking to that part of the yard, bent over and caressed the smooth wood as though the action might somehow make the memories more real. At length the realization came to him that he would never again play cards with his brother or do any of the other things they had done together. He sat down upon the stump and looked up at the clouds that sped across the sky first hiding then uncovering the full moon. There was no doubt in his mind that his brother was up there already, possibly trying to get up a card game with one of the other saints or perhaps with an unsuspecting angel. The thought brought a smile to his face. But then he began to weep and for the longest time he sat there alone, sobbing quietly. Then he wiped his eyes with his handkerchief and went inside and to bed.

Chapter III

But it rarely happens so easily or so quickly. In fact for some it never happens, and others go through life and only at the very end find where it was they should have been all along.

From Looking Out The Front Window, by Kassy Debbin.

*   *   *

SUMMER—1923

It was nearly the end of June and the weather was still pleasant. Mary went and sat on the front step to wait for her two men. They had come to the lake somewhat later than usual partly because of John's graduation and partly to interrupt the association with old memories. The setting sun was turning the sky into a rose colored screen covered with tufts of radiant orange cotton. A deep feeling of pleasure stirred Mary as she watched it move majestically down behind the trees. Then somewhere up the road a dove softly made his rain call. It was the only sound she could hear and the haunting character of it gripped her. She began then to think about Aloysius.

It was two years since he had died and Mary had not reconciled herself to the fact that they would never see him again. She tried to remember what it had been like four years before when all of her children had spent part of the summer at the lake. Then she began wondering what Eileen, now Sister Mary Charles, would be doing at that time of the day. She was comforted by the feeling that Eileen was very happy in the convent, but Mary missed her nevertheless.

Now she could see only the very top of the sun through the leaves, a beautiful soft orange arc, as the shadow of evening settled its soft mantle slowly over Mary's world. And the two men had still not arrived. She smiled to herself recalling how John had always reassured her while they waited for Pat. Now the two of them, John and Pat, were out there together. Just a trace of a frown settled briefly on Mary's brow as she considered the circumstances which had led to John's working with his father. It was always Aloysius who had been expected to follow in Pat's footsteps.

Actually Mary felt that, considering the situation in retrospect, Aloysius might not have done very well at it anyway. While he was certainly endowed with the gregariousness generally considered to be one of the absolute requirements for a successful sales career, Mary felt he might have lacked some of the patience and perseverance that also seemed to be necessary. John, by contrast, was friendly enough and, while he seemed quiet, had a knack for listening when someone spoke to him and for paying attention to what was being said.

At first Pat had made the observation that John wasn't forceful enough to be a good salesman. But after a few days he had changed his mind remarking to Mary that their son had his own way of doing things. He let the customer do most of the talking, smiling and interjecting a question now and then until he knew exactly what the person to whom he was listening needed. Then in a short time he was able to demonstrate how well he could fill that need. "He lets the customer sell himself," Pat explained.

Pat had long been responsible for a very large territory as the only outside salesman that Weller & Rex had ever had. Now the company was expanding and the owners were also enlarging the sales force. Pat was to occupy a brand new position. He would manage a sales staff of three men, the first of which would be John, the other two still to be hired as soon as John was trained to his father's satisfaction.

When the Packard pulled into the driveway the lights were on. Mary noticed that John was driving. Very carefully he applied the hand brake before stopping the engine. Then he turned off the lights. When Pat stepped to the ground from the passenger side Mary noticed that somehow he seemed tired. Well, she thought, he was not getting any younger nor, she reflected further, was she.

John, on the driver's side, bounded from the car, his enthusiasm and energy contrasting with his father's noticeable lack of it. "Hi, mom," he called to Mary. "Is supper ready?"

"It's been ready for at least an hour," she answered drily, then added smiling, "But never mind, it will keep."

Once she might have been inclined to scold because they were late, but it just didn't seem to matter that much lately. "What," she wondered to herself, "is wrong with me?"

While the three of them ate supper Mary mostly listened as the two men went over what they had accomplished that day. Pat's eyes twinkled as he observed that he had never realized how many of his regular customers had young women associated with them until John had begun making the rounds with him. Now, he explained to Mary, it seemed that the secretaries and female clerks were so much more attentive than they used to be. John said he hadn't noticed and Mary thought he probably hadn't at that. To her husband she remarked pointedly that she had never thought lack of female attention was something he had to worry about. It was something she halfway teased him about and over which they sometimes argued. She really couldn't understand this either because she trusted Pat completely.

Now when she looked at John he reminded her of a younger Pat O'Maury even though he didn't look much like him. Suddenly she appreciated what a tall handsome man her son had grown to be and how attractive he must be to the young women. With that knowledge came the realization that it might not be long before he would want to marry and leave them. The thought brought such a feeling of loss to her heart that she was afraid she might cry. Abruptly she rose and went to stand by the sink and look out of the window. She was afraid the other two would notice and wonder if something was troubling her but they went on with their conversation, apparently unaware of her distress. After only a few minutes she was able to overcome it and turned to watch them. Then she realized John had asked her a question and was waiting for an answer.

"What did you say, John?" she asked.

"I said the circus is in Bellefontaine. Would you like to go?"

Mary didn't like to do things on the spur of the moment. The idea of going to a circus appealed to her but not so suddenly. Such a trip had to be planned. Besides, as a practical matter, it seemed rather late to begin such a trip.

"I would really like to go to the circus," she said to John. Then she went over and sat back down at the table and added, "But don't you think it's pretty late to be driving to Bellefontaine? Look how dark it is already."

John glanced toward the window. "I guess it is kind of late at that," he admitted. "The show would probably start before we got there." Then the look of disappointment on his face was replaced by a broad smile. "But it will be there tomorrow and that's Saturday. Let's go tomorrow, but let's start earlier."

Pat had said nothing but he was thinking that going to the circus would be good for Mary. He knew that being at the lake was not as much fun for her as it had been when the whole family had been there. Now she was by herself most of the time and he realized she must be lonely. He wondered why she insisted on coming back every year but suspected that it was mostly because she enjoyed remembering a particularly happy period in her life. "Maybe that would be good for all of us," he said to John. "We will go early enough that you can take your mother on the ferris wheel before the show starts. You know she always liked riding on that thing."

"Mr. O'Maury," his wife insisted, "you know that is not true. It scares me to death. I would as soon go into the lion's cage." She looked so serious that both of the men laughed.

Pat asked, "By the way, John, doesn't your girl friend live in Bellefontaine?" The girl he was referring to was a young lady from the university whom John had mentioned a few times. As far as they knew he had never dated her but they knew he had at least a passing interest in her. Her name was Joan Gonetta. John reddened slightly and frowned. "If you mean Joan, she isn't my girl friend. She is just someone I know from school."

Pat winked broadly at his wife, but Mary didn't smile.

In the first place she didn't like for Pat to tease their son. In the second place linking him with a girl, even in jest, made her uneasy, perhaps even a bit jealous.

They sat at the table for a while longer discussing what time they would leave for Bellefontaine the next day and what they would take with them. John, as he often did, offered to wash the supper dishes but Mary, as usual, told him she would rather do them herself.

Pat had begun brewing beer at home in their basement and he had brought a supply of it to the lake. Now he took three bottles from the ice box where they had been standing next to the ice. He opened each one and poured the contents into a tall glass, carefully so that the yeast residue remained in the bottle. As the thick foam mounded up over the rims of the glasses the pungent smell of the homemade brew filled the room.

Many years later John would tour a commercial brewery in St. Louis and the aroma of the fermenting beer would trigger the recall of a picture in his mind. He would see the three of them sitting at the table with the supper dishes stacked and waiting to be washed. The deep darkness of the night had wrapped itself softly around the cottage so that John's world ended at the windows. The physical nearness of Mary and Pat evoked in John a feeling of security. But the feeling was less that of the impregnability of a fortress, and more the sanctuary of a church. He felt a spiritual unity with them that made him feel absolutely at peace.

They talked quietly of unimportant things for a while. Then Mary poured the last few swallows that remained in her glass into Pat's and stood up, announcing that the dishes had sat too long. Pat drained his glass and then he too stood up and yawned. He lit a small lantern which they would all use for the trip to the backyard.

Pat went first and while he was gone John watched his mother as she quickly washed and dried the dishes. When Pat came back Mary took the light from him and quietly went out. By the time she came back John had washed his glass and dried it. He took the light from her hand and he too made his way to the outhouse. When he had finished and started on his way back he looked up and noticed that the clouds had all left and because there was no moon the sky was filled with visible stars. He blew out the light he held in his hand and walked slowly back to the rear of the yard until he found the old stump where he and Aloysius had played cards.

Placing the lamp carefully on the ground John sat down on the stump and leaned back, gazing up. But the position was uncomfortable so finally he lay down on the ground by the lamp. There were so many stars he was overwhelmed by the spectacle of all the tiny lights. The area stood on a slight rise so that the canopy of the stars came down around the sides of the yard and gave John the impression that he was surrounded by the sky or, perhaps, lifted up very close to Heaven. Whenever he was in that yard alone at night John always felt very close to his brother. On this night, with the impression that he was lying among the stars, the feeling was even stronger. He also began thinking of Eileen and wondering what she would be doing—probably sleeping. Thinking of them and the good times they had had together brought about a feeling of melancholy and, as he often did, he wondered how he could feel so happy and so sad at the same time. A small tear trickled from his eye and rolled down across his ear. He wiped it away and got to his feet.

"Oh Aloysius," he said aloud but to himself, "I sure wish you were here." John picked up the lantern and went inside the cottage. His parents had already retired and he remembered another time when he had come in after they had gone to bed and Aloysius had been on his mind. It was the night his brother had died. John sighed deeply and shook his head.

As quietly as he could he made his way to his bedroom. Soon he too was in bed and asleep.

*   *   *

John drove. Mary realized that he seemed to do most of the driving lately. She and Pat sat in the back seat of the Packard and John was able to place his straw hat on the seat next to him so that it wouldn't blow out the window. He was, his mother observed, rather dressed up, in white trousers and a dark jacket. She wondered, somewhat defensively, if he hoped he would meet Joan in spite of what he had said about it.

The circus was actually set up on the outskirts of Bellefontaine (which the natives pronounced "Bell fountain") in several large vacant fields, probably part of someone's farm. From the road one could see only a cloud of dust where the cars were pulling off the road to park, and above the dust, in the distance, an orange and white pennant hanging limp and lifeless in the sun at the top of a tent.

Farther down an area with a few trees had been reserved for horse drawn vehicles so that the animals could be kept out of the dusty air and the sun's glare. Pat and John decided to drive across the field and get as close as possible to the other side so that Mary would not have so far to walk across the somewhat rutted field. She voiced her objection to what seemed to be their opinion that she wouldn't be able to "walk over an old field without falling down." Secretly though she was glad. She was over forty five and it wouldn't be long before she would be fifty, and the closer she got to that milestone age the more she consciously avoided situations where she might injure herself, perhaps even break a bone. She worried that she might become physically dependent on the others, a condition which she would consider a loss of her privacy. In addition she did not want to be forced into a position such that others would begin to think of her as getting old. It had nothing to do with vanity. She just didn't want to lose any of her independence.

The Packard bounced and swayed as John carefully steered it across the open space toward the other side. Mary held on to the back of the front seat with both hands and at the same time cast a wary eye toward the heavens, wondering what they might do if a sudden rain turned the field muddy. She needn't have worried. The brilliant sun stood high in a nearly cloudless sky.

John was more than a little disappointed. The structures he could see as they drove up were not what he had expected. They looked more like the backs of a row of small canvas covered sheds than tents, between two of which a mere trickle of people walked along to the other side. John had expected throngs. Well at least he could hear music off in the distance and the voice of a barker. He couldn't tell what the man was saying but there was no mistaking the fact that he was trying to get someone to do something. John and his parents joined the others and made their way in.

Once inside the perimeter formed by the canvas covered booths John was somewhat more impressed. The area was actually quite crowded, with people walking around a large oval shaped clearing, bound by the games and sideshow tents on the closest end and the rides and big top on the opposite end. John was caught up in the sights and sounds that assaulted him from all sides. Mary took Pat's arm and the three of them joined the sightseers. They walked slowly past booths where one could win prizes by throwing baseballs at wooden milk bottles or tossing darts at balloons fastened to the back wall. A young man wanted to guess Mary's age or her weight but she wouldn't let him and Pat teased her about that.

There was a booth where men were throwing baseballs at a black man's head, which was stuck through a hole in the back wall. For twenty five cents one could throw three balls at him and, if the black man was not able to get his head out of the way, win five dollars. Mary pronounced it "disgusting", and refused to watch. Actually the black man was rarely hit, although some balls came very close.

The three of them bought popcorn and ate it while listening to the spiel of the sideshow barker. At the other end of the oval the girl in the booth was selling tickets to the circus performance but Pat pointed out that the sign next to the booth indicated that the show would not start for more than an hour.

Probably if Mary had not been with them the men would have gone into the sideshow tent, but Pat was not sure it would be something a lady would want to see. Actually Mary was curious and would like to have seen the show but she thought it would not be ladylike to suggest that. Next to the circus tent was a stand with benches in front where a brass band was entertaining with some lively Sousa marches. Pat and Mary found a place to sit on one of the benches and John volunteered to walk back and buy three ice balls for them. As he approached the booth where the ice balls were sold his attention was drawn to a small group of people standing in front of it. There were four young men, one of them about John's height, the others well over six feet tall, and all of them could easily have been described as husky. They were dressed in dark trousers supported by red suspenders. They all wore white shirts with buttoned collars, but all had their sleeves rolled up, baring muscular arms covered with blonde hair sun-bleached almost white. Each wore heavy work shoes and a straw hat, the kind that most farmers wear for protection from the sun. Apparently they were brothers, and, standing in a loose circle, they laughed boisterously, talking with an accent that sounded German.

John was amused by the fact that the four men seemed to be having so much fun together that they were unmindful of everyone else. Chuckling, he started to make his way around them, but then he realized that they were directing some good-natured teasing toward someone in the center of their group. Mostly out of curiosity he moved nearer and to the side of the closest man so he could see whom they were surrounding. It was a girl.

The young woman's back was turned toward John so he could not see her face but he noticed that she was very small compared to even the shortest of the men around her. By comparison with the other three she was diminutive. On her tiny feet she wore leather shoes the tops of which extended up past the hem of her calf-length skirt. The skirt fell loosely over her ample hips which looked even wider because her waist was so narrow. She had on a white blouse with a high neck, but her arms were bare to her shoulders. All this John saw but later he would hardly remember anything about her except for her hair. It was gathered at the nape of her neck and fell to her waist, and it's color was the most golden blonde he had ever seen.

The girl had an iceball in her left hand and was holding it away from her as though she were worried about it dripping on her. Her other hand she held on her hip and her posture indicated that she was lecturing the two men in front of her with some vehemence. It also seemed that the bantering that had been going on had something to do with the syrupy confection she was holding in her hand.

Suddenly the young lady whirled and started out of the circle. Too late she realized that John was standing there, and that he was unable to get out of her way. She held on to the cone but its grape-colored contents splattered over John's jacket and shirt and down over his white trousers.

When she saw what she had done she dropped the paper cone and pressed the knuckles of both hands to her mouth.

Through her fingers she uttered, "Oh, my goodness!" She was obviously distressed and the four men, when they realized what had happened, stopped laughing. But no one seemed to know what to say.

Finally the one closest to John said, "Katie, I'm sorry ve make you do dat." To John he said, "Young feller, we figure out someway to clean you up. Don't you worry." He needn't have been concerned, though. John appeared anything but worried. From the time the girl had turned around he had not taken his eyes from her face. He would say later that he thought it was the most beautiful face he had ever seen.

The girl, whom the man had called Katie, at length realized that John was staring at her and that, in fact, he did not seem to be aware of anything that was going on around him. At first she thought the reason he was seemingly immobilized was that he was very angry at what she had done. But eventually she saw that he didn't even appear to know that his shirt and trousers were no longer white. At that point her apprehension began to turn to slight amusement and some amount of conceit, as she began to appreciate the way that he was staring at her face. But so intent was his gaze that finally she began to feel a bit embarrassed. She was not used to being looked at in that fashion. To cover her own confusion she began to give orders to the young men, all of whom were her brothers.

"Vendell," she said to the man standing at John's left, "go get the wagon. I will take dis man to our house and get the stain out of his clothes before it sets. Hurry."

Without a word, perhaps anxious to get out of a rather awkward situation, the young man whom she had addressed left. John, suddenly becoming aware of the fact that she was talking about him and about doing something to him which was very personal, began to realize that the others were waiting for him to react in some way.

"Wait," he stammered, "I can't do that."

The girl, Kate, put her hands on her hips and said, "Vhy not? Have you got some better way to get your britches clean? Or do you like to valk around looking like a peppermint shtick?" At this her three brothers who were still standing there started to chuckle but she quickly silenced them with a steady glare. There was no doubt who was in charge, at least for the time being.

Finally John said, "My father is waiting for me with my mother over by the big tent. I came to get iceballs for them."

Kate turned to the shortest of the three men. "Alex," she directed, "get two of dose sings and the tree of you take zem to his mama and papa. You should be able to find zem I sink. Tell zem he will be along pretty soon."

Alex left the group to do as he was told. John started to protest but one of the other brothers held up his hand.

"It von't do you no good," he told John. "She has already made up her mind. You might as well go along like the rest of us." And John did. He followed Kate back the way they had come in between the booths at the end of the oval. As they came out on the other side, in the field now nearly half full of automobiles, they saw Wendell. He was waiting for them, standing next to a hay wagon hitched to a pair of immense chestnuts. He put his hands on his sister's waist and lifted her onto the wagon as easily as if he were lifting a doll. John was left to use a wheel spoke as a step and scramble up next to the girl.

Wendell stood near the front edge of the bed of the wagon and untied the reins from the brake handle. "Get up dere, you horses," he commanded and the two chestnuts leaned into the harness. Almost without any effort on the part of the horses, it seemed, the wagon began to move across the rutted field. The motion caused John to bump into the girl sitting next to him. He wondered if she might think he was doing it intentionally. But he was reluctant to move farther away from her because he didn't want her to think he was afraid of her.

They crossed the road and started through the field on the other side. This also had some autos parked in it, but only next to the road. Farther back, twenty or thirty yards from the highway, corn was nearly eight inches high. Wendell steered the horses into a road which ran up the middle of the field.

No one spoke as they jolted along the dirt lane with corn coming up on both sides. A bump bigger than the rest caused John to lose his balance and in trying to regain it he inadvertently put his hand on Kate's knee for an instance. He took it away quickly, embarrassed.

Kate said, "Sometimes it is easier to stand up. You could stand next to Vendell and hold on to the rail." John noticed that when she said Wendell's name she made it sound almost as though it was spelled with a V. Her voice was soft and, when she was not angry or giving orders, she sounded as though she was about to laugh. John was glad to stand up and hold onto something to keep from falling off the hay wagon. And since it was her suggestion he wasn't embarrassed. He stood next to Wendell, wondering why he had even agreed to go with them. Then he turned and glanced at Kate's profile, with her golden ponytail catching the sunlight, and he knew why.

At the end of the road John saw a white house with a porch running neatly across the front and around one side, and a widow's walk on the top. As they bumped over a little rise he was able to see the rest of the Hoect farm.

The house stood alone surrounded by a yard of plush green grass and a very short white fence. There was a tall hickory tree in the middle of the front yard. In its shade a half dozen or so white chickens and a couple of guineas scratched for whatever they could find.

Outside the little fence stood a white barn, taller than the two story house and apparently just as well taken care of. Behind the barn and the house John could see other buildings, neat and clean, painted white and in good repair. Any one of the buildings looked as though it could be lived in.

As the wagon neared the gate in the fence Wendell pulled back gently on the reins. "Ho, now, ho," he called to the horses. They stopped obediently, standing in the sun, waiting for his next order. Wendell leaped down and lifted his sister to the ground, once again letting John take care of himself. Then, without a word, he turned the wagon around and left.

"We can walk back when we are finished here," Kate told John as he stood watching the wagon return down the road. "Come on to the house. I vill ask my mother for sure what I should do to your britches."

"Your mother?" John asked.

"Yah, my mother," Kate answered. She was walking ahead of him along a concrete walk toward the house. She stopped and turned to look at him. "Do you sink dose brothers of mine vould let me bring a man here by myself?" She tossed her head at the ridiculousness of the thought and laughed. Then she walked on, expecting him to follow.

There were five steps in front of the porch. Kate bounced up them and stopped. John came up behind her and stopped too. She was looking at someone sitting on the porch but instead of standing with her hands on her hips, as she usually did, she stood with them together in front of her. It made her look much less commanding and much more like a very young girl.

"Mama," she said, adding something else in German. In front of her John could see a woman sitting on a straight chair, close to the back of the porch, out of the sun. Her grey dress had long sleeves. She had on black shoes and a small grey cap. She did not look stout nor did she seem very tall, but she held herself very much erect. She did not wear glasses and she looked first at Kate, then at John, with clear dark eyes. She had been sewing something and she stuck the needle into the cloth, folded it and put in into a basket next to her chair. Katie asked her something else in German and the woman answered her in the same language. She looked at John again with little expression. Finally Kate's mother got up and went into the house. She had not spoken to John or even smiled.

Kate said, "She only speaks German."

John didn't know whether she was apologizing or just making conversation. He said, "Oh."

"Anyway she told me what to do," the girl said. "Come in the house."

She led the way along the porch to a side door. They went into the kitchen. She said, "You can keep your shirt on but you will have to take off the britches."

John looked at her with more than a trace of panic on his face and did nothing. She shook her head and put her hands back on her hips in the gesture with which John was becoming familiar.

"Well, go on," she ordered. "Do you sink I have never seen a man in his drawers before? We got to hurry or dat syrup sets. If you are bashful I'll get you a blanket to wrap around you."

John's problem was that, because of the warm weather he hadn't worn any underwear. It was a habit he had picked up at college. He didn't know how to explain this to the girl so he stood there, saying nothing, while his face turned crimson.

Kate said, joking, "Vhat's dah matter? Don't you have no drawers on under dose britches?" Then she realized that what she had said was exactly the problem. She put both hands over her mouth but could not keep from laughing. This, of course, made John even more embarrassed. He said later that he would not have been unhappy if a tornado had struck the area at that moment.

Kate laughed so hard that she had to sit down in one of the wooden chairs that stood next to the kitchen table. But at length she began to feel sorry for John. She wiped her eyes and got up. She said, "I'm sorry that I laughed. But didn't your mama ever tell you you should never go out without clean undervear on because you might have an accident? Or don't you pay attention to your mama?"

John had had enough. He turned toward the door. "Never mind," he muttered, "I won't bother you. I'll get my clothes cleaned myself." But the girl stopped him. She put her hand on his arm.

"No, no," she said. "I really am sorry. I know you only feel bad because you are a gentleman. I shouldn't laugh at you. But please don't go way yet. I did zis to you. I want to fix it. Please let me fix it."

She sounded so sincere that John stopped and turned back around. She still had her hand on his arm and she was looking into his eyes. What he wanted to do was put his arms around her but he knew that would not be acceptable. Nevertheless he would have done anything she would have asked him to do.

She said, "Wait a minute and I get you a pair of Alex's drawers to vear for a vhile. He vouldn't care." Slowly she took her hand from his arm, seeming to wait to see if he would stay or not. He could look in her eyes and tell that she was still amused but she did not laugh. She backed a few steps away from him before turning around and leaving the room. She was back in just a few minutes with a pair of long woolen underwear bottoms. "First take off the coat," she ordered. And John took off his jacket and handed it to her. She looked it over and told him, "Dis looks like it only got a little bit on it. I sink it would be better if you have it cleaned later. Maybe you better take off de shirt too."

John took off his shirt then and gave it to her. She said, "I take dis and work on it while you put de undervear on." Then she left.

John turned a chair around so the back was toward the door. He sat down on it and began to take off his shoes. Then he stood up and began taking off his trousers just as Kate came back in for a pan of water. Quickly he pulled the trousers back up almost causing himself to fall down. But Kate paid no attention to him, acting in fact as though she didn't know anyone else was in the room. She went back out and he finished taking off the trousers and putting on Alex's underwear. They fit him fairly well.

Kate brought the shirt back and took his pants. The shirt still bore the stain of the ice ball but it had become very faint. She felt that the next time the shirt was laundered the stain would disappear.

When she returned with his trousers he had already put the shirt back on. She had had the same good luck with the trousers but there was, of course, a large wet spot where she had removed most of the stain.

"You should leave on Alex's underwear," she suggested to John. "There is still a wet spot on your britches and it will feel funny if you don't have on underbritches."

John did not want to keep Alex's underwear but, on the other hand, he didn't want to discuss with Kate how a damp spot would feel like to him on what he considered a private part of his body. Besides that he would not remove the underwear while she was standing there and she didn't give any indication that she intended to leave. He put his trousers on over the underwear. Finally, without saying anything, he sat down on the chair and put his shoes back on.

By now, in spite of how he had begun to feel about Kate, he was almost to the point of wishing that he had never met the girl. But then Kate did a seemingly very uncharacteristic thing. She was standing in front of him and, bending over, she put her hands on his shoulders and kissed him on the cheek. Then she stepped back and looked at him solemnly. "I am sorry," she told him, "that I laughed at you. I know it vas not funny for you. I vould not blame you if you are sorry you ever saw me. But I want you to know I am not as crazy as you sink. I vas making jokes with my brothers who have been working very hard for weeks and needed to have some fun. Papa would have told zem to go to the circus today," she said wistfully. "So ve all vent. I should have been more careful and zis whole sing would not have happened. But I sink you are a nice boy and I am glad

I have met you. If you want to come calling on me I sink mama vould agree, and so vould I. But I vould understand if you vould not want to."

When she finished saying this she looked down at the floor. John noticed that her cheeks had turned slightly pink and he realized how hard it had been for her to say what she had. He knew that he would have to "come calling" on this girl and, for the first time in his life, he began to wonder what it would be like to be married.

John laughed. Katie had not heard him laugh before and she was relieved. He stood up. He said, "Katie, I'm glad it happened too. And I will be back to see you. You can bet on that." Then he added, "I have to bring back Alex's underwear anyway." And they both laughed.

John and Kate walked back to the circus grounds. They walked rather far apart and he did not touch her except when he offered her his hand as they climbed a slight ditch to cross the road. They talked very much though, actually Katie talking the most and John listening. She told him how her parents had come to America long before the first world war and had become citizens. Her father's parents had come with them but had never learned to speak English, nor had they become citizens. Katie's mother too had refused to speak anything but German and now had even forgotten what little English she had learned. But Katie said her father had resolved to be a "good American" and had been very disappointed when most of the people around them had regarded them with suspicion during the war.

Katie told him her family had worked hard to make their farm a success and she felt that now they were respected in the community. Her grandparents had both died.

John noticed that when Katie talked it wasn't only w's that she pronounced differently. Often she changed her th's to either z's or s's, but not always. It gave her speech such a soft sound it mesmerized John. He decided that he would like to study German and learn to talk like Katie.

Pat and Mary were sitting on the bench where John had left them, but they had not been there all the time. They had gone into the big tent and seen the circus performance and then returned to the bench. They had been waiting only a short time when John and Kate found them. Pat smiled broadly when he saw the young girl but Mary did not. Without being told and without even looking at John's face she understood that he and Kate were already more than just friends. And she was not happy about it.

The first thing she said was, "Your father and I have been worried sick. We didn't know where you were or when you would be back."

Kate had no way of knowing for sure, but she was fairly certain her brothers had told John's parents what had happened, as she had instructed them to do, but she could not miss the animosity in Mary's voice. Under no circumstance did she want to challenge John's mother. Yet it was not her nature to be completely submissive. She stepped ahead of John but not in front of him. She said directly to Mary, "It is not your son's fault." And it did not escape Pat's notice that she had referred to John as Mary's son. "It was all my fault. I spilled somesing all over his front. I had to take him over by my mama to try to clean him off." And Pat knew that she wanted them to know her mother was there also. She shook her head. "I just vonder vie dose brothers of mine did not tell you like I told zem to. Zey will hear about zis."

Pat felt it was time to intervene. He held out his hand. "You must be Kate. Two of your brothers did tell us, and they told us your name. They didn't give us too many details, though, and they didn't seem to know when John would be back. But everything's fine now, Except John didn't get to see the circus, and that's what he came for."

Kate let Pat take her small hand in his immense one. She knew immediately that he would be someone she would like. She smiled at him and said, "I am glad to meet John's papa. I am sometimes clumsy and dat is what caused the problem."

"Oh," Pat said, "sometimes things like that happen. I wouldn't be surprised if John wasn't watching where he was going either."

John had been standing next to Kate and had wanted to say something to his mother but had been waiting to see what might sound the best. Now he thought she might have been placated but he was wrong. She put her hand on his coat. "Look at this," she exclaimed. "We should get this to the cleaners as soon as we can. I wonder if it will come out. And what about your pants?" She pulled the coat open so she could see. The spots had mostly dried but enough color remained to show what had happened.

John said, "Katie soaked the spots to keep the color from setting. She said when everything is cleaned it should all come out."

"Well," Mary told them, still looking at John's shirt and trousers, "we'll see."

John wanted to see the circus with Kate but he was sure if he suggested that his mother would find some reason to disagree. He knew that she was about to suggest that they start back to their cabin and he didn't want to go. Pat, who understood how both his son and his wife felt, suggested that John drive him and Mary back to the cabin, change his clothes, and then come back to see the circus with Kate. He knew this would irritate Mary but he felt it was the best thing to do. Actually the fact that it was something Mary would probably not like was also one of the reasons he suggested it. Then he insisted that the young lady ride along with them because it would keep Mary from berating him all the way back. In fact Mary had almost nothing to say for the rest of the day.

John and Kate got back just in time to see the last performance of the day. Afterwards John drove her up the same long road they had traveled in the wagon and walked back on later. He helped her out of the Packard and walked with her to the foot of the porch steps. There was no one on the porch but John worried that members of Kate's family were not far off, probably waiting to see what he might do. He very much wanted to put his arms around the girl and possibly kiss her, but he did not want to give anyone who might be watching or listening the impression that he did not respect her. He remained standing on the ground while she went up the steps and then turned around to face him.

"Will you be coming back sometime?" she asked. Her hands were clasped in front of her the way they had been when she had talked to her mother earlier.

"You bet I will," John assured her. If I can borrow the car I will be back tomorrow after church."

Katie smiled and said, "Oh, I am glad for that." Then she quickly came down to the bottom step, reached out and put her hands on the sides of John's head. She pulled his head down and kissed him quickly on the mouth, and then ran inside the house, letting the screen door slam behind her.

John stood there for more than a minute before he got in the car and drove away. The next day he could not remember driving back to the cabin.

* * *

That night, as Pat had sat on the edge of the bed and removed his shoes and Mary sat before the mirror and brushed her hair, she suddenly sniffed, "Well you seem to like your future daughter-in-law."

Pat was very careful because he wanted to avoid an argument and he wasn't sure what would be the best way to do that. He couldn't tell if she wanted to say more about what she had asserted or if inviting her to do so would make her angry. He decided to take a chance. He asked, "Why do you refer to her like that?"

Mary put down her brush and turned toward him. "Well," she told him. "it seems plain to me that the boy is infatuated with that little blond. Can't you see that?"

Pat realized then that he would have to do something or risk letting Mary talk herself into a permanent dislike for someone who, Pat readily admitted, could very well be their future daughter-in-law. Rather sternly he said, "I don't think he is infatuated. And I don't think he is a boy. He has been grown up for a long time. Kate seems like a very nice girl to me. I know she is German but I think she is Catholic. And besides wasn't it the Germans then who helped the Irish in the troubles? Time will tell. I think

John will get to know her better and if she is as nice as she seems maybe they will get married. Would that be so terrible?"

Mary had turned clear around so that she sat facing her husband. As she listened to him she knit her brows, pursed her lips, and folded her arms stiffly. Pat could tell she was about to say something furious in rebuttal. But then a strange thing happened. She had been staring at him but suddenly she cast her eyes down and her hands dropped to her lap. Then her shoulders began to shake as she sobbed quietly. Finally she murmured, "I know he will marry her and I don't want him to. He is all I've got." Then she sobbed even more.

Pat had never seen his wife like this before. Through her parents' deaths and the news of the accident which had taken Aloysius she had remained calm. Now she looked so forlorn that he started to smile but stopped. It was obvious that, to Mary, the relationship between John and Kate represented a crisis. He got up, went to her, and knelt on the floor. He put his arms around her knees and looked into her face. "May I remind Mrs. O'Maury that she will still have me?" he asked kindly. "And at one time she said that was all she needed."

Mary continued to weep, but the sobs grew farther apart and much weaker. She stared through the window and into the blackness outside. Pat thought she was ignoring what he had said until she put her hand on the nape of his neck and began to knead it gently. It was something she had not done for a long time. Pat understood that Mary was trying to make up her mind about something and he knew it would not do to try to hurry her. It was, in fact, an accomplishment to get her even to consider changing her mind about anything. He put his head in her lap and remained kneeling with his arms around her knees for minutes, even though it was uncomfortable. At length he heard her give a deep sigh and she took her hand from his neck. He recognized that as a signal that she had come to some decision. Pat stood up without saying anything and finished getting ready for bed. When Mary finally turned out the light and took her place under the light coverlet next to him, she still had not spoken. But in the darkness she found Pat's right hand and pulled it up to rub it on her cheek. Then she released it before she settled down on her left side, facing her husband. He took his other hand and reached over his chest to touch her face again. She felt the roughness of his palm and it comforted her. She had been so occupied with what she felt she was losing that she had almost lost sight of what she had long ago begun to take for granted. Her husband was a rock of a man on whom she could always depend. And yet he was one of the most gentle people she had ever known. She had always been aware of this; it was why she had married him. But somehow she had let herself forget.

Mary turned over on her back but held onto Pat's hand. "Pat O'Maury," she began, "one of the things that upsets me most about you is that you are so often right. Not all the time, mind you, but often." Then she turned and whispered in his ear, "And I'm glad because it sometimes keeps me from making some big mistakes." Pat smiled to himself. He might have said something but he thought it might be better if he did not.

They lay in the darkness for a while with their own thoughts. Then Mary said, "I think, if we are going to keep coming here in the summertime we should be thinking about getting a bigger place. It may not be long before we will need more bedrooms."

Some time later, without saying anything more, they made love. Then Mary turned her back to Pat and he, turning toward her, put his left arm across her body and pulled her close. No matter what had happened during the day, to lie in bed like that, with her, always stirred in him a feeling of absolute peace. He cupped his left hand over her right breast. Perhaps it was not as firm as it had been when they had married, but it was not any smaller and it was as smooth as velvet, and it was his Mary's. Soon he was fast asleep. But Mary lay awake for a long time.

Chapter IV

…, he took it off the hook and looked at it for a minute. It was big enough to keep but he threw it back anyway. Then he put the line in the water without baiting the hook. He went back and sat down on the ground again, leaning on the old blanket folded up against the tree trunk. He pushed the rim of his formless hat down over his eyes. "Zeek," he said, "do you think it so bad bein' black an' bein' po?" Zeek answered him slowly, lethargically. "Is you crazy? Bein' black and bein' po the same thing. And they both bad." Amos' response was just as slow. "If we wuz rich we wouldn't be heah. We'd be someweah worryin' bout losin' owuh money. We can stay heah as long as we want. And when ah goes home ah can eat some catfish, or ah can fool aroun' wid de kids, or ah can grab mah wife's ass. Ain' no rich man can do mo dan dat." "Amos," said Zeek, "I do think you crazy." And Amos said, "You probly right. Maybe that why I so happy, cause I crazy." And they both lay there and laughed for five minutes.

From It Takes One, by S.A.S. Kowsky

*   *   *

1930
Sister Mary Charles

The old grandfather clock struck at half past two reminding them that it would soon be time for Benediction. John and his father sat on either side of a small round table with a marble top, near the ornate fireplace which had not been used in years. Sister Mary Charles sat on a straight chair facing a couch covered in beautiful brocade with pictures of flowers.

Her mother sat on one end of the couch and Kate on the other. Katie and her sister-in-law had become close, much closer in fact than Katie and her mother-in-law. But even that relationship was improving. Mary found it difficult to dislike the woman who had given her two lovable grandchildren and did not so far seem inclined to stop with two. Jack was more than a year old, starting to walk and getting into everything. Norman was only three months. They had been attempting to get Jack to say, "Aunt Sister," and he tried, but it was too much for the little fellow. Sister Charles held the sleeping baby on her lap. Pat had deposited his derby on the table so that he could hold Jack on his knee. Jack kept getting down and walking off, with faltering steps, followed by his father, and as soon as he fell on his well padded bottom John would bring him back and put him on Pat's knee and they would continue their conversation. It was May and being the first Sunday in the month it was visiting Sunday. They were in one of the parlors which the nuns were permitted to use to entertain company.

Kate said to Sister Mary Charles, "Are you sure you don't want me to hold him?" knowing the answer.

"Heavens no. I can handle them fine when they're sleeping. And he's such a doll." She put the end of a finger in the palm of one tiny hand and was pleased to feel the infant's fingers tighten around it. She smiled impishly and asked, "Katie, when is the next one due?"

At this both John and Pat stopped talking, wondering if they had missed something. But Katie probably disappointed Pat and reassured John by saying, "I hope not for at least another year. I still got verk to do on our house."

Pat said, "how do you like it by now?"

And John answered, "Oh, it's fine but it is a lot of work. Someday I would like to buy a new house, one where nothing in it needs to be fixed."

Then Mary said, "I don't think there is such a thing." They all laughed.

Sister said to John, "You are lucky you could buy a house. I understand a lot of people are out of work now. How is your job holding up?"

Pat broke in, "John should do fine. These bad times should not last long. In a year or two the whole country will be back in business better than ever. I think Hoover is just the right man to get us out of this."

John said, "It may not be as bad as some people think, anyway. I read the other day that Ford expects to sell nearly a million and a half cars this year." When he mentioned cars his sister suddenly remembered something. She looked at Pat. you were here?"

Mary looked at Pat and said, "Tell your daughter, Mr. O'Maury. Tell her what you have now." But without waiting for him to say anything she went on. "You know that your father never thought there was any other machine but a Packard. But now that he spends most of his time in the office where there aren't any young women to admire his automobile he decided a Pontiac was good enough for his family."

As usual Pat was irritated by his wife's teasing but, as he had been doing more and more often lately, he tried not to show it. Sister Charles though, who always wondered why her mother did these things, could not help but come to his defense.

"Now mom," she said quietly, "why do you say things like that? You know he never had eyes for anyone but you."

Mary knew, of course, that her daughter was right but she couldn't help herself. She sniffed and asked, "And how do you know that?" But then she let the matter drop.

Pat said, "The Pontiac is a very good machine. And it is really more than we need. I do very little traveling nowadays and when I need to go somewhere it is usually with John and we go in his machine."

At this John laughed and said, "Oh, yes, and you should hear him. He once saw a picture of one of those Studebaker Rolling Homes in a magazine, the ones that look like tents, and some movie stars were using it for a dressing room. So he's always asking me if Katie and I and the boys are going to live in our automobile." They all laughed, even Pat.

Sister asked, "So you bought a Studebaker? I understand they are very economical. How much did you pay for it?"

Katie then broke in, "actually more than we should have, I guess. But it was still less than seven hundred dollars."

"My goodness," exclaimed Sister Charles, "I'm glad I don't have to worry about things like that." Then she said, "By the way I've been meaning to ask you, when did you buy the cottage that you have now, the one," she lowered her voice nearly to a whisper, "with an inside toilet?" They all laughed a little at her obvious reluctance to say "toilet" out loud.

"Well, let's see now," said Mary. "I think that was about five years ago. John, wasn't it in 1925?"

John said, "I think so." His forehead was creased in thought a while. "Yes, I think it was."

Sister Mary Charles said, "You know I've never seen a picture of it? I've heard you talk about it but I don't know what it looks like. "It isn't near the one we used to rent is it?"

"It's on a different street, but not too far away," Pat told her. "We'll take some pictures and bring you one."

Mary asked, "If the old cabin had an inside toilet would you still have joined the convent?" They all laughed.

The conversation turned to other things. Sister asked, "Katie, do you still have relatives in Germany?"

"Oh, yes," her sister-in-law told her. "But I only know of zem because zey write my mama letters. I have never see any of zem."

"Do you know there is a man in Germany by the name of Hitler who blames all the country's problems on the Jews?" Sister asked. "I have heard he is attracting a lot of attention. Some people think he may someday run the country."

"Not a chance," said John. "I don't think anyone that radical could get anywhere in such a conservative country." No one disagreed.

At three o'clock they all went into the chapel for benediction. A nephew of Sister Mary Thomas, on Navy leave, served for the chaplain, Father Philip Regus, so John, who usually served, sat with his family. By thirty minutes past the end of benediction the last visitor had left and the nuns had begun to put the areas used by the visitors back in order. It did not take long; it mostly involved moving a chair, straightening a rug, or rearranging a cushion here or there. By five o'clock they were finished and most of the nuns had gone out into the courtyard in the back to wait for supper. Only Sister Mary Charles was near the lobby when the front doorbell rang.

Instead of answering the door Sister Charles went to a side window and looked out to see who might be there. She saw a black man seeming to be in his fifties or sixties, it was hard to tell. His beard of several days was a mixture of grey and white. He wore a hat and his dark hair stuck out from beneath the brim. His clothes were ragged and so dirty it was difficult to tell what color they were. The nun decided not to answer the door, hoping the man would go away.

While she stood watching him the man rang the bell again, and finally a third time. Getting no response he turned and stood on the step looking out toward the street, obviously wondering what to do next.

When the derelict turned around Sister Charles was able to see his face. He was not someone she recognized but then she knew very few blacks. There was, however, something in his face that would not let her look away. It was the absolute hopelessness she saw there. He stood, hardly moving, looking down at his feet. The only motion the nun detected was a slight swaying which she attributed to the effect of alcohol. "Not only is he a bum," she thought, "but he is drunk on bootlegged whiskey."

Sister Mary Charles was shocked by what the man did next more than anything she had ever witnessed before. In the fading but still ample light of early evening he went down the steps and, turning to face the low-growing shrubs alongside, urinated. From where she watched the nun could see him from behind and she noticed that the seat of his pants was wet. She had been reluctant to confront the man before but now she was so indignant she could hardly wait to get to the door. As quickly as she could she went around and opened it just as the stranger was fastening the buttons on the front of his pants.

With all the ire she could manage to put into her voice she said, "Just what do you think you are doing?"

He had not heard the door open and was startled by her voice. He looked up at her and with his hand still on his fly said, "Ah was jes takin' a leak. Ah couldn' hep it. Ah had to go. Ah's sorry lady. Ah jes couldn' hep it."

He was still swaying slightly back and forth, but suddenly he lunged with unstable steps back toward the door. His action frightened the nun and she started to close the door on him but as he reached the top step he fell on his knees and took his hat off. "Lady," he asked in a pleading voice, "does you bleeve in de Lawd?"

The door was almost shut but the stranger's words stopped the nun. "Why, what do you mean?" she demanded. "Of course I believe in God."

"Den gib me a glass a wattah and a piece a bread. I sweah I ain't had nothin' to eat in two days, nothin. Den please let me go down in you cellah and sleep by you fuhnace. I can sleep on de flo. It don make no mattuh as long as it a little wahm theah. Please lady. It still get cold at night and I ain got no place to go."

The man's curly grey hair was knotted and dirty. He had on an old jacket with one sleeve missing and there was a stain on the front that indicated he had vomited. His beard was matted with dirt also. Through the door came the odor of alcohol mixed with urine. The nun was disgusted. Yet she could not close the door on him. She heard a voice repeating something she had just read in the Old Testament. "He doth judgment to the fatherless and the widow, loveth the stranger, and giveth him food and raiment. And do you therefore love strangers, because you also were strangers in the land of Egypt." "Dear God," she thought, "why did you send him here? Are you testing me? I have never been to Egypt." Then she said aloud, "Come in." And she opened the door all the way.

The man scrambled to his feet and came inside, hat in hand, and stood in the hallway. Sister Mary Charles closed the door. She made herself take the stranger's arm and she pulled him toward the sitting room she and her family had made use of earlier.

The bell rang for supper. Sister Mary Charles heard it but she ignored it. Now that she had brought this man inside she would have to do something with him, she didn't know what. "Oh Lord," she thought, "thinking about charitable works is so much different from doing them." She had no idea how she would care for the man she had brought into the convent.

"What is your name?" she asked him.

"Samson," he answered. "It Samson Brown, lady."

"I am a nun," she told him. "My name is Sister Charles. Or you can just call me sister."

He stood in the parlor, still holding his hat in his hands. He said, "Oh, yes'm. That fine. Sistuh Chahles. Yes'm, that fine."

"I have to decide what to do with you now. We have no place here for men, but I'll think of something." The nun gritted her teeth. "Sit here," she said, indicating the exact place on the spotless couch her mother had occupied earlier. Samson sat down.

In another part of the building the rest of the nuns had finished saying grace and sat at the tables to eat their evening meal. Since many of them had entertained visitors there was much to talk about. The noise started slowly but grew sharply to a steady hum of conversation and laughter. Mother Theodosia, sitting at the head table with two of the older nuns, smiled. She was happiest when the others were happy. She knew which of them had had visitors and she looked around the room trying to see if any of them seemed depressed. She knew this often happened when family members left for home. She remembered when it had happened to her. One by one she located them and everyone seemed happy. She looked for Sister Mary Charles. Her place was empty. Mother Theodosia turned to the nun sitting next to her. "Michael, do you know where Charles is? She's not at her table." The other nun turned and looked toward the table at the far side of the room where Sister Mary Charles should have been sitting. It was true; the younger nun's chair was empty. Her cup was still turned upside down on its saucer. Sister Michael started to get up.

"I'll go see if I can find her," she said.

Mother Theodosia put her hand on Sister Michael's arm. "Never mind," she said. "I'll go. You just sit here and eat. I'm not very hungry anyway. "If I don't get back in time you lead the prayers, will you?"

"Of course," said Sister Michael.

Two sentiments tugged at the mind of the Mother Superior. The younger nun was breaking a rule; she had not been excused from joining the other nuns for supper. That was her first thought. But then she tried to recall whether Sister Charles had given any indication that she had not been feeling well. Theodosia could not remember anything unusual in the other sister's behavior.

As she reached the top step Mother Theodosia's long skirt rustled loudly. She was in a hurry, slightly irritated. She was being forced to give up something she very much looked forward to every evening, sitting in the refectory and listening to her charges enjoy themselves. If Sister Charles was not ill she might soon wish she were.

The hall was empty. Sister Charles must be in her room. The superior turned toward the rear of the building where the living quarters were, but then stopped short. She had heard voices and they seemed to be coming from a sitting room near the front door. One was a gentle murmur. Could that be Sister Charles? The other was unfamiliar. It sounded, in fact, like something that certainly did not belong in a convent. What in the world was going on? Mother Theodosia marched resolutely down the hall. But as she neared the sitting room she was slowed by the sounds which were becoming clearer. The soft murmur continued; it sounded like a mother, consoling a child. It was Sister Charles. She was saying tenderly, "Never mind. Don't worry. It will be all right. Everything will be all right." She said it over and over.

The second voice belonged to someone who was (could it be?) intoxicated. Yes, the man definitely sounded drunk. And he sounded like a black man. Could it be, a black man who was drunk, in a convent? The superior gathered herself to her full height and entered the doorway, but what she saw in the room caused her to stop.

Eileen had always been a kind person and, perhaps even thoughtful. But she had never been considered, by anyone, shy. By most standards she probably would have been thought rather bold. Nevertheless it was recognized by everyone who knew her very well that she did not have a strong stomach. She could not stand the sight of blood, her own or anyone else's. Further, if someone in her presence vomited, so did Eileen. She did not like strange odors or things that did not look clean. She often said that such things made her sick and most people believed this was literally true. But now she sat on the couch, her arms around the old black man, his head on her breast.

Samson's ramblings had stopped. Mother Theodosia stood in front of the couch and looked down. To her it looked as though the black man had become unconscious. Sister Mary Charles moved his head slightly so that she could look up at the superior and when she did so Theodosia noticed the stain on the front of the younger nun's habit where he had apparently vomited. The stench was very strong but, strangely, it did not seem to offend Sister Charles. She said, "Mother, this man needs something to eat. I think he must be starving."

Theodosia frowned. "I think he is probably drunk, don't you?"

Sister Mary Charles answered cheerfully, "Yes, I think he probably is. But he needs something to eat too." Then she asked, "Do you think George is downstairs?"

George Winters was a black man who lived in the neighborhood and worked for the sisters. He did many things, one of which was to tend the heating system. He sometimes slept on a cot in a small room in the basement. If one of the nuns needed him she would go partly down the steps and call him. He was big and amiable, a devout Baptist, and able to do many things.

"I think he is," answered Mother Theodosia, "Why?"

"I want him to take this man downstairs and clean him up, and let him sleep there tonight."

"Do you think that is wise?"

"No, I don't. But the alternative is to throw him out into the cold. What should I do?"

Mother Theodosia thought about this for only a second. She said, "I'll call George."

When Mr. Winters came into the sitting room Sister Mary Charles told him, "See if you can find some clothes for him. When he is cleaned up and dressed call me and I will come down and give him something to eat."

George was not enthusiastic but he was accustomed to getting strange requests from the nuns. And he liked working for them. Actually, given the time and the social climate, and George's particular situation, he often said he was happy to be doing work of any kind. He was able to pick Samson up, now completely unconscious, and take him to the basement.

When he had gone Theodosia said to Sister Charles, "You go to your room and change your habit. Put that one in the laundry. It smells terrible. I'll have someone clean the cushions on this couch."

"Thank you, mother," Eileen answered. "But," then she added resolutely, "I would like to clean this room myself. After all it was my doing. Would you let me?"

The superior stared intently at the younger woman's face trying to discover some sign of a hidden motive. Was she trying to be a martyr? Was she trying to appear better than everyone else perhaps? Or had she merely lost her mind? Theodosia could see only a person who had decided to do something and seemed happy to do it.

"All right," she said. "But first change your clothes. I'll go to the kitchen and see what can be found to feed him. You had better eat too. You have missed supper."

"Oh," answered Charles, "you are right, mother. And Sunday supper is my favorite meal. I wonder if the kitchen saved me something."

"I'll see that they do," she was assured by her superior, who added, "One more thing. You usually can't stand anything the least bit crude. You don't usually even like to help clean out the kitchen sink. What kept you from getting sick?"

"Oh, mother, you are right," Sister Mary Charles said, "I really don't know." She started to leave the room. Then apparently she thought of something else. She said, "Do you remember that old picture of the Sacred Heart that hangs on my wall? My father gave it to me. It is an unusual picture because Jesus looks so very sad. I can't explain this but that old man knelt down on the steps by the front door and when he did I saw something in his face that looked like that picture. I know he doesn't look at all like it but he did then. I can't explain it."

Mother Theodosia said only, "Go change your clothes."

"Yes, Mother," answered Mary Charles.

After Eileen had left Mother Theodosia remained deep in thought. She had wanted to throw her arms round the younger nun and shout, "Yes, my daughter, yes, you have done what we all are expected to do, see in the face of the needy, the face of the Lord. It wasn't the face in the picture on the wall, but the face of Jesus which you have in your heart. But even when you did it you didn't believe it. Before you could accept it you had to tell yourself it was the face in the picture. We are all like that. But why?"

She went back to the dining room to tell Sister Michael that she had found the truant nun, and to make arrangements for her and the black man to eat.

It would have been wonderful if only Samson had become well, had stopped drinking, had found a job and regained his health, but it was not to be. He stayed long enough to be able to help George do some things around the building, and he ate enough to regain his strength to a certain degree. But in the end he left. Theodosia gave him a bit of money for helping George and he used it to buy something to drink. Unfortunately much of what one could buy at that time which had alcohol in it was not fit to drink. When Samson died it was determined that his heart, his liver, and his lungs had deteriorated to the point that none of them was able to sustain life. The failure of any one of them could have been responsible for his death. When the sisters heard about it they were genuinely sorry. But Sister Mary Charles hardly wept at all. She went to the chapel and knelt down. She said, "Lord, thank you for taking Samson home with you."

Chapter V

Hooks was the only one in the store when Everet came in and the first thing he noticed was that the old man wasn't smiling. It was unusual. He said, "Why you lookin' so glum, Ev? It ain't like you. For the last month, with all the things that been happenin', your old barn burnin' down, losin' the election, that old heap you called a car gettin' wrecked, and then your wife Babe leavin' town, you had all the right in the world to be sad but you held up pretty good. Now, though, you look like you just found out the company you work for got sold to your brother-in-law. What's wrong?" And Everet looked at him for a long time. A tear rolled down the wrinkled cheek and he said sadly, "Ah, Hooks, sometimes I just don't know where to turn. Things ain't never gonna be the same again, never." He sobbed and another tear rolled down his face. Hooks grabbed him by both shoulders. "What in tarnation happened?" he said. The old man peered at his friend with red rimmed eyes. Finally he took a deep breath and whispered, "Ah, Hooks, my old dog Sylvia done ran off."

From When A Pair Beats A Straight, by Mitchell S. Brothers.

✶   ✶   ✶

Summer 1938

They had been in the newest cabin for almost a year. It was certainly an improvement over the last one, having four bedrooms as well as some other advantages. For one thing the kitchen was bigger and so was the bathroom. In fact all the rooms were at least a bit larger, and the bedrooms seemed immense. But for some reason Mary could not get used to it.

Probably she missed the old cabin they had used when she and Pat had brought their three children there for the first time. This one, and the one before it too, were better places in which to live but they just weren't like vacation homes.

Mary looked at Pat sound asleep in the old rocking chair on the other side of the room. For a sixty eight year old man he looked very good, a little overweight but still with most of his teeth and he still had a lot of hair. It wasn't white either, but steely grey. Mary got a light blanket from the couch and draped it over his knees even though she knew he wouldn't appreciate it because he still did not like the idea of other people doing things for him which he hadn't asked for. He was one of the most independent individuals she had ever met. And she loved him.

It was strange that in spite of his reluctance to accept help from others Pat was always ready to give it. Mary recalled how he had responded to Kate's mother's plea for help. That had been three years earlier in 1935.

Heidi was aware that she was dying and so was everyone else, but it was something that was never mentioned, at least not in her presence. With great difficulty she had made the trip from the farm to talk with Pat on that particular afternoon when she had been told she could expect him to be at the lake. Because she spoke so little English and Pat spoke no German at all, Wendell had come with her. Wendell, the second oldest, came because Alex, the oldest brother, was away at school. Actually though, Wendell usually seemed to take charge of things even when Alex was at home. Now he pulled the old Ford into the O'Maury driveway, turned off the engine and hurried around to the other side because he knew his mother would try to get down without his help if he was too slow.

Heidi Hoect had once been rather stout but her illness had taken its toll and her clothes were now all too large. Rather than invest in new clothes, which she knew she would not use for very long, she made do with what she had by taking some of her dresses in, with Kate's help, and in some cases merely by wearing a belt around her middle.

Wendell could have lifted her down from the seat but Heidi would not permit that. To her such a maneuver would have seemed undignified. In any event it would not have reflected the seriousness of their errand. He put his hands under both her elbows and allowed her to float to the black-topped surface. She stood erect as always but he was so tall that he had to bend down to offer her his arm.

Mary was waiting for them in the doorway. She came out on the porch as they came up the two steps. She put her arms around Heidi and said, "Hello, Heidi. It has been such a long time since we have seen you."

Heidi hugged the other woman. She said quietly, "Yah, yah." The two women had never been very close, neither of them being the kind of woman to encourage such a relationship. But they had a mutual respect and each recognized this respect in the other.

Mary said, "Heidi, I was just going to have a cup of tea. Would you have a cup with me?"

Heidi said, "Yah, dat vould be goodt. Danke." And she looked at Wendell. He smiled at her ever so briefly just to let her know he thought she had said the right thing.

Mary looked at Wendell. "Would you like a cup of tea?" she asked him. He looked uncomfortable. Max Hoect had always regarded tea as a woman's drink and his sons had always honored his memory by preserving many of his likes and dislikes. This was one of them.

Pat who had been standing behind his wife but so far had said nothing came to Wendell's rescue. He often drank tea, perhaps more often than coffee, but it was usually at night. "Wendell, how would you like a beer?" he suggested. "It is some I made. You know that I started making it during prohibition and it tasted so good I couldn't give it up. I was just thinking about having one myself but I don't enjoy drinking alone."

Wendell had always liked Pat. Perhaps it was because he reminded Wendell of his own father. He regarded Pat as a man, like Max Hoect, hard working and serious, who could laugh but saved it for the proper time. He teased members of his family but only when he thought they would enjoy the attention. He sometimes did this to others also but it seemed to be his way of showing that they were part of his circle of friends, and he never tried to hurt anyone. Pat also enjoyed drinking beer with his friends and his family, just as Max had.

Wendell smiled gratefully, first of all because Pat had helped him from an uncomfortable situation, but also because he liked Pat's beer. He had tasted it before with Pat and also with John.

He said, "That vould really taste good. I remember your beer dat you started making ven the country vas dry. My papa used to make some beer too. I think it's better dan any beer you can buy."

Pat said, "Why don't we all sit in the kitchen? Mary and I feel more comfortable there when we have friends, don't we mother?"

Wendell realized that Pat was trying to make him and his mother feel at home. He had called and talked to Mary but he had not told her what Heidi wanted to talk to her and Pat about, only that it was business. But Wendell knew that Pat was a shrewd person. He expected Pat to reason that their conversation would involve money. And, knowing that Pat was a sensitive man, he would anticipate that Wendell and his mother would be uncomfortable. Unfortunately this made the younger man even more uneasy.

Pat had noticed before that Wendell's German accent had become much less pronounced than it had been on that first day when they met him and his brothers at the circus. Pat suspected that when Wendell was completely at ease he probably had almost no accent at all.

Wendell and Heidi sat down next to each other at the big table. Ordinarily Heidi might have expected to see her grandchildren but she knew Katie and John would have taken them somewhere else, probably to the park, so Katie's mother and her in-laws could talk undisturbed.

Mary got cups from the cabinet and put them on the table. Ordinarily she would have used thick mugs but she didn't think they would have been appropriate for guests. She put the tea leaves in her old teapot and poured in the water which had been simmering on the stove. She was very old fashioned.

Pat went to the fairly new refrigerator and got bottles of beer for himself and Wendell. Usually he poured the beer into the glasses himself to make sure the yeast residue remained in the bottles but he was sure that Wendell would be familiar with the procedure so he set one of the bottles on the table in front of the young man and put the tall glass next to it. Sure enough Wendell carefully decanted the liquid into the glass and then raised it toward the window to admire the sparkling clarity of Pat's brew.

Wendell said, "Dat is like a crystal, beautiful." Then he tasted the beer. "And it is as good as any beer I ever had." He raised the glass toward Pat then in a sort of salute before resting it on the table. Pat smiled in satisfaction. He tried to act as though compliments didn't matter much, but it was difficult for him to hide his enjoyment when someone was pleased with his beer.

Heidi sipped her tea and remarked how good it was. Wendell and the O'Maurys talked about the weather but Heidi did not join in because she was afraid her English would be inadequate. The conversation soon waned and after a short period of silence Wendell looked at his mother and she gave him an almost imperceptible nod. He cleared his throat.

Wendell looked directly at Pat and Pat realized that the young man was trying very hard to look as though he did not feel as awkward as Pat knew he must have felt. "I vant to tell you somesing," he began. "I mean I vant to ask you somesing. Really my mama vants me to ask you somesing for her." He looked at Heidi and she nodded once more. He went on.

"Papa died eighteen years ago, only a little after the war." Wendell explained how hard it had been for Max during the war, how some people had seemed to suspect them of sympathizing with the Germans, or even worse. At one time someone had put a large swastika on their lawn with a little star of David in one corner. The police later found out that some youngsters had actually done this but that they had been urged to do it by a group of adults who wanted to build an airport on the Hoect farm. The adults were hoping a local Jewish family would be blamed but that the Hoects would have to sell their farm and move. Max though had been stubborn. He continued to work hard and helped his neighbors in every way that he could, and this did not go unnoticed. By the end of the war he had been accepted into the community. Unfortunately Max did not live long enough after the fighting stopped to do many of the things he had intended to do.

Max left his family with a mortgage which eventually they were able to pay off so the farm was theirs. However Alex, who would soon graduate from the University of Dayton, and Fred were both married but, with their wives, were still living on the farm. It was not a good arrangement. Besides Heidi knew Paul was thinking about getting married and she was certain that Wendell would do the same before long, although Wendell pointed out that it was only his mother's opinion. The farm, in short, was just not big enough for so many families.

Wendell said that his mother wanted Pat and Mary to know that she did not expect to live much longer. She was sure they already knew this but she wanted them to understand that she realized it and that it was part of the reason she had decided to ask for their help. As Wendell explained this Mary reached over to Heidi, who was sitting next to her, and put her own hand on the other woman's. For the briefest moment Heidi's head dropped and a look of sadness darkened her face. But then she put her other hand on top of Mary's in acknowledgement and she lifted her head with a look in her eyes so resolute it was almost defiant.

Heidi wanted her sons to be able to have places of their own. The only way she could do this would be to sell the farm. But a friend of theirs who was also a lawyer told them it would not be a good time to sell a farm. He said if she could keep it for a few more years, until the war in Europe would be over, they could develop it into a place for flying airplanes, the way the people who had wanted to buy it had planned. He saw that as a very profitable business in the future. And they agreed with him.

Actually Wendell did not mention it to Pat and Mary, because he did not think it made any difference, but the friend had been so enthusiastic about the whole idea, and so persuasive, that he had eventually talked them into it. And he had a plan.

He wanted the Hoect family to form a corporation. In fact he wanted to invest twenty five thousand dollars into it himself. He wanted them to buy two new farms, which were for sale, for the two married boys; Heidi could stay at the old property with the other two sons, who could still farm the long field that bordered the road, and they could use the rest of the money to turn the back part into an airfield. But they needed still more money and that was why they had come to Pat.

Now Wendell pointed out that they would consider it a favor if Pat would help them, but as a matter of fact it would be a business proposition that he thought would be very profitable to the O'Maury family in the long run.

Pat had listened very closely to Wendell as he explained all this. He had expected that Heidi was going to ask him to lend her family some money and he had wondered why, knowing that the Hoect farm had always done well. And even though the last few years had been hard on everyone the Hoects had actually been able to do somewhat better than most. But then he also knew that it was hard to make enough money from a farm to be able to save very much. The drought years had not helped. And before that prices had been down for a long time. He could understand how they might need money temporarily. But their proposition had taken him by surprise.

Wendell stopped and drained his glass. Without saying anything Pat went to the refrigerator and got two more bottles of beer. He opened them and put one in front of Wendell, then sat down again. He had not said anything while Wendell talked; now he did. "Might I be asking how much money you would need?"

Wendell answered him, "Ve been doing some figuring and talking to some of dem flying people. Ve think about fifty tousand." When Pat asked Wendell if they had tried to get the money from the bank Wendell told him they had. One problem was that farm property was not selling very well then and was hard to borrow money on. Another problem was that they could not have used any of the money to buy more rural property and put it in his brothers' names.

In the end Pat had done it. Mary thought it was partly because he wanted to help Heidi Hoect but also because he, after doing some research on his own, thought it would be a good investment. But he had had to borrow much of the money on their house in Cincinnati and on the stock he owned in Weller & Rex. And borrowing the money had kept him from retiring because he needed to keep working to pay off the loans.

He had put his share of the new company which they formed in John's name. He did this without asking Mary, as he usually did such things, but she didn't care. The other partner, the lawyer friend of the Hoects, was named Robert Westkamper. Pat had spent a good deal of time talking with him and had found him to be very likeable, and had judged him to be sincere. Unfortunately the lawyer's forecast of an early end to the war had proved in error. It dragged on and, in fact, seemed more and more likely to eventually embroil the United States. This proved both good and bad though. The country was becoming the supplier of almost everything to the countries in Europe and this was starting to provide some relief from the depression. But there was still very little production devoted to non-war items and the airfield had, so far, made very little return on their investment.

And Heidi had died that year. The official cause of death had been given as pneumonia but in truth something else had sapped her strength to such an extent that the pneumonia had been inevitable. By relating it in her mind to other events Mary was able to recall the year of Heidi's death as 1935. It seemed like such a long time ago. And Mary painfully remembered how the other woman had become more and more depressed because the airfield had seemed like such a poor investment. She was especially remorseful when she realized that Pat O'Maury would have been able to retire if he had not tried to help them.

Mary went into the kitchen and sat down at the table so she could look out the open window into the backyard. Kate had all her kids out there and they were playing. Jack, who was nine, and Norm, a year younger, were both helping to push some of the littler ones on the swings. Their joyous laughter made Mary smile.

Kate was expecting again, in January. When Mary had found out about it she had sniffed to Pat, "Well I guess you know what she likes to do all the time." Pat had smiled noting that she had said, "she likes", and not "they like." She seemed to think Kate had the babies all by herself.

Actually Mary had grudgingly come to appreciate her daughter-in-law, but she didn't want to admit it. Pat felt that she was a bit jealous of the younger woman. Not only did Kate have a larger family than Mary but she handled it so well. She was raising her children with obvious love but she was doing it in the same way she did everything else, with an organized and unswerving singleness of purpose that Mary considered typically German.

On the kitchen wall was the old clock that Mary's grandmother had given her. The pendulum made a steady muffled clicking sound as it swung slowly back and forth. In a few minutes it would chime eight times.

It being June there was still much light. Nevertheless Mary knew that soon Kate would be bringing them all in to get ready for bed. It was good that the bedrooms were so big. They could be used as dormitories, one for the girls and one for the boys. Sometimes the living room couch was made into a bed for the two older boys to sleep on. Of course John and Kate would use the other bedroom.

When they all came in Polly's eyes were already closed. Elleen and the twins seemed wide awake but Mary knew they would not be in bed long before they also would be sound asleep. Jack and Norm, being the two oldest, would be allowed to stay up for a while longer. They might even go back outside after they had helped get the younger ones ready for bed. Mary wasn't sure about Al who was only six.

Sometimes he seemed to have more fun than even the youngest; and at other times he was so serious that he seemed older than his years. This was one of those times. He came over and stood by his grandmother's chair and put his arm around her. She hugged him. She expected him to say something but he just stood there. Finally she spoke.

"What's the matter now?" she asked him.

"Oh, nothing," he said. She noticed something in his voice which she could not identify and she was suspicious. In many ways he reminded her of his namesake as a young boy. He had been what Mary called a conniver. He was very able and apt to use any situation which might seem to present the possibility for some advantage. She knew that the younger boy often did the same. She was aware that he did not want to go to bed with the little ones and she wondered whether or not he was trying to give her the impression that something was bothering him so that she might be encouraged to influence his mother to let him stay up for a while longer. She pulled him around in front of her so she could look directly into his blue eyes. He tried to meet her gaze but he could not do it for long. Like his brothers and sisters he was sure his grandmother could somehow look inside a person's head and see what the person was thinking. Not wanting this to happen he looked down at the floor. Mary recognized the maneuver. Smiling she hugged him and then turned him around so she could give him a gentle swat on his seat.

"You're a conniver like your uncle was," she told him. "There isn't a thing wrong with you. Go get ready for bed." Realizing the game was up he laughed happily and started to run off. Then he came back and kissed her on the cheek, and then ran into the other room. Mary shook her head happily.

Later Kate came back into the kitchen and sat down. For a few minutes the two women did not speak. Finally Mary asked where John was and Kate rolled her eyes and said, "Oh, he's working again, where he always is." Then she added wistfully, "I know he is doing it for us. But I would rather have him at home. His father and my father both worked so hard all dere lives. And what good does it do zem?" Mary said nothing but after a while she patted the younger woman's hand. Kate smiled at Mary and shook her head.

* * *

John had been able to make a very big sale, actually big enough to require the reorganization of the customer's office area. In order to cause as little as possible disruption to the work and to find it necessary to answer as few questions as possible from the staff John had agreed to go into the plant after everyone had gone home for the day and measure the facility so that a new floor layout could be drawn up.

Actually not everyone was gone. The manager could not be there because of a previous commitment, but he had asked his secretary to stay in his place. She was knowledgeable enough to provide John with whatever information he would need.

The plant, just inside the city limits of Wapakoneta, had a very small parking lot and John usually had a hard time finding a place to park when he called there during the day. But on this evening there was only one other car in the lot. A single light bulb illuminated the front door of the building. It was the only light that John saw. He got out of his car and walked toward it, the gravel crunching underfoot.

There was a small window in the upper part of the door. It showed no light and the thought occurred to him that no one was there. Perhaps the plans had been changed but he had not been notified. But after he knocked twice a light went on, he heard a lock turn and a bolt slide back, and the door opened.

Aimee Rennel had worked with the same company for nearly ten of her thirty years. Like most of the young women who still lived with their parents on farms in the area, she had thought about marrying but found that it was not very easy to meet eligible young men. One of the problems was transportation; there wasn't a lot of it. Another was, simply, time. Most of the men, young or old, spent most of their time either working or looking for work. And many of them had moved to one of the big cities where they felt jobs would be easier to find. Some of them had joined the army or one of the government work projects.

Aimee had considered moving to Cincinnati or Dayton. But her brother and her sister had both died before they had reached adulthood and she knew that if she left it would sadden her parents. Besides that she was really not the adventurous type. She felt comfortable in the security of the things around her which were so familiar. Still, sometimes, when she was alone in her room, she thought about what it would be like to sleep with a man.

There were many different kinds of animals on the Rennel farm so Aimee knew where babies came from and what caused them. Actually her observation of various animals engaged in mating had led her to conclude that the act of sex was not particularly enjoyable. The males usually seemed to be rather aggressive and in a hurry and the females most often seemed, at best, reluctant. On the other hand, once the act had begun the female never tried to get away. And afterwards, while the male seemed to lose interest almost immediately, the female usually waited for at least a few minutes before going back to whatever she had been doing before. To Aimee it appeared as though the females might have wanted to continue.

It would be erroneous to say that Aimee longed for a sexual experience; but it would not be far from correct to assume that she was at least curious enough to sometimes wonder what it would be like. She felt, however, that at her age she was at that point where it might be too late to hope that she would ever have the opportunity to find out.

John had seen Aimee twice before. To him she looked like a nice girl who wore long dresses and kept her hair piled on top of her head, probably to make her appear taller because she was rather short. He had never given her a lot of attention, partly because on both occasions he had been on sales calls and was concentrating on business. But he did vaguely remember what she had looked like. Now he was surprised to see that her long hair was gathered in the back but hung down nearly to her waist. She wore a woolen skirt that came down below her knees and a tight blouse that would have come up to her neck but she had left the top three buttons open. John, able to peer down on her, noticed that a good bit of cleavage was visible.

She said, I'm Aimee. I hope you are Mr. O'Maury."

"I am," John laughed. "But what would you do if I wasn't?"

She laughed too and opened the door a little wider for him to come through. He waited for her to close it and push the bolt back in place. Then he followed her down a dark hallway then through a doorway and into a large office with a half dozen or so desks. There was enough light for him to notice that the girl had sort of a round figure and that the calves of her legs were big, but not unattractive. She had on brown loafers and white socks. She walked ahead of him to a large desk from which everything had been removed but several sharpened pencils and a lamp. There were two chairs.

John had brought his catalogue because it contained the specifications for all the products he sold. He and Aimee's boss had already decided what items would be included in the sale, however, and he knew what their measurements were, so he put the large book on the floor next to the desk. He also had a tape measure which he put on the desk.

Aimee had already done a good bit of work. He could see that she had made a fairly detailed drawing of the room. It was lying on the desk. He said, "Well, it looks like you didn't need any help. I might as well go on home."

She giggled a little, a bit self-conscious but pleased to have her industriousness acknowledged. Her Methodist parents both regarded themselves as old fashioned Christians who believed that working hard was the only moral way to achieve success. It had rubbed off on Aimee. "I hope it helps," she said.

"Oh, it will," he assured her. "There are just a few things I want to add."

With his tape measure he checked a few dimensions here and there. What he was actually doing was checking Aimee's work just to be certain. But he was careful to hide that by making a few additional notations here and there on the paper she had left on the desk.

She had marked all the desks in the room and identified them by name he noticed. He asked, "Could you give me a short job description of all these people so I can jot them down under their names? What everyone does will make some difference as to where we put things."

He sat down in the chair that was in the middle of the desk. She took the chair next to it on his right. She watched as he put his pencil under one of the names and waited for her to tell him what to write. She pulled closer so she could follow what he was doing. John could smell a very faint odor of perfume and it was very pleasant, an aroma that reminded him of flowers, something he indeed would have associated with this clean, buxom girl.

It took only a few minutes for her to describe the functions of everyone represented on the chart, partly because several of them had essentially the same job. When she was finished he began making little notations next to the outline for each of the desks. She leaned back with her hands in her lap and waited to see what else he might need from her. The hem of her skirt had fallen on the floor and when John suddenly pushed his chair back so that he could get up and check something, he rolled over the edge of her skirt. Immediately he realized what he had done.

"I'm sorry," he apologized. "I hope I didn't tear your dress."

"No," she said, "it's fine. This skirt needs to be cleaned anyway." But she pulled it up a little toward her knees and tucked the sides in under her thighs. John got up and walked toward the end of the room. He was checking the windows and the heat registers. He was occupied for five minutes or so and when he returned to the desk Aimee had crossed her knees. As he walked toward her John could see the under side of her left leg. He was suddenly aware of the fact that she was not wearing stockings and that he could see a lot of attractive feminine bare skin. He tried to ignore it, and he sat back down. But then he thought of an excuse to return to the other side of the room so he could come back and look at her leg again. "What am I doing?" he asked himself. He sat down and went back to work.

While John worked Aimee watched him. When he had arrived his hair had been carefully combed but after a while it fell down in a short curl over his forehead. Now and then he would push it back but it wouldn't stay. Aimee thought it was attractive. She began to notice other things about him. He was tall enough and somewhat athletic. Actually he was good looking. Without thinking about it Aimee sat up a bit straighter, flattening her stomach and extending her breasts.

Sometimes, when people meet for the first time, they are immediately attracted to each other. They are often able to communicate this mutual attraction without saying anything, which makes it even stronger. This perception between them is often described in terms which give it an air of mystery. For instance it is frequently called a chemistry or, at times, a vibration which materializes between the two. Actually there is nothing at all mysterious about it. It is a matter of body language. And while we may not be entirely conscious of what it is, we are constantly sending and receiving these silent signals. It is a way one has of communicating feelings without making a commitment.

Aimee's chair had been pushed a distance away from John's. Now he was aware of the fact that she had pulled it closer and that she was watching what he was doing from next to his arm. In fact when he reached across the desk for a new pencil his right arm touched her breast. Instinctively he pulled his arm back but she didn't move away. On the contrary she did not react at all. He, therefore, reached out again and picked up the pencil, pulling his arm back slowly so that not only his arm but also the back of his hand brushed lightly against her breast. Her response seemed to be to lean forward a bit farther.

John was trying to concentrate on what he was doing but he could not help imagining what Aimee's breast might be like. The sensation he had received, through not only his shirt sleeve but also all of the clothes she had on, had been ever so slight. Physically it would probably have been indistinguishable from the feeling he would have gotten from touching her shoulder. But he knew that it was her breast he had touched and because of that his mind created pictures on its own. He imagined that her breasts would be large and soft but, at the same time, firm and round. He also imagined that Aimee was attracted to him, possibly attracted enough to want him to see her breasts. He wondered if that was really so.

This was by no means an example of burning passion. It might even have been only curiosity at first. But the thinking about Aimee's body stirred up erotic feelings in John. It was with great effort that he continued with what he had been doing.

Finally he was finished or at least at a point where he could complete the project at his own office or at home. He turned to the girl beside him and began to discuss in a general way what he had done. She leaned forward and seemed to listen but her eyes never left his face. John forgot what he was saying and he also began to look only into her eyes. She was so very close to him, and neither of their chairs had arms. He was able to slowly reach over and put his hands on her shoulders. She did not resist as he pulled her toward him and only when her face was inches from his did she close her eyes. He kissed her softly and then released her. But she put her arms around his neck and pulled his mouth down on hers. They stayed that way for a long time. Then he put his left hand on her right breast and massaged it gently. She began to unbutton her sweater, then her blouse. He reached inside her brassier and, rather clumsily, pulled her breasts free. They were so large that her nipples seemed tiny.

John continued to kiss Aimee and knead her breasts. She seemed excited. She would hold her breath for a while and then breath rapidly for a few minutes. John could feel his heart beating rapidly and his own breathing was irregular. He leaned over and put his mouth on her right nipple. It tasted faintly of perfumed soap.

John put his left hand under Aimee's right thigh. Her bare skin was soft and smooth but very firm, as her breasts had been. Slowly he moved his hand so that it was between her legs and slid it up toward her crotch, and she spread her legs slightly to accommodate him. Suddenly he realized that Aimee wore a girdle but was not wearing underpants. He had heard one of the girls at College say that some women did not wear panties, but he had not believed it. Apparently it was true. He could put his hand under her girdle and feel her pubic hair. He was becoming very much aroused, and so was Aimee. She was certain she was about to learn what it was like to be made love to.

Then they could hear the telephone start to ring from a desk on the other side of the room. John's first thoughts were to wonder how Kate had been able to find the telephone number of the office they were in and then to wonder why she was calling.

John sat back in his chair. Aimee uncrossed her legs and smoothed her skirt down over her knees. After the phone had rung a dozen times or so and did not stop she got up and walked toward the sound. John heard her say hello and then heard her say a few more words which he could not distinguish. He wondered what he would say to Kate.

When Aimee came back her breasts were hidden and her blouse was buttoned. She said, "It was a wrong number." She did not sit down but stood there, her feet together and her hands clasped in front of her. But she continued to look directly at him after she finished talking, apparently waiting for some sign from him as to what they would do next.

John looked away, first at her hands, then at the floor, and finally at the desk. He began organizing all his papers. He said, "I'm sorry for what I almost did. If I offended you I ...." His voice trailed off. Then he said, "I know you are a very nice girl. I don't know what made me ...." Again he stopped, unable to give a name to what had occurred. Either he did not know for sure, or he did not want to admit to himself, that he had actually intended to have intercourse with this young woman.

Aimee did not help him. She would have been willing to let him continue with what he had been doing but she didn't want to concede that, especially since he apparently no longer wanted to. She looked down at the floor but said nothing. She began to feel rejected, even a little angry, perhaps a bit as though she had been used. But she knew that later on, when she was alone, she would feel disappointment.

After Aimee had locked the front door and they stood by their cars he said, "Thanks for helping."

She answered, "Oh, that's all right."

They stood there for a few awkward seconds. Finally he said, "Look Aimee I really don't know why I did what I did. I know that you are a very nice girl. I feel terrible about this. I don't know what to say."

The girl smiled ruefully. She felt shamed by the fact that she was disappointed that he had stopped while he was sorry the incident had even happened at all. She felt an almost uncontrollable urge to throw her arms about his neck, to tell him that she did not mind what he had done, to beg him to make love to her there in the parking lot. She said, "I don't know what to say either. I could have told you to stop. I guess we should just forget about it."

He wanted to put his arms around her, to hug her and tell her that she was a good sport to take it that way. But he was afraid of what might happen. He nodded his head slightly and patted her hand before opening her car door for her. When she had started the motor and pulled out onto the road he got into his car and started home.

The excitement had gone away but not the memory of it. John was sorry for what he had done and for what he might have done. It occurred to him that he had been very much aroused, perhaps even more than he ever was with his wife, whom he loved very much. He had never done anything like this before. He was certain that if Kate ever found out about it she would leave him, and he would not blame her. He pounded the steering wheel with his hand and shook his head. "Oh what a fool I was," he muttered to himself. "I can't believe that I would ever do such a thing. And that poor girl. What in the world must she think of me?" He drove on in the night, in a hurry to get home, to see his wife and his family, to reassure himself that Kate was there, that nothing had changed. He resolved that never again would he allow himself to be drawn into such a situation. He had come very close to doing something he would have regretted for the rest of his life. He promised himself it would never happen again.

Still he could not erase from his mind the memory of the softness of Aimee's breast, the taste of her nipple, and the smooth firmness of her thigh. Even though he kept calling himself a hundred kinds of fool these things kept running through his brain.

*   *   *

During the night Pat coughed in his sleep. Then he groaned. It woke Mary and she was disturbed because she had never heard her husband do this before. She was worried and lay in the bed for a long time wondering if she should call someone. But Pat did not groan again and he did not seem to be awake. Finally Mary decided that there was nothing so seriously wrong that it could not wait until morning. But for the rest of the night she was uneasy. She slept only fitfully, awakening to lie there trying to hear his breathing, dropping off to sleep for a short time, and then waking up again.

It was still dark when she knew that he had died. At first it was his breathing, or rather the fact that she could not hear his breathing. She put her hand on his bare chest and there was no sensation at all. She could not feel his lungs expanding, nor could she feel his heart beating. She felt for a pulse on his wrist but she knew there would be nothing. He was still warm and she reached over and kissed him on the mouth. She said, "Oh, Mr. O'Maury, now you are in heaven I hope. And I hope you are happy. But I will miss you, old man."

The thought struck her that he often woke up in the morning with an erection. He said he thought it was not an uncommon thing but she sometimes teased him about it anyway. It was one of the very few personal things which had any sexual connotation about which they ever talked.

Now Mary wondered if Pat had an erection. Slowly she reached under his shorts and felt his penis. It was very stiff. When he had been in early middle age he would often say that they should not let such a thing go to waste, a reference to the fact that he felt he was not able to "perform sexually" as well as he could when he was younger, or at least not as often. This was, in fact, one of only two expressions he ever used in referring to the act of sexual intercourse. The other one was a reference to gaining merit.

Before they had married they had gone to visit Mary's pastor for their instructions. He had reminded them that sexual intercourse between a man and a woman married to each other, unhindered by any act which would prevent pregnancy, was a means of gaining spiritual merit. Therefore, he said smiling, it would be appropriate for one partner to ask the other to join in gaining a little merit. Pat used the term now and then. Mary, of course, never ever did. Now she said very quietly, "Too bad we have to waste that. We could gain a little merit."

In all the years they had been married she had never touched Pat's testicles, mostly because she knew how tender they were and how painful it could be to a man if they were not handled properly. But she had always wondered what they felt like. She moved her hand down further in his shorts until she felt his scrotum. His testicles felt much bigger than she had thought they would be. Even though she knew he was dead she was careful not to squeeze them.

Except for her days in the hospital with the babies or for the infrequent times Pat had taken short business trips, Mary had not slept alone since the day they had been married and it was something she had learned to appreciate. Before they had been able to afford a gas furnace Pat had kept her warm in the winter. He always seemed to generate heat. Now she would have to learn to sleep alone again. She wondered if she could do it.

Mary put her head on Pat's shoulder and pulled the cover up over both of them. She didn't want to get up. She put her arm across his chest and held him as close as she could. He was beginning to grow cold.

"Oh my Pat," she whispered, "my dear, dear Patrick." And, her tears running down over his shoulder, she wept quietly for a long time.

Chapter VI

Timmy was the junior server, officially still learning, but doing very well nonetheless. He handed Father Mannix a straight pin having remembered that the priest didn't trust the elastic in the maniple. Then the two boys held the old Greek style chasuble for him. He had to lean way down to get it over his head without putting his hair in complete disarray. Timmy beamed at him and said, "When I grow up I want to be a priest, just like you." Father Mannix smiled and encouraged him, "Timmy, I hope you can. You two guys are good servers. You'll make a good priest." He patted him and Ben, the older boy, on their shoulders as they started out into the sanctuary. Silently he prayed, "Oh God, save him from being like me. Rather grant me the grace to be like these two, simple, innocent, only wanting so hard to do things right, only wanting to serve the Lord."

From According To The Order Of Melchizedek, by Luce Andrews.

Fall 1944

John had thought about joining the Navy but had been dissuaded not by Kate but by the sailor in the recruiting office. Then, in 1942, he had joined an army reserve outfit. On his first exercise he had jumped off a tank and torn a ligament in his knee. After that he was told he ought to leave the soldiering to younger men. At first he felt as though he was letting his country and his family down, but he was made to realize that there were things he could do that were important to the war effort.

After Christmas in 1943 Norman had informed his parents and his brothers and sisters that he had decided to enter Brunnerdale, a prep seminary of the Congregation of the Most Precious Blood. He was fourteen years old. Not everyone was taken completely by surprise. Fifteen year old

Jack, for instance, rather expected it. He and Norman had often spent hours discussing what the two brothers intended to do after they left high school. Neither of them being close enough that a decision in the matter could be considered critical their discussions were always very general. Nevertheless Jack recalled that Norman seemed to be curious about how people in the religious life lived. The assistant pastor at their parish in Cincinnati was a Precious Blood priest and he had taken Norman and another boy to witness an ordination at the Society's major seminary at Carthagena. The ceremony had made a very strong impression on Norman. Jack was not certain but he felt that visit had been the occasion which had caused his brother to make the decision.

The ten year old twins, Billy and Fritz, only wanted to know if Brunnerdale had a football team and when they found out the school did not they said they thought going there was a bad idea.

Aloysius was twelve and in the sixth grade. He was not completely surprised either but he was not sure he would like it there. His primary objection to it was his not being certain how he would like the food. Aloysius liked the way his mother cooked and he was usually reluctant to eat anyplace where he thought the food might be different from the menu at home.

The older girls, Elleen and Polly, nine and seven, asked if there would be any cute boys there and when told that likely there would be they were pleased. Carrie, who was only five, didn't seem to care one way or the other.

John and Kate both were proud of their son. They were aware that his enrolling in a high school seminary only indicated his intention to explore the possibility of becoming a religious. Norman might, or might not, become a priest after twelve years of prayer and study. But they were proud that he was willing to try.

On the other hand they were both a little sad, Kate perhaps more than John, because they knew that they would be giving up their son. Brunnerdale was one of the religious institutions which did not allow the seminarians much time at home. Vacation consisted of two weeks in the summer. That was the only time the student was permitted to visit his family. And visiting at the seminary was restricted also, to the first Sunday of every month, and Christmas and Easter. There were very few exceptions to any of these rules.

The Rector of the seminary sent each of the newly enrolled a rule book which, among other things contained a list of things to bring. It was very specific regarding the number and color of socks, trousers, shirts, and underwear, etc., and also mentioned the obvious, toothbrush, wash cloths, towels, and razors for those who needed them. Dress shoes and work shoes were specified because the seminarians were required to help maintain the school building as well as the farm on which it was situated. It was in this way that everyone was able to avoid paying tuition. Everyone worked his way through school.

Norman and his family spent much of the summer of 1944 collecting the things mentioned in the rule book. And, as autumn, and the time of leaving,grew closer Norman and his parents grew partly excited, but also partly apprehensive. The realization that he would be leaving home, probably forever, began to occupy Norman's thoughts more and more. And Kate would sometimes cry but never when anyone else could see her.

Chapter VII

It was the place she always came to, where the creek wound around an old tree. If she sat down on the other side of the tree no one coming along the path next to the stream could see her before she could hear him coming. It gave her some privacy so she could think. The water was clear and it never dried up even in the hot days of summer when there was no rain. It must have come from a spring somewhere. She picked up a little leaf and threw it in. The rapid current took it round the bend so she couldn't see it any more. She wondered if far, far away someone would see the little leaf and know someone like her had thrown it into the water. Maybe they would try to imagine what she looked like. She wondered.

From One Road Down And To The Right, by T. S. Taylor.

Fall 1953

✳ ✳

There was a widower by the name of Chester Walker who lived in Huntsville and had been a friend of Max Hoect's. Mary had met him through the Hoect boys about eight years after Pat had died and he had started calling on her from time to time. He was rather distinguished looking and was reputed to be "rather well off". He was also at least a few years younger than Mary; she didn't know exactly how many. Apparently he was in love with her because he had asked her to marry him more than once, but she said she was not interested.

Chess, who preferred to be called that rather than Chet, was accepted by the rest of the family and was usually expected to take part in the family activities; and mostly he did. In fact they often teased Mary about him, suggesting that, since he lived a fair distance from the lake and even farther from Cincinnati, it would be a matter of convenience and good economics if she married him. Of course Chess encouraged this, even though sometimes it seemed to irritate Mary.

At seventy four she was healthy and active, perhaps a little overweight but with very few wrinkles, and more buxom than ever. She knew she was still attractive. And she liked to go out with Chess. Strangely she actually had a better time with him than she had ever had with Pat. They had learned how to dance and often did, something for which Pat had never had time. And Chess treated her differently than Pat had. Pat had obviously loved and respected her, but there was never any doubt that he regarded her as a dependent. Chess on the other hand regarded her with what bordered on adoration. And perhaps this is what the problem was. While Mary enjoyed his obvious affection when they went out together it was apparently not the kind of relationship she thought was a proper one on which to build a marriage. Chess did not realize this, nor did anyone else. Not even Mary did in all likelihood. It was a subconscious thing that prevented her from feeling about Chess the way she would have to feel before she could marry him. Nevertheless she liked him very much, perhaps even loved him, and enjoyed his company, even though she had told some of her family she thought he was a pest.

Chess had brought his new Plymouth and parked it in the driveway for everyone to admire. He liked cars. But the vehicle which he most often drove when he took Mary out was parked in the barn on his farm. It was a DeSoto Airstream Coupe convertible which would soon be twenty years old. It was one of the cars of which he was most proud and he kept it in tip top condition. He also owned another old car, one which he did not use as often, and the only one he had ever owned of which he had not been the original owner. It was a 1931 Cord L-29 Boattail Speedster and it was parked in the barn next to the DeSoto. Everyone, but especially the young boys in the O'Maury family, were fascinated by it. It was painted a flashy yellow and orange and it was unique not only in the county but probably in the state. Chess only drove it in parades, however. He often said he only kept those old cars because they would someday be worth a lot of money, but no one ever conceived of the notion that he might sell one of them for any amount.

Chess and Mary were sitting on the swing which John had put in the backyard of the newest cottage, with some help.

Jack actually had helped the most when he had come out from Cincinnati to spend one weekend in July. But Norman had also gotten in on the tail end of the project when he was permitted to come home from the seminary in Carthagena for a short visit. Norman was twenty three years old and expected to be ordained a deacon in a few years.

During the three years he had attended Brunnerdale Seminary the family had often traveled to Canton on visiting Sunday and, from Cincinnati, those had been long trips. John remembered them well with a combination of pain and pride. He had been so proud of Norman but, at least in the beginning, whenever they left the grounds on the long road which wound about from the lake and through the tall trees which immediately blocked their view of the front of the building, he would carry in his heart a picture of a forlorn little boy who stood at the end of the drive and waved goodbye to them. Fortunately the picture was not completely accurate.

It was true that Norman was often homesick but he was never desolate. He missed the way of life with his family which he had given up. Most of all he missed his parents but he also missed his brothers and sisters. And he knew that before long some of them would marry and there would be nieces and nephews which he would learn to love but would only see infrequently. But there were compensations which not everyone else was able to appreciate.

For one thing living at Brunnerdale was like having about a hundred brothers, some older and some younger; and Norman was already used to a big family. And Norman liked the regulated, steady, dependability of the way of life which was provided by the strictness of religious discipline. He often thought that if this had not been available to him in a religious atmosphere he probably would have sought it in the military.

Norman did not consider himself particularly religious; and this was true of most of the other students at Brunnerdale. What they had in common was the idea that they might someday want to become priests, and the desire to eventually become religious enough to do just that. Only vaguely did they consider what they would be giving up if someday, in a far distant future, they would indeed be ordained. It would probably have scandalized some people who in fact tended to regard them already as part priest if they realized the way in which many of these adolescent boys thought of girls. Perhaps a good example of this might be an activity which sometimes took place on the ball field.

It was customary on Sunday afternoons in the summer to get up a game of baseball. This may sound much the same as activities on the outside but at Brunnerdale it was different. For one thing it was easy to get eighteen players so that there would be two full teams. And there were always two or more boys who would agree to be umpires. The field on which the games were played was regulation and well taken care of, with grass on the infield. Besides this, to make it even more authentic, the school was in possession of official practice uniforms which had been donated by four teams from the National and the American Leagues. The players used these uniforms. The umpires had to provide their own apparel but no one minded.

On visiting Sundays one of the things boys who had visitors did was to take them down to the ball field to watch the game. And as often as not the visitors included girls in skirts who found it necessary to sit on the benches which were provided, or sometimes on the grass around the playing field. In either case there were usually a good many feminine legs made very visible by this. One of the activities popular among the boys who did not have visitors was to go down to the ball field and lie down on the grass, the position which provided the best prospective for viewing the girls' legs without being too obvious. Groups of them would in fact collectively decide who had the most interesting legs. They tried to be discreet and the games were usually exciting enough to attract sufficient attention so that the 'other' sport went unnoticed.

In February of their first year Norman and his classmates were invested with the black cassocks and Roman collars which made them truly feel that they were studying to be religious, but it didn't make them act much differently.

Then, in his fourth year, which was at St. Joseph College in Indiana, Norman learned how to smoke, because it was permitted and it was a novelty. Besides, his father seemed to enjoy his pipe, whenever he smoked it. But Norman smoked cigarettes. He also learned to play the slide trombone and marched in the band. At this time, in acknowledgement that they were becoming adults, the seminarians were permitted to take short trips into the small town of Rensselaer. And some began to pay more attention to the differences between men and women. And many of them decided they did not want to give up the right to take advantage of those differences and went home to stay. Norman did not. It was not that he was not attracted to women. It was just that he thought there was something else, something for which it was worth giving up any possibility for a personal relation with women, or at least with any woman he had met so far. There were, obviously, others who felt the same way. But Norman's class had been reduced by nearly half to less than thirty.

Finally, after six years of practicing to be a religious, Norman went to St. Charles, the major Seminary of the Society of the Most Precious Blood, at Carthagena, to seriously learn how to become one. By then his family had come to accept the fact that although they were still very important to him they were definitely second in line. John and Kate had seen their boy grow up and become a man. Now, because the seminary was so close they were able to visit much more often, and they did. And they still missed him in between visits. But there was never any question about where he belonged nor about whether or not he chose to be there.

Norman wrote to his parents nearly every week, even when he had nothing that he thought worth writing about. And he wrote nearly as often to his aunt Eileen, whom he referred to as Aunt Sister. Most of her nieces and nephews called her that, sometimes Sister Mary Charles. But John always called her Eileen.

Some things had changed for Sister Mary Charles. For one thing Sister Theodosia had died in 1950, and when she did it had been a great personal loss to Sister Charles. They had become very close, so close, in fact, that some of the other nuns, especially some of the older nuns, had resented it. In 1948, when Theodosia had stepped down because of the arthritis which was disabling her more than a few of the sisters had expected Sister Charles to replace her as Mother Superior. And, after Mary Dominic was elected instead, they blamed it on jealousy. Sister Charles, however, was not one of them. She sincerely felt she was unworthy and was relieved that she was not elected.

Besides Eileen liked Sister Dominic. She saw in her a dedicated, devoted, impartial, energetic religious. In other words Sister Mary Charles saw in Dominic exactly the kind of person that should run a convent, and the kind of person she would like to have been.

Chess had just asked Mary how she liked the new cottage, bought in 1950, bigger even than the O'Maury house in Cincinnati, which she still called home, and he was waiting for a reply. They were sitting on the front porch, Mary on the wicker swing suspended from the porch ceiling, and Chess on a wooden recliner, his feet propped up. Mary hadn't answered him immediately because she was trying to sort out how she really felt about it and why.

For one thing there was the bigness of it, the five bedrooms, the three baths, and the immense kitchen. And there was actually a family room next to the living room. For Mary these were unnecessary extravagances. She would rather have had a basement and perhaps an attic to store things in.

But Mary knew that she was not being practical. All the space encouraged the family to visit. The building was big enough, and the rooms situated in such a way, that they could always find someplace for everyone to sleep. It was built for a large family. But still The Manse, as they had started calling it, did not evoke in Mary the same enthusiasm it did in the others. There were many reasons.

For one thing she knew Pat would have been proud of it and he was not there.

There, she was able to put it into words, if only in her heart. Things would never be as good for her without Pat. He had worked so hard for all of them, why couldn't he be there to see how well his work had been rewarded?

She didn't want to explain this to Chess. It was too personal. And anyway there was more, some things that she could share with him and some that she could not. She said nothing and Chess did not press her.

One of the things she could not share with Chess was what had happened to Elleen in 1951 when the girl was only sixteen. And the reason she could not talk to Chess about it was that she was not able to talk to anyone about it; she did not even like to think about it. To Mary being raped was worse than being killed. She could not imagine that the anguish would ever go away.

Actually none of the family knew many of the details of what had happened because no one could ever talk to Elleen about it. She had gone with some acquaintances to the amusement park. One of them was a girl from Russels Point whom she had met at church. Another was the girl's sister. And the third was one of their neighbors. Mary knew that Elleen had never become more than an acquaintance with any of the three. What she did not realize was that Elleen had never even talked with any of them following what took place that night.

As it was all pieced together later on, Elleen had decided to walk outside the park, near the lake, where she could get a better view of the moon shining on the water. The other girls told her to be careful because the footing was not very good and she might turn an ankle. They also told her to hurry back because it was getting late and the band would soon be playing its last number for the night. They intended to wait with her in the parking lot for John, who would give them all a ride home. Elleen had not gotten far before she realized that someone was following her in the dark. She tried to run but immediately she felt someone grab her shoulder. She screamed but the band and the other sounds from the park were too loud for her to be heard, and then her assailant put his hand on her mouth. He dragged her into a small stand of trees and fell to the ground, pulling her on top of him. Quickly he pulled a piece of adhesive tape over her mouth. Then he rolled her over so that she was on the ground and he was lying next to her, his shoulder resting on her left arm while he was able to reach behind her head and hold her right wrist with his right hand. When she tried to struggle he pinched her nostrils with his left hand so she couldn't breathe. When she lay still he let her breathe. When she began to struggle he held her nose again. After a while, afraid she would suffocate, she began to lie still. Then he reached down with his left hand and began to remove her underpants.

Elleen was terrified. She began to cry and, once again to try to pull loose. But he clamped his hand on her nostrils again and she realized struggling was useless. She began to sob but it was nearly in silence because of the tape that covered her mouth, and it made her choke. Elleen could hardly see the man because he was in the shadows of the trees but after he had taken her pants off and moved over to get on top of her the moonlight fell clearly on his face and she could see him better. She knew that, if she lived, she would never forget what he looked like.

It was then that he said the only words he would speak to her, "That's it sweetheart, lie still and enjoy it." He didn't pronounce the "r" so "sweetheart" came out something like "sweethot".

During the next twenty minutes Elleen at first was afraid that the man would kill her but then, as the full realization of what he was doing came to her, she began to hope he would.

When he was finished he stood up and closed his pants. Then he leaned over and spat right in her face. Then quietly he ran off into the darkness.

Elleen waited a few minutes to make sure he was gone. Then she stood up and slowly, painfully, tore the tape from her mouth and threw it on the ground. She wiped her face with her skirt and then found her pants and put them back on, carefully avoiding contact with the place between her legs. The area was sore and besides she felt ashamed to even touch herself.

Elleen did not know what to do. Above all she didn't want the other girls to see her. In fact she didn't want anyone to see her. But she knew she couldn't stay where she was forever. She considered throwing herself into the lake and drowning but ridiculously the thought occurred to her that she would not drown but would float around on the water until someone found her. She stood in the darkness, sobbing, listening to the sounds coming from the park, of people having a good time. How she envied them. "Oh God," she thought, what did I do wrong that brought this on?"

She decided to walk back along the edge of the parking lot to the road. She had some money in the pocket of her skirt and she thought that perhaps she could locate a phone and call her father and he could find her without anyone else seeing her. She knew that nothing would ever be the same again but, she thought, if only she could get back with her family she would feel good enough to want to live. She longed to hear Kate tell her that she still loved her little girl no matter what Elleen had done.

She made it to the parking lot without getting into the open. She saw no one in any of the cars along the edge of the lot and started walking along, sobbing quietly, hoping to make it to the road without anyone seeing her when the door of a little Ford coupe opened suddenly and someone jumped out. It was a woman not much taller than Elleen. She threw her arms around the girl and said, "Hey, what are you doing? What are you up to? Why, you are only a child. Oh, my God! What's the matter?"

Marge Donovan was a nurse. She was also married to Harry Donovan, a Logan County detective. Because both of their work schedules were irregular Marge sometimes accompanied Harry on his job just so they could spend some time together. This was such a time. The amusement park had been bothered by some vandalism in the parking lot and the sheriff had told Harry to sit in his car in the lot to see if he could catch someone in the act of causing trouble. Harry had taken Marge with him because he did not think it would be a dangerous assignment and it would be less boring if he had someone to talk to. Also he reasoned a couple sitting in a car would look less like a policeman on assignment. While they had been talking he had noticed two young men who seemed to be arguing and he thought he might try to stop the argument before it became a fight. While he was gone Marge had seen Elleen. She seemed to be stumbling along as though she was not quite stable. Marge thought perhaps Elleen was doing something that should be investigated and as Elleen passed the car she had jumped out to apprehend her. It had not occurred to her that if Elleen had been doing something wrong she might have been dangerous.

When Marge put her arms around Elleen to restrain her the girl realized that she had been discovered but she was so miserable that by then she didn't care. She only wanted to go home. She put her head on the other woman's shoulder and began to sob violently.

"Oh, please," she said, "I want to see my mother. Can you take me home?"

At first Marge had thought that what she had was a young girl who, perhaps, had come to the park with a man and, for some reason had decided not to leave with him. She knew things like that happened all the time. But as she held this girl in her arms and heard her crying she knew that what she was listening to was not the sound of a bad romance but something rather more serious. "Sure, honey," she said, and she gently patted Elleen on the back of her head. "What happened?'

And Elleen was finally able to blurt out what she had thought she would never be able to acknowledge, "He raped me." Then she began sobbing again.

Marge gasped. "Oh, my God." Then she became indignant. "Who was it? Someone from around here?"

Elleen stopped crying and said, in a monotone, "No. Oh, I don't know. I never saw him before."

Marge was getting in over her head. "Donovan," she called, "Donovan, come here. Hurry!"

Marge's husband was on his way back to the car when he heard her. "What's the matter?" he asked her.

"Oh, Harry," Marge blurted out, "some guy raped this little girl. We've got to find him."

The detective separated the two women. He looked closely at Elleen's face, trying, in the darkness, to tell how old she was. "Are you okay? Are you hurt bad?" he asked her.

She said, "He spit in my face."

Donovan took out his handkerchief and gave it to Elleen. "Here," he told her gently. "You can wipe your face." Then he added, "How old are you?"

She said, "I'm eighteen."

Marge said, indignantly, "He ought to be..." but Donovan didn't let her finish.

Quietly but sternly he said, "Not now, Marge. We'll talk about that later. Right now we've got to get this girl to a doctor." He asked Elleen, "Are your parents here?"

"No, I came with three other girls. We were just going to listen to the music. And we danced a little. My daddy was going to pick us up later and take us all home."

"What's your name?"

"Elleen O'Maury."

"What's his name?"

"John O'Maury."

Harry patted her on the hand. He had never handled anything like this before. He was thankful that his wife was with him because he had no idea what to say to the girl. But he knew he had to find her father and tell him what had happened. "Where was he going to meet you?" he asked.

Elleen said, "By the bridge at the entrance. One of the girls is named Betty Dennister. I don't want them to know."

He tried to reassure her. "We won't tell them. I'll say you had an accident." Then he said to his wife, "I'll go find the father. You take Miss

O'Maury to see your friend, Doc Bester. Tell him to examine her and write down any marks such as bruises and things. And clean her up as well as he can." Then he added, his voice revealing his embarrassment, "Maybe he can wash her out, you know, so she doesn't get pregnant. I'll get her father and we'll meet you there."

Marge took Elleen around to the other side of their car and opened the door for her. When Elleen was inside and the door was shut Marge got in on the driver's side and started the motor. Before she drove out of the lot she put her hand on Elleen's knee. She said, "Honey, I can't say I know how you feel because I never been raped. But I know you must feel like it's the end of the world. If you want to cry you go ahead and do it. You cry all you want to. I'm going to take you to see a doctor who is a friend of mine and someone I work with sometimes. He's an old man who has seen just about everything I guess and he is the nicest guy you ever want to know. He'll take good care of you and then we'll get you home. Then tomorrow my husband will come out and talk to you about what happened so they can find the no-good that did this to you. And I'll tell you one thing, Harry will find him if he's from around here. And when he does the guy will be sorry he did this to you. I promise you that."

Harry Donovan had no trouble finding John, who was already talking to the three girls and was nearly frantic. Harry pulled him aside and told him that there had been an accident, that his daughter was not in any danger but that Harry had had the girl taken to a doctor anyway, to be on the safe side. John was alarmed because he recognized the detective's reticence to say more in front of the three girls. He followed the detective's instructions to take them home and return to pick up Donovan. While he was gone the detective asked to talk to the girl in the ticket booth and the parking lot attendants but was told they all had already left for the night. When John returned Harry knew nothing more than he had before. Harry Donovan decided that they should take Elleen's mother with them to pick up the girl at the doctor's.

For Elleen the last several hours had been a nightmare. Doctor Ben Bester had turned out to be a kindly old gentleman who treated her as gently as he could. And he explained everything he did so that she could be prepared. He asked very few questions except to find out where she felt pain. Finally he gave her some medicine which was a mild sedative and she was beginning to feel a little better. Nevertheless she burst into tears again when Kate came in because she was so happy to see her. Kate also began to cry when she saw her little girl sitting on the examining table in the doctor's office. But she knew that it would not help the girl to see her mother cry so she tried to stem the tears. She threw her arms around Elleen and told her everything would be fine. She even tried to believe it herself.

Marge and Doctor Bester left Elleen and her parents alone for a while as they went into the waiting room to talk to Harry. The doctor had made a list of bruises and scratches and other conditions that indicated that Elleen had indeed been forcibly raped. He also told the detective that he could tell her mouth had been taped shut.

Detective Donovan went into the other room to talk to Elleen and her parents. He explained that he needed to get as much information as he could while it was still fresh in the girl's mind but that she would soon be free for her parents to take her home. Elleen was able to give him only a general idea of where the attack had taken place. But she was able to give him a somewhat better description of her attacker. She said he was of medium height and very strong. She could not tell how old he was but she thought his hair was red because it did not look very dark and she thought he had a lot of freckles which red haired people often do. She remembered exactly what the man had said to her and the detective carefully wrote down the words. Finally he told her she could go home but that he would like to come and see her again the next day to see if she could remember anything else.

Before they left he took John aside and told him the description did not fit anyone he knew but he would ask around. John thanked him and Marge for taking care of Elleen. The doctor told them that he could not be certain but that it seemed unlikely that Elleen would become pregnant. John thanked Doctor Bester for being so kind to Elleen.

When everyone had left Harry took Marge back to the park and left her in the car while he searched for the site of the attack. The sun was starting to come up when he came back and woke her. He had found the piece of tape which had been used to gag Elleen.

The next day Harry went to see Elleen and her family. The only additional thing the girl could think of was the odd way in which the man had pronounced "sweetheart". Detective Donovan pointed out that it did not sound as though the assailant was from around the area. He said he and the other members of the sheriff's office would do all they could to find the man. To himself he thought that it would take some extraordinary luck.

Mary could never say this to anyone but she had always wondered what Elleen had done to cause the man to rape her. Surely there had been something which had caused him to pick her out of all the others. Of course though she was probably the only one who had wondered off in the dark by herself. If nothing else that is what she should not have done. She still loved her granddaughter very much but the girl should not have brought this disgrace upon her family.

After she had told Elleen how sorry she was that the awful thing had happened Mary avoided talking about it at all. In the end she was able to act as though it had never happened. After a while so were the others. But Elleen was not able to sleep in any room that had no light in it.

Something that occupied much of her thought those days which she could talk to Chess about were her two grandsons, Bill and Fritz. They had hardly seen this place and she would never feel good about it until they were able to enjoy it with the rest of the family.

They had been preparing for their junior year in high school the summer that John and Kate bought the new "cottage". They had not even been able to come to the lake until the football season was over and that was too late in the year to spend any time there. The next summer, 1951, was much the same. The football team was expected to be very good that year, partly because of the O'Maury twins, and practice started just as soon as it was permitted.

And there was the threat of the Korean "police action", as it was called. Every boy in the senior class expected to be drafted; most of them wanted to go. It was a feeling left over from the patriotism that had gripped the whole country during the second world war.

The team had done well, not as well as some had hoped, but better than the year before. And the twins had graduated shortly after they registered for the draft. They had spent that summer waiting, with their friends. Everyone checked his mailbox each day as soon as the mailman had passed. Then in the evening they would gather to find out who was going and when.

They had friends who were girls, but these were not girlfriends. The unstable climate of the times did not encourage the making of firm commitments. There would be plenty of time for that later, when they all came home, heroes with medals covering their military blouses. The country would be grateful and they would continue their lives knowing this, realizing that they had helped keep the world safe and free, and that the others appreciated what they had done.

The twins were drafted in the middle of October in 1952, after many of their friends were already in Korea, and sent to Camp Breckenridge, near Morganfield, Kentucky, for basic training. They were not in the same company but they were close enough that they could see each other regularly. They were allowed to come home for Thanksgiving and it was at this time that Bill met Jill. She was the sister of George Shannon, one of the trainees in his platoon, whose family lived in Cincinnati. She was two years older than Bill, dark and slender with beautiful legs. George and the twins had all driven home together on the Wednesday before Thanksgiving with a member of the cadre who was allowed to keep his car on the base. He left them all out north of the city where he planned to pick them up the next day for the return trip. Each of the boys had at least one member of his family waiting to take him home. Jill was waiting for her brother and as soon as Bill saw her he fell in love with her.

What followed was a true whirlwind romance, mostly by mail. Jill came down on a bus "to visit George" on the second weekend after Thanksgiving, but she hardly saw him. She stayed in the civilian quarters reserved for visitors, where soldiers are not permitted in the visitors' areas, but she and Bill spent all his free time together. They never left the base but they ate together in the PX, they attended Mass together in one of the theaters, they sat and held hands in the recreation room near the main gate.

The next weekend she drove to Breckenridge and she and Bill and George went to a party in Morganfield on Saturday night. The two boys did not have to be back until Monday morning so George stayed with a friend's family and Jill and Bill spent the night in the car, huddled together and now and then turning the engine on to keep warm. They had already decided to get married.

They were able to get the Catholic Chaplain to marry them on a Saturday, a week before Christmas, by telling him Jill was pregnant. After the wedding the two of them, and Fritz and George, had dinner together in a hotel in Evansville. Then they returned to a motel near Morganfield leaving Fritz and George to call the families.

None of their parents had been happy about the marriage, but Jill did the best she could. She met with John and Kate. The boys were expecting to be allowed to go to Cincinnati for Christmas and, at that time Billy intended to explain how he and Jill had been afraid to wait, afraid that perhaps they might never have another chance.

The twins had always pretty much done things together. Fritz had gone out for the basketball team. Billy had followed. Then Billy had made the football team and Fritz had done the same thing. Billy had seen an old clarinet in a pawn shop and bought it. Then, without taking lessons, he had learned to play it. Fritz had vowed to learn to play just as well as his twin and had done it. It had been that way with most of what they had done. When Billy and Jill were married Fritz was at first happy for them but when Jill rented a room in Morganfield he suddenly felt alone. Basic training was winding down and the two boys had most of their evenings free. Jill would pick Billy up and take him to her room as soon as Billy was able to leave camp. Fritz was always invited to come along but, although he liked Jill very much, he did not want to intrude. He would go with them to Jill's room but he would stay only long enough to say hello. On the first floor of the building where Jill lived there was a bar called The Black Apple, and he would go down there to drink beer and play table shuffleboard until it closed. Then he would go back upstairs and Jill would drive them both back to their barracks.

It was in the bar that Fritz met Paul Gains. Paul was a local who had been in the second world war. He was a mechanic, going steady but not married, and sympathetic to young soldiers away from home, especially around the holidays. He also liked to drink and he liked to play shuffleboard. He and Fritz teamed up against two other players, won a few games, and in the process became friends.

Christmas that year fell on a Thursday. On the Monday before Billy and Fritz were told that their company would be allowed to leave the camp for the holidays, but only on a local pass, because they might be on their way to Japan and the Far East Command. It was a terrible blow to both of them but probably harder on Fritz because he had to look forward to spending Christmas more or less alone, while Billy at least would have his wife.

Paul, who was only a half dozen or so years older than Fritz, was deeply concerned for his friend. He had an idea. Paul's girlfriend Sandy was attending college in Lexington. She was home only on infrequent weekends which, Paul said, was why he had so much time to spend at "The Apple". Sandy would be home at Christmas and she was going to have a small party on Christmas Eve at her parents home. Why didn't Fritz come to the party?

At first Fritz declined, pointing out that Paul would be the only one he would know and that he probably would feel like an outsider. But as the two talked, and drank beer, Fritz began to consider the prospect of spending Christmas away from his family. He had never done that before. He expected that he would spend most of the time with Billy and Jill but, seeing the two of them together would only emphasize the fact that he had no one of his own, a situation that did not seem to matter much until Billy and Jill had married.

When it was nearly midnight Paul decided to call Sandy and ask her to extend her own personal invitation to Fritz. Sandy lived in a dormitory and had to be called from her room by a dorm monitor to answer the phone. She was not happy about this and began scolding Paul very strongly as soon as she found out he was the one who was calling. She had been cramming for an exam and had been trying to get a few hours sleep before going back at it. Paul sounded properly repentant while talking to Sandy but whenever she talked he covered the mouthpiece with his hand and grinned at Fritz who was standing next to the pay phone. Finally Fritz heard the girl say very loudly, "Paul Gains I know you aren't listening to anything I'm saying, are you? What did you want anyway?"

"Why do you think I wanted something?" he asked. "How do you know I didn't just want to hear your voice? You know how much I love you."

"Uh huh," she answered skeptically. "And when are we getting married?"

"We'll talk about that when you get home," he told her, and grinned even broader at Fritz. Then he said to Sandy, "By the way I want to know if I can bring a good friend to your party."

At that Sandy's attitude seemed to change completely. She made a sound that resembled a slight scream, the way girls often do when they are very pleased. Paul took the receiver away from his ear. She said, "You must be a mind reader. Ginny is coming home with me and she needs a date. You know my roomie, don't you? She can't go home. She says she can't afford it. You think she'll like your friend?"

"She can't help it," Paul told her. "Everybody likes him. But I don't know if he'll like her. Isn't she kind of moody?"

"If you mean that she is serious, yes. She isn't exactly an airhead. But she's fun when she wants to be. And you have to admit she's good looking."

"Yes," conceded Paul, "She is one of the best looking broads I know. So I guess that means it's okay?"

Before they hung up Paul also told Sandy that Billy and Jill might come too. She didn't seem to mind.

So that is what they did. Fritz met Paul at The Apple shortly after six on Christmas eve. He and Billy had decided to wear their uniforms because they were the dressiest clothes they had, but Fritz had already pulled his tie down and opened the top button on his shirt. He and Paul were on their fourth bottle of Falls City Beer by the time Billy and Jill came downstairs to get them. They were all going together so that Paul could show them the way to get to Sandy's home.

They got to the party a little before eight. Fritz was introduced to Sandy and her parents, who proved to be very nice people, and offered a drink. Ginny was still upstairs "getting ready". When she finally came down Fritz was not disappointed.

Ginny Lowell was a small girl, very pretty, with dark hair and smoldering eyes. She wore a sort of peasant blouse and a full skirt that came down below her knees. She might have been a gypsy.

She said, "Hi," when they were introduced. She kept her hands at her sides and made only the faintest smile. Fritz could think of nothing to say. Finally he asked her if he could get her a drink. Then she surprised him. She took his hand and said, "Let's see what they have."

Sandy's family lived in Sturgis, which was "dry"; no alcoholic beverages were sold there. Nevertheless in the dining room was a table with glasses and an ice bucket, soda, ginger ale, coke, and several kinds of bourbon. They were told they could find beer and soft drinks in the refrigerator in the kitchen and that they should help themselves. The guest who told them this, they found out later, was a deputy sheriff.

It was a rather small party, not more than twenty people but they all seemed to be concentrated in the living room and dining room. Ginny mixed herself a rather strong drink and then she and Fritz began to look for somewhere to sit.

The kitchen was next to the dining room and they noticed that the door which led downstairs was open so they went down into the basement. It appeared to be part of the party area since the floor was painted and there was furniture, but there was no one else there. They sat down on a couch, Ginny in one corner with her legs tucked up under her. They talked for a while about college and the army. She disposed of her drink quickly and Fritz took her glass upstairs to refill it. By the time Ginny was on her third drink she had moved over closer to Fritz, and she had even begun to laugh now and then. But Fritz could never remember what had made her laugh.

Sandy came down looking for them. Fritz asked how his brother was doing and was told he had gotten into some sort of serious discussion with the sheriff's deputy; Sandy couldn't tell him what it was about. She went back up and brought them a small plate of snacks, in case they were hungry. She said she would be back later and left. Ginny and Fritz drank some more.

About eleven o'clock Fritz decided he would like to go to midnight mass. Ginny, who was not Catholic, said she would not mind going along to see what it was like. Fritz went and found his brother who agreed to go so that he and Jill would not have to go to Mass the next day. When they left Sandy and Paul and Sandy's parents told them to come back after mass. They said they would and started off to the church in Morganfield. By the time they got to the church there was one empty pew, which they thankfully took. But one of the ushers told them they would have to move because that pew happened to be reserved for "colored". This upset the two men and Jill; Ginny actually seemed to be amused by the fact that it bothered them. They all left and went to the camp where they knew there would be a Mass at one of the theaters. They had no trouble getting in the gate and finding where Mass was.

There was no music and, though there were a lot of worshippers, the Mass was very short. Afterwards Jill and Billy decided that they did not want to go back to the party but offered to drive the other two there. Fritz said he would rather take Bill and Jill back to Jill's room and borrow Jill's car, which was agreeable to Jill. But when they were alone Ginny said they didn't have to go back to Sturgis if Fritz didn't want to so Fritz took her into The Black Apple, which was still open but practically deserted. They took their drinks and went to a booth.

They sat and drank. Ginny's hand was on the edge of the table and Fritz reached over and held it in his.

"Have you ever seen what an army cot looks like?" he asked her.

She frowned. "Doesn't an army cot look like any other cot?"

"Yeah," he said, "I guess." He wanted to do something different, anything but just sit there. He said, "How would you like to see where I stay?"

"You mean where you sleep?" she asked. She was thinking that anything would be better than just sitting in a bar for the rest of the night. She wondered aloud, "Are you allowed to bring someone in there?"

He answered, "Tonight I think we could probably bring in a tank." Then he added, "Well, do you want to try?"

She said, "Yeah, I guess so. Why not?"

They told the bartender they would be back. He said they had better hurry because he intended to close up in half an hour. Actually he locked the door as soon as they left.

The MP at the front gate waved them through without even stopping their car. At Fritz's company area he parked in the little lot next to the orderly room and waited until the sentry walked past the back of the barracks. Fritz knew that whoever was C.Q. that night would be asleep in the orderly room by then. As soon as the soldier disappeared around the corner Fritz said, "Come on. He has to walk all the way around the whole company area. He won't be back for at least twenty minutes."

They got out of the car as quietly as possible and ran up the steps and into the building. They waited just inside the door to see if anyone had heard them, but the first floor seemed empty. They could hear no one breathing. Fritz was sure the upstairs was just as empty. They did not dare turn on the lights but the illumination from the lamppost outside the window was enough so that they could see where they were going. Fritz took Ginny's hand and led her to where his bunk was.

The alcohol had mostly worn off and they were both very tired. As often happens they began to feel giddy and Ginny started to giggle without knowing why.

"Shhhhh," admonished Fritz, "Someone might hear us."

But Ginny only laughed harder even though she tried not to. She sat down on the cot. She said, "I can't help it."

Fritz sat down next to her and he began to laugh too. Neither of them could stop although they both attempted to stifle the sound. Finally it wore them out and they stopped. Fritz took Ginny in his arms and kissed her.

Ginny whispered, "It's cold in here. Can I wrap a blanket around my shoulders?"

He whispered back, "You can get in bed if you want to."

She giggled again. She said, "can I take my shoes off?"

He told her, "I don't care if you take all your clothes off."

She stood up next to the cot and looked at him for a few seconds. Then she said,"Okay, if that's the way you feel about it, I will." First she kicked off her shoes and pushed them under the bed. Then she pulled her blouse over her head. Her skirt dropped to the floor. She unfastened her garter belt and pulled it off with her stockings still attached. Then she stepped out of her underpants. The last thing that fell onto the pile of clothes was her brassiere. She pulled the blanket covering the pillow away and quickly slipped under the blanket covering the rest of the bed, and the sheet. He could see her lying there staring at him but it was too dark for him to recognize the expression on her face. He considered what she had done at least partly a challenge, but he also thought it was an invitation. He was aroused and he had difficulty getting his clothes off but he did.

When he got into his cot he said "Damn it."

She said, "What's wrong?"

He said, "I'm on top of the sheet," which made her start giggling again. The blanket was tucked under the mattress on both sides in the usual military mode. He got up, pulled the blanket loose and got back in. This time he was next to her and he pulled her close.

She sighed, "Now I'm getting warm."

Ginny got pregnant that night but she never told anyone. They never, in fact, told anyone what they had done, except to say that Ginny had seen Fritz's bunk, and that much they told only to Billy and Jill.

Fritz expected to get married. He thought that because of what they had done together they ought to get married. But Ginny did not think it was quite that serious. She took it as little more than an escapade. It had been fun and that was about all there was to it. When she and Sandy went back to school she and Fritz wrote to each other. But their letters were different. He told her he loved her and that he wanted to be with her. Her letter was about school life and how glad she would be when it was over. It was not very personal. When she realized she was pregnant she thought perhaps she would find someone who would perform an abortion. But that proved to be very difficult. In the end she decided that she would have the baby and give it to someone, perhaps for money. It was not a big deal. She never told Fritz. In March she left school and although Sandy had wondered, perhaps even suspected, she never really knew.

In January the twins got their orders for Korea. They were allowed to go home first and Billy and Jill told both their families that she was fairly certain she was pregnant. John and Kate received this news with mixed feelings. They tried very hard to act as though they were happy for the couple. But they felt hurt that they had not been allowed to participate in any of the relationship that had developed between their son and Jill, and it was hard not to let that show. And yet they wanted both of them to know that they would be eager to welcome Jill and the baby into the family. And this relationship was put on hold to a certain extent because of the fact that the twins were going to Korea.

Fritz finally made up his mind that he didn't love Ginny. She was after all probably rather loose. And besides that she was unpredictable. He had no idea how to take her. He had thought that she liked him. Why else would she have slept with him? He and Billy both mentioned Ginny to John and Kate and the rest of the family. They said that she had gone to church with them on Christmas Eve. Little more was said about her. The family would hardly remember her name. No one expected to hear from her again. No one else in the family had ever gone to war. Only John had ever even been in the military. Jack and Aloysius had wanted to but both, for various reasons, had been prevented from going. Now the two of them were both apprehensive that their younger brothers were going, but they were a bit jealous that they weren't going too.

No one else in the family was married. Jack, who was twenty four years old was going with Marilyn and they had decided to get married but it was not official yet. Aloysius, three years younger than Jack, was going with several different girls but none of the relationships was serious.

All of John and Kate's family who could had gathered at the house in Cincinnati. Mary was at her own home. She would see the twins in the morning, before they left. Norman had talked to them on the phone because he was not permitted to leave the seminary. They had gone to the convent to see Sister Mary Charles.

Jack and Aloysius would drive them to the airport, and the three girls, Elleen who was eighteen, Polly, sixteen, and fourteen year old Carrie were going to squeeze into the car and ride along. John and Kate had decided that they would say their goodbyes at home. Jill also, knowing that she would not be able to maintain any control of her emotions, had told Billy she would stay behind. He agreed that it would probably be best for both of them.

They were to leave on Sunday. On Saturday evening Billy found his father sitting alone in the living room. Everyone else was in the basement playing darts, except Kate. She had gone to church for confession and she was not back yet.

There was no light on but even in the gloom John looked every bit of his fifty years, which was unusual. He was staring out of the window and, although he heard his son come into the room, he continued to peer into the front yard. Billy put his hand on John's shoulder.

"Dad," was all he said.

After a while John put his hand on Billy's, then he sighed deeply and turned around. "Ah, well," he said.

"Don't worry, dad," Billy tried to assure him. We'll be okay. We both know how to take care of ourselves." At this John smiled. He thought young people always make everything sound so easy. But then perhaps that is why they could live in a world so full of problems and not go insane. He tried to remember how he had felt when he was the same age as the twins. He could not.

He said, "Your mother will worry about you," which Billy knew meant, "We will worry about you."

"I know, dad," he almost whispered. He sat on a footstool next to John's rocker. For a while they did nothing. Then Billy said, "will you keep an eye on Jill and the baby for me?"

"You know we will," John answered. "How could we not?" He was quiet for a short space, trying to think how to put into words what he wanted to say. "It is not easy for us to get used to all of this at once, but we will. Your wife has her own family but I want her to think of us as her family also. Perhaps we can get to know her in the next few months. And perhaps you won't be gone a long time. The people at Panmunjom have been trying to arrange a cease-fire for so long. Maybe this time it will work and the fighting will be over soon."

"We'll just hope for the best," offered Billy.

"Be sure and go to church when you can," John urged his son.

"Don't worry, dad," Billy assured him. "We both will. Being in the army won't change us."

"No," John agreed, "I don't expect it will. I don't think being in the service really changes anyone, although some people will use that as an excuse." It was nearly dark in the room. Neither of them wanted to turn on a light though because neither wanted the other to notice the tear which now and then he brushed from his cheek. John asked, "Do you need a rosary?"

Bill did not smile at this. He said, "No, dad. My rosary is fine. The case was starting to come apart but I had Mr. Reising at the shoe shop sew it for me. It's good as new. And he did it for nothing."

When Mary came in they were still sitting quietly in the dark. They both had had so much they wanted to say, but neither of them had been able to say it. They went with Mary down to the basement to be with the others.

*   *   *

In May some of them had gone to the lake. The weather had been too cool to do much but they had gone up because there had been a few warm days and it had the effect of starting them all thinking about summer. So on Saturday John and Kate had taken Mary, Elleen, and Carrie with them to the cottage. Elleen had been driving for nearly a year and she so liked to do it that John let her take the wheel and he sat in the back with his mother and Carrie and enjoyed the trip. They went through Mason, Lebanon and Kettering, avoiding Dayton because that city was growing so it would have taken nearly half an hour to get through it. Springfield too was getting congested enough that John resolved to think of some way they could bypass that area also. From there to Bellefontaine, past Urbana and West Liberty on Route 68 the countryside was plowed fields and winter wheat, budding trees and fields of Timothy turning green. It was a good time to be alive.

By every report available to the public the action in Korea was winding down. There was every indication that an armistice would be signed before the end of summer. The family expected the twins to be home by the end of the year and everyone was looking forward to Christmas just in case they would be allowed to come home by then.

But in the meantime there would be the summer and this would be a planning trip. Even though they could not do a great deal they could make an assessment of what needed to be done, all the things that had been put off with the promise to, "wait until next year". Now was next year.

John busied himself in the yard, picking up fallen branches and inspecting the garden. The tulips had been especially good that year if the number of dead blossoms he had to cut off were any indication. And it looked as though the peonies and the irises would do very well. He expected to be there to enjoy them.

The women decided to get out the linens and make all the beds, then cover them up with old sheets. They would have washed all the dishes in the kitchen also but John didn't want them to turn on the water. They made a list of everything that they would need to bring along the next time, to finish getting ready for the summer season.

It was nearly two o'clock when they decided to sit in the sun on the front porch and eat the food they had brought in the picnic basket. It had grown much warmer than they expected it would, but they knew it would get cold as soon as the sun went down.

Not long after three Mary and Kate began to talk about leaving for Cincinnati. Both of them said they had many things they needed to do at home. John could not imagine what his mother had to do that was so urgent but he realized that perhaps the one thing that kept her from growing old was that she continued to maintain a list of things she intended to do. If these things were not actually written down on paper they were most certainly in her mind.

John was still sitting on the porch step. Mary and Kate had gone back inside. Elleen was gathering up what would be put back in the basket. Carrie was standing on the walk near the road when the unmarked Chevrolet passed the cottage but turned around and came back to park at the edge of the lawn.

The door of the car opened and a man in uniform stepped out. He was dressed in sharply creased officers pinks and an Ike jacket with three rows of ribbons. As he closed the door he put his overseas cap on his head and adjusted it to the proper position over his right eyebrow. Pinned to it was the stylized figure of an eagle.

The officer approached Carrie and, referring to papers he carried in his hand he asked her something which John could not hear but to which she nodded her head, and then she pointed to her father. The officer said something else to her and she ran up the steps, stopping only long enough to say to John, "He wants to talk to you and mom," and then hurrying on inside. John felt a coldness clutch at his heart.

All four of the others came out. John started to get up but the officer came up the walk and told him that perhaps he should stay seated. Kate, who also could feel a trembling start inside her sat down next to John and took his hand.

John put it into words for all of them. "It is one of the twins, isn't it? One of them is dead."

The officer stood before them, ramrod straight, his insignias and his medals shining in the afternoon sun. He saluted and started to speak. But then he bowed his head and covered his face with his hand. His body shook and he said, "Oh my God, this is the hardest thing I have ever had to do in my life." He took his hands from his face and they could see tears on his cheeks. In a choked voice he said, "It is both of them. They are both dead. I am so sorry."

They were all stunned. Mary, who was standing, began to stagger, but Elleen put her arms around her grandmother and held her. Kate said, "Oh, mein Gott! Oh, mein kinder!"

The Colonel still stood there, his feet close together as though he stood at attention, but his hands were at his side, his head was bowed, and his whole body slumped.

John stood up. He said to the soldier only, "I'm sorry."

The man said, "I'm Colonel Sam Wong. I'm the commander at Fort Thomas. I went to your house in Cincinnati because I didn't want you to get this in the mail. When they told me you were up here I drove up. I am supposed to say something but I don't know of anything that would do any good. Will you forgive me?"

Mary was able to lean against the post at the top of the steps. She had regained her composure to a degree. Elleen took her arm from Mary's shoulder and said to Colonel Wong, "We would like to offer you a cup of coffee but the water is not turned on yet."

He seemed embarrassed. He said he had to start back. He looked at all of them to see which one might be in charge with whom he could make further arrangements. He decided it would be Elleen. He gave her a card and told her to call him in a few days to make plans for bringing the twins home for burial. Then he left.

All the way back to Cincinnati John kept wondering why Colonel Wong did not look Oriental. This thought kept him from thinking of anything else. And he desperately wanted to avoid thinking of anything else at all.

*   *   *

October 1953

It was probably the first fall they had ever been glad to close up the cottage for the season. It had been a terrible summer. Most of the weekends had been rainy. And, of course, the memory of the twins haunted them. Details of how they had died had answered some questions but had not made them feel any better.

Corporals Bill and Fritz O'Maury had both been killed on routine patrols, within days of each other. Kate and John had received personal letters from friends of both of them. They were well liked by the men with whom they lived and worked, and respected as soldiers. Neither was given to taking chances and neither was considered reckless. In both cases the patrols on which they had been engaged had not been considered dangerous. But, in both cases, they had surprised enemy personnel and had been unable to react in time. Also in both cases the enemy soldiers had been killed by other members of the scouting parties.

The boys' bodies had been returned in August and had been buried in St. Mary Cemetery in St. Bernard. They had been offered the service of a full military funeral but Kate had declined. She wanted to bid her sons farewell without a great deal of pomp and to grieve in solitude with only her family around her. Colonel Wong came to the funeral with some other officers and men from Fort Thomas. They were all in dress uniforms with ribbons and insignia. And although they all kept in the background they added a certain dignity to the service. When the caskets had been lowered into the ground and the family had been preparing to leave, Sam Wong, his face streaked with tears, handed Kate a flag which he told her had been sent from the men in Fritz's company in Korea, and had flown over their base. After he gave it to her he stepped back and saluted smartly but she threw her arms around him as though he were an old friend and he burst into tears. She too sobbed but was able to whisper, "Come and see us when you can and tell us how it was in Korea where our boys were."

He could only answer, "Yes, yes, I will. I promise I will."

October had started out as though the winter would be early and severe and infringe on autumn. But then it had turned a bit warmer. As John puttered around in the backyard and planned what changes he would make for the next year most of the rest of the family concentrated on the inside of the cottage.

Two of the rest of the family consisted of Mary and Chess who sat in the swing watching John and now and then offering advice. Eventually Chess would offer to drive Mary back to Cincinnati but he knew she would decline because it would be such a long return trip for him, and she would not allow him to spend the night in her house because it would not be proper. He had asked her to marry him again and once again she had turned him down. She would have been disappointed if he had not asked. He would have been surprised if she had accepted.

Jack had made an unexpected appearance and brought Marilyn. They had decided to make their engagement official and told everyone. They were a bit disappointed that no one seemed to be very excited about it until Kate pointed out that everyone already thought of Marilyn as one of the family and the wedding would be only a formality. But when Carrie heard about it she squealed and threw her arms around Marilyn and said it was the best news she had ever heard. Although Marilyn had at first tried to act hurt she couldn't pull it off. She had grown to feel too comfortable around Jack's family to be upset for long about anything like that and they knew it. And, besides, not only Carrie but Elleen too helped her feel that her marriage to their brother would indeed be special. Later on Kate also put her arms around Marilyn and told her how happy she had always been that Jack had found her.

There was another distraction. Bill's widow Jill had brought Billy, one month old, and the girls could not let him alone. Whenever he was awake they insisted on holding him. Jill had been spending more and more of her time with the family because of the connection it gave her with Bill's memory.

As it started to get dark someone suggested that they cook supper on the grill in the back yard. Those who had intended to leave early knew that this would mean they would get home very late but no one wanted to go anyway. With little Billy there, and Jack and Marilyn's announcement, it was the first time that summer that they had really felt like celebrating.

Chess and Jack offered to take charge of the grill.

While they were eating John decided to light the lanterns which still hung over the picnic table and only needed to be turned on from inside. Carrie, who was standing near the back door told him to stay seated and let her do it. Just as she opened the door they all hard the doorbell. She stopped and said, "There's someone at the front door." Everyone laughed.

"Well, go see who it is, Dopey," said her sister, Elleen. This, of course, caused everyone to laugh a little more, even Carrie. She made a face at Elleen, reached in and flipped the switch that controlled the lanterns, then ran around to the front of the building. After what seemed like a very long time she came back, walking very slowly and carrying a large basket. She said, "You'll never believe this."

Elleen laughed and said, "Try us."

Carrie put the basket on the table and reached in. She pulled out something wrapped in a blanket. "Look!, she squealed, "It's a baby."

It was everyone else's turn to gasp. Even Elleen had nothing to say. Finally John said, "What?"

Kate said, "Who's baby?"

Carrie had pulled the blanket away from the infant's face. "It's just a little one," she told them. "I don't know who's baby it is."

Chess had gotten up from where he had been sitting at the end of the table and looked into the basket. "There might be a note or something," he suggested. "Look here. There is a little piece of paper." He pulled it out and held it up. Then he unfolded it and tried to read it but the light from the colored lanterns was much too dim. He handed it to Elleen. "Here take it inside and see what it says."

Elleen took the small paper and went into the kitchen. They all saw the light go on and waited for her to come back. So excited were they that no one even said anything. Finally Elleen came back slowly.

Carrie asked, "Well, what does it say?"

Elleen handed the piece of paper to John. "Here," she told him. "I think you should take a look at this."

John started to laugh but he saw that his daughter had been shocked by something. He said, "But I can't read it out here. Tell me what it says."

Elleen took a deep breath. She pointed to the bundle which Carrie held in her arms. "That's Fritz's little girl," she announced quietly. "Her mother must have left her on the front porch and ran away."

Chapter VIII

She got off the old mule and walked up the dirt path. He was sitting barefoot on the edge of the porch, whittling on a stick from the old willow tree. He said, "What you doin' heauh?" She said then, "Momma done got a boyfriend. She thinkin bout marryin him. Don't you cayuh?" He said, "Shuh I cayuh. Daddy only been dead three yeah. Ah bet momma's boyfriend old and ugly, ain't he?" She giggled and said slowly and dramatically, "Well he do own the only stowuh in Tobey's Landin'." He stopped whittling. He said, "That so? He probly ain't neauh as ugly as Ah thought."

From *The Truth Of The Matter*, by Chuck Francess.

1956

★★★★★★★★★★★★★★★★★★★★★★★★★★★★★★★★★★★

The family began seeing much more of Norman after he was ordained in 1956. Most of the family had been there in the chapel at Carthegina when Cincinnati's Archbishop Alter had placed his hands on the head of each of the nineteen Deacons and made them Priests, by fiat of the Lord, in the order of Melchizedek. All of his family were very proud of Norman.

A few days after the ordination, Norman had been able to officiate at a double wedding. And immediately after that he had left for Rome to study at the Society's Motherhouse. But one year later he was back and was now an assistant at St. Joseph, in Wapakoneta.

The four people who had been married were his brother Jack, to Marilyn, and his sister Elleen, to Dan Frankl.

Jack and Marilyn appeared made for each other. They were both shorter than average, both rather slender, both very dark, and both very good looking. Jack had met her when they were both members of the Coast Guard. They were both in the first year of their second enlistment and seemed to like the military life. They were stationed on Lake Erie and were able to get to Indian Lake often.

Elleen had met Dan through a mutual friend, Muriel, who had been one of Elleen's high school classmates. Muriel was dating Dan at the time and brought him to a party at the O'Maury house in Cincinnati. Elleen did not have a date that night, in fact she was not seeing anyone at the time. And when Dan and Muriel stopped dating months later, Dan remembered Elleen and called her.

It had not been easy. Elleen had not gotten over the trauma of her unfortunate experience to the extent that she was able to go anywhere alone with any man outside of members of her family. Every time Dan called she politely but firmly declined to go out with him. But Dan was persistent. He kept calling and even drove up to the lake to see her when he knew Elleen was there with other members of her family. In the end his persistence had worn her down.

Dan could best be described as having the body of a bear and the heart of a Santa Claus. He was only a few inches over six feet tall but well over two hundred pounds of mostly muscle. And his chestnut hair was so unruly that he would have looked dangerously wild except that a friendly smile seemed to be a permanent part of his face.

From the beginning Dan realized that Elleen had been exposed to something which had done severe damage to her spirit. He longed to know what it was because he was sure he could help, mostly because he had such a strong feeling for her from the very start. But he knew that if she would ever tell him what had caused her such pain it would have to be on her terms and only when she was ready. Obviously it was something very personal. When she finally told him it was just after he had asked her to marry him and it was because she felt she needed to explain to him why she was not going to accept his proposal.

They were sitting on the steps of the front porch at the lake. It was rather late and Dan had actually said goodbye to the family inside more than an hour earlier. Elleen had walked with him outside to his car where it was expected he would offer her a more personal farewell before he began the long drive back to Cincinnati. But before he squeezed himself into the little Bel Air he had asked Elleen to sit with him on the front steps for a few minutes because he had something to ask her. It was then that he had taken the tiny box from his pocket and held it out to her without saying anything by way of explanation.

But she had needed none. Before she opened the little box she already knew what was inside, the modest but beautiful diamond in its simple setting that sparkled in the light from the front window. Quickly she closed the box and held it out to him. But he wouldn't take it.

"What's wrong?" he asked. "Don't you like it?"

She did not cry aloud but a few tears found their way down her cheeks as she looked miserably at him. "Oh, Dan," she uttered quietly, "It is beautiful, but I know it is an engagement ring, and I can't marry you." Then her whole body shook as she sobbed. "I can't marry anyone. I was raped. I was raped. I have been used." And she buried her face in her hands, tears spilling through her fingers.

Dan ached to take the girl in his arms and tell her that it didn't matter. But he felt certain that she had been told that before, and it was apparent to him that she didn't believe it. It had been told her by people who loved her and wanted to make her feel good, who had a reason for telling her that she had nothing to worry about. But he felt instinctively that if he and Elleen were to be happily married she must be certain in her heart that what had happened meant nothing to him. Otherwise he would never be able to object to anything she did without her wondering if the fact that she had been raped had anything to do with his anger. So he asked her if she wanted to tell him about it, and she told him.

She told him how it had started, how she had been having such a good time with the other girls and how she had decided to go off by herself to enjoy the lights on the water. She admitted that it had been a foolish thing to do; but that's the way she always was, doing things on her own, perhaps at times to prove that she could. She told him about the man who had seized her from behind, everything she knew about him, his build, his hair, his face, and the way he talked. It wasn't much. And she told him what the man had done.

"Then he held me down and he raped me. Dan, he raped me," she said, her lips trembling. "Then to show how little he thought of me he spit in my face and left." Then she covered her face with her hands again and sat there in silence, shaking.

Dan, sitting on the step below her, moved closer and took her small hands holding the little box in his giant ones and pulled them away from her face. He said, "Elleen, look at me. Look at my face. I love you. Do you believe me?"

"I don't know," she said. Then, desperately, "I want to."

"Then believe it," he insisted. "I love you more than anything I know. Now I want to ask you something. Did you ever see this man before?" She shook her head. He asked, "Did you do anything to encourage this man at all?" She tried to pull her hands away but he wouldn't let her.

"No, no, no, never," she said. "How could you think that?"

"Oh, Elleen," he assured her, "I didn't think that. But I wanted you to say it to yourself. You had nothing to do with what happened except that you were there. It was not your fault. Why should I love you any less for it?"

For a long while they sat there, saying nothing. Elleen still held the box with the ring in it. Dan could not tell what she was thinking or what she had decided to do. Finally he could wait no longer to find out.

"Elleen, will you keep the ring?" he asked her. "Will you marry me and let me love you and take care of you for as long as I live?"

She leaned forward and threw her arms around his neck. "Oh, how I want to," she answered. "You are so good to me. I don't deserve you, you know. But, yes, I will marry you anyway."

He smiled and reaching up put his arms around her, pulling her toward him as if she weighed nothing. He squeezed her and whispered in her ear, "I don't want you to ever say that again, that you don't deserve me." Then he laughed and added, "But I don't care if you think it sometimes."

The others inside had wondered where Elleen was and why they had not heard Dan's car leave. When the couple came back in they noticed that Elleen had been crying but no one mentioned it because they also noticed the ring on her finger.

But John understood. While the women were admiring the ring and all talking to Elleen at the same time he motioned to Dan to join him in the kitchen. He told him he thought the occasion called for a toast and wanted his help in opening a bottle of wine and some soft drinks. But before they took the drinks back into the front room he took Dan by the arm and said, "I'm glad she finally told you. Now we have that out of the way and we can put it all behind us." And he congratulated Dan, told him how much he liked him, and how happy he was for both of them.

But even after Dan and Elleen were married she was afraid to sleep in the dark.

****

1957

When Polly married John Comstock in June, 1957, it caused some confusion for a while, there being two Johns in the family and one Jack, who was really also another John. But they got used to it. By special permission they were married at St. Joseph where Norman was still an assistant. He could have gone to Cincinnati of course and officiated at the ceremony in the O'Maury's parish church, but the Comstocks and most of their friends were from Columbus, and Wapakoneta seemed close to halfway between the two cities. Besides Polly had wanted to have the reception at the cottage.

It was a beautiful day for a wedding. The weather was unusually warm and they were able to have most of the celebration outside. It lasted far into the morning. Polly had wanted all of her sisters to be in the wedding but Elleen had decided she had better not since the wedding date was so close to when her baby was due. Billy and Tammy, both four year olds, were in the wedding, Billy as ring bearer and Tammy as flower girl. Late in the evening both of them were put to bed while the party continued downstairs and in the backyard. About every fifteen minutes one of the grownups looked in on them and although both the little ones said they couldn't they went right to sleep and were apparently undisturbed by the noise.

Far back in the corner of the yard John O'Maury sat on a lawn chair under a colorful string of lanterns and smiled at the sight of his family and their friends enjoying themselves. Probably half the guests had left but those who remained, although they had quieted down from earlier, were still partying. Jill relaxed next to him on a chaise. It had been a busy day for her with both of the little ones to be dressed and brought to the church on time and then kept an eye on afterwards. Actually she had had lots of help, but she was glad when they were finally in bed and she could pay some attention to what everyone else was doing.

Pensively she said to John, "This is a lot different from when Bill and I got married down at Breckenridge."

It took John by surprise. She rarely mentioned anything that had happened between her and her husband anymore. But then, John reflected, actually they didn't see her often enough to talk about much of anything. Still he wondered what had prompted her observation. He turned and looked curiously at her profile but it revealed nothing. She continued to look impassively at the people in the yard, with little expression. But she knew he was watching her. She turned with a hint of a smile.

She said, "Are you surprised that I still think of him?"

"No," he answered slowly. "Actually I would be surprised if you didn't. But I was only wondering if something in particular made you say that just now."

She seemed to be considering this for a long time before she told him, "It's just that seeing everyone having such a good time at Elleen's wedding, all Bill's family I mean, I understand why everyone was so upset that they weren't asked to be at ours." She was silent for a few seconds. Then she added, "But I'm not sorry we did what we did. I hope you don't hold that against me. If we had waited we might not have gotten married. We might not have Billy either."

John's eyes drifted to the upstairs window behind which he knew the two infants slept. His heart swelled with love as he thought of them and considered once more that they were all he had left of his twin sons. He chuckled. "No, "he assured Jill," I don't hold it against you. I can't imagine not having those two kids. And if you and Bill had not been married, who knows, we might not have either of them."

A few more guests were getting ready to leave. They came over to where John sat and told him how much they had enjoyed the party. They told Jill how cute they thought the youngsters had been in the wedding. When they were gone John asked, "Has anyone ever heard from Tammy's mother?"

She answered, "No, at least not that I know of. As I remember, the people you hired were able to trace her through Denver and St. Louis. Is that right?"

"Actually," he corrected, "they found she went to Chicago too, but that was the end of the trail. She had been on drugs and in a hospital for a while. But after she got to Chicago she dropped out of sight. She had been working as a call girl and they thought she probably changed her name. She might even be dead."

It was Jill's turn to cast her eyes in the direction of the upstairs window. "That poor little tyke," she said.

"Oh," John told her, "she could be much worse off. You are doing a wonderful job with Tammy. I can't imagine that her mother could do any better."

"I know, I know," she admitted. "I try to treat her just like she was my own. I couldn't love her any more. But someday she will have to know, won't she?"

"Yes," he agreed. "She will have to be told. I am surprised you haven't told her already."

She sighed. "I just didn't know how. And I guess I don't really want her to stop calling me mommy." She smiled wryly. "But I have decided I will do it as soon as we get home."

It was nearly dawn before the last guest had left and quiet settled over the cottage.

And, as it turned out, Elleen need not have worried about being in the wedding party; or so everyone told her afterwards. Libby waited two days after Polly's wedding to put in an appearance.

****

1958

Without letting Elleen know, Dan had several conversations with Harry Donovan, the detective telling Dan everything he knew of what had happened on that terrible night. He also told him that, in the detective's opinion, they would never see the rapist in the area again. Donovan was convinced the man had been alone and on his own and had no reason to return. The detective, who was now a sergeant, had grown to like Dan and he promised that if he ever had any news of the rapist's whereabouts he would be sure to inform Dan.

Dan was sure that the Detective's opinion was correct, based on the facts of the case as well as Donovan's training and his instincts, and that they would never see Elleen's attacker again. But he was, for some reason he could not explain, continually drawn to the place where the attack had occurred. Often, if he was alone on his way to the cottage, he would park his car in the lot and sit on the bench next to the ticket booth watching the people as they approached, certain that he would recognize the man if he did appear, even though the passage of time would certainly have altered the way he looked. On one evening in August, during the middle of the week he was doing just that.

Dan had told Elleen that he was going to drive around for a while, explaining that there was a problem at work which he needed to think about and he could best do that while driving. This was not entirely a falsehood and it was enough in character that Elleen did not voice any objection.

After about an hour the steady stream of laughing faces had melted into one. The happy voices, the music, and the lights would have lifted Dan's spirits were it not for the fact that he was constantly reminded that just such an atmosphere had been the background to Elleen's attack. Already Dan had decided to call it a night and go back to the cottage; but he closed his eyes for just an instant and soon he was almost asleep. It was then that something brought him abruptly wide awake. It was a voice that said cheerfully to the young lady in the booth, "Okay, sweetheart." But the speaker elided the R so that the word sounded like "sweethot."

Dan opened his eyes and stood up. But before he was able to see what he looked like the speaker was gone. All Dan could see was the man's back as he walked toward the park entrance. He was of medium height and build. Because of the colored lights Dan was not able to tell what his hair looked like.

Dan got in line but there were three people ahead of him and by the time he could get a ticket the man had disappeared inside. Dan ran through the gate and began pushing through the crowd, searching.

Nearly an hour later Dan was beginning to panic. He had not been able to locate the man he had seen come in and he was afraid that somehow he had lost him. Perhaps he had already left. Dan decided to try the dance floor once more; and that is where he saw him.

Dan realized that it had probably been an accident that the rapist had been able to attack Elleen in the area outside the park. There was no way he could have known the girl would go out there alone. So he wondered whether, if this truly was the man who had attacked Elleen, he expected the same situation again. Why else would he have come back?

Dan found a bench where he felt he could sit and think while keeping the individual he suspected under observation without being noticed. He soon realized that his caution might have been unnecessary because the man he was watching seemed neither nervous nor in a hurry. Perhaps he was, after all, the wrong one.

After the year and more Dan had spent looking for the rapist he had no idea what he would do if he found him. For one thing how could he be sure? And if he was not sure he certainly could not apprehend the man. Could he call the police? If he could get in touch with Donovan the detective would probably look into it, but it was doubtful that anyone else would, merely on Dan's suspicion. And what else did he have besides a physical description several years old, and a few words spoken with an accent which, although unusual around Indian Lake, was certainly not unique in other parts of the country. Dan actually considered calling the detective but he had no idea where a phone was. And anyway by the time Donovan got to the lake the man Dan wanted him to see would probably be long gone. It seemed Dan had no choice but to wait for the suspect to do something incriminating. So Dan waited.

Every few minutes the roller coaster on the other side of the park reached the top of the first drop. Dan could hear the clicking of the chain as it moved over the sprocket and pulled the car to the crest. Then there was the loud scream as the riders looked down and anticipated the thrill of falling. It was always the same scream, as though the same group of people rode on the roller coaster every time.

It was dark. The day was almost over, but not to the people in the amusement park. There was much time left. Dan looked at the crowd. Where did they all come from?

Sound was all around, laughing, teasing, cajoling, flirting, the pleading of the barkers, the good natured skepticism of those who knew better. Although one could not decipher the words, one could still tell what was being said by the tones of the voices. And it was a collection of happy sounds. There was pleasure in the air.

But that was in a different world, not in Dan's world. The pleasure in Dan's world had been suspended for a while. For such a long time there had been something he had hated intensely but which he could not identify. It had affected everything he did. Now he thought, now it had an identity. But he didn't know what to do about it.

So many times he had imagined that someday he would come face to face with the man who had raped Elleen and that somehow he would know. And it always ended the same way. The man would eventually be led away in chains to spend the rest of his life in prison. He would somehow be made to feel the helplessness and the humility he had imposed on Elleen, and probably on other women as well. And the man would know that it was Dan, the husband of the criminal's victim, who had caught him and sent him to prison. In Dan's dream it was always so certain. But now that it was about to become reality, could Dan be sure? He felt strange sitting there on the bench, surrounded by the sounds of gaiety and absolute joy, but feeling none of it. How could there be, in this small space, two worlds so different, one of pleasure, one of hate, and no one could see it but him? In fact no one could see him.

And Dan was reminded of another time and situation with somewhat similar connotations. There was a little hill behind the house in which his family had lived when he was a boy. Sometimes the boy would go up on the little hill and lie down in the tall grass. He would listen to the sounds around him. It was so strange to hear a screen door close, to hear people talking without hearing words, to hear the sound of a saw or a hammer, and know that the people who were responsible for the sounds were not aware that he heard. They were the sounds of people living. It was children asking mothers, and mothers telling children, and children telling other children. It was people working but he could only hear the sounds. He could not distinguish the words.

Before long Dan began to wonder what the man he was watching was going to do. Why was he sitting there so long? Then it became clear. He was watching the dancers on the open floor. Many of the couples consisted of two women rather than a woman and a man. They were probably from groups of women vacationing together. Women like that often did things they would never consider doing at home. They were very likely hoping a man would notice them and try to pick them up. Even if they declined it would make a nice story when they went back to work or school. Dan's suspect was undoubtedly looking for someone who would likely be receptive to an overture from him. Once Dan realized that he began to feel more confident that he was chasing the right man. Of course he still didn't know what he would do. There was nothing wrong with trying to get a woman to dance with you. Dan knew it was done all the time. No one would arrest the man for that. But perhaps he would do something worse: Dan was not able to decide what this might be, but in case it happened he thought he could apprehend the man and ask someone else to call the police.

In a little while the man got up and approached two women on the edge of the floor. He talked to them for a little while and they both giggled but did not seem to encourage him. He did not persist for long but went back to his seat. This happened several times. Then as a pair of women who appeared to be in their late thirties danced near the side of the floor another man approached them and asked one of the women to dance. After only a brief discussion the man and the woman went off together toward the middle of the dance floor leaving the other woman standing alone and looking rejected. It was a golden opportunity and Dan's suspect lost no time in trying to exploit it. He walked up behind the woman who now peered after her partner and apparently wondered what to do next. He touched her elbow and she turned, obviously startled. Dan, who could see her clearly, noticed that she was not particularly attractive or unattractive. She probably considered herself very average. In a group of women she was likely accustomed to being the last one who would be approached by a strange man with any kind of a proposition. She was vulnerable.

Dan watched as the two talked. He noticed that the woman did not giggle the way the others had. She kept looking out on the dance floor for her companion but it was too crowded. Although he was too far away to hear anything they said Dan could tell by their expressions that the man had asked her to do something besides dance and she was reluctant but had not absolutely said no. The look on his face said he was still hopefully waiting for an answer. Finally she must have agreed and off they went, his hand on her arm. Dan followed close enough so that he could be sure he would not lose them.

First they stopped at a refreshment stand. He wanted her to drink a beer and she did not want to, but finally she let him buy her one. Then they threw balls at milk bottles and tried to win a stuffed animal with no luck. They walked around for a while. Then they had another beer. By now she seemed to be starting to relax a bit. She even laughed now and then. He suggested that they go somewhere else, where they could get something to drink besides beer, and something to eat besides hot dogs. Finally she said why not.

Dan, who had been able to get close enough to the couple to hear most of the conversation was not sure what he should do. He wanted to follow them to wherever they went but he was afraid that he would not be able to find his own car and then find the man's car so that he could follow it, since he had no idea what it looked like. He decided to trail them on foot so that he could get a license number which he could give to Harry Donovan so that they could identify the man Dan was sure had raped Elleen.

As he walked a short distance behind the man and the woman he heard the man ask her if she had a car that they could use. She said yes but she and her friend had come together and if she took the car the other woman would have no way to get back to where they were staying. Then he said that would probably not be a problem since her friend's dancing partner would probably want to take her home. Then he told her that the vehicle he was using that night was a small pickup truck that he used for work and that it had tools and some old clothes in it. Perhaps she would rather ride in her car and after they had eaten and had a few drinks she could bring him back to get his truck. To Dan she did not sound very enthusiastic about this but she agreed anyway. Dan realized though that under this arrangement he could not get the man's license number until the two came back to get his truck. He felt that the only thing he could do then was to follow them to the woman's car so that he would know what it looked like and then try to get back to his own car in time to be able to follow them. If he lost them he would have to make the rounds of all the eating places that were open to see if her car was parked there and then wait for them to come out so he could follow them back to the amusement park lot. If they stayed in the area this would not be too difficult because there weren't very many places to eat near by.

When they departed the front gate they were in a small crowd of others who were leaving which made it possible for Dan to stay close to the couple without them becoming suspicious. But as they moved along and some of the others found their cars the crowd thinned making it necessary for Dan to drop farther and farther back to keep from being noticed. When they found the woman's car Dan was too far back to even see it, much less to be able to recognize it in the dark. He waited until they were inside and then approached carefully crouching as low as he could. But he realized he would not be able to read the plate until they pulled out because another car was parked so closely behind them, so he stayed down behind the second car and tried to remain inconspicuous while he waited. Fortunately they were nearly on the edge of the parking lot where not a great number of people could be expected to be walking by and wondering what Dan was doing there.

After nearly five minutes Dan's legs grew so tired that he felt he must straighten up or when the time came for him to move he would not be able to walk. Cautiously he stood up and tried to see what they were doing. He was sure that since it was so secluded where they were the man would be trying to do something besides talk with the woman he had enticed to leave the amusement park, but from the bits of conversation Dan managed to catch he did not expect her to be very cooperative. Then it occurred to him that maybe the man was trying to force himself on her. Maybe he was trying to rape her just as Dan was convinced the man had raped Elleen. Dan's heart began to beat so hard the blood pounded in his temples. He wanted to grab the man while the woman ran for help. Dan was not afraid since Donovan had told him that he didn't expect he would be carrying a weapon of any kind. But even in his anger Dan knew he had to be certain so he stood up slowly and, in a bent over position, neared the car on the passenger side, where he expected the man to be.

The windows were rolled up but Dan could hear the woman. Her voice was loud enough that he could tell she was protesting something. Then he heard the man's voice, quieter but insistent. And then she screamed so loudly that he understood the words, "No, no, what are you doing? Let me go." And then he thought he heard her start to cry.

That was enough for Dan. He was certain he had the right man. And to Dan the person sitting in the car with the rapist was a young girl named Elleen. He seized the door handle and yanked the door open. The man held the woman next to him by the shoulders and was leaning over her. The light was very dim but it was strong enough that Dan could recognize the terror on her face. He was furious. He put both his hands on the man's shoulders and pulled but the woman could not get away. So Dan put his left arm around the man's neck and jerked his head back. The woman was free. She threw open the door on her side, fell onto the pavement, then picked herself up and, sobbing, began to run toward the lights of the park.

Dan had pulled the woman's attacker back much more violently than he needed to. Now, with a strange feeling, he realized that the man was not moving. Dan released him and the man fell forward onto the seat, his head at a strange angle. Dan realized that the man's neck was broken.

The rage that had filled him now left just as suddenly as it had come. He felt very peaceful. He closed the door of the car. He took out his handkerchief and wiped the door handle. Then he went to the other side and closed that door also, with his handkerchief. Then he walked slowly to the other side of the lot, looking for his own car. It was not hard to find since the lot was beginning to empty. When he found it he drove away.

At the cottage everyone was in bed except Elleen who was waiting for him on the front porch. She said, "Where in the world have you been? We were worried enough that we almost called the police."

Dan was very calm. He took both her hands in his. He said, "Well I had a problem that has bothered me for a long time and I finally settled it. It just took longer than I thought."

Something in his voice sounded different. She couldn't tell what it was. She searched his face in the light from the window. "Is it something you could tell me about?" she asked.

"No," he answered, and then he laughed quietly. "But that's only because it's a long story and I'd rather go to bed now. I'll tell you sometime, though. I'll tell you all about it."

But he never did.

The next evening when Dan came back from his office Detective Donovan was waiting for him on the front porch. He was by himself. He was drinking a glass of iced tea Kate had given him. He said he had been waiting for nearly an hour. He had some good news for Dan.

"I wanted to tell you this without saying anything to your wife. You can tell her later. I think the man who attacked her is dead." As he talked he watched Dan's face intently.

Dan sat down slowly on the step. He said, "Are you sure?"

The detective answered, "Yes, I'm sure. He fits the description pretty well. And there's something else, something that I probably couldn't use in court, but It's something I think is a clincher."

He took a little envelope from his pocket and opened it. Then he shook something from it onto his hand. It looked like a little piece of adhesive tape. "This is the piece of tape that creep put on your wife's mouth. I looked all over the next day until I finally found the right place. I know exactly where it happened. I found his footprints and your wife's footprints. And I found this piece of tape too. There was a bloody thumb print on it but it was smudged so we couldn't do a fingerprint match. But look at this." He held it close so Dan could see. "Look at this mark, like a little cross. You can see it better under a magnifying glass."

Dan said, "Yeah, I see it."

Harry Donovan said, "Well, the guy we found had a little scar on his thumb that looks like that mark, almost exactly, anyway close enough for me. I'm sure it was the guy alright."

"Who was he?" Dan asked.

"His name was Clinten Hills. We aren't sure where he was from. His car has a Texas plate on it but his driver's license is from Arkansas. We are checking into it. It takes a little time."

"Did you say how he died?" Dan asked the detective.

"That's another thing," Donovan told him. He had picked up some woman from Dayton in the park and got her out in the parking lot and he was trying to rape her. Some guy who was passing by must have heard them and pulled him off of her. Then somehow he broke the guy's neck."

"And you say the fellow who killed the raper didn't even know the woman?"

"Actually we don't have the man who did it. But she doesn't know who it was. It sounds like a perfect accident, lucky for the woman, unlucky for Hills."

Dan gave a little whistle. "Boy, I'd say that was lucky."

The detective started to leave. Then he stopped. He asked, "Oh, by the way, and just for the fun of asking, where were you last night about eleven thirty?"

Dan frowned as though trying to think. "I'm not really sure. I was out driving around, doing some heavy thinking on a problem at work. Why? Do you suspect me?"

"Oh, no," Harry told him. "I don't see how you could have known he would be there. So it couldn't have been planned. It's just that whoever did it must have been someone very strong. But it would have to be someone who was able to kill a man with his bare hands. You're much too good natured for that. We would like to find him though. We might want to give him a medal."

Dan promised, "If I hear anything I'll let you know. And thanks for telling me about it. I know Elleen will feel better and I feel better already."

They shook hands and the detective left.

Later Dan told Elleen what the detective had told him.

Elleen looked closely at Dan's face when he was finished. She waited. Then she asked, "Is that all?"

He looked puzzled. He said, "Yes. Why?"

"Oh nothing," she answered. "I was just wondering. It's nothing."

In a few days she began to turn all the lights out in their bedroom before she went to bed.

✶✶✶✶✶✶✶✶✶✶✶✶✶✶✶✶✶✶✶✶✶✶✶✶✶✶✶✶✶✶

It was Sunday and Norman was sitting in the backyard with his parents after everyone had eaten lunch. He was slowly sipping a glass of lemonade. Dan came out of the house and, standing by the steps, motioned to the priest. Norman got up and came over to where Dan stood.

Dan said, "I want to ask you something. Let's go sit in your car."

Father Norman could not imagine what Dan could want to ask him that he would not want the rest of the family to hear, but he followed Dan out to the road where the priest had parked his car. They got in.

Dan asked, "Do you have your purple stole with you?"

Norman laughed. He thought Dan was kidding. But he assured him, "I always have it with me." He opened the glove compartment and took out the stole and unfolded it.

Dan said, "Put it on. I want to go to confession."

Norman started to laugh again. But then he saw that Dan was very serious. He asked, "Dan, can't this wait?"

But Dan insisted, "No. I want to go to confession right now."

Father Norman realized that whatever it was seemed serious to his brother-in-law.

Someone came partly down the driveway and started toward the car but noticed that the two men were in quiet conversation and turned around and went back. After only a short time Dan got out of the car. Father Norman, his face pale, started the engine on his little Chevrolet and put the car in gear. With a crunch of gravel he pulled away. Dan joined the others in the backyard. He was smiling.

Kate asked him, "Where is Norman? Did he go inside?"

Dan shook his head. "No, I don't know what got into him. All of a sudden he said there was something at the parish he had forgotten to do that was important. And he took off."

Well, for goodness sakes," said Kate.

Dan chuckled to himself. Then he said to no one in particular. "I think I will go in and get myself a beer. Would anyone else like me to bring them anything?"

※※※※※※※※※※※※※※※※※※※※※※※※※※※※

1958

They sat in one of the parlors ordinarily used for visitors even though it was not visiting Sunday. It was in fact not even a Sunday but a Wednesday. Everyone else must have been in a different part of the building because Carrie could hear no sound except that of the pendulum as it moved back and forth in the great clock in the hall, its rhythm precise and unchanging and, possibly because of that, somehow reassuring. It had become so familiar to her in visits to the convent that she knew exactly where it was and what it looked like. As a child she had been fascinated by it. Then the melancholy thought occurred to her that she might never see it again.

Carrie sat on one of the small sofas with the elaborate brocade, her hands folded in her lap, her eyes cast down. Sister Mary Charles sat next to her, slightly turned so she could watch her niece. She reached over and put one hand on both of the girl's and squeezed them. She said, "Oh, Carrie, I'm so happy to hear that. I have always prayed that you would have a vocation. My prayers have been answered."

The girl smiled. "Then you're not upset?" she asked.

"Upset?" asked her aunt. "Why in the world would I be upset?" Then she knew what the answer was and she laughed. "Oh for goodness sake. Is that why you have been so nervous ever since you came in the door? You thought I wouldn't like it because you aren't coming here." She pulled Carrie to her and put the girl's head on her ample bosom. "Carrie, Carrie, I'm so glad Jesus has called you to His house. And you will make a good Little Sister. I have noticed how well you get along with old people. And they do such good work with the poor. OH, you will be so happy there. Have you told everyone yet?"

"Only mom and dad." Carrie sat up straight and turned so she could look at her aunt. "I wanted to tell you first. You know it was hard to decide. I always thought I might come here. But then some of us from school went to sing for the residents at Christmas time at the home on Riddle Road. You should have seen those old people. They were so happy to have us there. They made us feel good. It made me feel so happy. I just knew then it was what I always wanted to do but I never realized it before. I don't know how to explain it."

Sister Mary Charles laughed. "No need. I know exactly what you mean." Suddenly the years melted away and she saw another young girl who stood in the front hall, outside the very room in which they now sat. Her father held the little valise for her, reluctant to put it down because he knew that when he did it would be taken to another room and with that act his daughter would no longer be only his. He would have to share her with the Lord. Or even perhaps it was the other way around. Perhaps it would be the Lord sharing her with him.

In the end Pat had not had to put the bag down. The nun who was in charge of novices was tall and slim and looked as though she would be very strict. She hurried down the hall, her habit swishing as she walked, stern and efficient. Mary, who had been standing behind Eileen, knew she was going to cry so she fished her handkerchief out of her purse. The nun took the imitation leather bag from Pat's hand.

"Thank you Mr. O'Maury. I will take this up to Eileen's room for her," she said. Then she smiled but it seemed that the smile hardly reached her eyes. "You may say goodbye to her now. It is nearly time for evening prayers and she should go in with us. I will take her things to her room and then come back for her." With that she was gone.

Eileen remembered how she had felt, wondering whether anyone ever laughed anywhere in the building, but feeling in her heart that, no matter what, it was where she belonged, that it was her new home. And, of course, she had soon learned that the convent was in fact a very happy place.

Sister Mary Charles looked fondly at Carrie and patted her hand. "You will be fine. I am sure of it. And I'll bet John and Kate are so proud of you."

"I hope so," Carrie told her aunt. "But I'm not sure. They both seemed happy when I first told them. But I have caught mom crying. I hope they won't miss me too much."

Sister Charles hugged Carrie again and laughed. "Goodness, child, they will miss you very much. They love you. But they know that Jesus needs you and they will be glad to share you with Him. I would think you would be disappointed if they didn't miss you. And you will be homesick at times, sometimes very homesick. I remember how I was. But I found out that I could go to the chapel and sit in front of the statue of Our Lady and tell her all about it. It never took long and I felt better again. "But," she added wistfully, "I always thought about mom and dad, and John, and wondered what they were doing. And then when you kids were born I though how much I would have liked to be there to watch all of you grow up." She sighed then and smiled. "But there is always so much to do. I really didn't have time to be homesick for very long."

They sat and talked for a while about many things such as what Carrie could expect in the convent. Sister Charles admonished her not to forget to write to everyone, not to ever lose touch with her family.

John had dropped Carrie off at six o'clock and told her he would be back to pick her up at seven thirty. Both of the women knew that when Carrie left they might never see each other again because of the restrictions both orders had on travel outside the convents. As the time passed the hour they both grew pensive. At length Sister Charles put her hand once more on her niece's. She said quietly, "You know Carrie I have been so eager to tell Our Lady about this I can hardly wait. Before you leave let's go in and tell her together. She will be so glad."

Carrie would never forget how the fading light slanted in through the windows as the two of them walked quietly down the corridor to the chapel. They went straight up to the side altar where the wide candles burned in the tall blue glass holders, and knelt in front of the pure white statue of Mary. The nun, now in her fifties, and her twenty year old niece looked up at the figure and smiled.

There were three other nuns scattered about the chapel but Sister Charles nevertheless spoke aloud, "Mother, we have something so very special to tell you. This little girl is going to join The Little Sisters Of The Poor. She is going to spend the rest of her life with you and Jesus, working with old people who need her. I am asking you to help her just as you always helped me. It is not easy to leave your family and your friends. Do you remember when Jesus left you, how hard it was for you when you remembered all the things you had done with him and Joseph, when Jesus was growing up? Now it will be like that for Carrie's mother and father, won't it? We ask you to help them. But most of all I ask you and Jesus to make Carrie as happy as you have made me. Ask the Father to give her love to share with the people she will care for. And ask the Holy Ghost to give her the wisdom and understanding she will need. And finally I ask you, mother, to keep this little niece of mine close to you, and safe. And I thank you for loving me all these years."

Carrie thought she had never ever felt closer to God than at that moment. She felt a tear fall on her hands which were folded in front of her. She wondered if the nun noticed that she was crying and she glanced up quickly to see. But Sister Charles was still looking happily at the statue. And though she was smiling radiantly there were tears on her cheeks. Carrie stood up and hugged her. "Oh, Aunt Sister," she sobbed, "I am so happy." And then they both laughed and hugged each other. As the two left they could not notice it, but the other three nuns in the chapel were also weeping silently.

Chapter IX

Actually it is likely no one in the world could make goetta the way Aunt Bea could. People came from all around just for that one thing. They even put it on the menu that way, "Aunt Bea's famous fried goetta." And when Aunt Bea died they didn't change it. Everyone knew Aunt Bea was gone and someone else was doing the cooking, but no one had the heart to mention it.

From That One Little Town, by Francis Christop

1965

Polly and John's little girl Joan had been born in 1962, the same year that Pam said she talked Aloysius into marrying her. Of course everyone accepted this as a bit of humor. Aloysius had been fascinated by Pam ever since he met her at St. Charles Seminary, of all places. Aloysius had gone there with Father Norman to visit a priest who had been one of Norman's teachers at Brunnerdale. Pam was one of the old priest's nieces and she happened to be visiting him at the same time. The priest was in the infirmary.

Her last name was White, but white certainly was not descriptive of her appearance except for her teeth which were indeed white, but the only part of her that was. She might have been Spanish or perhaps part Indian or Negro. Her slightly wavy hair was so black it sometimes seemed blue and her skin never lost its tan. Pam always looked as though she had just returned from vacationing in the south.

She seemed taller than she was because she was so slender, certainly not voluptuous. But in the way she moved there was a certain manner that suggested animalism. She did not walk, she flowed from one place to another. Her dark eyes seemed to flash but on closer inspection one might determine rather that they merely twinkled.

When Norman and Aloysius came into Father Gregory's room Pam was there, with her mother, one of the old priest's sisters. After they were all introduced the five of them chatted for a while but it was not long before two separate conversations developed, one between the two priests and the sister and the other between Pam and Aloysius. Finally Aloysius suggested that he take the young lady, who had never been to St. Charles Seminary before, on a tour of the building and the grounds. By the time they returned, nearly two hours later, he knew everything he wanted to about Pam White. That had been in the fall of 1960 right after the family had bought the last cottage.

It was on Pokey Lane and the name was only at times appropriate. In 1960 Pat had been dead for twenty-two years, give or take a few months. John was fifty-seven and only now and then acted as though he was beginning to slow down; Kate was fifty-six and never did. Mary, who had just celebrated her eighty-second birthday would have become somewhat sedentary but Chess would not allow it. However they only went dancing about every other month and they sat out more dances than they used to.

The new cottage had six bedrooms, two of them very large, and a family room. But it had neither basement nor attic and Kate constantly complained because of the lack of storage space. And this was one of the many things she and Mary had found they could agree on.

Those two women had become closer year after year. By 1962 Heidi Hoect had been dead for twenty-five years but her daughter still thought about her often. Heidi had always maintained a sort of reservation in her relations with her children and it had prevented her and Kate from being as close as they might have been. Kate loved her mother very much and respected her even more, and she always regretted the fact that she had not done more for Heidi when she was alive. It was probably because of this that she became so attentive toward John's mother.

Mary and Kate were sitting inside the gazebo in the backyard, sipping lemonade and talking. It was a hot July day, three weeks after Pam's wedding. Mary stood up and looked at two month old Joan who slept in a basket on the picnic table. She smiled and shook her head. She said, "I just don't know how those babies can sleep like that when it is so hot."

Kate chuckled. She was aware that the thermometer had been creeping up over the eighty mark. But they were in the shade and there was a slight breeze moving the leaves on the trees. She did not feel terribly uncomfortable. It was her opinion that Mary had said what she did more because it seemed the thing to say than that it was the way she felt. But Kate did not respond.

After a little while Mary said, "She is so cute, isn't she?"

"Uh huh," Kate agreed. She did not add that Mary had said the same thing, without fail, about all her grandchildren and great grandchildren. Mary went back to her chair and sat down.

From the direction of the lake they could hear a dove. When the bird stopped, the call of the cicada, apparently one who didn't know it was the wrong year, rose to a crescendo and then tailed off. To Mary these were summer sounds, soothing by their familiarity and the fact that they were there when they were expected. Mary closed her eyes. The sounds made her feel comfortable because she could have been anywhere in the area and, with her eyes shut, felt that she had been there before.

Mary asked, "How well do you remember your father-in-law?"

The question surprised Kate. But then she perceived that Mary had been listening to the sounds around them and those sounds had reminded her of all her years at the lake. That must have made her think of Pat.

"I remember him very well," she answered.

Mary, her eyes still closed, leaned her head against the back of her chair. After a time she said, "He liked you very much. I think you knew that, didn't you?"

Kate said, "Yes. And I thought a lot of him too."

Mary opened her eyes and looked directly at her daughter-in-law. "When you and John first met I didn't want him to see you again. I could tell how much John was smitten." She smiled at the sound of the word, "smitten", and went on. "I guess I was worried that I would lose him. And I didn't want to lose another son."

Mary reached over and put her hand on Kate's. She said, "I'm glad my husband was able to make me realize that it was not my job to decide who was to be John's wife. If John had waited for me to give my approval for someone he would still be single I guess." She patted Kate's hand. "And I couldn't have picked a better wife for him anyway."

A sudden feeling of love for this strong-willed woman brought a tear to Kate's eye. She knew full well how hard it had been for Mary to say what she just had. Kate almost whispered, "And I don't know how I could have found a better father-in-law or a better mother-in-law."

Mary leaned back and closed her eyes again. The sound of a motor boat droned across the water. As its steady but muffled tone drifted in off the lake it sounded tired. The boat must have been moving away because the sound of the motor slowly diminished until it could no longer be heard at all by the two people in the gazebo.

A beautiful butterfly sampled the four o'clocks by the fence and then disappeared over it into the next yard. A tiny finch hopped around in front of the garden for a little while but couldn't find anything interesting and flew off.

John came out of the house and started to say something but Kate pointed to his mother by way of letting him know she was asleep, and he understood. He motioned to her to come outside the gazebo so he could talk to her without disturbing Mary. He held the screen door for her and noticed that her eyes were a bit red.

As they walked toward the front of the house he asked, "You look like you were crying. Is something wrong?"

She wiped her eyes and laughed. "No. Nothing's wrong. It's your mother. She said something sentimental and it caught me off guard."

"Yeah," he said. "She can do that now and then." He took her hand and they walked around to the front porch.

Kate asked, "You're home early. Is something wrong?"

Now it was his turn to laugh. "No, nothing is wrong. It's just that my work was all caught up." Then he stopped and turned to look at her directly and added slyly, "Besides, don't you think a vice president can take an afternoon off now and then?"

"Oh, John," she exclaimed, "you did it. You got the promotion. Did you act surprised?"

John chuckled again. "Actually I was surprised. It took the old man so long to do it I thought he had changed his mind. You know I wasn't supposed to know about it anyway."

Kate gave him a congratulatory hug and then they continued on to the front of the cottage where they sat down on the steps.

John said, "There is something else I want to talk to you about, It's the old Hoect farm."

Now John had Kate's complete attention. They very seldom talked about the deal that never had seemed to work out the way anyone had planned. The airfield had attracted some business, more than enough to keep the facility in operation, but there was just not an extraordinary demand for small commercial air traffic, nor was there any great surge of private plane ownership and a need for storage. Everyone had generally conceded that the idea had been good but the location had perhaps not been the best. According to Kate's brother Fred, who had always handled the business more or less on his own, maintenance and incidental expenditures for running the facility had eaten up most of the profit. With every accounting it appeared that the expenses had about kept up with the income and the books had never shown much of a profit.

Kate was of course very conscious of the fact that Pat O'Maury had, to some degree, jeopardized his family's future by trying to help her family. And he had, in any event, been forced to postpone his retirement because of it. However, whenever the subject came up, which was very seldom, John was always quick to point out that the family had really not lost any money since they had continued to maintain part ownership in the airfield and besides he always felt that Pat had never wanted to retire anyway and by continuing to work he had left his estate with almost no bills at all to pay when he died.

John asked, "Do you remember Bob Westkamper, your brothers' lawyer?" Kate nodded and he went on. "He came over to the office to see me today. I have always thought of him as a very honest man and I still do. I think that anything he tells me is at least something he believes. We talked for quite a while and he made us an offer for our share in the old property. I'm not sure what we should do."

Kate asked, "Did he want to buy it?"

John changed the subject, "You know what would taste good?" And when Kate smiled because she knew what he was going to say he answered his question, "A cold beer." He looked toward the screen door. "is Billy here?" he asked.

Their first grandchild, then nine years old, was indeed staying at the cottage, not with his mother, but with Elleen and Libby, who was only five. He was big enough to get his grandfather a bottle of beer from the refrigerator. Kate went to the door and called inside. Billy came and looked out and when his grandmother explained to him what John wanted he ran off to get it. Kate was aware that the boy was still young enough to like to be allowed to do grownup chores and was just a little surprised when it was Libby who brought the beer out. Kate imagined that Libby had asked her cousin if she could help and he had obliged the youngster he seemed to think of as a little sister. When Libby came out Kate could see they had opened the bottle for John and Libby carried it with a glass on a tray. But one of them had put two ice cubes in the glass. Her grandfather smiled and said nothing about the ice. He poured the beer into the glass, took a big drink and said, "Boy that tastes good. Thank you, young lady."

Libby said, "If you want anything else call me. I'll ask Billy to get it for you and he will." Then she smiled at Kate and added, "You too, Grandma."

Kate grinned and told her, "Well I hope 'me too'. Us women have to stick together." Then she said, "You're a doll," to the young girl as she went back inside.

John said, "Now where were we? Oh yes, Bob made us an offer to buy our share if we want to sell it. First he said that he thinks he has someone interested in buying the property for a good deal of money. He said he thinks they want to build a shopping center on it. When he said a lot of money he mentioned millions. But he said no one has made a real offer and, although he is fairly sure they are going to do it eventually, he isn't sure when. He isn't even sure it will be this year or even next year. But he said he has the money now to make us an offer if we don't want to wait. He said he could give us a hundred and twenty five thousand for our share. That's two and a half times what dad paid for it." He stopped and took a swallow of his beer, poured what was left in the bottle into his glass and put the bottle back onto the tray.

Kate thought for a moment and then said, "That is a lot of money, isn't it?" John said nothing. She added, "What do you think now?"

John answered her slowly, "I'm not exactly sure whether Westkamper wants me to sell the property or not. I think I know him fairly well and I really am convinced that he wants us to do what is best for us, which would be for us to hold on until we can make the big deal he seems to expect. What I'm not sure of is how sure he is that this is going to happen. You know that he has always seemed to feel that he helped talk dad into putting his money into this even though the two of them really didn't talk much about it directly. I think now he would like to make amends sort of. I just can't tell for sure if he would like to do that by letting us get out now or by engineering a big deal later. I wonder how your brother Fred feels about this, or if he even knows about it. I wonder about Alex and the rest of your brothers too."

Libby came to the door and asked her grandfather if he would like another bottle of beer. When he said he would she asked Kate if she could bring her something. Kate decided on a root beer. This time both the kids came out and they also had drinks for each of themselves. After they had served John and Kate the two of them sat down on the bottom step and joined in the conversation.

Billy made a gesture in Libby's direction and said to his grandparents, "She is so funny sometimes." Kate and John looked at each other and smiled. No more was said about the old farm until the next day.

It turned out that Alex was indeed aware of the possibility of the property being sold to an outside party and turned into a shopping center, as also were his brothers. Alex in fact had been very active in making the initial contact with the interested party and in trying to develop a deal. He was very enthusiastic and seemed convinced that it would happen. He was, however, just as uncertain as the lawyer, Mr. Westkamper, as to when that might be.

In the end John decided that although there was the possibility of some sort of deal in the offing it was somewhat nebulous. He was convinced that Robert Westkamper and the Hoects wanted to buy John and Kate's interest because they felt it was the honorable thing to do. But he also thought they were exaggerating the probability of a financial windfall so that John would not have to feel that he was deserting the others by selling out.

Kate was not so sure. She talked to all of her brothers but they would not try to influence her and John either way, apparently because no one of them wanted to feel responsible for talking the two of them into another poor decision. So Kate went along with John. They used the money to pay off some bills and invested part of it in a relatively conservative fund.

*   *   *

Pam had lost her figure early in 1964. It had not been difficult to tell that she was pregnant. But still it didn't seem that she got very much bigger until the ninth month. Toward the end though she was obviously uncomfortable. And Aloysius wanted so much to do something for her, but there was nothing he could do. And then, late in October, all of a sudden her time was up. Aloysius barely got her to the hospital before Dennis was born.

All the girls were taken with the little guy, especially Libby. After all she was seven years old then and could help take care of him for her aunt and uncle.

And Mary took a special interest in him too. What she especially liked to do was have Pam leave Dennis with her at her house in Cincinnati on a day when Libby could be there too to help feed him and even change a diaper. Then while the baby slept, which was most of the time, Libby would tell her great grandmother about school and sometimes even read to her from one of her school books. Or at other times Mary would get out her old pictures and the two would look at them together. Libby reminded Mary of Eileen when she was a little girl.

Billy seemed to have so many other things to do that he was not able to spend as much time with the rest of the family as Libby did. It almost seemed that by default Libby took his place as the oldest, even though Billy also continued to see as much of all of them as he could.

The winter of 1965 set no records but it was worse than most. There was a lot of snow. For some of the older people this proved to be a significant problem and Mary was one of them. She was homebound for much of the time. Chess, on the other hand, didn't seem to mind it at all. He called on Mary several times a week. He would come in the early evening and either they would go out to eat and to a movie or, now and then to dance, or Mary would fix supper for them and they might watch television for a while. Chess always left early enough that he could get home before midnight.

The others at times visited Mary also but it was mostly during the day. They were not trying to avoid Chess, actually all of them, especially John, liked talking to him. But most of them were still speculating that Chess might be able to get Mary to agree to become his wife and, without really taking sides in the matter, they didn't want to interfere.

Mary had a little arthritis in her hands but for a woman of almost eighty seven it was rather mild. However it did cause her to have a bit of trouble getting around and it irritated her that Chess did not seem to have any mobility problems at all.

Sometimes Mary wondered what Pat would have been like if he had lived to be eighty seven. As a matter of fact she seemed to spend more and more time thinking of "Mr. O'Maury." Her final conclusion was that if he had lived to be very old he would have developed problems in his joints and he would have become harder and harder to get along with. But still she missed him and would have been glad to have him back.

One day in the middle of November as she was putting away a few dishes she had used for her lunch Mary heard a knock on the door but before she could go through the living room to the front hall and open it Elleen let herself in with the key her grandmother had given her years ago. Mary was pleasantly surprised to see the young woman.

Elleen met her coming out of the kitchen and hugged her and then kissed her on the cheek. She said, "How are you feeling, Grandma?"

Mary said, "Oh, I'm feeling just fine." Then she decided to tell nearly the complete truth. She said, "Well actually my rheumatism has been acting up a little, but I can stand it." She started to tell Elleen about the tingling she had felt a few times in her arm—let's see now was it the left arm or the right arm? But it didn't happen all the time and it was probably nothing. She decided it wasn't worth mentioning. She just added, "How are you?"

Elleen pulled out one of the kitchen chairs and sat down. She said, "Terrific."

Mary said, "I have just had lunch but we can have a cup of tea, and I could make you a sandwich."

Elleen said, "I've already eaten, Grandma, but the tea sounds good. It's cold outside."

Mary added water to the pot which still held some hot water from her lunch and turned on the flame underneath. She set out the old mugs and put tea bags in them. By that time the water was boiling and she poured it into the mugs. Then she sat down at the table across from her granddaughter.

They talked for a while about the family and the way the great grandchildren were growing up. There were eight of them then with Robert only a few months old. Mary laughingly remarked that Pam was already pregnant again. Elleen laughed too. As they drank their tea Elleen noticed that Mary coughed occasionally. She said, "Grandma, that cough doesn't sound too good. Have you had it long?"

Mary waved her hand as if to dismiss the question. "It's nothing. It will go 'way in a day or two. It's already going away."

But Elleen was concerned and looked at her grandmother more closely as they talked. In truth the woman did not look as though there was anything seriously wrong with her. They talked for a while longer and finally Elleen said she was on her way to a class and had to go. Before she went out the front door she made Mary promise to see her doctor if the cough didn't clear up by the end of the week. She would have been more concerned except that she knew Chess would have taken Mary to a doctor himself if he had thought there was reason. She was unaware that he was out of town on business and would not be back for another week. And Mary did not tell her.

It had started to snow and there was even a light accumulation on Elleen's car when she got in and drove away.

When Elleen came home Dan was listening to Libby's homework. Four year old Millie was already in bed and Danny, who was six, had been playing on the floor but he ran over and threw his arms around Elleen's legs, nearly causing her to fall. She laughed and picked him up and hugged him. Dan said, "Well, how did it go tonight?"

She said, "Oh, class was fine but did you know the snow is getting deep out there? I had a little trouble getting home. How I envy you, going to Baton Rouge for a week. What kind of meeting did you say this is?"

"It's not really a meeting, more of a conference, and I wish I wasn't going. I don't like being away over a weekend but a new machine is being installed in one of our plants down there on Saturday and that is what the conference is about. We have to be there to see it in operation for the first time. Some of us have worked on this for a good while, trying to develop systems that best use its capabilities. I couldn't get out of it. I tried."

Libby said, "Can we stop now dad?"

He grinned at her and messed up her hair playfully. He said, "No we can't stop, not until you're finished."

She pushed his hand away and smoothed her hair. Then she said, "But we are. I was just doing extra work."

He looked at her suspiciously and said, "You wouldn't kid your old man would you?"

She closed the book from which she had been reading and assured him, "Oh no, I would never do that."

He was still skeptical but only a little. He knew Libby well enough to be sure she might tease him but she would never lie to him. He let her put away her books. It was nearly time for her and her little brother to get ready for bed anyway.

Dan got Danny ready and tucked him in. While Libby took her bath he and Elleen sat at the table and Elleen had some coffee and a piece of cake, both left over from supper.

Dan said, "I see you're off your diet."

Elleen acted hurt, "Are you saying I need to be on a diet."

"No," he defended himself, "you said you do. Don't you remember?"

"Oh yes," she admitted. "But that was yesterday. And I didn't think you were paying attention anyway."

Dan got up and poured himself a cup of only slightly stale coffee and sat back down across from his wife. Her cheeks were still pink from the cold air outside and her eyes sparkled. He marveled at how good God had been to him, giving him his beautiful wife, his fascinating little girls and boy. He had an idea.

"Why don't you go with me? We will have a lot of time for ourselves and there's an indoor pool at the hotel."

Elleen thought it over for a few minutes. She took a sip from her cup. "It would be fun, but what about the kids? Libby and Danny are in school," she pointed out.

But Dan had thought about that. "Let them stay with Kate. All four of them would like that. So would John in fact. And they'd make sure they got to school, and that Libby got her homework. Millie isn't any trouble. I think Kate is a little miffed that we don't let them stay over there much."

"It would be fun," agreed Elleen. "Do you really think we could do it?"

"Actually I think Henry Ostin is taking his wife. There won't be a lot for some of us to do except observe the operation in case we have to make changes in the control programs in the future. Do you know Clara Ostin? I think you met her before. Henry's a good guy. The four of us could probably go out some night together to eat or something. Maybe we could even get Chick Lutton, our boss, to pay for it. You'd have to stay away from him though. He's divorced and always on the lookout for good looking women."

Elleen went, "Oh pooh, I know Chick. I think I can handle him." Then she grinned. "If I can't I'll sic him on Clara."

So they made plans. Then they called Kate to make sure she had no plans that would interfere.

Kate was ecstatic and later when they told Libby the little girl was overjoyed also. She always looked forward to staying with her grandparents. The old house was filled with interesting things, many of them mementos of Indian Lake. And she promised that she would help look after Millie, but not Danny. He was too wild, she told them, rolling her eyes.

During the week Dan and Elleen were gone it snowed more than an inch on two different days. It was just enough snow to limit some people's traveling but not enough to cause much concern. No one saw Mary for three days or called her on the phone. When Chess came back from his trip the first thing he did once he was unpacked was to drive to Cincinnati to see her. He did not take the time to call first and when he knocked on the front door and no one answered he thought that perhaps she had gone to stay with someone until the weather improved. He knocked several times and still there was no response. He did not know why but suddenly he began to feel uneasy.

Jean Fullerton, who lived next door, was younger than Mary but they were very good friends. Chess walked across the snow covered lawn, which had not a footprint on it yet, to use Jean's phone. He called John.

"Hi, Chess. Glad you're back safely. How was the weather where you were?"

"Oh, it was worse than it is here. But this was one of those deals where we spent most of the time in the hotel. Actually I'm glad to get back home. What I called about is I'm down at your mother's and no one answers the door. I was wondering if she is staying with someone."

John didn't answer for half a minute, all the things going through his mind which could be reasons for Mary not answering the door. He asked, "She didn't know you were coming down, did she?"

Chess answered, "No, I was in a hurry. I just thought I'd come on in to town without calling. Now I wish I had called." His voice was beginning to sound worried.

John tried to reassure him. "Well I don't think it would have made any difference. If you had tried to call her and she didn't answer the phone then what would you have done, called the police?" They both laughed. "Look, there's a spare key in the back that dad put there once when he locked himself out. It's in a crack in the foundation of the garage. If you can find it why don't you go in and look around?"

Chess said, "I can find it. I've seen it. Your mother got it out once while I was there and I saw where she put it. But I didn't think it would have been proper for me to go into her house unless someone else knew about it. You know what I mean?"

John smiled to himself and said, "Sure, Chess, I know what you mean. But I think under the circumstances it would be okay." Then he added, "After you look around would you call us back and let me and Kate know what's going on?"

Mrs. Fullerton had discreetly withdrawn to another room while Chess used the phone but she could tell by the tone of his voice that he was uneasy about something. When he thanked her for the use of her phone she asked him if something was wrong but he merely said he hoped not. He let himself out the front door.

Mary had used the spare key once when they had come back from dancing late at night. She made no attempt to hide from him the place where she got it and then replaced it. But she had never indicated in any way that he could use it so he continued to carry on as though, in fact, it was not there. It was there though, where he expected it to be, so he retrieved it and let himself in the front door.

While Chess stood in the vestibule, wondering where to look first he heard the thermostat click and then the furnace turned on. There was no other sound. In a few minutes heat began blowing from the register under the steps to the upstairs. Light from the cut glass window over the door colored the floor.

Chess called rather quietly at first and then a little more loudly, "Mary! Are you home? Mary?" There was no answer.

Chess could not shake the feeling that he was an intruder and that Mary would not like it, but he tried to ignore it.

He could not decide where to look first. Finally he stepped hesitatingly into the living room. Everything there was in order. He was gathering courage. Next he went to the kitchen. It was Mary's kitchen, nothing out of order, the teapot ready on the stove, each piece of furniture where it belonged. The dining room too was in impeccable order. Chess acknowledged to himself that he had to look in the bedrooms no matter how embarrassed he might find himself in the end.

Slowly he climbed the stairs and walked down the hall, peering into every bedroom on the second floor except Mary's, saving that until last. Her door stood slightly ajar and, with trepidation, he reluctantly pushed it open. "Mary," he almost whispered. Then he saw the form beneath the covers on the bed. At first an impossible dream crossed his mind that perhaps it was not Mary. Maybe it was someone he didn't even know. But he knew better. He called loudly, his voice pleading desperately for an answer, "Oh, Mary, Mary," and rushed to the side of the bed.

Mary lay on her back, her eyes staring at the ceiling. She was alive but there was no way he could tell whether or not she could see anything. She had no expression on her face and she made no sound except that of rather shallow breathing. He took one of her hands which lay outside the covers and rubbed it. It felt very cold to him. Tears welled up in his eyes and spilled down on Mary's bed. "Oh, dear Mary," he said over and over. "Then he said, "I will be right back."

Chess ran back down the steps to the only phone in the house. First he called the fire department and gave the person who answered, his name and Mary's address. He said he thought she had had a stroke. Then he called John and explained the situation to him. Then he went back upstairs. He knelt down by the side of the bed and took Mary's hand again. This time she turned her head toward him. She seemed to look at him and smile, and he thought she tried to say something. She made no sound but to Chess it appeared that she was saying, "Oh, Mr. O'Maury." Then suddenly her eyes widened and she was gone.

Chess sobbed quietly for only a few minutes. Then he kissed her on the cheek and put his face next to hers. Finally he put her hands together on her bosom and went downstairs to wait for the life squad.

In less than twenty minutes John pulled into the driveway and ran inside. The big red truck from the Fire Department stood at the curb but John did not see Chess' old car anywhere. He raced up to the second floor and into his mother's room. One of the crewmen was pulling the cover up over Mary's face. When he saw John he pulled it back down and stepped away from the bed. Kate came slowly into the room and stopped, realizing that they were too late. She began to weep quietly.

John knelt down and looked at his mother's body. Then he crossed himself and said a short prayer. He was not crying. Finally he stood up and the fireman once again pulled up the sheet.

The fireman said, "I'm sorry, there was nothing we could do."

John said, "Oh," and then added, "well," but nothing else. Then he asked if there was someone else there. The fireman told him there had been a man downstairs when they came in. He had appeared to be almost in shock and they had told him to go into the living room and sit down. But later when they had looked for him he was gone.

It was later, much later, when Kate called and was able to find Chess at home. He told her that he held himself accountable for Mary's death, maintaining that if he had not been so foolish about the key he might have been there in time to get help before it was too late. He refused to listen when Kate insisted that it would most likely have made very little difference.

When Mary was buried there were people from the church, and people who were in politics, people from Cincinnati and from the area around Indian Lake. The solemn high Mass was celebrated in Latin. It seemed that everyone was there, except for Chester 'Chess' Walker.

Chapter X

"I give her this. She took good care of her kittens. Once Brewster, that big dog of ourn who was five or six times her size or more, started nosin' around the basket they was in. Now he wouldn't hurt a bitin' fly but she didn't know that. She jumped on his head and dug in, and that dog took off straight through the bottom of the screen door, screechin' like his butt was on fire, which, most likely the truth of it was, he'd have rathered. She'd do things like that. But then donchaknow she jes' up and died after them kittens was all big enough to go off on their own. We never knew what she died of. Jes' one day, after we got rid of the last one, she went out on the porch and laid down in the sun and died. Jimbo buried her out in the back, right next to grammaw's old lilac."

From One General Store, by A. J. Tagge

* * *

1968

Dennis had been born in 1964 which was a little over two years after Pam and Aloysius had been married. Everyone, including Pam, had begun to think that perhaps those two would never have any children. But Robert followed Dennis by only a year and little Clint came a year after that, and then everyone was saying it looked like Pam was going to show all the rest of them how it was done.

It was Saturday afternoon at the lake, for a June day rather warmer than one should expect but the backyard was shady and comfortable. At least it was where John sat and listened to the conversation between the four year old Dennis and two of his older cousins. One of them was seven year old

Millie who loved to talk with "the little kids" because they always "Say the cutest things". She was there without the rest of her family who would be up from Cincinnati later in the evening. The other one was Joan who was a year younger than Millie. She didn't get to see her cousins quite as often because her family did not live as close. But Polly and her husband John Comstock had decided to make the trip and spend the weekend. It was a sort of short vacation.

They were inside the cottage with Kate. She had shown them the latest letter from Carrie, for the last eight years known as Sister Dominic. Polly remarked how hard it was to realize that her own baby sister was a nun and that it was nine years since she had entered the convent. According to the letter she was as happy as ever and getting used to her new assignment in Cleveland. John and Kate had found that drive easier than the drive to her previous station in Missouri and had already visited her twice. The last time they had spent nearly a week.

When the three came outside they heard Joan ask Dennis to say Rice Krispies for her. It came out "Rice Krippies", which made them all laugh. But it was about the twelfth time in the past hour someone had asked the little boy to say the name of the cereal and, although he enjoyed the attention, he was getting tired of being asked to repeat the same thing over and over. He went and stood behind his grandfather's chair. Kate carried a tray with iced tea for everyone except the three smallest ones, Dennis, three year old Robert and two year old Clint. They were served lemonade. Even Joan and Millie had iced tea, with lots of sugar, as they had requested. Dennis came out from behind John O'Maury's chair to get a sip of his mother's tea, but it was hardly sweetened at all. He made a face and went back to his lemonade.

All but the three little boys found seats and the conversation turned first to the weather. When that subject was exhausted they talked about the plants in John's garden some of which were more than a foot above the ground. In fact the tomatoes in the corner were already covered with yellow blossoms. Finally John Comstock asked his father-in-law what his first impressions were of the Vatican Council. Kate rolled her eyes heavenward and said, "Oh my goodness I wish you wouldn't ask him that." And at this they all laughed, even John O'Maury.

He asked, "Do you really want to know what I think? You don't really, do you?" And they all laughed again.

Millie who had been sitting on the edge of her grandmother's chair with Kate's arm around her said, "I think now I'll be able to understand all the prayers at the mass." They all looked at John to see how he would answer the little girl. He took a long drink of his tea and put the glass down on a bare spot in the grass next to his chair.

He looked at Millie with a slight frown and shook his head as though he felt the statement was really a question. But that feeling didn't last long. She was only a child. At her age it was unlikely she would have very serious thoughts about anything, much less about theology or whether the liturgy was in Latin or English. Probably what she had said was not something she would have thought of on her own. In fact it was a question he had heard, and answered, before. Obviously it was something she had heard and, most likely, didn't even understand completely. But it deserved an answer, both for her and the others who were still making up there own minds about what was being done in Rome. Besides that he loved his granddaughter. Whether or not she had any constructive thoughts on the subject was immaterial. She had brought it up and he would never give her the impression that he thought her opinion was not important to him.

"Oh Millie," he began patiently, "I wonder if you really will understand the theology of the sacrifice of the Mass just because the prayers will all be in English. And anyway the missals always did have English translations printed next to the Latin prayers. What will be the difference?"

Millie looked at her grandmother first, but Kate just smiled at her. She was apparently on her own. She bailed out. "Well," she said, "that's what Sister Mary Thomas told us the other day."

John groaned at this but then he smiled. "God bless our helpful but misguided nuns," he said. He took another sip of his tea and added reflectively, "What seems to have begun with good intentions on the part of John 23rd, has somehow gathered steam and veered off in the wrong direction. I hope someone has the good sense to stop it before it destroys the Church."

In the middle of the afternoon John and Kate got the old Studebaker out and drove to Wapakoneta for some groceries. The car was a 1958 Golden Hawk which John had paid more than three thousand dollars for and, with only two doors, one of the very few things in his life that could be considered an extravagance. It was still in good condition because he had taken loving care of it. Even Kate liked the long rear fenders and the distinctive little grill that set it apart from other cars. They both considered it "their car". How sad they would have been had they known that Studebaker would only be in existence for a short time.

The rest of the family drove over to the beach to look at the lake, taking along a few chairs so they could sit a while and let the kids play in the sand. Although the air was warm the water was a little too cool for swimming and there was no lifeguard on duty yet anyway.

On the way back from Wapakoneta Kate was unusually quiet and John asked her what she was thinking. She didn't answer him immediately but stared out the window watching the passing landscape for such a long time that John thought she hadn't heard him and was about to repeat the question. Then she said, "Oh, I was just thinking what a good life we have, you and me togedder, sometimes."

John chuckled at her German accent because it had been so long since he had heard it. And he liked it. It took him back to that day at the circus when he had met her. Now it was his turn to seem lost in thought, thoughts from his youth. He remembered how hard it had been for him to face the days, after Aloysius had been killed. His brother had been such a source of surprises that John constantly looked forward to seeing him. After his death it seemed to John that nothing very interesting would ever happen again. Then he had met Kate and his world had once more become bright and exciting.

Kate's skirt was pulled up over her knees and John, smiling, and without taking his eyes from the road ahead of them, put his right hand on the inside of her left thigh. "Yes," he said suggestively, squeezing her leg, "sometimes we have a very good life."

Kate put her knees together and told him, "I know what you are thinking but I don't want us to have a wreck. You better put two hands on the wheel."

Reluctantly he removed his hand from Kate's thigh and put it back on the steering wheel. He told her, "I could stop the car on the side of the road."

She laughed her slightly throaty laugh and pulled the skirt down over her knees. "Oh, you want us to get arrested?" He laughed but he didn't say anything else for a few miles. Then what he said was almost prophetic, "Is that what you would say if you thought it was the last time I would ever get to take your pants off?"

She was watching the fences and trees and the grass as they passed by the window and she didn't turn her head to look at him, but when she answered he could hear something in her voice. "Sometime it will be the last time we ever will have love together won't it?"

It didn't sound like sadness in her voice but she sounded rather pensive. She sounded so reflective, and a bit apprehensive. He wondered what, if anything, she was worried about? It concerned him, and he took his eyes from the road for a few seconds to look closely at her face. But then she turned and smiled and he was sure he had only imagined it.

They loved each other. But if both had known what was about to happen, in fact was already happening, their responses would have been very different. They might both have agreed indeed to stop the car on the side of the road. But he would have wanted to take her in his arms and hold her as long as he could, doing nothing except reminding her how much he loved her and how difficult it would be for him ever to face life without her.

She, on the other hand, would have insisted that he pull her skirt up and slide her pants down and off her legs. She would want to have intercourse because to both of them it was the ultimate surrendering of a woman to a man and it was involved with the memory she would like him to keep forever, that they had always been totally each other's, but that each time they had made love she had always felt she had given herself to him anew without question.

They did not talk any more and each was lost in thought. But when they were almost to Pokey Lane John looked at her and noticed that her head was against the back of the seat and her eyes were closed. He asked her if she felt well. She told him she was fine except for a slight and very rare headache. She wanted to get back to the cottage so she could get rid of it with an aspirin and not ruin everyone else's holiday.

The others had not come back yet so John put the groceries away. Kate took two aspirin tablets and told him she would lie down for a while until the kids returned. Then, when they did, he went up to get her but she told him the headache had not gotten any better, in fact a little worse, so she had taken two non-aspirins from Walgreen's. Now, she said, she was beginning to feel clumsy, as though she was losing control of her muscles. "I think it is because I took two different kinds of medicine. I think that does it sometimes. I think I will keep lying down for a while until it goes away. Then I will come downstairs." John wanted to call a doctor but she wouldn't let him.

For the rest of John's life he blamed himself for not calling Doctor Lighter, who lived not far away. But he was told over and over that it would have made no difference.

John told the family that Kate was lying down because she had a headache and that she intended to join them later. For supper they ate cold roast beef and macaroni salad that Kate had made that morning and orange sherbet from the freezer. Then, since it was still warm, they returned to the backyard to sit and talk. Eventually, of course, the others noticed that John was even less talkative than usual. Someone asked him if he was worried about mom. He said he was not but they noticed that his response was not immediate. And then he said he would go upstairs to make sure she had not changed her mind about coming downstairs. But he only stood in the hall and listened at the bedroom door and since she seemed to be breathing normally he decided not to wake her.

When it was time for the three little guys to go to bed Aloysius started to get them together but Pam told him not to get up but to stay there and talk to his father, that she could handle the job herself. She also promised to look in on Kate and report back. Actually she was back very shortly. The boys had had a busy and tiring day and had hardly been able to keep awake long enough for their baths. Pam assured everyone that Kate was still sleeping and they all agreed that, since the hour was late there didn't seem to be much point in waking her.

John could not decide whether to go up and make sure Kate did not need anything or to stay and talk to members of his family whom he did not see very often. He made up his mind that Kate, being asleep, would probably not appreciate it if he woke her up to ask her how she was feeling. And it was just about that time that Elleen and Dan drove into the driveway with Libby and Young Danny. It took a while for Millie to tell her parents what she had done all day. Dan said he was thirsty and asked John if, by any chance, there might be a beer in the refrigerator, to which one of the women remarked, "Is the Pope a Catholic?" at which they all laughed. And John said, "Since I have been reading about the council sometimes I wonder," and then they all groaned. Dan went in and got beers for everyone who wanted one and came back out and sat down. Everyone talked at once for a while and while the conversation became a little lighter in content its volume rose considerably. Eventually Elleen noticed that Kate was missing and wanted to know where she was. And when she was told Kate wasn't feeling well she wondered aloud whether Kate might not be getting to the age when she was overwhelmed with having so many people around at one time. Someone else said she shouldn't let Kate hear her say that and everyone laughed again.

John appreciated nothing more than listening to his family having a good time together. He leaned back in his chair and when they laughed he laughed. But he kept glancing toward the house looking for any sign that Kate was awake and would join them in the yard.

Finally someone yawned and started an epidemic; one by one they all yawned. Obviously it was time to retire.

First the women went in and assigned the sleeping areas. The men turned all the chairs over to keep the dew from gathering on the seats. Then they went in and sat in the kitchen and had one more beer while they waited for a signal from upstairs that they were allowed to use the bathrooms.

John was one of the last to slip into his bed next to Kate. She still seemed to be sleeping normally and John was careful not to wake her. He would have felt much better if she had awakened and told him her headache was gone.

It was nearly half past two when John was wakened from a fitful sleep by Kate's hand on his arm. He turned on the light that stood on the table by the side of the bed and leaned over on one elbow to look at her face. He was shocked to see that her eyes were open but seemed filled with terror. She clutched his arm again with one hand and pointed toward her face with the other. Her mouth moved but she seemed unable to talk.

"Oh my God," uttered John, "what is it? What is the matter?"

Then Kate said the last words John would ever hear her say. Although they were really unintelligible he would always insist that what she said was, "I love you. I love all of you." And, considering everything about Kate the wife, the mother, the grandmother, and Kate the woman, he was probably right.

John had always thought that in any kind of crisis he would be able to remain calm and see that whatever action needed to be taken was indeed taken. He saw himself as a steadying influence in a world that revolved around him in turmoil. That image was destroyed completely on that particular early morning. First he ran into the hallway and knocked on Elleen's door. When she answered he shouted, "Come quick. Something is wrong with mom."

Of course everyone else heard him and soon all the women were in the hall, still pushing their hands through the arms of robes. Elleen was the first to reach her mother's side. She felt her mother's pulse and told the others, "I don't know. I think she is having a stroke. Someone call the fire department and see if they have an ambulance." Then she added, "And call Doctor Lighter too."

The man on duty at the fire station said it would take too long for their ambulance to respond because the volunteers would have to get there first. But he called Kibby, the undertaker, who immediately sent an ambulance with two men.

The drivers from the undertaker did not have room for anyone to ride with them to the hospital. As soon as they left the family held a conference to decide who would go and who would stay with the kids, still in bed and sleeping soundly. It did not take long for them to decide Pam and Aloysius should stay because their boys were the only youngsters, and would probably feel better with their parents when they woke up. All the other adults and Millie and Joan rode together in Dan and Elleen's new van. They left with the promise to call as soon as they new heard any news, good or bad.

At the hospital they were directed to a waiting room and told one of the interns would be with them as soon as he had examined Kate. It was nearly five o'clock before anyone came to talk to them and it was Henry Lighter, the doctor who lived on the road to Bellefontaine, and who knew John and Kate well. When he came in John stood and shook the doctor's hand. Doctor Lighter nodded to everyone there and even smiled a little. He shook his head and looked down at the floor. He said, "I'm sorry but it does not look good. Kate has an aneurysm inside her brain. The only way we could do anything is if it would stop by itself. In that case we could find it and make some permanent repair. But, unfortunately, that does not seem to be happening." He looked at Polly and Elleen who were sitting on a couch, holding hands and weeping softly. He said, "Your mother is paralyzed. She does not seem to be able to do anything. It is possible that she can hear you, though. We have put her in a room and I have called a priest, Father Angelo Yaccabucci. He will be here shortly. If any of you would like to see her I will take you there." As they seemed undecided who should go he added, "You can all go if you want to. Unfortunately I don't think anything you can do will make any difference at all but it certainly won't hurt anything." To John he said, "Norman is already on his way but I called Father Angelo first because he is closer."

When he said that Polly began to sob and her sister embraced her. Then they both got up and followed Doctor Lighter with the others straggling behind. No one spoke. Dan put his hand on John's shoulder and squeezed it as they went out the door. John acknowledged the gesture by turning his head, by touching the younger man's hand with his own and smiling ever so slightly.

Once in Kate's room Doctor Lighter listened to her heart with his stethoscope and felt her pulse. Her mouth was open and she hesitated before every breath. Doctor Lighter gave them no reassurance. He said, "I will be back as soon as Father Angelo gets here." Elleen asked him to call the cabin and tell Aloysius what he had told them. She wrote the phone number on a little piece of paper she found in the waste basket. He took the paper and patted her hand gently before he left.

When the priest came into the room they could see he needed a shave. Indeed he looked as though he had only a little while ago been in bed. But he had been able to put on his collar and a black coat. He came in quickly, unpacked his kit, and donned the small purple stole. Then he lit the little candle. Everyone knelt while he gave Kate absolution. Then he administered Extreme Unction, the last sacrament.

When he was finished he told John he would be available if the family needed anything at all. He shook John's hand and said to the two girls, "Now your mother is in the hands of God. She will either get well and soon be back with all of you, or her soul will be with Jesus and His mother in Heaven." These were hopeful words, words he had used many times to many people gathered around the sick beds of loved ones in hospitals and homes, words he believed with all his heart, words meant to give comfort, but words he dreaded saying. But they were the only words he had. The first few times Father Angelo had administered the Sacrament to someone who was dying he had grieved with the family, not because he knew the patient well enough to feel their sadness, but because he was a sensitive man and he had felt their grief. He had identified with those who were losing a loved one.

But eventually he had learned to shield himself from the sorrow of others, no longer shedding tears at death watches and funerals. So his voice did not falter and his eyes were dry even though he spoke quietly. Still, when he left the hospital, even knowing that this woman would soon be in heaven, he did not feel happy about what it meant. Because of his faith, watching someone enter heaven was easy; but, nonetheless, watching those who loved her say goodbye was very difficult. He would not feel good the rest of that day.

The family's vigil continued until the middle of the afternoon. Then Kate's breathing became more and more labored, and finally she breathed her last. Since they had put her on the stretcher to bring her to the hospital she had never opened her eyes.

*   *   *

It was a day halfway between springtime and summertime, somewhat warm for the one and a bit too cool for the other. Kate would have said, "Why doesn't it make up its mind?"

The solemn funeral Mass at St. Mary Of The Woods Church was celebrated according to the old system by Archbishop Elko who came up from Dayton. Norman served as Deacon and the Pastor, Father Tombrinker, was the subdeacon. There were eight servers and Father Angelo acted as Master of Ceremonies. He told Norman he had not filled that position since his seminary days, but he had not forgotten how.

After Kate's casket was lowered into the grave in a plot next to her mother's everyone was invited to the house near the Lake. It was still early in the day and the women served lunch. One by one and two by two the guests began offering their condolences with promises to help in any way they could and starting home. And after a while Carrie, who, under the new rules, had been permitted to leave the convent and attend her mother's funeral, noticed that her father was missing. She asked Elleen if she knew where John was. Elleen thought for only a minute before she said she did. "There is a place on the shore where he and mom used to go sometimes, just by themselves, in the early spring or the late fall when there weren't likely to be many others there. It's a good walk but I'll bet that's where he went." So she and Carrie got Dan and all the grandchildren and put them in the van and went to get Grandpa.

It was nearly a mile to where a narrow path ran in a zigzag path down to the beach. They all got out of the car and walked single file toward the water. As Elleen had expected John was sitting on the sand, looking out across the surface of the lake that reflected a gloomy sky. The three grownups stopped and let the grandchildren go on ahead. The older ones who were there, Libby, Danny, Millie, and Joan, sat down quietly behind the old man. The little ones, taking their cue from the others, said nothing as they sat down around him but closer. Clint put himself right between John's feet. Three year old Robert put his hand in his grandfather's and John, who at first did not seem to have noticed them, looked at little Robert affectionately. Then he looked around at all of them. Finally he said softly, "Your grandmother loved you so much. What are all you little guys going to do now?"

And four year old Dennis, sitting next to his brother, asked, "But Bindah, don't you love us too?"

And John realized that from then on he would love the family enough for both himself and for Kate. He said, "I sure do, young feller. I sure do." And he reached out and put his hand on Dennis' head, ruffling the boy's curly hair. "Let's go back and see if they saved us anything to eat."

When John got up and turned to go he saw the other grandchildren sitting behind him and around him, and the three adults by the bit of hedge at the back of the beach. He smiled at them and nodded his head in understanding at the three grownups. Libby and Millie hugged him first, one on each side, then Danny. Gathered around him they all started walking toward the car. But just before the group left the beach John turned around and looked out across the water. Dan said quietly to his wife, "Do you think he is looking for your mother out there?"

Elleen's answer was, "No, I think he is just saying goodbye to all the things they did together here." Then, after everyone but Dan had started to walk toward the van, she said, "Goodbye, mom." She was not looking at the lake, though, but up toward the sky.

Chapter XI

Being the biggest frog in a small pond might have been worth something but being the only frog would not seem to be as much fun. I would have thought even frogs wanted company. But this little guy didn't seem to mind. I suppose it was an advantage not having to compete with another frog for the insects that seemed so plentiful there. On the other hand if something hungry came down to the water that wanted frog on its menu there was only that one frog to choose from. Anyway one day I poked around under the rocks where I usually found him but he didn't jump out, and I never saw him again. I don't know whether he got to be someone else's dinner or if one night he just heard some romantic frog singin' to the lady frogs in another pond and decided to go see what all the fuss was about.

From Where The Reeds Grow The Longest, by Lindsen Taylor

The Second Love (1971)

Kate had been dead for nearly three years. Since her death John had slowly gotten into a routine, doing nearly the same things every day. Actually he had two routines, one for when he was at home in the city and one for when he was at the lake.

One of the things he did almost every day when he was at the lake was to walk to Arlen's Park in the afternoon when the weather allowed. He would go there and find a bench and sit and think. He missed Kate and being away from the cabin allowed him to imagine that she was there waiting and that when he went back he would see her.

The early June sun was warm and felt good on John's knees. He had a little arthritis but he knew that for a man of his age he was in very good health. He leaned back and closed his eyes, trying to remember if it had been on such a day that he had met Kate. Yes, he thought, even though it had been much later in the summer, the temperature had been about the same. It was several years after Aloysius had been killed.

Those had been bad years for the whole family, but probably they had been hardest on him. His parents had, he knew, been very much affected, especially his mother. But they had each other. And Eileen was somewhat insulated by the fact that she lived in the convent, since there was little there that she could associate with her brother. With John it was different. Nearly everything he did reminded him of Aloysius.

But then he had been able to find Kate and everything had changed.

He remembered now how it had made him feel guilty, the way she had distracted him from mourning for his brother. But he knew that mourning does no one any good, neither the mourner nor the mournee. He didn't know if mournee was a word and thinking about that made him smile.

John must have heard a sound that was out of place because he suddenly had the feeling that someone was near him. If that person had seen him smile with his eyes closed he or she must have wondered what such an old man could be dreaming about. Slowly he opened his eyes and saw that it was a girl, but she was not watching him. She was, in fact, peering off to his left, looking somewhat perplexed.

She was a young girl, John figured not much older than thirty. Her hair was light brown, not particularly striking, but it fell to her collar in soft waves that caught the sunlight as it filtered through the trees. Actually she was, in fact, not especially attractive, John thought. In spite of the warm temperature she wore rather loose fitting slacks which, although they gently outlined a rather round derriere, revealed little else of her figure. And her short sleeved blouse was so full in the front it could have covered a fairly ample bosom without showing much of it. In other words from the profile which John saw she was just a girl, without any outstanding features and possibly, he thought, a bit overweight.

John remembered another young girl; her name was Aimee Rennel. That had been a long time ago and John was then thirty five years old.

After that one experience with her John had never seen Aimee again except at a distance. But for a long time he had often thought about her. He had gone to confession the next Saturday but he had never been able to lose his feeling of guilt. Nor had he been able to completely lose the desire she had stirred in him. Sometime after Kate's death John had thought about trying to find Aimee but he was sure she would have been married by then. Besides he was sure that because of the way he had treated the girl she probably would not be pleased to hear from him.

He was sorry for what had happened. But wasn't he also sorry he would never know what making love with her would be like? He wasn't sure.

The girl who stood in front of him now brought back memories of Aimee. This young girl was probably close to what Aimee's age had been then. She seemed a little taller but they probably had much the same build. And Aimee might have been prettier than this young lady.

She stood on the walk about six feet directly in front of the John's bench. And he knew immediately what her problem was. In that small park, although there were only six benches, rarely were they all occupied. On this particular day, however, each of them had at least one person on it, possibly because of the pleasant weather. John assumed, from the book which the girl carried in one hand, that she was looking for a place to quietly sit and read, preferably on an unoccupied bench. He moved as far as he could to one end of the bench.

"Young lady," he said, "I see that the park is a little crowded. You are certainly welcome to share this bench. I might go to sleep, but I promise I won't snore."

She might have been startled by his voice but she gave no indication. She would have preferred to share a bench with another woman but the only females she saw were with small children which she thought would disturb her reading. There was one younger looking man, sitting by himself farther down the walk. The girl did not want to sit there for fear her reason for doing so would be misinterpreted. Besides he would probably be married and that might make him uncomfortable. This man, she thought, was probably old enough that she need not worry about either his intentions or what someone might think hers were. She smiled and turned toward him.

"Thanks," she said. "You had your eyes closed and I didn't know if you were sleeping. I didn't want to disturb you."

Her voice was low and a little throaty. Her face was a slight oval, her eyes dark green and her teeth white and even. When John saw her from the front he decided she was after all much prettier than he had at first thought, even though not quite the most beautiful woman he had ever seen. And her voice was exciting. The thought suddenly crossed his mind that he must have looked very old to her and he was sorry. He would like to have said something clever but could think of nothing. He said, "No, no, I was awake. Just sitting here thinking."

She sat down on the other end of the bench. She thought she should say something. Finally she did. "It sure is a nice day, isn't it?"

"It sure is," he answered. "It's a good day for sitting in the sun and reading." He gestured toward her book. I guess you are on your lunch hour, aren't you?"

"Yes," she answered as she opened her book.

"Well I won't bother you then. You probably don't have much time."

"Actually no," she told him. She looked at her watch. "I will have to leave in about half an hour. I should be back to work by one o'clock." She opened her book and took out the bookmark. But then she seemed to change her mind. Without closing the book she added, "Do you come here often?"

John turned toward her, putting one arm up on the back of the bench but being careful not to look as though he was reaching out toward her. He said, "Nearly every day." He didn't want to say that he was retired even though it should have been obvious to her. He was glad he had gotten into the habit of wearing a hat too because he didn't want her to see how he was losing his hair. He said, "It isn't usually this crowded."

Once again she started to read and changed her mind. This time she put the bookmark back and closed the book. She had lost interest in it. For some reason which she did not understand she would rather talk to this man. She wanted to look at him more closely but she would have had to turn around and face him and that didn't seem right to her. She said, "I have only been here a few times. But I am only here in the summer. I work for an accounting firm in Cincinnati and they do the accounting for the amusement park." She laughed a little, sort of a deep chuckle. "They send me up here for the summer. I get to spend my summers here and get paid for it."

"Aren't you lucky?" he answered. "I'm from Cincinnati too. And I spend most of the summers here with some of my family." She didn't really know why but she was glad he had not said with his wife. He added, "From now on when it looks crowded I'll reserve a spot for you."

"That would be nice," she said and laughed again. He liked to hear her laugh.

They sat there for a few minutes without saying anything. He took his arm from the back of the bench and she was sure he had closed his eyes again. But she still would not turn and look at him. She glanced at her watch. "I guess I'd better get back," she told him. "I'll see you again." She stood up and took a few steps. She was so curious that she could not leave without seeing what he looked like. She turned and reminded him, "Don't forget to save me a place."

She could tell he was old, probably over sixty. But he looked trim and something else she could not define. It was much later that she realized the word she was trying to think of was "exciting". He had wrinkles around his eyes but it looked like they were from smiling a lot.

"Oh, I won't forget," he promised. "Just ask for John."

"My name is Monica. But most people call me Moni. I spell it M-O-N-I but it does rhyme with money. I don't know why people call me that. I guess they think I'm a gold digger."

"Are you?" he asked.

"No," she answered and then laughed her short deep laugh again. "Well," she added, "maybe sometimes." With that she waved and turned and, smiling, started up the path toward the parking lot.

John watched her until she went around a bend and out of his sight. From the back he could definitely see that she was overweight. It was hard to see where her waist was. But John decided that she was cute, whatever the hell that meant.

When John got back to the cabin Elleen was standing on the porch. She said, "Did you see anyone you know today?"

"No not today," he answered.

"Well, maybe tomorrow," she encouraged him. "I'll fix you a sandwich if you are hungry. We have already eaten and Danny and Millie are out in the back. They have been watching for you."

His mind seemed to be somewhere else. He did not appear to have heard what she had said. "Elleen," he asked, "do you think I look old?"

"Why whatever made you ask? Did some good looking young lady call you grandpa?" John glanced at his daughter's face, trying to tell if she was just teasing or if she knew something she was not telling him. He was embarrassed and Elleen could tell. She moved closer to where he stood and put her arm around him. "Dad," she kidded, "you don't look a day over sixty eight."

"No, I'm serious," he persisted. "Maybe I should start exercising more, or take more vitamins. I don't mind looking my age but I don't want to look decrepit."

Elleen started to laugh, but then she realized he was in earnest. She thought something must have happened. Perhaps someone had offended him in some way. It might have been some kids. It was just terrible the way kids were. They seemed to have no respect for older people at all. Elleen knew how much John liked children too. He talked to all of them and sometimes even got into their games. It could be that some thoughtless youngster had told him he was too old to play with them. Elleen was glad her three had never been like that. Of course Libby was fourteen and almost grown up. Elleen saw that John was waiting for her to say something else. She stepped back and looked at him. He was less than six feet tall but he held himself erect just like he always had. And there was probably not an ounce of fat on his whole body. She knew he was losing his hair but he wore a hat most of the time so it was hard to tell. And what one could see below his hat was steely grey as was his trim moustache. Elleen thought he could best be described as dignified. But that was until he smiled. Then the lines around his dark blue eyes deepened and his whole face seemed to light up. And the thing was he seemed to smile a lot. Did he look old? It was hard for her to tell because she knew how old he was. Perhaps he did look his age but on him it was not a reason for regret but a badge.

Elleen said, "Dad, you don't look very old to me. You get lots of exercise and it shows. I'm surprised that some woman hasn't tried to pick you up in that park you go to all the time."

He smiled. "most of the women over there," he pointed out, "are probably married. They usually have a lot of kids with them."

"I guess," she answered. "But these days that doesn't always make much difference you know. And anyway not all women who have kids are married. It isn't like it used to be in the old days."

She was going to mention Vatican II but this didn't seem to be the right time. It was funny how that was turning out to be somewhat of a disappointment. When they had first heard the Holy Father, John the Twenty Third, proclaim his intention of holding a council to "update" the church they had generally been encouraged. The feeling was that the old rules would be redefined with a view to including many new concepts. But now that some of the original declarations of the bishops were being "interpreted" by the press many old catholics were wondering how much of their church would survive. John had several times expressed his alarm at some of the things he had heard. Elleen hoped he was wrong but she too wondered at times.

What Elleen had said about his appearance seemed to reassure her father. He said, "I think I will have a sandwich. Then I'll see what the kids are going to do."

*   *   *

The next day was Thursday. John got to the park shortly before eleven and stayed until nearly two o'clock but he did not see Moni. On Friday he got there only a few minutes after ten and did not leave until almost three without seeing her. When he got back to the cabin Elleen was sitting on the couch in the living room, her feet propped up on a footstool, reading.

'You're late," she said, hardly looking up from her book. "Did you fall asleep?"

He seemed preoccupied just as he had on Wednesday. She closed her book, keeping her place with her index finger, and looked at him closely. He seemed to be looking at her but not seeing her. Finally he asked, "Is there anything to eat?"

"We ate oyster stew. There's some left. Do you want me to heat it up?"

"No," he answered. "I can do it." He walked out to the small kitchen. She put a bookmark in her book and put it on a table and followed him.

She said, "You know Dan is coming out tonight as soon as he gets off work and picks up Libby. Do you want to go out or should I fix something to eat here?"

John was getting the oyster stew out of the refrigerator. "let's not make Dan go out," he answered. He poured the stew into a bowl and put the bowl into the microwave oven. He punched the buttons to set the timer and then started it. Then he turned around. "I know how tired he will be when he gets here. If you want to we can go out and eat tomorrow night."

"Oh," she said suddenly, "we got a letter from Jill today. She is coming out tonight with Billy and his new girl friend. He wants us to meet her. I'm sure they intend to stay all night. We will have to do some shifting with the sleeping arrangements."

John sat down at the table. When the oven bell went off he started to get up but Elleen told him to stay seated. She got the bowl out of the oven and put it on the table. Then she got him a spoon and some crackers. "Be careful," she warned, "it's hot." He smiled because he knew she was so used to saying such things to her children that she said them to everyone. Since he had set the timer he was sure it wasn't too hot for him. He tried it and he was right.

"Is she a nice girl?" he wondered.

" I never met her," Elleen pointed out. "Jill seems to like her though. Her name is Ann."

"Nice name," John said between spoonsful of stew. "Nowadays a lot of people have names I never heard of and don't know how to spell. I think they make them up."

"I think they do too," Elleen agreed.

"How old is Billy, Ell?"

"Let me think," she answered. "he was born in July of 1953. That would make him eighteen wouldn't it?"

"Don't you think that is a little young for someone to be introducing his girl to the family?" the grandfather asked.

"Yes. Yes I do, dad," was her slow response. "but you know things are different nowadays."

He shook his head before answering. "Yes I know. But I don't know why they should be."

Elleen walked to the window and stood looking out at something far, far away, something that was only in her mind. "Billy and his father never saw each other, did they?" She seemed to be thinking for a while, then added, "I think it is so nice that Jill has stayed so close to us. Actually I think we have gotten much closer after Bill was killed. Don't you think?"

"Well," he reminded her, "we only met her about a year before he died. We couldn't have known her very well, could we? As a matter of fact they probably didn't know each other very well." He finished the stew and put down his spoon. "I will never forget the night we found out, both of them." He shook his head remembering. "I was not sure your mother would be able to stand it."

Elleen turned around. She said, "Mom always said the same thing about you. I guess you kept each other from falling apart." She took his bowl and his spoon to the sink to wash them. He might cry as he often did when someone talked about her twin brothers. It didn't bother her but she realized he didn't like for anyone to know. But he didn't cry. He pushed his chair back and stood up.

"I think I'll go and see what the kids are doing," he told her.

Jill arrived with her son and his girl friend at about seven o'clock. And Dan and Libby were only a few minutes behind them. Jill was introducing the girl, Ann, to John and Elleen and the two kids but all the conversation stopped when Dan came in. Because of his dimensions, and his beard, and the way he combed (or didn't comb) his hair he always had that effect on people. It was as though a grizzly had walked through the door.

The first thing Dan did was to pick Danny and Millie up, one on each side, and hug them. Then he hugged his wife and Jill. To his father-in-law he said, "Hi, Bin."

Billy said, "Hey Uncle Dan, How's it going?" He liked Dan pretty much, as most people did.

Dan, mimicking his wife's nephew answered, "Hey Bill it's going pretty well. How's it going with you?"

Billy pointed to Ann, who was actually standing next to Dan and was hardly visible. He said, "I want you to meet Ann Groblenski." To Ann he said, "This is my uncle Dan. I told you about him."

Dan took the girl's hand in his. It disappeared. He asked, "What did he tell you about me, that I knock things down a lot?"

She smiled and looked him straight in the eyes. "No," she told him. "Actually he said you were very big but your heart is as big as the rest of you, and he also said that sometimes you get a person's hand and the person never sees it again."

Dan laughed and let go of her hand. He was not often caught off guard but this was one of the times. "Billy," he warned, "you have to watch this young lady. She is not at a loss for words, is she?"

"No, not usually," Billy admitted. As everyone moved away from the door he caught Ann's eye and winked as if to say, "You did okay." And as soon as enough of the crowd had moved to the other room she came over to where he stood and took his hand.

Now everyone went to the kitchen. Dan and Libby had not eaten and both admitted to being starved. Elleen had fixed a salad and a seafood casserole and, when the others said they had already had supper, seemed disappointed. In fact she appeared to be so disappointed that in the end all the newcomers sat down and ate.

By the time they were finished it was nearly nine o'clock. As usual John indicated that he would like to turn in. Elleen had worked out the bedroom assignment. Since there were twin beds in both of the rooms the kids had been using she put Libby in with Jill in one of them. Libby regarded Jill with something between adoration and the feeling she might have had for a big sister. And if Jill did not enjoy the relationship she did a very good job of hiding it. In the other room Elleen put Ann and Millie, hoping that, since she was at the talkative stage, Millie would make the older girl feel at home. Billy and Danny would sleep on the folded out sofa in the living room. They didn't mind because that was where the only television set in the place was, and they knew they could watch it if they didn't make too much noise.

John was in his room reading his Douay Rheims version of the bible a little after ten, which was a bit late for him, and everyone else was in bed before midnight.

     *   *   *

John had intended to walk over to the park on Saturday morning even though it seemed very unlikely that Moni would be there. Actually he tried not to admit to himself that he was going there to see her. He told himself that he needed the exercise. But in any event he decided not to go but to stay at the cabin and help entertain the company. He found Jill relaxing on a chaise lounge in the backyard. The book she had apparently been reading was turned over on her lap and her eyes were closed. But she opened them when she heard John come into the yard and sit down at the table.

"It feels so good to just not do anything for a change," she said. "But I feel guilty. Elleen was making sure everyone got breakfast and I offered to help, but she said she didn't need any help."

John chuckled. "You know Elleen pretty well," he reminded Jill. "She usually says what she thinks. If she needs help she will be sure and let you know."

"I know," Jill agreed. "But I still felt like I ought to do something. I guess the guilty feeling was a little like eating too much chocolate though. You know how you can feel like you shouldn't have done something while, at the same time, you can feel good about what you did."

"Yes," he said, "I think I know what you mean."

"Oh, by the way," she changed the subject, "Tammy had to go to an orientation at Mount Saint Joseph. I guess you know she won a scholarship there. She really wanted to come with us but she couldn't. She wanted you to know that. She made a point of telling me to explain that to you. She said she will be up here for a visit as soon as she can, maybe next week."

John was looking out at the trees which stood at the end of the yard. He could see that they needed to be pruned. That was something he should have taken care of in the fall, one of the several things he realized he had gotten into the habit of putting off if they were not urgent. He decided to do it soon but not right away. He wanted to ask Jill something but he wasn't sure that he should. It would bring up old memories which might be painful. Finally he made up his mind.

"Jill," he said slowly, "Does she ever ask about her mother, and about Fritz?" Jill noticed that John had called Fritz by name but had referred to Ginny as Tammy's mother. She wondered if that had been intentional or if it meant anything at all.

"She hasn't said anything about them for quite some time now," she answered John. "she used to once in a while. But she seems to have accepted me as at least a substitute mother I guess." Then she added, "And you know I always think of her that way too, as my daughter I mean. After all I have had her for a long time."

"Yes," her father-in-law agreed, "you have that. And you have done a good job too. Sometimes we forget that you and Billy lost someone then too." He stopped for a moment and Jill knew that he was waiting until the surge of grief had passed so that he could control his voice. She waited for him, knowing that Bill was much more real to John than to her because John had known him much longer. He could remember Bill as a baby and as a boy growing up, and later as a young married man and a young soldier. Her only vivid memory of her husband was the picture of the grown up boy in uniform, just out of basic training. And that picture, she knew, would have faded long ago had she not kept the photograph on her dresser.

Actually there was something else she remembered, something so personal she would never mention it to anyone else. It was not an image of Bill but it involved him. It was the memory of their wedding night which had been spent in a motel near Morganfield, Kentucky. They had spent that Saturday night there, and the next day too, because Bill's pass had been good only through Sunday. On Monday morning he would have to be back with his training company at Camp Breckinridge. When they had slept together on that night it had not really been the first time. They had actually had sex before, but only once and that time it had been very different. It was after a party and they had both been drinking, she much less than him, but both enough that their guard had been down. It had not taken him long to overcome her resistance. For her the experience had been so different from anything she had ever known before that she had been overwhelmed. If he had wanted to she would eagerly have done it again. But he was remorseful. It was apparent that he felt he had taken advantage of her by making her do something they were not supposed to do, and he was sorry. He did not actually apologize but the only reason he did not was because he didn't even want to talk about it. He was sure she had only done it for him and could not have enjoyed it because she was so good she could not possibly have taken pleasure in it. She never was able to get herself to tell him that she had indeed enjoyed it.

On their wedding night it had been different. Both being able to give themselves so completely to each other there was no reservation by either of them and no second thoughts. Because of the time before, she had worried about what he might think of her if he realized that she enjoyed sex. But it was not a problem. He may have been surprised but he did not seem disappointed. It was obvious that the woman he had married would be anything but cold and he was glad. They would enjoy life together. They never ever talked about it but she knew that he appreciated her responsiveness.

They had gone to Mass on Sunday and then to breakfast. After that they went back to the motel and made love again. Then he had slept for a few hours and when he woke they had sex again. By late afternoon the insides of her thighs had begun to feel sore. Finally Bill had suggested that they go out and find something to eat. She remembered now how certain she was that she had walked funny and that everyone must have realized why, and known what they had been doing all day. And she thought suddenly how much she wished that her legs would hurt now for the same reason they had hurt then.

Before they went to bed that night Jill had packed their bags. On Monday they both woke very early and they lay in bed, holding each other close. They made love one more time but it was not the same. There was too much urgency. They got up and Bill put his uniform on for the first time in four days. He put the bags in the car and then went to the office and settled their bill. When he came back she was waiting for him just inside the door. He kissed her tenderly and then he went out the door without looking back. But she stood in the doorway for several minutes, looking first at the bed, then at the bathroom door, then at the desk where she had written notes to her mother and her sister but had never mailed them, then back at the bed where they had made love so many times. Then she went out too and closed the door.

It was still dark. Bill had to get back to his company in time for reveille. With Jill driving they stopped at the guardhouse just inside the gate. The M.P. who walked over to Jill's window and bent over stiffly to look in wore white gloves, and gleaming white spats below his bloused, sharply creased trousers. He glanced quickly at Bill and then waved them on seemingly with official indifference. But in the light that shined from the guardhouse window Jill was sure she detected a slight smirk on his face, as though he too knew what they had been doing for three days. But she told herself she didn't care. Actually she felt proud to have had sex with Bill. It was sort of an initiation, she thought. Now she felt more than ever before that she was a women, and she didn't care who knew that.

She drove him to his company area and stopped on the road next to the wooden orderly room. They both tried very hard to hide the tears but neither did it very well. The time they had spent together had gone so swiftly. He kissed her one more time and then got out of the car.

He looked in the open window and said, "I love you so much." And then he was gone. She watched him in the dim light as he went around the side of the orderly room and up the steps in the back of the barracks. When he was inside she had reached over and rolled up his window. She put the car in gear and drove through the intersection to the next company area and pulled over. Then she put her head down on the wheel and for nearly five minutes she sobbed in the darkness. Then she took a handkerchief from her pocket and wiped her eyes, and drove slowly out of the camp, up the road through Evansville, and on home. Eventually she would rent a room in Morganfield so that they could be together when Billy was off duty, but in her heart she knew that there was little time left for them to be together.

Jill tried to recall what the last thing was that her father-in-law had said. Then she remembered.

"Really," she said slowly, as though she had been thinking about it for the last several minutes, "Billy doesn't have any idea of what his father was like except for the things all of us have told him. And sometimes I have a hard time remembering.

But I know how you are Bindah. You'll never let go of Bill's memory will you?"

He smiled because it was one of the few times she had ever called him by his nickname. "No," he said thoughtfully, "and I don't think you will either. After all you have never remarried and I will never believe it was for lack of opportunity."

"Is that a hint?" she asked with just a touch of humor in her voice. "Are you getting tired of seeing me around?"

"No, no," he asserted. He looked closely at her, trying to see if she was serious. "I hope you know that you are welcome here anytime. I feel that you are part of my family as much as anyone."

Jill was troubled by the concern in his voice. She knew how much he worried about all his inlaws, but especially her and Billy and Tammy. The realization came to her that he probably also worried more about Ginny than any of the rest of them because no one ever knew where she was or what she was doing. Jill herself had always felt close to him especially after her own father had died. But she remembered that in the beginning she had worried that perhaps he didn't approve of her and her relations with his son. After all she had been older than Bill and they had married in pretty much of a hurry, even though it had been in church. And Billy had come so soon she knew a lot of people thought she had been pregnant before the wedding.

Suddenly she blurted out, "Did you ever think I was pregnant when Bill and I got married?"

It took him by surprise, so much so that he didn't know what to say. Actually he had thought it was a possibility but since he didn't know for certain he assumed she was not.

She saved him from embarrassment by saying, "Well, I wasn't. Actually I got pregnant on the weekend we were married. At the time I was sorry but after he...," she stopped talking, suddenly overwhelmed once again by the grief that she thought she had long ago learned to suppress. Then she went on, "I was thankful. It was a part of him. It was all I had."

"Jill," he said, "I am so glad we have you." It was all he could say to her.

*   *   *

On Sunday evening, when everyone left, Elleen went home with Dan and Libby. She had asked her father earlier if he would mind watching Ginny and Pat on Monday while she took care of a few chores. Of course he didn't mind and told her so. Actually he was thinking about going to the park and looking for Moni on Monday. He even thought that perhaps he might take his grandchildren with him, as he had done before on several occasions. But although he was proud of them and usually liked to show them off he really didn't want Moni to see them. He would not admit to himself why he felt that way, but he called himself a foolish old man, and he didn't go to the park.

They fooled around most of the morning and after lunch he took them fishing. The fish weren't biting though and the two youngsters soon lost interest. They had walked over to the lake and he hadn't realized how much of a walk that was for them. By the time they got back to the cabin the kids were tired and eventually they both went to sleep. He knew, of course, that they would probably not want to go to bed early that night so after they ate supper he asked them if they wanted to go to a movie, which of course they did. So he put them in the truck and drove to Wapakoneta. One of the neighborhood theaters was showing Chitty Chitty Bang Bang which had been made in 1968. John, knowing very little about movies, judged that it would be one he could take his grandchildren to without running the risk of being offended. He was right of course. In fact they went to sleep before it was over even though later on they both said they enjoyed it very much. By the time he got them home and in bed it was after midnight.

The next morning Elleen was there before ten o'clock. The two little ones were just finishing their breakfast but they jumped up from the table to throw their arms around their mother and tell her about everything they had done the day before. Elleen hugged them tightly and told them how much she had missed them. While the two of them both talked at once she looked at her father and rolled her eyes. "It's strange, dad," she said over the bedlam, "how I can be gone for just a couple of days and when I get back they seem to have grown at least an inch. Why is that?"

John Laughed. "I don't know," he told her. "But I'll think about it and if I come up with anything I'll pass it on."

"Were they any trouble?" she asked him, of course knowing his answer.

"These two? Why they never are. They're my buddies. You know I found out something though. All the old neighborhood theaters are closing up. There are only a few left in Wapakoneta and I had a heck of a time finding one I'd take kids to. We saw Chitty Chitty Bang Bang."

"Oh, yes," Elleen said, "that old Dick Van Dyke show isn't it? How was it?"

He made a sort of a face and then grinned. "The kids liked it, they said anyway." Elleen laughed.

With Elleen back in control John was free to go to the park. He was there before eleven o'clock, sitting on the bench where he had first seen Moni a week ago. He kept telling himself that he didn't really care if she came but he kept looking toward the bend in the path where he had last seen her.

The park was nearly deserted. Way down at the other end a young woman relaxed on a bench while her two little ones chased a flock of Canada Geese. John smiled wondering what would happen if one of them caught a goose. Finally he leaned back and closed his eyes. He thought there was no way he could go to sleep, the back of the bench was too short to support him. Actually those benches weren't very comfortable.

Every now and then John would open his eyes and look at his watch. It seemed as though several hours had passed before it was a little after twelve. Once again John began to watch the curve in the path. And finally he saw her.

She was wearing a light green blouse and tan slacks. Her hair was pulled back and she wore glasses. It made her look some older and John wondered if that was on purpose. She looked every bit of thirty. He stood up and waved.

Moni had come around the bend and stopped. She had no expression on her face at all but she looked immediately in John's direction and, when she recognized him, she smiled and it was as though a ray of sunshine had broken through the trees for the express purpose of shining on her face.

She came down the path and they stood facing each other. "Where have you been?" she asked.

"I came back both days last week," he answered. "You weren't here."

"Oh, I know. I had meetings on Thursday and Friday. That hardly ever happens." She sounded apologetic. "But I was here on Monday. You weren't here."

"I had to baby sit," he told her. He almost told her it was for two of his grandchildren but he didn't. He had a strong urge to take her hand but instead he sat back down on one end of the bench. She sat on the other end and turned toward him. They talked for a few minutes about the weather and other things which neither would remember later. Then they were silent for several minutes. She looked at her watch.

"Do you have to leave?" he asked.

"Not yet," she told him. "I have a little while yet."

After a few more minutes she suddenly asked, "Are you married, John?"

The question took him by surprise. "Well, I was," he answered slowly. "I was married for a long time. Katie died a couple of years ago."

The girl looked down. She realized that he must wonder why she had asked the question. Unfortunately she couldn't tell him because she wasn't sure herself. Since they had first met it had always been a question in the back of her mind and all of a sudden it had come out without her actually thinking about it.

"You seem to have a lot of free time," she said as a sort of explanation. Then she added, "You must miss her very much."

"Yes, I do," he agreed. But he realized that for days he hadn't really been thinking much about Kate. Did he really miss her? He thought he did but he wasn't sure. It made him feel disloyal. It was something he would have to consider later. To make up for the feeling of disloyalty he told her about the kids.

"Yesterday I was watching two of my grandchildren. One of my daughters stays up here with me most of the summer and they are her kids. Her husband works so much it was his idea. He's a computer programmer and he teaches besides. But he gets here most weekends.

"Are they boys or girls?" Moni asked.

"Both," he answered. "Let's see now. Danny is about twelve and Millie must be ten I think. They're good kids."

"Why don't you bring them along with you? she asked.

Now it was his turn to be embarrassed. Actually he didn't know why he hadn't brought them to the park except that he rarely did. In the beginning the walk had seemed too long for them. Then he had gotten used to the idea of being by himself so he could just sit and think about Kate. But that wasn't it. While Elleen had been gone it would have been a reasonable answer to the question of what to do to entertain them. But he hadn't wanted to do it. He was involved in two different worlds. Moni represented one, perhaps a dream world, and his family represented the other one, the real one. He wasn't sure why he didn't want them to touch one another. Perhaps he was afraid that if the dream world ever mixed with the real one the fantasy world would disappear.

"Oh, I thought they might bother you," he began lamely. "The next time I come I will bring them. Will you be here tomorrow?"

"Oh, I forgot," she told him. "I have to go to Cincinnati tomorrow, actually tonight. I won't be back until next Tuesday. I have some meetings I have to go to."

He tried to hide the disappointment he felt by making a joke of it. "I don't know if I can get along without you for that many days."

She knew he was exaggerating but she thought he would really miss her. At least she hoped so. "I think you will be able to find something to keep you busy," was what she said.

They talked for a while longer before she had to go back to work. He wanted to ask her if she ever went out on a date and if she was seriously involved with anyone. But he could not do it. It was none of his business and he could not think of any way to make the question sound casual. Finally she left and he walked back to the cabin slowly.

On Thursday Elleen had a call from Dan. Someone was coming on Friday to give them an estimate on putting a new roof on their garage and Dan could not be there. Elleen thought it would be a good opportunity to take Danny and Millie home for a few days. Their friends had been asking about them. She wanted John to go along. John thought it was amusing that she never had any second thoughts about leaving the kids with him, but she never wanted to leave him by himself. It made him wonder, when he was baby sitting, who was watching whom. He told her he had some things he needed to do and it would be a good time to take care of them. Perhaps he would prune the trees at the edge of the back yard. Elleen would rather he had gone with them but she knew it was usually no use arguing with him. She made sure he had plenty to eat for the weekend and they left after supper. The kids were excited at the prospect of seeing both their father and their friends, not necessarily in that order. After they left John drove the truck over to Russells Point and parked it in the parking lot in front of the amusement park. But he didn't get out. He listened to the music for a while and then he drove back to the cabin.

On Saturday John actually did get his pruning tools out and trimmed a few branches from some of the trees. There were too many leaves to do a very good job because with the foliage so dense it was difficult to see what branches needed to be cut. He dug a hole in the back yard and put up a bird feeder that he had bought in Wapakoneta the year before. He knew that Millie especially would be pleased to see it because she liked the birds. He made a little platform out of wood so that she could stand on it and put seed in the feeder.

When he came in the door after church on Sunday the phone was ringing. It was Elleen. She wanted to tell him that the roofer was going to put the roof on the garage on Monday so they were going to stay until Tuesday. Was that all right with him? Of course it was. He was fine. He didn't mention the bird feeder because he wanted to surprise Millie.

After lunch he drank two bottles of beer and watched television for a while. Then he got the truck out and drove around for several hours. It had been some time since he had done that. He hadn't realized how much the area had changed since Kate had died.

He ate supper and went to bed early. He missed Elleen and the kids.

On Monday he took the truck into Russells Point and had the oil changed at Buck's garage. When it was finished he wanted to talk to Buck for a while but Buck was too busy. John bought a paper and took it back to the cabin. He ate lunch. Then he read the paper and worked the crossword puzzle. He got his pipe out and sat on the front porch and smoked it. The tobacco seemed a little dry. Before he put the pipe away he soaked a little piece of tissue in water and stuck it in the canister where he kept his tobacco. After that he got out the sweeper and cleaned the whole cabin. It didn't need it. Elleen kept the place so clean you could eat off the floor. But she would notice that he had cleaned it anyway. She was so neat and orderly, the exact opposite of Dan. That was probably why they got along so well.

When John went to bed that night he lay awake for some time thinking about seeing the two kids the next morning. Right before he drifted off he thought about Moni. He wondered what she was doing.

Elleen didn't get there until after lunch and Dan was with her and the kids. When John saw Dan he was genuinely pleased. Although he would never admit it, even to himself, he probably liked Dan the most of any of the people his children had married. He always looked forward to seeing him. But the first thing he thought of now was that Moni would be back on Tuesday and if Dan was there John might not be able to go to the park to meet her. It turned out though that Dan had to attend a conference in Columbus on Tuesday, Wednesday, and Thursday. He was going to take Friday off and spend a long weekend at the cabin. John showed the kids the bird feeder and they both wanted to take charge of keeping it filled with seed. Eventually a schedule was worked out so that they could share responsibility.

On Tuesday Elleen was in the kitchen looking at some of her mother's cook books when she heard someone come in the front door.

"Is anyone home?" Elleen was sure she recognized the voice.

"Tammy, is that you?" she called out. "I'm in the kitchen." But she didn't wait for the girl to find her. She put the book she was holding on the table and went into the living room. It was indeed Tammy who had come in. Tammy put the bag she had been holding on the floor and she and her aunt embraced each other warmly. "How did you get here?" Elleen wanted to know.

"Oh, it wasn't hard," Tammy explained. A friend of mine from the college was going to a conference in Columbus and he gave me a ride."

"I'll bet it's the same conference that Dan is going to. What's his name?"

"Oh, Elleen, do you really want to know?" asked Tammy. "You may never see him. It was just a ride." Elleen laughed at the girl. It was so typical of her. She never seemed to take anything, or anyone, seriously. And yet Elleen knew that Tammy was much shrewder than she seemed. She was always keenly aware of what went on around her. And for someone her age she had an extraordinary amount of self-confidence. But she didn't like small talk. She usually got right to the point.

"Where's Bin?" she asked looking around for her grandfather.

"He's at the park," Elleen told her.

"What park is that?" Tammy asked.

"It's a little place on the way to Russells Point," Elleen explained. "He goes over there a lot especially in the afternoon. I think mostly he sits and thinks about grandma. Or maybe he watches all the little kids and remembers when we were all growing up."

"Why doesn't he take your kids with him?"

"Sometimes he does. It's a bit of a walk for them. And I don't think there is very much for them to do there anyway."

"Do you think I could find it by myself?"

"Yes, I think so. It's right on the road. You know I think there is a sign, but right now I can't remember." Elleen closed her eyes and tried to recall what the entrance to the little park looked like. She couldn't. "Were you going to walk?" She asked Tammy. "You could have taken our car except Dan has it."

"I thought I could take Bin's truck. Do you think he would mind?" Tammy wondered.

"Did you know it is a stick?" Elleen asked her.

"Sure, Aunty. Don't you think I can drive a stick? Remember I'm almost in college now." Tammy teased her aunt.

"Oh, yes," Elleen said rolling her eyes. "You college kids can do anything. I forgot." They both laughed. "Put your bag upstairs while I see if I can find some keys for you."

Fortunately John had backed the old Dodge truck into the driveway so Tammy was able to drive it out going forward. It jumped a little when she put it in gear but the engine didn't stall. Elleen was standing on the porch watching and Tammy saw her make a face. Tammy waved at her as she pulled out onto the road.

When she got all the way to Russells Point she realized she had missed the park so she turned around and went back. This time she noticed the Logan County sign that was partly hidden by some bushes. She pulled slowly in and found the parking lot. She parked the big truck and turned off the ignition, rather pleased with the fact that she had had no driving problems. She could see no one and sat there for a few minutes wondering what to do next. Finally she opened the door and climbed down from the cab. She made sure she had the keys in her hand before she locked the door.

There was a narrow path that led off through the trees and since it appeared to be the only way to get into the park she started along it. She had not gone far when she went around a bend and saw the area with the benches. She stopped to look for her grandfather and saw him almost at once. She started to call to him and run forward but then she noticed Moni and stopped. There was something about the scene which made her back up around the bend, hoping that they had not noticed her. But there did not seem to be much danger of that.

At first Tammy could not tell what it was about the two figures on the bench that caused her to stop. They were sitting as far apart as they could get, one at each end. And they were not touching each other. In fact they both seemed to be making an effort not to, neither reaching out in any way. Nevertheless they inclined slightly toward each other and each seemed engrossed in what the other was saying. There was absolutely nothing wrong with what Tammy saw but it seemed so out of character for her grandfather. And from where Tammy stood the girl looked so much younger than John that what she appeared to be witnessing did not seem reasonable. She backed up even farther, making certain that she could not be discovered. She knew she was spying on her grandfather, but she didn't know what else to do. She didn't want to go back and tell Elleen that she couldn't find the park. And she felt that if she allowed herself to be seen by John and his companion he would be embarrassed.

Moni had begun to realize just how much she had missed seeing John. What she could not understand was why. To herself she acknowledged that he was an old man. He might have looked younger than his actual age, but it was still obvious that he was long past middle age. Could it be that he reminded her of her father that much? She did not think so. Her father had died when she was in her teens. She tried to imagine what he had been like. The images she had of him were very graphic but she could not associate them in any way with the man who sat there in front of her on the other end of the bench. What she did feel was that he was interested in her, and that he was interested in her as a woman.

Moni did not date much. She thought that she was not beautiful, a little overweight too. Because she was so conscious of this she had at first worried that men would not like her. She had been so eager to be appreciated that it had become obvious and seemed to discourage the young men she had liked. Then, realizing how appearing anxious had not worked, she tried to change and started to seem indifferent, which had not helped either. Finally she had decided she would probably never meet anyone she would want to marry and who would also want to marry her.

John could only think of one thing and that was that he enjoyed the company of this young girl. He did not think that there was anything wrong with the way he thought about her because he told himself that his thoughts about her were only platonic. He would not allow himself to think about her in any other way.

The two of them talked intently about things neither of them really cared about, but which kept them from talking about anything personal. Before Moni left they agreed to begin taking turns bringing lunch for the two of them and eating together. There were many places in the amusement park where Moni could get something for both of them to eat. John, who of course would have more time, could go wherever he wanted to.

When Moni finally got up to leave and they said goodbye they still did not touch. They did not even shake hands.

Tammy, feeling she was doing something dishonest, hid in some bushes along the path as Moni went past. As soon as Moni was gone Tammy approached her grandfather. At first he seemed apprehensive. Was that a guilty look on his face, thought Tammy? She hugged him with genuine affection and told him how glad she was to see him. He seemed relieved and asked her to sit down. He asked her how she had gotten there and laughed when she told him. "Well," he said, "You can drive us back and let me see how good you are."

They sat and talked for a while, he about the park and how often he went there, she about what she had been doing since she had last seen him.

When they got back to the cabin she pulled into the driveway instead of backing in the way he had done and just before they got out of the truck she said, "Bin, I saw the girl."

"What...I...," he began and then stopped, taken completely by surprise.

"Don't, Bin," she said. "You don't need to tell me anything at all. It's no one's business but your's anyway."

He thought about it for a few moments before he said, "Actually there isn't much to tell. We meet each other in the park and talk. That's really all there is to it. And I'm not sure whether there could be anything more, or whether I would want there to be. Do you believe me?"

She looked into his eyes and she was sure she could tell he was being as honest with her as he could be. "Yes, Bin. I believe you. But it wouldn't make any difference anyway. No one will ever know anything about this from me. And I intend to forget it unless you bring it up again sometime."

He took her hand in his. "Tammy, you are much older than your years."

"Oh, Bin," she told him, "that's the nicest thing you could have said to me. I want to be treated like a grown up. Let's go in." Then she stopped him one more time and put her hand on his arm. She grinned and said, "Oh, Did I forget to tell you? I thought she was very cute." Then she got out of the truck and went in, leaving her grandfather to shake his head and smile.

Tammy did not see Moni again. For the rest of the week she ignored the fact that John was gone for several hours in the middle of the day. At the end of the week Dan came back from Columbus and spent the weekend with them. On Sunday evening he went back to Cincinnati and Tammy went with him.

John and Moni had seen each other on the last three days but on Saturday John had stayed at the cabin with his grandchildren. He was sorry to see both Dan and Tammy go home. He knew he would see Dan again before long, but he was never sure when he would see Tammy. He spent a good deal of time with her but they never discussed Moni and it really did seem as though she had forgotten all about what she has seen at the park.

All during the next week John and Moni had shared lunch in the park and talked. They sat closer together on the bench but still never touched each other. On Friday all morning it had looked like rain but no rain had been predicted. Neither John nor Moni had brought an umbrella and both were surprised when, just as they were leaving, there was a loud clap of thunder and without further warning the rain poured down on them. Before they got to Moni's car in the lot they were both soaked. They sat in the car with water dripping on the seat and running onto the floor. It was still raining heavily.

Moni looked at John and noted that his hat was so wet the brim was turned down and the entire thing had lost its shape. She said, "I don't think you ought to walk home like that. Can I drive you?"

"Let's just wait a little longer if that's okay. Maybe it will stop," John answered.

"I have a better idea," she said without looking at him. "Let's go to my apartment and try to dry off some. We can get something hot to drink. If I call work and tell them what happened they will understand." Then she looked at him. "I don't have to tell them I wasn't by myself."

John didn't say anything. He didn't want to go home soaking wet because he knew Elleen would be upset with him. He would rather try to get dry somehow and tell her he had managed to stay out of the rain. While he was thinking about it Moni started the engine and drove out of the parking lot. "I don't live very far from here," she told him.

Moni's apartment consisted of a small kitchen, a sitting room, bedroom and bath in the basement of a house owned by a middle aged woman who worked with Moni. She parked in the driveway and unlocked the side door. As soon as they were inside she called the amusement park and told them where she was and that she would be in as soon as she could change her clothes and dry her hair. She was told not to hurry. She went into her bedroom and quickly changed her clothes. When she came out she had a robe and a towel in her hands.

John was standing in the middle of the sitting room. He no longer dripped but his clothes were so wet they stuck to him. He grinned at her. "I'll bet I look like a wet hen don't I?" he asked.

"More like a wet rooster," she answered. "Look, I have my dad's old robe. I kept it just to have something familiar of his. I think it should fit you. Go in my bedroom and take all your clothes off and put this robe on. I'll put our things in Betty's dryer. They should dry in half an hour."

John said, "Do you think you should dry our clothes together?"

Moni laughed. "I was going to. Why? Do you think there is something wrong with that?"

"Well no," he lied. He really did but he didn't know what it was. He just didn't think their clothes should be together in the dryer, at least not their underwear. But he didn't know how to say it. He looked at the robe. "I'll feel funny running around here with just this on," he admitted.

She made a face. "You probably will look funny," she told him. "But I won't look at you if you don't want me to. Okay?"

He smiled weakly. "I guess," he said and walked reluctantly into her bedroom.

John emptied his pockets and put the contents on Moni's bed. He took his shoes off and put them on the floor. Everything else he removed and rolled into a bundle, with his shirt on the outside, before drying himself with the towel and putting on the robe. He did not take his scapular from around his neck.

He walked back into the living room. Moni started to laugh at his bedraggled mein and then remembered she had promised not to look at him. She took the bundle, noting that he had hidden his underwear under his shirt. With both of their wet clothes she went upstairs.

John wanted to sit down on the couch but the robe came just below his knees and it made him feel uncomfortable. Finally he did sit down but when Moni came back he stood up.

"I'm going to make some hot chocolate," she said. "We can drink it while our clothes dry." She went into the kitchen.

When she came back she had a small tray with two mugs and a pot on it. She poured chocolate into the mugs and gave one to John. She said, "Be careful, it's hot." John laughed and she asked, "What's so funny?"

He held the mug with both hands, feeling the warmth of it. "It's just that one of my daughters says things like that to me all the time. I thought it was because she is so used to saying it to her kids. But I was wrong. Maybe it's something all women say." He took a sip of the chocolate. "Boy," he said, "that is hot."

He started to put his mug on the floor to let it cool. Moni noticed that he seemed uncomfortable. She said, "Wait a minute. I have a little table."

Carrying her own mug she went into the bedroom and came back with a small table which she unfolded and put in front of him so that he could put his mug on it. she said, "I hardly ever get to use it." She went back into the bedroom and got her own chocolate from where she had left it. When she came back she sat down on the couch so she could set her mug on the little table too. "There," she said.

As they sat there drinking the chocolate they both slowly realized that they were sitting closer together than they ever had before. Moni put her hand on John's. "For a while," she told him, "my hands were cold. Your hand is very warm."

He didn't pull his hand away. He said, "It wasn't very cool today anyway, was it?"

"No," she answered, "it wasn't." Then she said, "Don't you like me?"

"What?" he gasped. "What do you mean? I like you very much."

"But you never touch me. You always stay so far away."

John took his hand from under hers. He turned and looked at her. "Moni," he said. "How old are you?"

"I'm nearly thirty," she told him.

He laughed. "Do you realize that I am nearly old enough to be your grandfather? I probably am old enough."

"Yes," she agreed, "I know you are a lot older than me. But we get along so well. Let me ask you something. Didn't you ever want to kiss me?"

John suddenly stood up and turned around so he could look at her directly. Moni could tell he was struggling to say something. Finally he blurted out, "Moni, I have wanted to kiss you since the first day I met you. I looked at your mouth and thought it was so sweet and soft it would be like kissing a rosebud. But I was afraid to." He walked to the other side of the room and turned around again.

"What are you afraid of?" she asked in such a low voice he could hardly hear her.

"I'm afraid that if I ever kiss you I will fall in love with you," he answered in a voice almost as low.

Moni stood up too. Slowly she walked over to where he stood until her chest was against his. "Try it," she said softly. "Try it and see."

Very slowly John brought his hands up from his sides. Bending over he gently pulled her head closer to him. He closed his eyes and tenderly put his mouth on hers. They stood like that for several moments and she put her arms around him. He took his mouth from hers and straightened and put his arms around her shoulders. She turned her head so that one ear was on his chest.

"I can hear your heart beating," she said. "It's beating very fast." He said nothing but held her close. Then she said, "See? You should have done that before."

He took her by the shoulders and held her away from him so he could look at her face. "Oh, Moni," he said, "I'm an old man and you are a beautiful young girl. It just doesn't seem right."

"What if I told you I love you?" she asked him.

"I would tell you you were crazy," he answered.

"In that case I must be crazy," she said.

Then John kissed her again, this time almost fiercely. She sighed and opened her mouth a little.

When he stopped she said, "Now what should we do?"

He put his face in her hair. "What do you mean?" he asked in a muffled voice.

"I mean have you ever thought about getting married again?"

John's hands dropped to his side and he stepped back from her. He shook his head and laughed. "I must say," he told her, "you sure don't mind saying what you think."

"Well, have you?" she persisted.

"Do you mean marry you? Do you mean you'd marry me?" he asked. "You really would?"

"Yes," she assured him. "Oh, I know there will be a lot of people who will roll their eyes and snicker. But I don't care. Do you?"

John thought about Tammy. Then he thought about the rest of his family. He wondered what they would say. He didn't think they would approve. He couldn't think of anyone who would.

He thought of something else. "I guess we would have to take pre-Cana instruction. Now that would be interesting. And every time we went to a restaurant the waiters would probably ask you if you wanted to order for your grandfather."

"That sounds like fun to me," she said. Then she paused to listen. "I didn't hear the buzzer but I think our clothes should be dry by now. I'll go get them."

She went back upstairs. When she returned she had all the things folded. She held his out to him. "Do you want me to help you get dressed?" she asked impishly. But he was embarrassed.

"No," he said gruffly. "You wait here." He went into the bedroom and put his clothes on. He left the robe on her bed and put all the things he had left there back into his pockets. He looked into her mirror and used the edge of his hand to smooth down the hair around the edge of his head.

When she saw him again she said, "Well, now you look much more dignified."

John wanted to leave then but she talked him into sitting down on the couch with her. "If we got married," she pointed out, "we could do this all the time." She put her head on his shoulder. He could not decide how to consider her. He could not make up his mind whether he should think of her as a woman or as a child. He twisted sideways so he could look at her face. She pulled her feet up under her and sat facing him. He held her face in his hands and kissed her.

"You have the prettiest face I have ever seen," he told her.

"MMM," she murmured. "I don't believe you. But I like to hear it."

John knew he should either go back to the cabin or call Elleen. But he didn't want to leave Moni and he didn't want to call because he could think of nothing to tell Elleen without avoiding the truth. Moni turned around and put her head on his shoulder again. He held one of her hands in both of his. He decided that he indeed loved her very much, but he could not decide what he should do about it.

"Well, what are we going to do?" Moni asked him. "Are you going to marry me?"

John smiled. To her it probably seemed simple. Just get married and live happily ever after. The trouble was that they had no idea how long "ever" after was going to be. It occurred to him that when he was ninety years old Moni would only be fifty. He wondered how healthy he would be then. How much care would he need?

"When you are fifty years old do you really want to be stuck with taking care of a ninety year old man?" he asked her.

"Yes," she said, "if you're the ninety year old man."

Finally John was able to come to at least part of a decision. He felt that Moni was serious about everything she had said to him. He believed that she at least thought she loved him. And he knew that he loved her. She made him feel as if all the years had been swept away and he was a young man again. But he thought that neither of them had thought much past the present. No matter how young he felt, he was still an old man, and nothing could change that. It was a fact they both had to consider.

"Let's do this," he said. "Let's not see each other this weekend. I want you to think about what it would be like living with someone who has different tastes in music, in food, in clothes, in just about everything. We don't even think the same about religion."

"But we are both Catholic," she interrupted.

"Oh, I know," he answered. "But you probably will welcome all the council changes. And I do not. And on the other hand maybe I am wrong about that. Maybe you will be just as old fashioned about it as me. There are still all the other things. And I will always be forty years older than you are. Anyway let's think about this over the weekend. If both of us want to, on Monday we will go see Father Tombrinker. We will ask him what to do next."

"I just thought of something," she told him. "I won't be here on Monday. I have to do some work in our Cincinnati office on Monday. But I will be back on Tuesday. Would Tuesday be too late?"

"It sounds like you're afraid I might not last until Tuesday," he teased.

"No," she answered, "I just don't want to wait. I want to marry you. I don't want to put it off. I won't feel any different next week."

"I don't think I will either," he said. "I don't want you to get away."

They decided they would not meet in the park on Tuesday because it would be too public for what they wanted to discuss. John was to come to her apartment and they would begin making arrangements and consider how they would tell their families. Moni drove John nearly to the cabin and kissed him goodbye. Then he went on down the road while she turned around and went to work.

It was a long weekend for John. He had told Elleen that he was late because he had had to find shelter with someone else and after the rain stopped couldn't find anyway to leave. He could tell she would have liked for him to provide a few more details but she had not insisted.

John tried to make the time go faster by spending as much of it as he could with his grandchildren. It helped that Aloysius and his wife and their children, all three of them, Dennis, Robert, and Clint, between the ages of seven and five, came out on Saturday morning. They were on their way from Chicago to Charleston to visit Pam's parents. And they had gotten Polly and her husband John to come up from Lexington and bring along their daughter, Joan. Joan was too much older to have much in common with Aloysius' kids, actually twelve years older than Dennis, but she said it didn't matter. She had reading to do for the classes she would begin in the fall at the University of Kentucky. It turned out she didn't get much reading done after all but she didn't seem to care. They all went to church together at St. Mary Of The Woods church on Sunday morning. John thought about asking Father Tombrinker if he would be available on Tuesday to talk to someone about a wedding. But there was really not much opportunity and he really didn't want to do it anyway. He had no doubt that he and Moni would eventually be talking to him. But he was not anxious to do it. There would be too much explaining to do.

Everyone waited until the middle of the morning on Monday to leave. Elleen's kids, as usual, were sorry to see their cousins go and, in order to help them get over it, John and Elleen drove them to Lake St. Mary for a picnic in the afternoon. It was nearly dark when they got back.

In the morning John asked Elleen if there was anything she wanted from Bellefontaine because he was going there for some garden things. Actually this was stretching the truth. He wanted to get Moni some flowers. Elleen said she could think of nothing she needed.

John bought Moni a dozen coral roses. He got a card and filled it out and fastened it to the blooms. The clerk at the store asked if he wanted them delivered but he told her he would deliver them himself. He was very happy when he left the store.

When John passed the park it was nearly noon. It was only a few minutes later when he parked his truck in the driveway next to the entrance to Moni's apartment. He was surprised to see that instead of Moni's little blue Plymouth in the driveway there was a slightly newer and bigger Ford. He waited for a few minutes, expecting the Plymouth to appear any minute. He was getting more and more excited. Perhaps, he thought, her car was at the garage being serviced and was waiting for him inside. He took his flowers and got out of the truck. He pushed the doorbell next to her door. Nothing happened. He pushed it again. After he rang the bell three times and when he was ready to turn away the door opened just a crack. When the middle aged lady who stood there saw him she opened the door all the way.

"I'm sorry," she apologized, "I can't always hear this bell in my place. Did you want to see someone?"

"Well, yes," John said, starting to feel as though something was wrong. "Is Miss Baller here?"

The woman didn't answer him right away. She looked curiously at his face. Finally she asked, "Are you a friend of hers?"

John began to feel uneasy. Clearly there was something wrong. "Well, yes," he said haltingly. "I am a friend. Is something wrong?"

"You obviously haven't heard," she said. "Please come in. I am Betty Fraly. I was her landlady." John noticed that she said she "was" Moni's landlady. He felt the blood leaving his head. He followed the woman up some stairs and into her living room. She sat on the couch her feet together and her hands folded in her lap. He sat down across from her. He was glad to do so because he thought he might be about to faint.

She looked at him for nearly a minute. For the first time John noticed that she looked like she had been crying. She said, "There is no easy way to say this. Moni is dead." She reached into her pocket for a handkerchief and covered her eyes with it. "I'm sorry," she said, trying not to sob. "I thought a lot of Moni. She was almost like a daughter."

John felt more than ever that he would faint. He fought off the feeling and sat there, not able to speak. He wanted to ask how it had happened, but he could not. The woman sobbed a few times. At length she seemed to gain control of herself. She asked, "Was she a friend of your family's?"

"In a way she was," John answered. "I haven't known her very long actually." Finally he managed to ask, "Can you tell me how she died?"

She began to sob again. Finally she said, "It was a terrible thing, just an awful twist of fate." The woman looked down quietly for a few seconds. "She died of shock," she explained. "she had just gotten home in Cincinnati last Friday when it happened. There was no one in the house and she went down to the basement, no one knows for what, and she musr have tripped at the bottom of the steps and broken her ankle. It was a rather severe break but the worst part was that she couldn't get back upstairs and no one could hear her call for help." Mrs. Fraly had to stop again and she twisted her hands in her lap. Finally she blurted, "She died of shock. They found her finally but it was too late. If only she had not been alone. And she seemed so happy about something, no one knows what it was." With another violent sob she added, "And now no one will ever know."

John now felt a wave of grief sweep over him. The idea that Moni would still be alive if he had not let her go home alone tormented him. He thought he would cry but he fought it with all his strength. He thought it would be too hard to explain. They both sat there in silence. From another room John could hear a clock ticking. He thought it was probably a grandfather clock. He was torn by an impulse to get up and go look at it. He wanted to do anything that would give him something to think of besides Moni. But he could not get up. All he could do was sit there and think of Moni, Moni, Moni. The name blocked everything else out of his mind.

He took a deep breath. "The funeral," he whispered. "Can you tell me?" his voice drifted off.

She looked at her watch. "It is going on now," she told him. "I wanted to go but I couldn't. Moni and I were working on something that had to be taken care of today. Oh, I should have gone. I was no good at all, no good at all. I had to come home. I should have gone." Her whole body was racked by sobs. Then she said, "I'm sorry. Can I get you something. You don't look well. Have you been ill?"

John hardly heard what she said. He looked at her and slowly the words penetrated his mind. "Yes," he said. "I have not been well. But I'll be all right." Still they sat but nothing more was said. It seemed to John that there was nothing more to say. He stood up. "I'm sorry," he said, "Moni must have meant a lot to you. I'm sorry." He tried to think of something else to say but could not. "I'm sorry," was all he could think of. She let him out the front door.

John walked around to the driveway and got into his truck. He backed out and started to drive down the street. He had gone more than a block when he realized he was going in the wrong direction. He steered into a parking lot and turned around. As he came out onto the street again he noticed two young boys playing on the sidewalk. He got out of the truck and called to them. They came over to where he stood but stayed some distance away. He asked, "Do you two live around here?"

One of them, the bigger of the two, answered, "Down the street."

John asked, "Are you brothers?"

"Yeah, we are," the other youngster told him.

"Is your mother at home?" John asked.

"Yeah, she's home," the same one said.

John held out the flowers. "Here," he said, "give these to her. Tell her you got them from an old man." The two boys looked at each other and laughed nervously. Slowly they both came closer and one of them held out his hand. Then John said, "Wait a minute." He pulled the card off the flowers and threw it into a trash can which stood by his truck. Then he gave the boy the flowers. He got back into his truck and drove off. How strange, he thought, he loved Moni but he would never really know what even her legs looked like. He had not loved Aimee and he could even remember what her breasts were like.

The boy who did not have the flowers reached into the receptacle and took out the card John had thrown there. "You want to know what it says?" he asked his brother. The other boy nodded. "It says, 'Moni rhymes with money. And it rhymes with honey, too. Love, John.' I wonder what that means?" He threw the card back into the trash can.

Chapter XII

He was surprised when he started to put the blanket on the little horse because for some reason the pinto stood completely still instead of shying the way she usually did. He always assumed she acted that way because when he put a bridle and saddle on her she knew they were going somewhere that might be exciting. Now the thought came to him that she must realize he didn't know where they were going, only that they were leaving. He looked out the window of the old barn and saw the bunkhouse which had been his home for the last eight years. It still would be too if it hadn't been for the note he found on the door when he came in from the range the night before. "1. Either clean yer boots or take em off before you come in here. 2. Make sure the bed close gets warshed evry week. 3. Change yer socks and yer drawers at least two times evry week and get em warshed." There was no name on the note but he knew it was from Darcy, the girl Stanley had brought back from town the week before, and they would all have to do what it said. Stanley was the foreman and he and the girl were probably going to get married. He led the pinto outside just as Stanley rode up and jumped off the big roan he always used when the grey mare was in a family way. Stanley said, "Where you goin' Deke?" And Deke climbed up on the little pinto and then said, "I ain't rightly sure." He shot a stream of tobacco juice toward the fence, away from the horses, and added, "But I'm goin away from here, that's fer sure." As he clicked his tongue and the pinto started to walk out of the barnyard Stanley said, "Why Deke? Somethin' happen?" And over his shoulder Deke said, "You done changed the rules. I don't cotton to somebody changin' the rules after somebody gets used to the way things was." He touched his spurs gently to the horse's sides and she began to trot across the field.

From Nothing's Forever, by Molly N. Kennedy.

*   *   *

May 1975

Father Norman O'Maury turned a page in his breviary and continued to read the Latin prayers. Shortly it would be time for him to go to the rectory for dinner. He had heard about two dozen confessions which was average for Saturday evening. The door opened and he turned off the light and put the book on his lap before he opened the slide. A mild scent of perfume drifted through the screen and a soft voice said, "Bless me father for I have sinned. My last confession was about three months ago." There was no sound for what seemed like half a minute. Father Norman was about to ask if there was a problem when he heard a deep sigh. Then the voice blurted, "My husband uses birth control when we have relations. Father, we can't help it. What should we do?"

"Why do you say you can't help it?" he asked her.

She said, "We already have three children and we can't take care of any more."

"Have you tried rhythm?"

"Yes, father."

"And?"

"Well, it didn't work."

"Is your doctor a Catholic?"

"Yes."

"Have you discussed this with him?"

"Yes."

"And what did he say."

"He said he could tie my tubes."

"That is against the laws of the church."

She almost whispered, "Yes, father, I know it is."

"Your doctor should know that too."

"He does, father. He said sometimes it is allowed. Isn't that true?"

Father Norman frowned and shook his head. But she couldn't see him. "Under rare circumstances it might be allowed. But it would never be allowed if the intention is to prevent conception. Is your husband a Catholic?"

"Yes, father."

"How does he feel about this?"

"He doesn't want any more children, but he doesn't want to do anything wrong. He doesn't go to communion."

From the other side of the screen Father Norman heard her weeping quietly. It tore at his heart. He could not tell if this woman was from his parish, but he knew dozens like her, sincere young Catholics, desiring to please God, but also wanting the same things that their friends had. And they felt that one desire stood in the way of the other. And didn't they have friends who thought the same way they did? Some women just didn't seem to get pregnant as easily. And some men could afford bigger families. Why were they punished for wanting to do what was right? It wasn't fair. How many times had he heard that?

He asked, "Have you asked your doctor to help you with your rhythm schedule?"

"Yes, father. He said that never works."

"That is not true. I know many people for whom it works."

"I went to a priest once who told me that the church only expects us to follow our conscience. Is that true?"

"Yes," said Father Norman. "But you must make certain that you have formed a right conscience."

"What does that mean?" she asked.

"Essentially it means that you have used all the sources available to you to help you decide what is right. In your case one of the sources is the teaching of the church. And the church is pretty clear on the subject."

"Then what you mean is if we practice birth control we can't go to the sacraments. We have to do what the church says, not what our conscience tells us. Isn't that right?"

The priest took a deep breath. More than a sigh, it was almost a gasp. The little confessional had become a box that kept closing in on him. It got closer and closer yet never quite squashed the life from him. He felt that if he didn't escape soon he would smother.

How could he explain this thing? To him the theology, the moral philosophy seemed so simple. But he could not possibly explain it to her in a few minutes. And she probably didn't want an explanation anyway. She wanted him to tell her that she had done the best she and her husband could, that God did not expect them to do the impossible. If, in their good conscience, they were convinced they could do no more, then they were not expected to do more. And God will understand.

But God would not understand. In fact understanding was not an activity of God, rather God was understanding itself. More to the point even, God made the rules and we didn't have to understand them, just follow them. To the woman taken in adultery Jesus did not say, " you are forgiven because you don't realize that what you have been doing is wrong." He told her she would be forgiven if she resolved to sin no more.

"No," Father Norman said, "you must in the end follow your conscience. If you truly believe you have exhausted every means at arriving at the truth and you are still not convinced, you must follow your heart. But you should be aware that you may be saying that you know more on the subject than the church, and all the teachers and theologians in the church."

"But," she said, "a friend of mine has a book that has a lot of writing by theologians in the church who do not think that birth control is wrong. I read it."

"Ah, yes," he answered, "but the church has said that they are wrong and condemned such teaching."

"Then why aren't they thrown out of the church? Why are they allowed to keep on teaching and writing books like that?"

"It's called maintaining dialogue," he answered dryly. "The church wants to give them every possible opportunity to change their ways."

There was silence for a little while. Then she asked, "Is that all then?"

He said, "Yes. Remember that in the end God is your judge. I am not. Do the very best you can." He could not bring himself to say, "and He will understand," as he knew so many other priests could bring themselves to say. He knew that by telling these people that they were not committing a sin, the priests were taking the sin on their own shoulders and throwing themselves on the mercy of Jesus. He hoped it worked for them, but he could not do it himself. He gave her a penance and then said the words of absolution.

"Thank you, father," she said, sounding as though a great weight had been lifted from her shoulders. But, as she left the confessional, he felt as though a greater weight had descended on his.

*　　　　　*　　　　　*

June 1975

Billy and Ann were back from their honeymoon. They had seen Jill as soon as they arrived in Cincinnati on Saturday morning and now had come out to the lake on Sunday to see John, and Elleen's family, and whomever else was there. Actually Elleen's family consisted of Millie who was fourteen years old and had just graduated from the eighth grade. The other two, Libby, an eighteen year old high school graduate, and Danny who was just sixteen, both would be out on Wednesday with their father.

Elleen had been teasing Ann about writing thank you notes and, when Ann had asked Elleen why Billy didn't have to help, Elleen said she thought he should and told him to get busy. Billy made a face but it was good natured and he sat down at the kitchen table and the two of them got started. Ann opened the box of cards and bits of wrapping paper with notes on them which she had kept as wedding present reminders so they wouldn't have to try to remember who gave them which gifts.

Millie came in and sat and watched for a while. Billy said, "you want to help?"

Millie said, "How much will you pay me?"

Elleen, who was standing at the sink cleaning strawberries, heard her. She said, "Millie! What a thing to say."

Millie laughed and told her mother, "Oh, mom, I was only kidding. I don't mind helping. There isn't much else to do anyway. The water is too cool to go swimming."

The three of them developed a system. Millie took a printed thank you card and an envelope and put them with one of the notes which would associate the proper guest with the gift. She gave these to either Billy or Ann who consulted the notation before writing a short message on the card thanking the person for the gift, signing both their names, and addressing the envelope. Then Millie sealed the envelopes and stamped them. They were finished in about an hour.

Elleen glanced at the old wall clock and then at them. "It sure didn't take you very long," she pointed out. See what you can do if you work together?"

"We couldn't have done it without Millie, either," Billy added. "Tell you what. Ann and I are going to Wapakoneta for a while, maybe to a movie. Since you were such a big help we'll take you with us if you want to go."

"I'd like to go," Millie told them. "I haven't been to Wapa for a while. And Ann can tell me all about your trip."

"What about you Aunt Elleen," Ann asked. "Do you want to come with us?"

"No," Elleen smiled. "I still have some things I wanted to finish and I think I should stay here with dad. He's still out in the back. Every year it takes him a little longer to finish spading up his garden in the beginning of summer."

"How old is Bin now?" Millie wanted to know.

"Oh, he's seventy two," Elleen told them after she thought a while. "But it isn't his age that slows him down. It's just that every year he wants to change something, put in something new, you know. So he digs for a while, and then he gets out all his catalogs and looks at them for a while, and then he goes back to digging. If he didn't have so many catalogs to look at it wouldn't take nearly as long and he gets at least one new one every year. And every year the catalogs are bigger."

Then she added, after thinking for a half minute, "But there is something you can do for me. I'm making strawberry shortcake and we could use some whipped cream. Your grandfather likes shortcake with whipped cream and so do I. As a matter of fact I guess all of you do. Maybe you could stop and get some on your way back?" And she added, "Do you think you could get back early enough that we could eat it before we go to bed?"

Billy laughed. "Gee, it's only the middle of the afternoon. I think we could handle that unless you intend to go to bed before it gets dark."

"Well don't forget how far it is to Wapakoneta," his Aunt Elleen reminded him. You'd better get going."

"I remember all right," Billy reassured her.

Ann had an idea. "Aunt Elleen, if you have so many things to do why don't you let us bring something home for supper? We could stop and get chicken at Bernie's. Isn't that the name of the place Billy and I went to the night I let him talk me into marrying him?"

They all laughed at that, Billy the hardest. Elleen admitted with a smile, "You know something? I do have a lot to do. That would be a great idea. Let me get my purse."

"No," Ann insisted, "Let Billy pay for it. Remember we're still on vacation sort of."

"Well, I'm not exactly sure what that has to do with it and you two should be learning how to save your money. But I don't want to hurt your feelings. I'll let you have one last fling."

As they were on their way down Pokey they saw Father Norman driving his car in the other direction. They waved and he waved back but kept on going.

Billy said, "It's a little late for him to be coming out here. But maybe he had a baptism or something this afternoon."

Millie asked, "Did you notice he wasn't smiling. Usually he smiles a lot. I wonder if something is wrong."

After the three had left Elleen stopped for a moment and looked once more at the clock on the wall, but this time she wasn't looking to see what time it was. She had just remembered something she hadn't thought about for a long time. That old clock had been Kate's but it had been given to her by Mary who had gotten it from her own mother's mother. Elleen did a quick calculation and realized that meant the clock had come from her own great, great grandmother, making a connection that stretched back through five generations. And who knows where it had come from to start with? The connection might even be from much farther back than that. The idea that she was looking at something so old, something that had been used by so many people in so many different circumstances overwhelmed her. The thought made the tick, tick, tick, tick so measured, so unaltered and stable, seem almost eternal and, because of that, somehow sacred. Mary, and Kate too, were both gone, and yet, to Elleen, looking at that ancient clock, it seemed they would never be gone.

Father Norman came through the front door rather quietly, not the way he usually came in. He stopped in the kitchen where Elleen was sitting on a chair, still looking at the old clock on the wall. He kissed her lightly on the cheek and squeezed her shoulders. Then he sat down at the table across from her and looked into her face without speaking. Elleen noticed there was something different about him but she could not identify what it was. He seemed to be looking for something.

Elleen asked, "Norman, is something wrong?"

He was thinking about something far away and her voice pulled him back to the kitchen, but he didn't answer right away. Then he smiled and shook his head. "I need to talk to dad about something. Is he here?"

When he smiled she decided there was nothing wrong. It had only been her imagination. "He's out in the yard working on his garden. He's been out there most of the morning and all afternoon since lunch. It's a little late in the season for him and maybe he intends to catch up."

Father Norman stood up. He said, "I'm going out and talk to him. I'll see you before I leave."

He went out the back door. Elleen realized that he had not even looked into the refrigerator. She was now convinced that something certainly was not right.

John leaned his spade against the picnic table and sat down. Seed and nursery catalogs were spread out all over the table top.

The old man took his hat off and put it on the corner of the seat. His shirt was a little damp in the back from perspiration but except for that he hardly looked as though he had been working.

John's garden was all the way in the rear of the fenced yard. As he glanced back there he saw in his mind where everything would go. As he had done year after year for a long time, he would try something that was appearing for the first time in one or the other of the catalogs lying on the table. He still liked to try new things.

He heard the door close and then footsteps approaching from the house. He turned around and when he saw Norman he smiled at the priest.

"Hi Norman," he called. "I didn't think you were coming today after it got past three o'clock. Did you have a baptism?"

"No, I just had something I wanted to take care of before I came over here." He sat down across from his dad. "Actually it was something I have been trying to decide and I finally made up my mind."

There were two wooden lawn chairs next to where John had been working. Norman pointed to them. He said, "Dad, let's go back there and sit. Is that okay with you? I want to tell you something."

The older man recognized something in the priests voice that alarmed him. He didn't say anything but he nodded his head. He picked his hat up from the seat and stood up. He walked toward the rear of the yard and sat on one of the chairs. Father Norman pulled the other chair around so that it faced the one which his dad occupied and sat also.

John said, "Okay, what is it you want to ask me? How much money do you need?" He was trying to introduce a little humor into the situation but he knew that Norman was not after money.

Norman looked directly into the older man's eyes. "I'm going to leave the priesthood," he told his father, and he heard the old man hold his breath, but only for an instant.

"Well," began John. "This is definite? You have made up your mind?"

Norman nodded his head once. He said, "Yes, I've made up my mind. Actually I made up my mind many times, one day one way and the next day the other way. But finally I realized that I was not doing a very good job. I have decided, this time for good. I should leave before I hurt someone I should be helping." Norman looked toward the house and then at his father. "I think I would like a beer. How would you like a beer?"

John smiled wryly. "I don't exactly feel like celebrating. But yes, I think I would like to have something to drink. My throat is very dry."

Norman walked slowly to the back door while his father sat, his hands in his lap, staring at the ground before him, lost in thought.

When Norman went into the kitchen Elleen was sweeping the floor. She said, "When I looked out the window a minute ago the two of you seemed to be discussing something very serious out there."

"We are," Norman admitted. "And I'll tell you about it later. I came in to get a couple of beers."

When Norman had sat back in his chair and he and his father had each taken a drink from his bottle of beer, he sat his on the arm of his chair. John asked simply, "Why?"

Norman shrugged. "There are a lot of reasons. I guess the biggest one is that I just don't enjoy it any longer, but that sounds so selfish, doesn't it? Maybe the best way to explain this is to say just what I said a few minutes ago. I am not able to do a very good job any more."

John held up his hand in the gesture that means "wait". "Does this have anything to do with Vatican II?" he asked.

"Oh, pop, you know it does. It has a lot to do with it. The church we have today is not the church I signed up to work with thirty years ago, not anything like it even. Sometimes I feel deserted by it."

"So do I," said John. "And it must be a lot harder on a priest who has to interpret all that nonsense for people who don't seem to care anymore anyway."

Norman took another sip of beer. "You're disappointed, aren't you, dad? That's the hardest thing about this. I know how important this was to you, how important the church is. I wanted you to be proud of me. I wanted to be such a success for you and mom. I wanted to so much. Now I guess you'll be ashamed of me won't you?"

"Ah, Norman, I could never think of you as a failure as long as you keep trying to do what is right, and I think you will always do that.

"What is a success anyway? Your mother and I raised a big family and we all stayed close. That is what I consider being a success. Other people might not think so but I do. It wasn't always easy. The house we lived in wasn't the nicest but it was big enough. And we always had enough to eat. We didn't need anything else." He stopped talking for a moment and looked at his son. He shook his head slowly as though he had just thought of something he wanted to say and he was considering how to say it best.

"Norman," he said, "Just look what you are able to do. You can call Jesus down on the altar at Mass. Not even the angels can do that and you have done it many times. And you have helped souls go to Heaven. I cannot imagine anything else a person could do that would be more of a success. I would rather do that than build the biggest bridge or sail the biggest ship, or anything else. But I was not good enough to be a Catholic priest."

"Stop it, dad," said Norman, irritation creeping into his voice. "I am not good enough to be a priest either. I thought I would be, but I'm not. And even worse, I don't know if I ever really understood what it is to be one. Oh, the part about saying Mass, and preaching sermons, baptisms and weddings, wearing fancy robes, all the pomp and circumstance, that I am good at. But speaking for God when what I have to tell someone is something he doesn't want to hear, that I'm not worth a damn for." His voice softened to little more than a whisper as the impatience left him.

"Why do these things happen to good people?" thought John. "why don't they just happen to people who aren't trying to do what they are supposed to?" He looked at Norman and his heart was wrenched by an intense feeling of affection. He could sense that Norman was very close to despair and he felt the desire to help him, but at the same time he knew that there was nothing he could do. Norman must find his own way through this problem.

At the same time John felt the strong need to help his son, he was confused by another thought. This man was a priest. He was supposed to be able to solve problems for other people. Why couldn't he solve his own? "If you are the Son of God come down from the cross." Isn't that what the thief had said to Jesus? But then he remembered the other thief had reprimanded the one who had taunted the Savior. And anyway Norman was not Jesus. Right now he was just John's little boy and he needed help. And unfortunately it was help John could not give him. He prayed silently, "Oh please dear God, what should I tell him?" But the voice that so often whispered in his ear was still today. John was on his own. Was the Lord testing him? Did He want to see if John had learned anything in all the years God had been leading him by the right road?

John asked quietly, "What do you have to do now?"

"First I will have to talk to the Provincial, Don Vogel. I will probably be told to take some time off and think it over. I guess they will want me to make a retreat. I may go down to Gethsemane for a week. But I know I won't change my mind. Then I will talk to the Archbishop in Cincinnati. I know him pretty well. In the end I will petition the Holy Father to be laicized. That will take a while. After that I will still be a priest but I will not be allowed to say Mass ever again." He added, "I will be allowed to hear someone's confession if he is dying."

Slowly a very strange realization began to impress itself on Norman. The thing that had been bothering him the most about what he was doing was not that he would have to face his provincial, or the Archbishop, or even that he would have to petition the Holy Father. To him the worst ordeal all along had been that he would have to tell his own father. It had always been that way, his mom and dad were always the ones he wanted to please. He always studied hard for an exam because he didn't want to tell them that he had not done well. Now it was just John.

Actually it had always been pretty much that way in fact. He had loved his mother the most of all. But it had been his father's approval he had always sought first. He didn't know why it had always seemed so important to him, but in the back of his mind there was always the feeling that if dad approved of whatever he was doing everyone else would like it as well. It didn't always work out that way but he always expected it to. Whenever the family had visited him at either of the seminaries it was always his mother about whom he had talked the most beforehand. But when everyone got out of the car it was always his dad's face he looked for first. Perhaps it was that he always felt that it was John who set the standards for the family. He really didn't know and until now he had never really thought about it. The strange thing was that John had never been demanding. His attitude had seemed to be that whatever they were happy with, as long as it was legal and not contrary to church law, was fine with him.

Now that Norman was talking to John about his leaving the priesthood the heavy weight that had been on his shoulders for so long seemed to be slipping away. But then he wondered if what he was doing was passing the weight onto his father's shoulders. Was it just like in the confessional? He knew that John always accepted the shortcomings and the disappointments of his children as at least partly his own responsibility. Norman wondered if John would now consider that Norman was a failure and, therefore, that John himself had failed.

Norman took another sip of his beer. The bottle was nearly empty. He said, "Dad, are you sure you don't think I'm a failure?"

John seemed startled by the question. He had been looking down at the ground, seemingly lost in thought. At Norman's question he looked up suddenly but he didn't answer him right away. He stared at his son for several heartbeats before he spoke. "No," he said slowly, then, "I said I thought you were a success. I still think so. I will never think you have failed. A failure is someone who tries to do something and gives up because he finds out it's too hard a thing for him to do."

"Well, don't you think that is what I'm doing?" Norman asked.

John leaned far forward in his seat and put his hand on Norman's shoulder. "No," he said quietly, "I don't, not if I understand what you have been telling me. I think you did what you set out to do and now that you are doing it you decided that it isn't what you wanted. I don't think it helped any that the rules were changed. After all being a priest now isn't what it used to be before Vatican II."

"What about the rest of the family?" Norman asked him. "Do you think they will be disappointed?"

"Oh, I think they will feel sorry for you because I think they all thought you were doing what you wanted to do. You know you always did a good job of making it seem that way. But they will like having you home more. And no one will think you have failed. They know what is important to the family. It is to love God, to love each other, and to show the little ones in the family what good is. You can still do that. And I think you will. It is a matter of being as good as you can, of helping the next generation to know what we have learned about good, and a matter of being a good example."

Norman drained his bottle and stood up. He didn't say anything but he held up the bottle and looked at his father with eyebrows raised in a question. John drained his glass also and held it out to the soon-to-be ex-priest. He smiled but not very broadly. He said, "Why don't you ask Elleen to come out. She must be dying of curiosity and I think it is time she knows, don't you?"

Norman smiled, also weakly, and nodded his head, sighing resignedly. "Yes," he agreed. "It is time everyone knew. I can use as much moral support from my family as I can get on this." He started off toward the house and John stretched out his legs in front of him, folded his arms against his chest and contemplated the ends of his old shoes.

A million thoughts seemed to hurry through John's brain, most of them questions, but none of them stopped long enough for resolution. "Has he really made up his mind? Will he be happy when it is all settled? Or is this something he will always regret? Should I have seen this coming? Would his mother have seen it coming? And what difference does that make? Is he just telling me all this to talk about it with someone or does he want me to try to talk him out of it? How will he get a job? Can I help him at all? Will he get married?...."

Of course it was the last question that was the most troubling to John. No matter what else Norman did most people would be sure he had left the priesthood because he had found it impossible to remain celibate. And perhaps that was true, but John was sure it was not.

It now occurred to John that this had been coming for a long time but he had not been able to see it. The outcome of the Council called Vatican II had upset many serious Catholics, John one of them, and they had complained as each new change was implemented but they still went to church. People like John, although they didn't like where their church seemed to be going, sometimes laughed about it because in the end it didn't seem very serious. The early changes in liturgy and regulation often seemed cosmetic, mostly shallow and often silly. But they didn't seem very substantial and John for one expected that, as the people in charge realized how counter productive the changes would turn out to be, one by one they would abandon them and the church would return to sanity. But he realized now that Norman saw more than he did.

Norman and his friends in the clergy read more than the average layman and they discussed what they read. And, what was perhaps more chilling to people who felt the same way Norman did, they were able to see what was being done in the seminaries. After all it was there that the real changes in the church would be effected. The bishops, even the Pope himself, could say what they wanted to and Catholics all over the world would nod their heads in agreement. But what the average catholic actually did depended on what his own priest said from the pulpit and, perhaps even more to the point, how the implementation of what he said in his sermon was explained particularly in the confessional. And John remembered how Norman had told him about changes in what was being taught, some subtle and some not so subtle, which had been taking place in the seminaries, where Norman still had friends whom he often saw.

Many of the changes were not even official. For instance Norman had been told that, although the official language of the church was still Latin, and that it was still the rule that Mass should most often be celebrated in Latin, it was generally known that the study of the language would soon be discontinued. And any seminarian who showed an interest in the old traditional rite, being termed the "Tridentine Mass", would find himself in disfavor with his superiors and face possible dismissal.

Every seminarian was also led to believe, unofficially of course, that it was only a matter of time until the rule of celibacy would be discontinued. It was not difficult to understand how such an atmosphere would result in the seminaries attracting, and keeping, a type of man much different from those who had wanted to be priests in the past, people such as Norman.

The priesthood was seen to be on its way to becoming more occupation than vocation.

And it had not taken long to see the effects of all this. The numbers of men seeking ordination had already begun to dwindle. Where large groups of young men, as many as thirty or more, had routinely joined the priesthood year after year, now there were only one or two ordained. It was already predicted that by the year two thousand there would not be enough priests to staff more than half the churches in the Archdiocese of Cincinnati. The thought that perhaps the fear of being overworked was what was causing Norman to leave the priesthood brought a wry smile to John's face. He shook his head. No that was not it. He was sure he knew his son better than that. Norman had never been afraid of work. And he had not changed. Rather it was the idea of the priesthood having changed, maybe even, in fact, the idea of dramatic alteration in the Catholic Church. The Church as Norman had known it was gone or soon would be.

To John it sometimes seemed that most of the world's problems were caused by the council. He had been involved, during the time Vatican II's outcome was first being made public, in a study of the Catholic Church by a group of Methodist men. He had been invited to answer questions. One of them had asked him if he didn't think that for the Catholic Church to allow for a less rigid rule of order by its members would be to signal an end to autocracy in the Church. And further, for the Catholic Church with its long tradition of strict conformity to do such a thing would suggest that perhaps there were not so many absolutes after all, in which case a lot of other areas in which satisfactory behavior depended on the traditional respect for established authority would find themselves losing a means of maintaining order. John had laughed and made the observation that the questioner seemed to have a lot more respect for the influence of the Catholic Church than John did, at which they all laughed. Now however John wasn't so sure. Perhaps it was the fact that the authorities in the church, by encouraging the impression that there were not really any absolutes for many teachings of the Church had also managed to create the impression that there were no absolutes at all. And they had certainly done that. When asked a question fifty priests might give you fifty different ways to look at the same question in the Church. Who runs the Church? What is the point, the relevancy? It was the rigidity of the rules that once provided stability. When there are no rules how does anyone play the game? Or if no one knows the law how can one stay out of jail?

Actually that question might even be irrelevant, he mused. It used to be, "Do what is right." Now it is, "Try to stay happy."

Was it possible that Norman might even leave the church? John knew that for someone with strong principles like Norman it was very possible. It was usually people such as he, or, on the other hand, those who had no principles at all, who could be pushed to do something so serious. It was the ones in the middle, those who only cared enough not to want to change, who would stay and put up with what they would consider little more than an inconvenience.

Norman and his sister walked slowly back in the yard to where John was sitting. Elleen carried two bottles of beer and a glass of iced tea. Norman had a lawn chair which he unfolded and sat upon so that Elleen could use the big wooden chair.

John thanked her for the beer and then said, "Has he told you the news?"

Elleen shook her head and sipped her tea. From the tone of her father's voice she understood that "the news" was not good. She said, "No. What's going on?"

Norman looked at his dad and shrugged his permission for John to explain. John said simply, "He's quitting his job." Norman smiled and shook his head at his father's rather simple way of expressing something somewhat more complicated. And then maybe, he thought, it wasn't that complicated after all.

Elleen continued to sip the tea and looked at Norman over the rim of the glass. She was sure there was more to the story than what she had heard and that Norman would be the one to supply the details.

Finally, when no one added anything she asked, "Well, is that it?"

"Yes, I guess it is," Norman told her softly. "I'm bailing out." A hint of a smile lingered for a moment on his face as he looked from his sister to his father. Then a tear spilled down his left cheek; then one on his right cheek. Then the smile was gone and he put his face in his hands and wept. Through the sobs they heard him say, "I'm so damn glad mom is not here for this."

John and Elleen both began to weep silently. Finally she stood and went to Norman's side. She put her hand on his shoulder and waited for him to regain his composure.

The sun had nearly reached the horizon. The shadows had gotten long and deepened near the fence. Soon it would be dark. Elleen stood with her hand on her brother's shoulder and looked around the yard. Everything looked so familiar to her, so comfortable. But it wasn't just what she could see; it was what she could feel, all the things she knew, that made her feel so at ease. It was her family and her friends, everything around her that made her feel good. It was the way things were. But change made her feel uncomfortable, not the fact that what things turned into was not as good as before, but the changing itself. Eventually she would get used to the new situation and would feel comfortable again. That was the way it had been after her mother had died. She would always miss Kate but she had learned to live happily with the way things were. She knew she would get used to having Norman around until such time as he decided to go somewhere else and then she would feel uncomfortable with that.

Norman took a handkerchief out of his back pocket and wiped his eyes and blew his nose. He patted Elleen's hand on his shoulder but did not say anything for a while. He took a drink from his beer which was beginning to get a little warm. He stood up just as they heard the car stop in the driveway.

Father Norman said, "I think I'll get back to Wapa. I don't feel much like a party. Will you explain for me?"

Elleen nodded her head and Norman hugged her. He said, "We'll talk more about this in a few days. I'll be back." She nodded again. Norman went over to where his dad sat and bent over to put his arm around the old man's shoulder. Neither of them said anything but John reached up and patted his son on the cheek. Norman walked around the house to his car, parked on the street, and drove away. John and Elleen gathered up the bottles and glasses and went inside.

Soon the backyard was completely dark and looking around there one could not see anything to indicate that only a little earlier the hearts of three people had been painfully twisted but not one of them had even been slowed down. Perhaps, after all, the news had not been as bad as it had at first seemed.

On the way back to the parish house in Wapakoneta Father Norman thought about the problems he soon would be facing. In truth he could hardly remember how it was to belong to the world, to worry about people's approval, to try to keep in style, to find a better job, to worry about getting a raise. He didn't know, in fact, what kind of job he might be qualified for, with a doctorate in philosophy and theology. He was somewhat excited by the challenge, but worried about not being able to handle it. Might he find himself in a homeless shelter somewhere? He knew his family wouldn't let him starve, but would they let him live his own life enough to keep his self respect? He hoped they would.

When the three who had gone to Wapakoneta came laughing into the kitchen John and Elleen were sitting at the table, not even talking. The laughing stopped abruptly. Billy put the bag he was carrying on the end of the table. He said, "Is something wrong?"

Before either Elleen or her father could answer Billy, Millie asked another question. "It's Norman isn't it? We knew he was worried about something. We saw him on the way out. He was coming in. They're going to send him somewhere far away aren't they?"

Elleen looked at John to see if he wanted her to respond and he nodded his head. She said, "He's leaving the priesthood."

Ann had a smaller bag in her hand. It had a container of frozen whipped cream in it. Slowly she walked to the refrigerator and opened the door. Then after thinking for a bit she closed the refrigerator door and opened the freezer for the container. She realized they would not be needing it that night.

Chapter XIII

He was the most faithful usher they had ever had at St. Sabastian's. He never missed a Sunday or a holy day, or any special service where there would be a collection. Father Grandiel had many times said he wished he had a dozen more like Clarence. The others did not exactly resent that but it could be assumed they were not extremely unhappy when the news came out after Clarence died that all those years he had been skimming a little off the top of the collections. As near as the accountants could figure out he had taken two dollars from every collection and deposited it into a savings account at the bank. It was not at all clear what he had intended to do with the money. He had only one living relative, a sister who made her home in North Dakota, and he had left no will. The sister insisted that the rather small but not insignificant sum of money be given back to St. Sabastian's. Poor simple Father Grandiel could never believe the awful truth, that Clarence had been robbing the church. He always thought there must have been some extenuating circumstance which never came out. He died believing that.

From Our Priest, by M. C. Paula

*   *   *

1980

The first thought John had was how Kate would have felt had she still been alive. But then he realized that she probably would have been more stoic than the rest of them. Or at least she would have concealed her grief better. She always seemed to be able to do that. Nevertheless he knew she would have been saddened when the news reached them that Fred Hoect had been one of the passengers on the Jumbo Jet that plunged into the sea off the California coast. He was only a year younger than Kate and the two of them had always been very close.

Then there was some question concerning why Fred had been on the plane, actually why he had even been in that part of the country. But John had no doubt there was good reason for whatever Fred had been doing.

The funeral Mass was held at the church in Bellefontaine, the crispness of the early fall air and the color of the leaves giving the trip to the cemetery a feeling of urgency.

John had been staying at the cabin and Tammy had met him there and she drove John's car to the church and later to the cemetery. Afterwards they started to drive back to the cabin so Tammy could pick up her car and return to Cincinnati. Everyone else had gone back to Cincinnati as soon as the funeral was over.

On the way to the church Tammy had teasingly told her grandfather she had something interesting to tell him but that it could wait until after the funeral. John hadn't forgotten. Once they started on the road back to the lake he asked her, "Well, what was it you wanted to say?"

"It isn't such a big thing I guess. I just wanted to tell you I am going to start nursing school. I have been accepted and classes start in a couple of days. I thought you should know."

He said, "What do you mean it isn't a big thing? I think it is a very big thing. In fact it's the best thing I've heard for a while. I would think you'd be excited about it?" He tactfully avoided mentioning the fact that she was a bit older than most nursing students.

But she didn't avoid it. "Yes I am excited, but only a little. I have been thinking about this for so long that I guess I've worn out the excitement part of it. And I guess you know I will probably be the oldest one in my class. But I think I can handle it. At least I hope I can. And I will try hard."

"Yes," he nodded enthusiastically, "I'm sure you will. You've never done anything part way. We are all proud of you."

Then he smiled broadly. To John Tammy's announcement had made the trip somewhat of an occasion. He suggested that instead of going directly to the cabin they continue on into town so that he could buy her an ice cream soda in celebration. She agreed. Obviously she was amused by her grandfather's enthusiasm.

As they sat at a marble-topped table in old man Clement's ancient drug store, sipping their drinks through straws, John told his granddaughter, "Tammy, just out of curiosity, I'd like to ask you something." But it was Tammy who seemed to be curious.

She had been scooping the soft ice cream out of her glass with her spoon. She put the spoon down and rested her hands on the edge of the table, waiting for John to finish what he had started to say.

She felt very close to her grandfather usually, but sometimes it was nearly the opposite. There were times when she felt that John acted almost aloof with her, and also with her cousins. She did not know for sure but she got the definite impression that he did it on purpose. Perhaps it was partly his way of trying to keep from sounding as though he was meddling in their personal affairs. But if that was the case she was sure it was a hard thing for him to do because, more than anyone else she knew, he took a personal interest in what each member of his family did.

"Now I don't want you to think I am suggesting anything at all, but how old are you Tammy? You're about twenty-seven aren't you?"

Tammy laughed. "Oh, so that's it?" She picked up her spoon and started after the ice cream again. "I'll bet you're wondering why I'm not thinking about getting married, aren't you? Why is it that fathers and grandfathers always seem to worry about their daughters and granddaughters not getting married? I think mothers are just the opposite. Anyway, yes I was just twenty-seven. And I might get married some day, but not now. Honestly, Bindah, I have too many things I want to do first." Her eyes twinkling she added, "But I'm glad you are worried about me just the same."

John seemed embarrassed. "No, Tammy, I'm not worried about you, at least not that way. It's just that you never bring a young man around for us to meet. I don't think you ever go out, even with any girl friends. I just wonder—". He pushed his glass aside to get it out of the way. He appeared to be clearing the deck for some serious discussion. He put his forearms on the table and leaned forward. "I just wonder seriously if you work too hard. That's all. Remember you are only young once. Believe me I know."

Then Tammy laughed again, the sound of it, like a little bell, tinkling merrily through the nearly empty store. She said, "Oh grandpa, when did you get old? You never will."

He sighed deeply. "I wish you were right. Everyday my arthritis gets worse." Then he grinned at her. "But maybe you are right. Maybe I won't get any older, at least not this year." They both laughed.

John felt comfortable with Tammy. He couldn't tell if it was because she made him think of her father or whether it was some mannerism that reminded him of Kate. Whatever it was he enjoyed talking to her. She obviously felt the same way about him and now she gave no indication that she was ready to leave when they both finished their drinks. For a few minutes they sat without talking watching people pass by the big front window.

Mr. Clements, who had been polishing glasses and placing them one by one in front of the mirror that stretched from one end of the long counter to the other, took off his apron. He folded it carefully and put it underneath the counter top and out of sight. Then he walked around the end and over to the window where he stood with his hands behind his back also looking out into the street. Everyone seemed to be in a hurry, possibly because it was getting close to supper time.

Finally Tammy asked, "Didn't you ever think that I might decide to go to the convent?" John was absent-mindedly polishing his spoon with his napkin. Thoughtfully he answered her, "I suppose I did at times. I've always thought about the girls in the family becoming nuns. But I hate to admit that since Vatican II it is not something I have been very enthusiastic about." This did not surprise Tammy.

"You don't much like all the changes Vatican II made in the Church do you?"

John put the spoon down on top of the napkin and looked out the window again without seeing anything. He seemed not to have heard her. Finally he looked at her and sighed softly. He said, "Actually it was not the council itself but what some people made of it that caused the most trouble. And I suppose it could be said that what the council did was give them an opportunity to do all these crazy things. But still it wasn't actually the council. It was some bishops who had lost track of what they were supposed to be doing, teaching, representing Jesus and His Church, and becoming obsessed with making names for themselves. Unfortunately it was those guys that the press heard. And it wasn't just the secular press either. Some of the worst were the diocesan papers," and he added ruefully, "like our own. Then of course some theologians used the strange ideas that found their way into the news as an excuse for them to stick in their own hare-brained schemes too."

"Bin," Tammy said, "I'd like to know something. I know you pray a lot, but do you ever pray for things?"

John had been very serious but now he grinned at her. "Well," he said, "what kind of 'things' did you have in mind?"

Then Tammy laughed lightly. "Oh, you know," she tried to explain. "Do you ever ask God to give you things that you want?"

"Sure I do sometimes," John answered, grinning more broadly. "Why do you ask? Is this a theology question?"

"Well," Tammy told him, "I heard you telling Aunt Elleen the other day that we can't change God's mind. It seemed like you were saying that sometimes praying is a waste of time."

Now John laughed too. "So that's it—why should we pray. Actually I do have a problem with that. Given the fact that God is eternal, with no future and no past, everything He could do He is doing right now. In other words He does not intend to do things. Whatever He wills is done by His willing it. Therefore it would seem to be impossible for one of us to convince Him to do anything, wouldn't it, because if He willed it it would already be done and if He didn't will it it would never be done? And besides I believe that the good Lord always does whatever is best for us no matter what we ask for. You are familiar with the bible quote about God never handing you a stone if you asked for bread. Well if you asked for a stone He wouldn't hand you one either. He would still hand you bread. So it does seem as though there is no point in praying.

"The only problem with all this is the fact that the bible is full of instances when Jesus admonishes us to pray. He was even pretty specific about how we should pray wasn't He? So it is rather obvious that it is something we are supposed to do."

"Well," Tammy asked, "then what is the answer?"

"I guess," John admitted to his granddaughter, "I really don't know for sure. In the first place I have often prayed for things that seemed pretty hopeless and got them—not anything very big you know—but things I thought I couldn't get without God's intervention. In other words it seemed my prayer had really worked. So I could be wrong about the whole thing. While it is true God has already willed everything that will happen and he will never change that, He also already knows everything we will ever do so He must know every prayer we will ever make to Him too, and every time we will ask the Blessed Virgin and the other saints to intercede for us. Who is to say then that our prayers which God sees in advance have no influence at all?

"I'll tell you one thing, though. A lot of us use public prayers as opportunities to make political statements."

"You were in church today. Do you remember the petitions? The reader asked God to stop abortions because an abortion ends the life of an unborn baby. Actually I think the Lord already knows that. Don't you?

"Oh, here's a really good example, a convocation, or something like a blessing given by the congressional chaplain. That will have more whereases than a resolution. It always sounds as though the guy who is praying is trying to explain the prayer to God. But if God doesn't already know He never will. So he must be explaining it to the other people."

"Don't you think the people who do that are just trying to make as much of the opportunity to talk in front of a big crowd as they can?" Tammy asked with a smile.

John smiled too. "You're right, Tammy. You're exactly right. And I guess I make too much of this."

Suddenly John's attitude changed. He reached across the table and put his hand gently on his granddaughter's. "Come on," he said quietly, "let's go. I know you want to get back to town and I think I will go on in too. I was going to stay all night but…"

His voice almost broke. Tammy thought she saw a tear in the corner of his eye before he looked down. "What's the matter, Bin," she asked quietly. Then she added, "Did something make you think of grandma?"

John looked up and smiled grimly. "Oh, little girl, everything makes me think of your grandmother sometimes. I was just thinking how proud she would have been to know you are going to be a nurse." Then his smile broadened. "I guess I'll just have to be proud enough for both of us, hm?"

Then Tammy smiled and warned him, "Don't get too excited just yet. I only said I was accepted. They didn't promise me I would ever graduate."

And he answered, "Young lady, if you don't graduate at the head of your class I'll think there's something wrong with that school."

"Oh grandpa," she said, "I'll bet you tell things like that to all your girls." And they both laughed.

*   *   *

Earlier in the day, at the St. Ursula convent on McMillan Street, the nuns left the chapel after the regular visit which always followed the midday meal. Sister Charles leaned on her cane in the hallway outside the chapel door and watched as most of the other nuns bustled off. The teachers, of course, were already in their classrooms but most of the rest of the sisters would have jobs to do also, somewhere else in the building. She waited until the hall was empty, then, in obvious pain, hobbled toward the elevator. She didn't want anyone to see her use it. For her one of the things getting old meant was not being able to do things like hurry up and down the stairs.

What Sister Charles didn't know was that Mother Cecelia was standing on the other side of the swinging doors at the end of the hall and watching her. The superior was peeking through the space between the doors to make sure that the older nun got on the elevator without mishap.

She was worried about Sister Charles. It would have been better for her to make use of a wheelchair but she would not even consider it. How many times Mother had tried to convince her that if she wouldn't think about the wheelchair she should at least use the walker which the order had provided for her. But to Sister Charles the walker would have seemed too much a concession to weakness or, God forbid, to creature comfort. The wheelchair would have been even worse for another reason. Sister Charles knew that the younger nuns would want to help her by pushing her chair whenever they could and she was well aware that since the effects of Vatican II had begun to permeate the church, vocations to sisterhood had nearly disappeared. There were far too few young nuns at St. Ursala for all the jobs they were expected to do. She didn't want to contribute to a frivolous use of that dwindling resource.

But what offended Sister Charles the most was that although she was far from the oldest nun in the building she was the most crippled by arthritis. It didn't seem fair.

Furthermore, something she never mentioned to anyone, she didn't want John, her older brother who still visited the convent at least once a month, ever to see her in a wheelchair. After all she had her pride.

When the elevator door shut the superior sighed, shook her head, smiled resignedly and turned toward her tiny office. There was work for her to do too.

The elevator creaked to the second floor and the door slowly opened again. Sister Charles was standing as close to the door as she could without touching it so that as soon as it started to open she could get at least partly out before it began to close. Once she hadn't made it in time and she had to ride back to the first floor and up again. She had been so afraid someone would see her and think she had forgotten to get off, or forgotten to push the button, or forgotten to do some other thing.

She got off and the door closed behind her but the elevator did not move. Apparently no one was waiting for it. That was another thing that bothered her, that she was one of the few who needed to use it, and probably the youngest. She sighed deeply and ambled slowly down the hall to her room. The door was not locked; she turned the knob and pushed it open.

Her room, like those of the other nuns, including Mother Cecelia's, was sparsely furnished. It had a cot to sleep on, a straight chair next to the cot on which she would sit after evening prayers to remove her shoes and stockings, and a small writing desk with another straight chair.

There was a shelf full of books, that reached the ceiling. There was another little table in the corner on which stood two statues, the Virgin holding the little Jesus, with Joseph standing next to them. In front of the statues was a little blue glass votive candle holder. It was empty, being reserved for emergency petitions. Alongside the little table and pushed against the wall was a kneeler.

One piece of furniture seemed out of place in the room and represented, in fact, a bit of a concession from both the mother superior and from Sister Charles. Or perhaps that was not exactly true, at least not on the superior's part. It was a reclining chair and although putting it in the nun's room officially required special permission Mother Cecelia had actually insisted that Sister Charles take it when the advance of arthritis in her knees, her hands, and her right hip, had become rather obvious to the other nuns. At first Sister Charles had loudly and regularly expressed her disapproval. She didn't want to be treated any different than the other nuns, at least the ones in her age group, not yet eighty-five year olds. But she finally gave in, more or less gracefully. And, truth be told, once she had used it she was glad she had accepted the chair.

With its back to the door the chair faced the only window in the room, one which looked out directly onto a tall oak tree standing in the grassy area between the convent building and the fence which ran along McMillan Street.

Sister Charles sat down painfully in the big recliner and looked out the window. A bright red cardinal sat on a branch and seemed to peer back at her through the screen. Then it flew off and a finch took its place. This was very unusual. She had often seen the little yellow birds when they drove to Metamora in Indiana, but Sister Charles did not ever remember seeing one in Cincinnati. But then, she ruefully acknowledged, there were many things she couldn't remember, which didn't mean they had never happened.

The books from which Sister Charles said her private prayers were lying on the floor next to her chair where she had left them that morning. As she always did after lunch Sister Charles began her devotion with the beautiful prayer from the gospel of St. Luke, the prayer of the Blessed Virgin in which she praises the Lord, the Magnificat. She opened the book with all the ancient devotions to the Mother Of Jesus which her father had given to her before she had entered the convent. She always read the inscription on the title page before she started to pray, "To Eileen from papa. Stay close to the Virgin Mary and you will always be close to her Son, Jesus. Your mama and your papa love you." She could hear Pat saying the words as she read them and it warmed her heart. Then she turned to the page where the Magnificat was printed and began to read the prayer in Latin as she always did.

"Magnificat anima mea Dominum. Et exultavit spiritus meus in Deo salutari meo." "My soul doth magnify the Lord. And my spirit hath rejoiced in God my Savior."

"Quia respexit humlitatem ancillae suae, ecce enim ex hoc beatem me dicent omnes generationes." "For He hath regarded the humility of His handmaid. For behold from henceforth all generations shall call me blessed."

Then she closed her eyes and continued to recite the prayer, as she had so many many times, from memory.

When she opened her eyes and replaced the little book on the floor next to the chair she felt a pain in her arm that was more severe than usual but she paid it little heed. She picked up the Imitation of Christ by Thomas A' Kempis and tried to continue reading but decided it was too dark. This surprised her because she had thought it was supposed to remain sunny for the rest of the day. Ordinarily she would have turned on a light but today for some reason she felt too tired to get up and walk over to the wall switch. She put the Imitation Of Christ back on the pile and, taking her beads from her pocket, said a decade of the rosary instead. Her shoulders were starting to hurt a little and she tried to change her position against the back of the chair to make herself more comfortable. It didn't help and, to make matters worse, she felt a sort of constriction in her chest. She decided that if it continued she would certainly mention it that evening to Sister Amelia who was the nurse.

Sister Charles put her head back and closed her eyes again. The Lord would not judge her too severely if she took just a short nap and then continued her devotions. She began to recite the doxology she had heard the Trappist monks at Gethsemane use when she and some of the other nuns had visited there once. "Praise to the Father, the Son, and the Holy Ghost, the God who is, who was, and is to come at the end of the ages."

Sister Charles opened her eyes and tried to say something aloud but she could not. Her hands opened and the rosary she was still holding slipped to the floor. Her mouth and her eyes remained open and her head leaned to one side. She looked very uncomfortable but it made little difference. For Sister Mary Charles, Eileen, O'Maury, the end of the ages had come.

It was late in the afternoon when old Sister Philomena knocked on the door to Sister Charles' room. She was the oldest nun in the convent and was slowing down. She found it necessary to use a walker all the time and had no regular assigned duties except to give advice to Mother Cecelia as she had to several of Cecelia's predecessors. The advice was not always followed she knew.

Sister Philomena had also taken on the job of keeping tabs on all the other nuns whom she considered "older". She had noticed Sister Charles had not been out of her room since lunchtime and although this was not unusual for most of the older sisters it was for Charles. So Philomena had decided to check on her.

When she got no answer to her knock she opened the door and saw her friend in her recliner. She started to say something before noticing the uncomfortable angle of the other nun's head. It was apparent to her that Sister Charles had died.

The first thing the old nun did was recline the chair so that she could put Sister Charles' head in a more comfortable position. Then she closed the nun's eyes and her mouth. Something from her stomach had apparently been ejected from her mouth and soiled her chin as she died. Sister Philomena found a box of tissues on the little table and used some of them to wipe off her friend's face. Then she knelt and quietly recited the Lord's Prayer, an Ave Maria, and a doxology, followed by, "May the soul of Sister Charles and all the souls of the faithful rest in peace. Amen."

By bracing herself on the arm of the recliner with one hand and on the top of her walker with the other Sister Philomena pulled herself back up. She said aloud, "Oh, Charles, how I envy you." Then she went out, leaving the door to the corridor open.

Sister Philomena would use the elevator to go to the first floor and walk to the chapel where she would say a few more prayers before the Blessed Sacrament—first things first. Then she would go to Mother Cecelia's office and tell her that another one of the sisters was in Heaven praying for her friends.

*   *   *

When they arrived at the cabin Tammy and John walked up the drive and into the back door as most of the family usually did. Tammy collected a few things she had intended to take home with her and came back out the same way, got into her car and started home. John left the cabin only about an hour after Tammy did.

Tammy hadn't wanted to start home until her grandfather was ready to leave too and hadn't either until he assured her repeatedly that he was fine and that he had only some straightening up to do before he got on his way. What he really wanted to do was go through every room in the cottage before he went out and locked the front door. He was never sure that this time would not be the last time and each room had some special memories he wanted to recall one more time; the sound of a laugh, a word whispered to keep from waking a baby, a sob from a little one who needed that special attention which would make him or her as good as new, a sigh that might have signalled impatience or might have shown the beginning of passion, or just a bit of a wink from an eye long since closed for good, but one which John could still see, because instead of getting weaker every year in his mind all the old images grew more indelible.

And he could close his eyes and imagine himself in other cottages where he and Kate had spent so many hours laughing, and dreaming and planning, sometimes crying, and sometimes making love.

Finally he opened the front door and stepped out onto the porch. But before he closed the door and locked it he smiled at the picture of Kate hanging on the wall across from he door. Quietly he said, "Goodby, my beautiful wife. I'll be seeing you again soon."

When he closed the storm door John noticed a little piece of paper taped to it that he realized must have been there when he and Tammy went in through the back of the building. He took it off, unfolded it, and read it. It was from Leonard, the patrolman at the police station in Russells Point. The convent in Cincinnati had tried to call John at the cabin but had learned that the phone had been disconnected. So Mother Cecelia had called the police and asked if they could ask John to call the Mother Superior. That was all the note said but John had a slight feeling of uneasiness nevertheless. He locked the door and drove to the gas station next to the highway to call Mother Cecelia.

It took a few minutes to get her because she was in chapel. When she came to the phone she was very business-like. She told John that his sister had died very peacefully a little after the mid-day visit to chapel. "John," she added, "Sister Philomena found her and she said it was apparent your sister had died while she was saying her rosary. I can't think of any better way to die, can you?"

"No, I can't," he answered softly.

They talked for a few minutes, discussing funeral arrangements. Then the nun said, "God bless you," before she hung up.

It was not yet dark when John got into his car. He sat for a few minutes before starting the engine. Then he turned and went back in the direction of the cabin. Pokey Lane was only a short distance from the street he had just left but it suddenly occurred to him that he hadn't been by the old place in several years. On impulse he drove there and parked on the street directly in front of the first cabin they had ever used. It was obviously empty and still had no fence. He got out of his car and walked up the driveway. For several minutes he stood remembering; the day Aloysius had come home from school and John had left the ice on the porch, Eileen in the car with Aloysius' friend (a story they had never heard completely), waiting on the steps for Pat, and sitting in the kitchen with his parents after Aloysius had died. Then he remembered when he had walked into the backyard that night and lay down on the grass to look at the stars, wondering if Aloysius was looking down at him. He still didn't know.

John walked into the backyard. The old stump was still there but the bark was all gone and there was a big piece of wood missing from one side. John thought about lying on the grass and looking at the stars as he had done on that night so long ago. But it was cloudy and he knew he wouldn't see all the stars. Besides it would be hard for him to get back up again. He sat on the stump instead. So many things had changed. So many people had come and gone. It occurred to him that he was the oldest male member of the O'Maury family. He was the O'Maury "himself". He wondered what Aloysius would have thought of that.

He would miss his sister. He loved her. More than brother and sister they were friends. A tear dampened his cheek but he didn't wipe it away. It was the least he could do for Eileen.

Funny but all of a sudden he didn't remember her as an old nun slowed by arthritis, but as a vibrant young lady. Which was better? He didn't know. He didn't think it made any difference now anyway. He waved at the sky and said softly, "Eileen, see if you can find Aloysius and Kate and let them know how things are going down here." Then he stood up stiffly and left. It was just starting to get dark.

Once he was on the road to Cincinnati the thought of Fred and the mystery surrounding his death took his mind off Eileen. "Well," he thought to himself, "there is an explanation which will probably be very simple after all."

* * *

But it wasn't nearly as simple as John had hoped.

When the Hoect family had decided to develop the land occupied by the family farm into an airport it was Fred who had volunteered to take over the job of managing the operation. He had even gone to Miami University at night to learn enough accounting to be able to keep the books without help from anyone else. The others accepted without question his regular reports on the status of their investments.

But sometimes it did seem strange. They never appeared to make a great deal of money even though the airport did a good bit of business at least for short periods. And on the other hand even during the slow times they never lost any large sums of money either, according to Fred's reports. But even though this might have seemed unlikely it was not beyond the realm of possibility. So his figures were never questioned. In truth everyone seemed to be too busy to even worry about it. What it came down to was that they all trusted Fred completely.

Then a few days after the funeral, when bills had to be paid, Alex reluctantly unlocked Fred's small desk in the corner of the airport office to get out the checkbook and write some checks. He ended up spending nearly the whole day trying to make sense of what he found there. Eventually he was forced to admit to himself, and later to the rest of the family, that his brother had been taking money from the airport account and investing it under his own name in a stock fund. What was puzzling to Alex was that Fred had apparently never actually realized any benefit from the apparent embezzlement. All the money which had been taken from the business owned by the family and invested separately was still there. In fact the total amount had grown substantially over the years until it represented a very comfortable sum. According to the records Fred had never withdrawn anything from the fund. So, Alex wondered, what had been the point of the manipulation? Then, by noticing the date of Fred's first transactions and remembering what also had taken place at the same time, the very plausible conclusion was reached that the entire charade had been for the purpose of making the project look like a poor investment. Further, the timing pointed to the added conclusion that the whole plan was directed toward getting John and Kate to relinquish their interest in the family property. But since Fred and Kate had been so close there was little doubt that if some animosity had caused Fred to do what he did it had been directed only at John. Yet there was nothing in any record or in anyone's recollection of anything Fred had said to provide a clue as to what his specific motivation had been.

It was understood that John and Kate had not lost any money in the transaction. The problem was that they had not made any and, having severed connections with the operation, could never do so no matter what happened. More and more it seemed that in his heart Fred had harbored some unidentifiable resentment toward John which had not permitted him to allow his brother-in-law to participate in any success the family might realize. Perhaps it had been jealousy. But no one would ever know for sure.

The surviving members of the Hoect family were, of course, shocked by Alex's discovery. They refused to believe that such a thing could have happened. Mr. Westkamper, who had been enthusiastic about the investment in the beginning and had carefully avoided influencing John and Kate to relinquish their share in it, was devastated by the disclosure.

At first the Hoects could not discuss the matter with anyone from the O'Maury family. And as often happens in such situations for a short time they even seemed to resent John as though he was not the victim but the cause of Fred's deception. But Alex would not allow this to go on for long.

John was working in the yard in the early spring. He was the only one at the cabin. He heard the doorbell ring once and he picked up an old towel to wipe the dirt from his hands before walking around to the front of the building to see who might be there. But as he began to walk toward the gate that stood at the end of the walk the three Hoect brothers came through it and into the backyard. Wendell was first. The next was Paul, the youngest. And Alex, the oldest, was last. As he followed the others through the gate he carefully closed it, so typical of someone who had spent his entire life on a farm where livestock was kept. The Hoects were so tall that, as usual, they made John feel as though he were standing in a canyon as they walked past him. Only Alex shook hands with John, rather solemnly John thought. While gripping John's hand Alex asked him, "Are you too busy to talk? We have something we would like to talk over with you if you have the time, John."

Surprised and a little nonplussed John answered, "Why sure Alex. I was just doing a little work out here in the yard. We can go inside if you want to or we can sit in the chairs back by the garden."

Alex let go of John's hand and told him, "Out here would be fine." He smiled and added, "You know we are pretty much outdoors people."

When the Hoects were all seated John waited for someone to say something but everyone seemed reluctant to start. Finally he told them, "I was getting a little thirsty and I was about ready to go inside and get a cold beer. Would anyone like to join me?"

Wendell and Paul both looked at Alex who nodded his head and said, "That would taste good I think. That would taste fine."

Before he went into the kitchen John asked, "Everybody?" and the other two brothers also nodded their heads but still said nothing. John was beginning to feel uneasy as he walked toward the house. The brothers seemed nervous about something as though, he thought, there was something they had come to discuss but now no one wanted to bring it up. The thought occurred to him that perhaps someone had died. John was certain that they were such good people that a death of a close relative, even the death of someone he did not know very well would be very difficult for them to talk about. He went on into the kitchen, put the drinks and glasses on a tray and came back out.

No one said anything as John put the tray on a little table. Each of them took one of the opened bottles and began pouring the contents into a glass. Alex didn't even taste his but before the glass was half filled put it on the arm of his chair and uttered, "John you are our brother-in-law and our little sister's husband. You are a good member of our family." He stopped and pulling a large handkerchief from his pocket used it to wipe his forehead. He didn't put it back into his pocket but held it in his hand as he continued. "We got something to say to you." He looked around at the others but none of them said or did anything that seemed to alleviate his obvious agitation. Our brother Fred did something to you what we don't know why, or don't know what he meant by it. He made the figures in the books he was keeping for the airfield look like we weren't making any money so you would sell out." Alex picked up his glass, took a sip and set it back down and then said, "That's what he did, and we don't know why." With that he leaned back in his chair and sighed.

John, who had not even had time to sit was startled and confused by what Alex said. The announcement had been so abrupt, with so little said to prepare him for the disturbing assertion which was made concerning Fred Hoect that he was not able to even decide how he felt about it. No one else said anything for what seemed a long time, the Hoects looking intently at John as if waiting for him to begin some dialogue. Then Paul blurted, "I know my brother. He must have had some reason for what he did that we don't know about. Some day it will all come out. Then we will know." And with that, in a gesture of defiance, he lifted his glass and nearly drained it."

The other two brothers stared at him in disbelief. Alex gasped. Wendell shook his head slowly and said quietly, "Mein Gott, Paul, why do you say that? We already have decided. Why do you do this now?"

Paul looked at him, then at Alex, and finally up at John. Then he said, "All our lives we have been looked down on because we don't talk as good as everyone else. When ever something goes wrong it is our fault. It is always something. And now our own brother gives everyone something that will remind others of of." He extended his hands with both palms up. Then he lowered his head moving it slowly from side to side. He dropped his hands into his lap and looked up again. "John," he said, "I forget how we came to be here today. It is not something you have done. It is something our own brother did. What I said right here is wrong. I don't know why I say this thing to you. It is because I feel so bad and I don't know what else to say. If you never want me to come here again I think it is every right of you that I never come back here. I am sorry for what I said to you."

John was now so touched by what Paul had just said that he moved forward and put his hand on the other man's shoulder. "Oh, Paul," he said, "I have already forgotten the whole thing. I am sure it was some sort of misunderstanding. Whatever it was it should not affect us. What would Katie say? She would probably say we were all making a mountain out of a molehill. That was one of her favorite expressions. As far as I am concerned it is a closed book. Let's forget it."

Paul stood up. He took John's hand in his and squeezed it without saying anything. Neither did he smile. Then he sat back down.

Alex said, "Okay," and also stood to take John's hand. Then Wendell did the same.

For a little while the four men sat and the Hoects tried to tell John how what Fred had done had come to light. They offered him the option of reclaiming his stock in the enterprise but John, expressing his gratitude, demurred. He said he didn't think it would be necessary and that he thought the business should be owned by those who had the ambition to help run it. Besides, he said, he was comfortable with what he had.

John went into the kitchen and brought out more beer. Finally one of the brothers looked at his watch and said it was time to go. They all stood and shook hands with John again. He thanked them for coming and asked them all to come back before long when he would try to get as many members of his family to join them. It had been a long time since they had all been together. They should see how each other's kids had grown.

As the Hoects walked down the driveway to their car John stood beside the porch steps. As Alex opened the door on the driver's side to get in he waved to his brother-in-law. John waved back, happy that the rift which had apparently opened between him and his wife's family had been closed and the connection between the two families had remained intact. It gave him a comfortable feeling. But then, as Alex's door closed, John had the feeling that in fact he and the Hoect brothers would never be close. They would all see each other at funerals and weddings, and they would remark how long it had been since the last time they had all been together. And they would promise sincerely to keep in touch. But they would know that they would never do it.

By the time the Hoects left it had begun to grow dark. John went back to the yard and gathered the bottles and glasses onto the tray and took them into the kitchen. He washed the glasses and put them in a rack on the sink to dry. The bottles he dropped into a lined bin. Then he sat by a window and watched the shadows as they crept from the fence and across the yard. He was profoundly shaken of course by what he felt he could assume his brother-in-law had done. He and Fred had never been close, but he knew that Fred and Kate had been because, being so near in age, they had shared so many memories of their growing up years. Over and over John asked himself what he had done to cause bad feelings to develop on Fred's part. He blamed himself even though he could think of nothing he had ever said or any action on his part which would have caused such animosity. After a while the old man got up and walked into the front room to stand before the picture of Kate. Her eyes twinkled but her mouth smiled only slightly. He had never noticed this before. Her expression actually seemed to show disapproval.

"Oh, Katie," he murmured softly, "I'm so sorry." And then he began to weep a little.

Later on as it continued to grow dark John sat in the living room and tried to make sense of it all. The objects in the room slowly became unrecognizable.

John took his rosary case from his pocket, unzipped it and took out the brown beads. As he started to pray the picture of Kate began to fade too in the darkness. Before he finished the second decade he was asleep in his chair.

Chapter XIV

After all that, he went back anyway. It wasn't that all the things he had told them, how they didn't understand him, and they were mean to him, and he hated them, it wasn't that all those things weren't important anymore. It was just that something else seemed more important. The last lift he got was with a train conductor on his way home who went out of his way to drop him off at the house, maybe just because it was already two hours into Christmas. It was even starting to snow a little, the way it is supposed to. He knocked on the door a couple of times before a light went on upstairs. Then the hall light went on and the door opened a crack. He knew who it was. He said, "Mom it's me, Tig. Can I come in?" She undid the chain and pulled the door back all the way. After he hugged her and kissed her on the cheek he said, "I want to tell dad I'm sorry for what I said, real sorry. Do you think he'll talk to me?" And she said, "Oh Tig you're too late. We buried him just last week. And Tig sat on the hall steps and cried. His mother sat down too and put her arm across his shoulder. She said, "Before he died he said he loved you. He wanted you to know that." And Tig cried harder than he ever had before in his life.

From Essays On Going Home, by Marianne Pip

October 1983

Tammy had finally lost all hope of ever seeing her mother. That had been long ago actually, and it had amounted to nothing more than being practical. But she would always wonder what had happened to Ginny. She was fully aware of the little the family had been able to find out about the woman. And although Tammy felt a good deal of compassion for her it was certainly not very personal. It was hard for her to feel very much fondness for someone she had never known. But she was still curious.

Tammy always thought that Ginny had most likely died very young, probably from something connected in some way with her use of drugs or alcohol. In fact she often let herself believe, charitably, that Ginny had expected that such a thing would happen and had given up her daughter for that very reason. Tammy seldom talked to anyone about this. Jill, of course, was the only one who had known Ginny at all. But since the two of them had not been very close she had little to tell. So there was no one to whom Tammy could talk about her mother from whom she could learn much more than she already knew.

John was sitting far back in the yard, enjoying the end of the season. It occurred to him that there were advantages to growing old. Not many years before he had had to return to Cincinnati nearly every week all summer to care for his yard. Now he let his grandson Billy, who was thirty, take care of it for him, and he himself needed to make fewer trips back and forth. He remembered that when he was younger he used to wonder how it would feel to be eighty years old. Now he was able to say with authority that it was not very bad. Oh, there were a few aches and pains that had crept up on him, but those he could put up with.

He was sipping a small glass of burgundy. As Tammy got near where her grandfather relaxed on the chaise he noticed that she had a tall glass of iced tea in her hand. She stirred it as she walked and this caused the ice to tinkle against the sides of the glass. The sound made the drink seem particularly refreshing in the unseasonably warm evening air. John's first thought was that he should have taken the same drink out to the yard, rather than the wine. But, then he thought, after he finished the wine he would ask someone to get him some tea. Perhaps he could ask his great grandson, who was seven and eager to help. He wondered if they would eventually call the little boy William the Third. That had a rather aristocratic ring to it.

Tammy sat down in a lawn chair and sighed. John chuckled and said, "That was a terrible sigh for someone so young."

She laughed. "I guess that did sound as though I am about to collapse. But I'm not. I have been working pretty hard lately but I don't mind that very much. Maybe it's just the heat." She took a long drink and put the glass on the table that separated them.

They sat in silence for a while, watching the young ones playing at the other end of the yard, closer to the cottage. Suddenly Tammy asked, "Bindah I remember once when I came out here I saw you in the park with a young woman who seemed to be a friend of yours. I was wondering what ever happened to her."

The question took him by surprise. For a while he had carried Moni's death notice in his wallet, but it had become worn and nearly unreadable and finally he had thrown it away. He wondered out loud, "What ever prompted you to ask?"

She said, "Oh, nothing in particular. It seemed to me she was someone you liked pretty much. But we never, or at least I never, heard anything about her after that day."

John took another sip of his wine and put his glass on the table across from Tammy's. He said, "You're right. I was very fond of her. The reason you never heard anything of her was because there was nothing to hear." He stopped for a moment before going on. He had never talked to anyone in the family about Moni. He had not even thought about her for a long time. Finally he answered succinctly, "A short time after you saw her she died."

Tammy did not know what to say. She could have said she was sorry but that would seem to make the relation between the girl and her grandfather more personal than he had sounded as though he wanted it to be understood. Instinctively she felt that might very well have been the way it was, but she didn't want to acknowledge the fact that she suspected it. Finally she just said, "Oh," and, a few minutes later, changed the subject.

She asked him, "Bin, what did you think of my mother?"

This surprised him even more than the first question had. He said, "Actually I never ever met her. None of us did. Jill, you know, was the only one who even knew her. And she must not have known her very well or I doubt she would have introduced her to your father." John did not know what he ought to tell Tammy. Finally he decided the best thing to do was be completely candid. He said, "I suppose that I was not very happy with her. How could I be fond of a woman who allows herself to get pregnant but does not want to marry her baby's father." He paused and then went on, "But the worst thing was when she gave her little girl away. I could never understand that. How could someone just abandon a little one, not knowing what would happen to her?" Then John sat up straight on the side of the chaise so he could look directly at Tammy in the shadows. He added, "But I can't say I am unhappy that she left you with us."

Tammy smiled, acknowledging the sentiment, and said, "Sometimes I feel sorry for her, even though I didn't know her at all." Her voice drifted off. She took another sip of her tea.

John tried to recall everything he had ever known or thought about Ginny and opening the door to that particular single area of his past allowed a dim light to reflect on everything else around that place in his memory. And then he became lost in thoughts of the total past. Once again it was the first time he had ever been to Indian Lake and he could see Mary and Pat and Eileen, waiting for Aloysius to join them. Then, out of proper time sequence, he could see the young twins, and then the infant Tammy lying in the basket. Then his mind drifted like smoke on a gentle and changing breeze, still farther back, and he could see himself at the circus with colored syrup on his shirt and trousers and the beautiful Katie trying so hard not to laugh.

Tammy asked, "Bin, what in the world are you smiling about?"

John chuckled. He said, "Oh, I guess a lot of things, your great grandparents, your grandmother, my brother and my sister, and the twins. Yes, a lot of things, a lot of people." He drank the last of his wine. "Tammy," he said, "I have had a lot of good times with my family." Then he added wistfully, "I wish they had all stayed around longer to enjoy them with me." Then he grinned and said, "Is there any more tea? That looked good."

She said, "No, but it won't take long to make some. You just sit here for a while and think some more good thoughts. I'll be back in a jiffy."

* *

December 24 the same year

Tammy came on the floor before she was due to start so that Amber, the girl she was relieving, could go home early enough to attend Midnight Mass with her husband if she wanted to. The section was not very crowded which surprised Tammy. She wondered if death sometimes took a holiday for Christmas.

The two of them went over all the charts before Amber left. It didn't take very long. While they worked Tammy ate cookies from a tray someone had left in the nurses' room. "Boy, those are good," she said as she brushed crumbs from her hands and her mouth. "Who made them?"

Amber said, "Jamie brought them in but I think her mother made them."

"I've got to quit eating them," Tammy said, but she took one more.

Amber laughed. "Don't worry about it," she told Tammy. "After all it's Christmas, isn't it?"

Tammy rolled her eyes and remarked, "Uh huh. That's what people have been telling me for days, as if that will keep a person from getting fat."

When they were finished they wished each other a merry Christmas and Amber left. Tammy got all her medicine out and organized it on the cart.

The other two female nurses were in the lounge area with a couple of nurses aides and Alex, a male nurse. Tammy knew that some of the staff suspected Alex of being homosexual but she knew better. She had known Alex for some time and she was sure that his somewhat effeminate behavior was the result of his being raised by a very possessive mother after his father had left them when the boy was very young. In any event Tammy felt that Alex was a good nurse, homosexual or not.

Another thing Tammy knew was that Alex had a better than average bass voice, and now she could hear it. He and the two aides were singing carols, quietly at first but, gaining confidence, starting to get a little louder. Tammy's first thought was that this might disturb the few patients they had on the floor but the singing sounded rather pleasant and, she reflected, the other nurses were senior to her and they apparently didn't object so why should she? She smiled and started on her rounds.

All of the patients were considered terminal except Harry Ferrel who had been moved there temporarily from surgery. He had had a leg operation and would be able to go home in a day or two. Mr. Ferrel was in his fifties and well enough to flirt with the nurses, but he was not a problem.

The only other man was Reginald Hanks. He was suffering from cancer in its final stages and was heavily sedated and in an oxygen tent with his eyes closed. Tammy had no medicine for him and had only to check on his condition and try to make him as comfortable as possible.

The final patient on her list was Mary Smith. As Tammy approached Mary's room the singing group began to break up because their replacements had arrived and they needed to start their briefing procedures.

Mary Smith was new to the ward. Tammy looked at her chart. The woman was suffering from many things. She was a recovering alcoholic and a drug user. She had gotten over tuberculosis but it had left her weak and underweight. She had a stomach ulcer and was suffering from congestive heart failure. As a nurse Tammy felt a deep compassion for her. But as she looked at the chart she recognized the woman for what she was, someone who had probably never tried very hard to help herself and, in the last analysis, an individual on whom it was not worth expending a great deal of effort because she would likely never change. Actually she could probably not be saved from whatever demons tormented her because she didn't want to be saved.

Tammy pushed open the door and went in. In her most cheerful voice she said, "Well, are you feeling any better today?" The woman on the bed only looked at Tammy with brooding eyes. She did not smile. She said nothing.

Tammy noticed that the woman's hair was grey and thinning in places. And her face was wrinkled. Tammy thought she must have been at least eighty, possibly older. But she could see that her teeth, although somewhat discolored, appeared very straight and still strong. Then she remembered that there had been some mystery about the woman when she was admitted to the hospital.

For one thing she appeared to be indigent. Such patients were often admitted at Good Sam but usually from other institutions, such as the Little Sisters Of The Poor for instance. According to one of the other nurses, whose boy friend Chuck Linde worked in accounting, Mary Smith had been admitted by a middle aged man who had assumed responsibility for all her expenses. He told the volunteer in admissions that he was an attorney representing someone who wanted to make sure Miss Smith was taken care of. He declined to give the name of his client. He also said he could not give them Mary Smith's date of birth because he had no knowledge of what it was himself. The volunteer had typed "unknown" in that space on the entrance record.

The nurse took the patient's temperature, measured her pulse, and listened to her heartbeat with the stethoscope. All were in an acceptable range and the last two seemed rather strong. Tammy asked the woman if she would like to sit up but Mary Smith did not answer. Tammy made her lean forward anyway and fluffed up the pillows. As the woman leaned back she sighed deeply. Tammy was going to tell her that her grandfather often said there was an old Irish saying that such a sigh meant someone had just walked over the sigher's grave. But she thought that would not be the best thing to say to the woman on the bed. On an impulse she pulled a chair close alongside and sat down on it. She took the woman's hand in hers and said, "what's the matter? Don't you have any family? If you want me to I can stay here for a while and we can talk." But Mary Smith only looked at the younger woman as though she did not comprehend the words. Finally she closed her eyes and appeared to drift off to sleep. Tammy waited a few minutes and then patted the back of the gnarled hand before putting it under the cover. Then she replaced the chair and started to leave the room. At the door she turned and looked once more at the old woman. She thought to herself that her own mother, by dying so young, had been spared ever looking like that. That would certainly have been a blessing.

Every two hours Tammy made her rounds, checking vital signs, listening for changes in breathing patterns, and making sure that water containers were not empty. At three o'clock Mary Smith was lying on her back, slightly propped up, inhaling and exhaling loudly through her mouth, negating the effectiveness of the tube which delivered oxygen to her nostrils. She did not look comfortable and Tammy moved the pillow behind her head slightly so that the woman could lie back at less of an angle.

According to the others Mary Smith had no visitors, not even the attorney who had brought her in. "The poor old lady," Tammy thought. "How sad to be all alone on Christmas Eve." Then it occurred to her that it was Christmas, not Christmas Eve. She walked to the window and looked out at the lights from the houses that stretched around the bend in the street and on toward downtown. Ordinarily most of the homes would have been dark by then. But on this night many of them were lighted both inside and out. Suddenly a feeling of loneliness tugged at her heart. She remembered something she had heard in a sermon from an old priest at Midnight Mass when she was younger. He had said that almost universally at Christmas everyone feels a need to be with those he loves, pointing out that even the wanderer says, "I must go home."

It was true she thought. There was something about this particular holiday that made a person want to spend it with his family. Tammy felt a little shiver even though the room was rather warm. She wasn't cold, but lonely. She had not felt so all alone for a very long time, perhaps never before.

Actually she was certainly not alone. Besides all the patients there were two other nurses at the station and four nurses aides. She had plenty of company. But the feeling persisted. Why was it? She guessed it was because she was not near anyone she loved. Oh she often said she loved these patients for whom she felt responsible. But that was different. She loved them because she could see Jesus in them. She loved them for Him, not for themselves.

She had never thought about that before. She suddenly realized how much she really did love them, even if it was for the Lord. She walked near to Mary's bed and in the shadows she could almost see His face on the pillow. Was this the sleeping Jesus, exhausted from His torment on the cross? Or was this Jesus who had died? And did He now rest on the bosom of His Father? But when she looked closer all she could see was the face of an ancient woman who had wasted her life and waited now to die.

The poor unfortunate derelict, at one time she could have had the same potential as Tammy, possibly even more. What had made her waste it all? Tammy realized she would never know. Maybe Mary Smith did not know. It could be that she did not even remember at what point in her life she had accepted the realization that she would never attain any of the things she dreamed and that she would never be anything but a failure. How she must have hated herself after that.

"How sad," thought Tammy. Her eyes filled with tears but she wiped them away with the back of her hand before they spilled over. She moved the chair back to the side of the bed and sat down.

Suddenly she felt a hand on her shoulder and she started. "Sorry," said a familiar voice, "I didn't mean to scare you. I just wasn't thinking. I saw you in here and just came in. I was trying so hard not to make too much noise in a patient's room I guess I was too quiet."

Tammy stood up and turned around. It was Norman. She threw her arms around him putting her head on his shoulder. "Oh, Uncle Norman," she said, her voice muffled in the cloth of his heavy overcoat," I can't tell you how glad I am to see you. What are you doing here at this time of the morning?"

He patted her gently on her back. Then he pulled away from her slowly and began to unbutton his coat. It was black, as was his felt narrow brimmed hat. But the jacket he wore underneath the coat was a somber grey tweed. "I went to midnight Mass at the cathedral by myself. Afterwards I drove around for a little while looking at the lights. When I realized I was near the hospital the thought struck me that you might be working tonight and I could stop in and wish you Merry Christmas. So here I am."

Tammy was so happy that when she spoke she sounded as though she was about to laugh. "I'm so glad to see you." She hugged him again.

Then Norman laughed. "Well if I had known how much I'm appreciated I would have come earlier."

They walked outside and he took the coat off. Tammy went to the nurses' station and told the other nurses she was going to take a short break. Then the two of them went to the deserted lounge and he dropped his coat on a chair. When he took off his hat Tammy noticed his hair was beginning to turn grey but it was still as thick as always. They both sat down.

Tammy told him, "I have been so lonely tonight. I don't know why but I guess I needed someone from my family to be with because it's Christmas."

"Well," grinned Norman, "I hope I'll do."

And she giggled and patted his hand which lay between them on the couch. "Oh Uncle Norman you'll do just fine. How long can you stay? I'm not very busy. For a change we aren't understaffed."

He looked at his watch and then shook his head slowly. He got up and walked over to the window and looked out for a few seconds without saying anything. Then he came back and stood looking down at his niece. "Actually I have all the time in the world." He plopped down again at the end of the couch and stuck his long legs straight out in front of him. "This is still strange to me, you know? I can remember when Christmas was the busiest time of the year for me. No—actually I guess Holy Week and Easter was the busiest, but Christmas was close. Now, since I was laicized, I have to look for something to do. It has changed my life very much."

Tammy realized that her uncle did not expect her to say anything. He was stating a fact, sharing something with her. But no comment from her was expected so she said nothing. Then suddenly Norman's mood shifted and he turned to her and smiled. "I'm still glad I came here. I can stay a while as long as I don't get in the way. And you can tell me if I do and I will leave. How does that sound?"

"It sounds just fine to me," Tammy told him. I've got an idea. I have to do some paperwork right now. Why don't you sit here for a half an hour or so while I do that? Then I want to tell you about the patient in the room we were in just now. Maybe you can help me with a problem I have with her. Don't worry, I won't ask you to hear anyone's confession."

She didn't wait for his answer. She stood up and started toward the door. But before she went out she turned and smiled at him and said once more, "I am so glad to see you." Then she was gone.

Norman suddenly felt a peace he hadn't been able to experience for years. He noticed for the first time the tree in the corner with its colored lights, and how it reflected off the window. It really was Christmas and that special comfort which, even on such a day as Christmas, comes only sometimes, enveloped him. He knew that for the rest of his life he would always remember this night, and this feeling, and this experience. He didn't want to leave. He put his head back and closed his eyes. Soon he was asleep.

Then Tammy was shaking his shoulder. "Wake up," she said, "I need your help."

For just a split second he was back in his bed in the St. Joseph parish house being wakened by the pastor, Monsignor Muldoon who Father Norman was sure heard the telephone before it rang. Then he realized where he was. "What is it?" He asked. "What's wrong?"

"It's one of my patients, the one I started to tell you about. I think she is dying and I want to call a priest but she won't let me."

"Is she a Catholic?" Norman asked standing up.

"Oh, I don't know," Tammy said. She took his hand and pulled him through the lounge door. "Can't you help her?"

"Can't I help her?" thought Norman, "can't I help her?" He realized that in all honesty he didn't know. He wondered if he had ever helped anyone. Had he ever gotten anyone into the 'Pearly Gates'? Or had he at least made someone happier in this life even a little? Was there any way to find out really? Well, no matter, he would have to try again.

Tammy took him into Mary Smith's room. The plastic tube still delivered oxygen to the woman's nose while she lay back on her pillow and breathed laboriously through her open mouth. The gasps came several seconds apart and each one seemed to be the last she would take.

Tammy said, "Dr. Russell, the intern, was here. He said she would probably not last more than a few hours. A little while ago she opened her eyes and I told her I was going to call a priest. She grabbed my hand and told me to mind my own business. I could hardly hear her she is so weak, but I know what she said next. It was, 'Let me die in peace.' Please, Uncle Norman, can't you hear her confession?"

Norman ran his hand back through his hair. "Yes," he said sitting down in the chair next to the bed. "I could hear her confession, but not if she didn't want me to. Anyway you said you don't know if she is even a Catholic."

"Then let's baptize her and make her a Catholic," Tammy insisted.

Norman laughed quietly in spite of himself. "You can't do that," he told her. "you can't make someone a Catholic who doesn't want to be one."

"Why not?" she whispered loudly.

"Well," he was whispering also, "you just can't go around committing someone else to living a Catholic life who doesn't even know what it is. It wouldn't be fair to the person, would it?"

"But we do it to babies all the time."

"Yes," Norman explained, "but only if there is a good chance someone intends to bring the child up in the faith."

Tammy frowned. "Can't you just assume she's a Catholic and hear her confession? Would that hurt anything if she isn't?"

"No," Norman told her quietly, "it wouldn't hurt anything." He took Mary's hand and leaned over so that his mouth was close to her ear. "Mary," he said gently, "can you hear me at all?"

Suddenly the patient opened her eyes. At first she stared vacantly and unblinking at the ceiling as though she could not see anything. Then she blinked twice and turned her head so she could look at Norman. He said, "Mary are you a Catholic?" Then she turned her head back and fixed her eyes on the ceiling again.

Finally after what seemed like several minutes she said very clearly but without looking at Norman, "Yes, I'm a Catholic. But I don't go to church."

Norman still held her hand in one of his. Now he put his other hand on hers also. Her hand felt as cold as ice. He said, "Would you like to go to confession?"

Impatiently she said, "didn't you hear me? I said I don't go to church." Then she turned her head and looked at him again. Tammy, who had been standing next to her uncle's chair left the room without saying anything to either of them, to go and sit in the nurses' station.

"That doesn't matter," Norman assured Mary. "What you have done before doesn't matter now if you are sorry for all your sins and ask Jesus to help you live your life in Him from now on."

She made a sound that was very much like a chuckle. She said, "From now on? Do you mean for the rest of my life? Don't you know I'm dying? Don't you know it's too late for me? It's too late for me to change my life."

"Oh, Mary," he assured her, "it is never too late to come home to the Lord. He is waiting for you. He has always been waiting for you to listen to His voice. Do you want to go to confession now?"

Then, without saying anything else the old woman on the bed nodded her head slightly.

Norman noticed that Tammy had already left. He got up and closed the door. Then he sat back down, made the sign of the cross, and took her hand in his again. He said, "Mary try to remember when was the last time you went to confession."

This time she looked at him for what seemed to be more than a minute without saying anything, and without any expression. She seemed to be trying to make up her mind about something. Finally she began to talk. At first it was to him but after a little while she seemed to be talking to no one in particular. Her voice became stronger as she went on. After nearly an hour she stopped talking for a few seconds then she began again. She said, "For these and all the sins of my past life I am heartily sorry."

Norman was surprised to hear this old ending for the woman's confession but then he realized that she had last gone to confession before vatican II and the words had then been common. He had been listening while she talked and was shocked at what he had heard. More than a list of the woman's sins it had been the condensed story of her life. While she talked she had pulled her hand from his so that she could gesture with both of hers. Now he took her hand back in both of his. He said, "Mary, for your penance I want you to say the rosary as soon as you feel strong enough. Can you do that?"

She was lying back on the pillow, once again staring at the ceiling. A tear started in the corner of her eye and ran down the side of her head and over the top of her ear. She said, "I would say the rosary right now, Father, but I am so ashamed. I don't even have a rosary."

Norman was so happy that he began to weep also. He squeezed her hand in his. "Oh, Mary, Mary," he said, "wait."

He reached into the side pocket of his tweed jacket and pulled out a small pouch worn a little around the edges. He unsnapped it and turned it over in one hand allowing a black rosary to fall onto the other palm. He held it out to her. "Mary, this was left me by my mother when she died. It had been given to her by my grandmother O'Maury. It was blessed by Pope Pius the Tenth. My grandmother's name was Mary too. I know she is in heaven now and I can almost hear her and my mom telling me to give this rosary to you. Here, take it. It is yours now." He put the beads into her hand and closed her fingers around them.

The old woman squeezed the rosary in her hand and with her other hand took his and kissed his fingers. She said, "Oh thank you Father. Thank you for everything. I have not felt so good for so long. Now I am ready to die. But I am going to say the rosary first." Norman was embarrassed. He did not want to tell her that he should not be called father because he had left the priesthood. But he was afraid she might think her confession had not been valid. Better to let her go on thinking he was still a priest. After all that was not untrue really. "Once a priest, always a priest" was the old saying. It was just that he was no longer permitted to act like one. The woman closed her eyes and seemed about to drift off to sleep so Norman quietly stood up.

Then without opening her eyes Mary asked "Will you come back to see me later on?"

Norman answered, "You bet I will." Then she smiled and in a short time her regular breathing through the tube at her nose told him she was sleeping. He went out but left the door open.

Norman found his niece at the nurses' station. She was alone, just sitting at the desk, waiting, and when Norman came round the corner she looked up at him expectantly. The first thing she said was, "How is she? Is she okay?"

Norman put his hand on the gate in the low barrier next to the counter and waited, his eyebrows raised in a tacit question, until she nodded for him to enter the staff area. He pushed a chair next to the desk and dropped into it. He put his elbows on her desk and leaned over close to Tammy. Then, with a wave of his hand, he dismissed the question she had asked him. "Yes," he said perfunctorily, "yes, she is. But there is something she told me that I must tell you. Oh, don't worry. This was not part of her confession. I will not be breaking the seal. It was actually something she told me she had done that she was proud of." Norman looked round to see if anyone was near. No one was. Nevertheless he leaned toward Tammy and lowered his voice nearly to a whisper. "Tammy tell me, have you ever thought that possibly that woman might be your mother?"

Tammy looked away from him. He could not tell if she was avoiding his question or trying to think of how she might answer it. Finally she turned back toward him and stared into his eyes. "I think I wanted to think that," was Tammy's answer. "But I didn't think my mother would be as old as that. Why?"

"Because," he explained slowly, "She told me almost her whole life story. She is not nearly as old as she looks. And she told me that she had a little girl whom she left on someone's porch in a basket. I think it could have been you, Tammy. She didn't remember exactly where it was except that it was in Ohio. And she couldn't remember the exact date either. But as much as she did recall was in the range. It sounds like more than just a coincidence."

Tammy stood up. "I have to go see her," she told Norman.

"Wait" he insisted and put his hand on her arm. "I didn't tell her anything about you. I'm not sure how she would react to finding her little girl. She thinks that giving her to someone who would take care of her was the only good thing she ever did in her life. I got the feeling she didn't want her daughter to know what kind of a woman her mother was. She might still not want you to know. Besides she was sleeping peacefully when I left her. Would you want to wake her up?"

Tammy shook her head. "No," she said slowly. "I will let her sleep. But I want to talk to her later. I'm not convinced. But still it could be." Norman reached out and patted her hand. Then he stood up and went back to the waiting room. When he returned he had on his hat and his overcoat.

"I think I'll go home and get a few hours sleep. This has been an interesting night to say the least. Will you be at your grandfather's today?"

"I don't know," she answered. "I'd like to go but I may come back here tomorrow just to see how everything is."

Norman smiled. "You mean how everything is with Mary Smith don't you?"

"Well, yes, I guess so," she admitted. "But with everyone else too."

At that Norman laughed. Then he gave her one last hug and left for his apartment and bed.

The old woman slept peacefully until the breakfast trays were brought into the hall. And when she awoke a nearly miraculous transformation had taken place in those few hours. All her vital signs had improved so much that the resident, who had been monitoring her condition closely throughout the morning, said it was difficult to believe. Then he said she no longer needed the oxygen.

Tammy, who had been at Mary's bedside when she woke up had the woman's breakfast tray of high protein liquids changed for one with orange juice, bacon and eggs, sliced peaches, toast and marmalade, and coffee. Then she sat there and helped her eat it. But, she noticed, the woman needed very little help. Her entire condition seemed to have changed completely. She actually smiled. And although she did not act happy, she at least appeared contented. She talked with Tammy, although not about anything personal. They discussed the weather, and the hospital food, and some politics, and the fact that neither of them was interested in which teams might be in the super bowl or the NCAA basketball finals or the World Series. Neither of them mentioned anything which even suggested that they might be related.

It was a happy time for Tammy. After a few days she decided it was more than a possibility that, in this unfortunate woman, she had indeed found her mother. And she began to feel genuine love for her.

Tammy had not been scheduled to work on Christmas Day or the day after but came in anyway just to see Mary Smith. The next day, a Tuesday, she was scheduled to work. The ward was nearly full and Tammy was very busy but she spent all of her own time, even her lunch period, with the woman she had almost decided was really her mother, but she still had not mentioned to her anything that Norman had told her. Nevertheless she was making plans to take the old woman to her own apartment so she could care for her as soon as she was able to leave the hospital.

Norman had come in to see Mary on Christmas afternoon and again on Monday morning, very apprehensive that she might ask him something about his dress, which was definitely not clerical. But she never mentioned it. They too talked about the weather and the hospital food, and how nice the staff was, particularly Tammy. But she said nothing which referred to his being a priest. He told Tammy that he would be out of town for two days on job interviews. Norman had been trying for years to get a different job than the state Welfare caseworker one he had. He told her that he would be back in town on Wednesday.

One of the things which Tammy had not decided was when, or exactly what, she should tell Jill, whom she had come to think of very much as a mother. She had been able to convince herself that Jill would understand and even help Tammy make the other woman feel at home. Tammy began to believe that the woman, who at first seemed almost ancient, might, in reality, be only about the same age as Jill.

On Tuesday afternoon John came to the hospital. Although he had been in Good Samaritan many times before it was the first time he had ever visited the section in which Tammy was working. She was surprised to see him. She said, "Oh Bindah, did Uncle Norman tell you?"

He was in the midst of taking off his overcoat and he stopped and looked at her with a puzzled expression on his face. She added, "Then I guess you're not here to see my mother."

"What did you say?" John asked her, then, "Wait a minute 'til I get my coat off." He hung it over the arm of a chair. "Now what was that you asked me? I was on the sixth floor to see an old neighbor who has been operated on and I decided to stop in here and find out how you're getting along, since we didn't see you at all over the holidays. Jill said you have been working yourself to death. Now, what was that about your mother? I don't think you meant Jill since I just talked to her a day ago."

"Oh now I've done it." Tammy said. "I guess I shouldn't have said anything until I was sure. Look, let's go into the lounge and sit down. I'll tell you the whole story."

Tammy told one of the other nurses that she would be off the floor for a few minutes and she and her grandfather went into the same lounge in which she and Norman had talked on Christmas Eve. John sat down in one of the chairs and Tammy pushed an ottoman around in front of him and sat on it so she could look directly at him while she told him about Mary Smith. "Oh, Bindah," she finished, "I'm sure she is really my mother."

At first John didn't know what to say. In fact he wasn't sure whether he was at all happy to hear Tammy's story. Many questions plagued him. Was the woman really Tammy's mother, his son's lover? If so would the woman turn out to be someone Tammy would be proud of, or would Tammy be ashamed of her? Would John be able to forget what she had done to his son? And what would Jill feel after so many years of mothering Tammy?

But it was obvious that Tammy was ecstatic so John decided to keep his reservations to himself. He realized that Tammy would ignore any advice he might give her which was not based on the premise that she had indeed found her mother and should try to take care of her. And, since she was an adult, he accepted the fact that she would make up her own mind as to what would be the best thing for her to do.

Tammy, of course, understood that John, and most likely the rest of the family, would be skeptical at first. And even if they eventually accepted the woman as her mother they might always be reluctant to forgive her for what she had done. After all the only thing they really knew about her was that she had "seduced" their son and brother and uncle and abandoned his, and her own, daughter.

Tammy looked at her watch. She knew she had to get back to work. She asked John if he wanted to see the woman she was convinced was her mother. She was relieved when he said he thought it would be uncomfortable for Mary since she apparently had no idea Tammy was even considering the possibility that the two of them were related. He told her he thought Tammy should try to discover as much as she could about the woman and make certain of the facts before she told her what she was thinking.

"But what do you think about it?" she asked him.

He chuckled and said, "You know I have a rule about serious discussions like this. I try to avoid telling the other person too much. After all if I tell her everything I know then she will be smarter than me because she will know what she already knew besides what I just told her."

But Tammy just laughed. "You could never tell me everything you know in that short a time. So that would never work the way you said it would."

Then he laughed. "See? You're smarter already."

It was early New years's Eve and already it was starting to get dark. Norman parked his car on Clifton Avenue and walked around on the driveway and up the steps to the front door of the hospital. Mary Smith's remarkable recovery had elated him almost as much as it had Tammy. It had made the entire Christmas season a special one.

He stopped for a minute just inside the door to look at the small creche in the old lobby. Not one of the figures smiled, not even the infant, although the faces of all the others bore expressions which reflected deep reverence and awe at what they were witnessing as they gazed at the little Savior.

Norman glanced around at the empty lobby. There was not even a volunteer to give directions to visitors. Everyone was apparently somewhere else, either getting ready to welcome in the new year or, possibly, preparing to spend a quiet evening ignoring it. He walked on down the hallway to the elevators.

"How is our patient?" he asked Tammy as soon as he saw her upstairs.

"Oh, Uncle Norman, she is doing so well I can't tell you how good it makes me feel," his niece answered. "She is even starting to put on a little weight. She will be able to go home in a few days I think."

"So what do you intend to do then?" he wondered. "Is she going to your place for a while?"

"I don't know yet," she told him then. "I still haven't mentioned anything to her. I just don't know how she will take it. Oh, Uncle Norman, I just don't know what to do. I just don't know."

"Can we sit and talk for a few minutes?" he suggested. "I think we had better have a serious discussion."

"Yes," she agreed, "I think so too."

Tammy told one of the other nurses she would be in the lounge for a few minutes. Then they both went into the same place they had been a week earlier, just before Mary's miraculous recovery had started. The Christmas tree still spread its cheery light on the rest of the room. But now there were three other people there, sitting close together, talking quietly, obviously waiting for something to happen.

Norman dropped his black coat onto the same chair as before but he and Tammy sat in chairs on the other side of the room from the group who seemed to be watching and waiting.

"Well", he started, "what's the problem? Why haven't you told her?"

Tammy shook her head. "I just don't know how. I'm not sure if she will like it. And what if it turns out not to be real after all? Then what will I do? I was so certain that I started to really like her. Now I don't want to find out it isn't so."

Norman reached out and patted Tammy's hand but he could think of nothing to say to her.

After a few minutes Tammy said wistfully, "She seems so happy. She has taken communion nearly every day from Sister Mary from the chaplain's office."

Norman said, "Has she ever asked about—you know—about my hearing her confession? Has she ever said anything about my not wearing a collar?"

Tammy giggled. "No, " she told him. "Your secret is safe."

Norman grinned sheepishly. He said, "Well, I'm glad of that. If she found out I'm not a real priest she might resent it."

"I doubt it," Tammy tried to assure him. "I get the impression that she is very happy the way things have turned out."

Norman felt that Tammy's mood had changed now. She seemed less ill at ease. He took his hand from hers and patted her on the shoulder. "You should be very happy that what you are doing for her looks like it was the right thing to do," he told her. "I am proud of you. You may have been instrumental in saving her soul."

"But I still don't know what to do," Norman's niece admitted. "I don't know if I should tell her anything, or how I should tell her either. I just don't know."

"Sometimes these things have a way of working themselves out," Norman said, and stood up. "I wanted to see her but maybe I should wait a little longer, until we have a better idea of what she will be doing."

Just then Shirley, one of the other nurses, called to Tammy through the door, "something has happened to your favorite patient. We may be losing her."

Tammy stood up. She said, "Oh, my God, no!" and ran out into the hall with Norman behind her.

At the same time they reached Mary's room an emergency crew got there. They wheeled their cart up next to the bed. Mary did not appear to be breathing. Quickly they went to work trying to decide what they might do to help her. Another nurse came in and looked at Tammy. She said, "There is a priest visiting Mr. Clothin down the hall. Should I ask him to come in here?"

Norman saw that Tammy was about to tell her no and suspected that she was going to tell the nurse that Norman would take care of Mary. He shook his head at her before she did. Very quietly Tammy said to the other nurse, "Yes, ask him if he would give someone the last sacraments." Then she looked at her uncle and he could see a tear slip from the corner of her eye before she turned away and wiped it with the back of her hand.

It was nearly an hour later when Norman decided to leave. Mary's body had been taken away. To everyone but Tammy and her uncle the ward had returned to normal. Actually for everyone else it had never left normalcy. After all for someone to die there was not an uncommon occurrence.

Tammy shed no more than a few tears. She would later, they both knew. But now she was on duty. Norman did not want to leave because he was worried about the girl. But finally he realized that she was under control. She had to go back to work.

Norman picked up his hat and coat from the chair in the lounge and put them on. Tammy stood in front of him with her head down. Finally she looked up. She said, "I guess now I will never know."

Norman shrugged his shoulders. "No, I guess you won't," he agreed.

She smiled grimly and started to say something else, but then she just sighed deeply. Finally she said, "Oh, well."

"Tammy," Norman began, "does it matter? What is important is that you tried to do something for someone you thought was your mother. You did your best and it might have been whom you thought it was. You were prepared to take care of your mother and you would have. You could have done nothing more."

"I know," she agreed. "But, Uncle Norman, I wanted it to be her. I really did." She squeezed her eyelids together tightly to keep the tears from spilling out again and before he could say anything else she turned and walked quickly away.

Norman watched her hurry down the hall. Outside one of the doors she stopped and took a wadded up tissue from one of the pockets in her dress. She wiped her nose with the tissue and then stuffed it back into her pocket. Once again she wiped her eyes with the back of her hand. Then she smiled and disappeared into the room. Norman heard her say cheerfully, "Well, Mr. Demmons, you are looking so good today. Are you feeling that well?

As he sometimes did when there was no one else around Norman addressed his Guardian Angel, "Well Mike, I guess she's going to be okay. Actually I think she's a pretty tough kid." When, as expected, the angel didn't answer him directly Norman turned and walked toward the elevators. It was three o'clock in the morning of the first day of a brand new year.

The lobby was deserted. Norman stopped and looked again at the little Lord Jesus lying on His bed of straw in the creche. "Well, he whispered for no reason, "was she or wasn't she? I'd like to know too. But then I guess it really doesn't make any difference, does it? Tammy did the best she could for one of the least of our brothers and sisters. She might have wanted it to be her mother but she didn't know if she was or she wasn't. And, do you know, I think it wouldn't have made any difference. What do you think?"

Norman looked closely at the little figure in the shadows. He had the distinct notion that the baby was smiling.

Chapter XV

When they stopped going around he jumped down. His dad had told him that next year, when he would be five, he would be permitted to ride one of the horses that went up and down. He looked forward to that but he also remembered that he had been riding the same horse for two years. Suddenly he stood on his toes and reached up to pat the wooden muzzle. "Don't worry," he said tenderly. "Next year I'll come back and see you anyway."

From The Best Of Times, by Pat Belles

BREAKING CAMP 1987

"Well, should we tell gramps it's time to go?" asked Libby. Her mother sighed deeply, then slowly she stood up. "yes, I guess so," she said, "I think we've put it off long enough. I suppose you or your grandfather took care of the mail."

"Oh, no!" Libby answered. "I completely forgot. And the phone has already been disconnected."

Elleen put her hand on Libby's. "Well, that's okay," she assured her. "The post office should still be open. We'll just go by that way, pick up any mail there is, and tell them we're leaving for the winter. It's hardly out of the way." But just at that moment they heard someone come up onto the porch and speak to John. "Maybe that's the mailman now," Elleen said. They both ran to the door. John was holding an envelope and talking to the young man who had handed it to him. They heard John say the family was leaving for the winter. The mailman then went to his little car and got a change of address card for John to fill out but John, because of the stiffness in his right hand, gave the card to Libby to fill out and sign. When he gave the card back to the mailman John remarked how lucky they were that he had come along just at that time.

As soon as the postman had left John took a small knife from his pocket, unfolded it and slid the blade under the flap of the envelope, neatly opening it. While the others waited he pulled a paper from inside and unfolded it. Then he took his reading glasses from his shirt pocket and turning, the paper over, glanced at the bottom of the page. "It's from Ann," he told the others. Then he handed the letter and the envelope to Elleen. "Here," he said, "you read it for us."

Elleen glanced quickly over the letter then started to read from the top. "Dear Bindah and everyone, the weather is so hot here I wish we were there at the lake. I thought summer was over and it would be cooler. I'm sorry we didn't get to come down at all this year. The kids missed seeing all of you but Fritz especially looks forward to seeing Ginny and Pat since the three of them are so close to the same age. Just imagine, he will be in the second grade this year. It seems odd that Pat will only be in kindergarten. They are so nearly the same size and Pat always seems so smart for his age. I guess that's it mostly. Anyway I miss everyone too. One of the best things about my marrying Bill was that I inherited a big family.

"Now comes the good and the bad news I guess. The reason Bill isn't writing this is he is at Beldsun's main office with his boss and his boss's boss. He is being promoted. We were pretty sure that this was going to happen but not absolutely sure. That is why he hasn't told anyone (except I think he did mention it to Libby's husband George the last time they were together. But he asked George not to tell anyone because he didn't want the whole family to be disappointed if it didn't go through). He is very excited about this because he will be an assistant manager in a big branch office and it will be a big raise. I won't say that money has been a big problem for us (I mean the shortage of it) but sometimes I have wondered if we might not be able to pay a bill here or there. But God has always provided. I guess He doesn't want me to have to go to work any more than Bill does.

"Now the bad part. The new job is out on the West coast, near San Diego. They tell us it is really nice, a nice place to live and everything. But it is so far from the family. And the kids (except for Fritz) have so many friends here. We tell them they will make new ones, but we both know it isn't the same. To tell you the truth Bill and I both talked about turning this down but he was afraid to. Beldsun is a good company to work for but not many people leave so he can't expect many vacancies at the top. And they really wanted him to do it. Now we have to get out there and find a place near a church to live so we can get the kids registered in the school.

"I know this is sudden and we won't have time to say goodbye to everyone. But we are hoping everyone will come out to visit us. Maybe if everyone comes out we can rent a bus and go to Disneyland. When we told Grandma O'Maury (Jill) about it she at first said she might move out there too. But there is Tammy to think of. Now that Tammy knows she doesn't have Ginny anymore Jill is the closest one she has to a mother. Of course she has all the rest of you too.

"The nearer it gets to the time we have to leave the worse I am going to feel. Bill will feel bad too but he has his job and this is all so exciting to him, learning it all, it will take a while for him to realize how far away we will be. We'll probably be flying back here whenever we can. Who knows, you may see more of us now than you used to.

"Anyway remember us in your prayers. It would be terrible if this didn't work out for us. Oh, but it will I know. Love, Ann".

When Elleen read the last line she folded the paper and put it back into the envelope. She noticed that her father took a handkerchief from his back pocket and wiped both of his eyes. She knew that it would sadden him to realize that another grandson and his wife, and three of his great grandchildren would be going so far away. It was especially painful for him because of the way the twins had died. He had never been able to get over that even though it had happened nearly thirty five years ago. Elleen watched him as he looked out across the road. She knew he was looking at the familiar things around him and thinking about all the things which had happened to him since he and his parents had started spending their summers near Indian Lake. She could see him adding up all the good things that had happened to him over the years. She wondered how he counted the things that had happened that were not so happy. Did he subtract them from the other things and try to come up with a balance? Whatever it was he always seemed to smile in the end.

And he didn't disappoint her this time either. Elleen saw him look at her grandchildren, Ginny and Pat, and smile broadly, and she understood that he had resolved to concentrate on what he still had rather than what he had lost over the years.

"Well, young fellow," he said to Pat, "are we ready to leave?"

"No," answered the boy, and his great grandfather laughed.

"We're going to stop on the way and eat. You could get a hamburger." Pat thought that over before answering.

"Can I have a hot dog, Bindah?" he asked.

"You can have a gourmet hot dog," John assured him. "We'll stop at Bernie's. And I think I'll put my teeth in and have a steak sandwich."

At this Ginny, who had been listening, giggled. "You already have your teeth in," she pointed out.

And John said, acting surprised, "Say, you're right. I do."

And all three of them laughed.

* * *

John sat in the back between the two little ones. Libby drove and Elleen sat next to her. As they pulled away John closed his eyes and leaned back in the seat. Pat and Ginny both stared out the windows, sorry to leave but eager to get home and see the friends they had not seen for several weeks, and, in fact, had not spent a great deal of time with for the entire summer.

Elleen noticed that John had closed his eyes. "All three of them will be asleep before we get to Bernie's," she said quietly to her daughter. They both laughed. Then she added, quieter still, "Look. Pop's smiling. I wonder what he's dreaming about."

The trees and other shrubbery moved swiftly past the window. The scenery was all so familiar to John, and then he saw Kate standing on the side of the road. It was a strange thing to see because the car kept moving but they didn't leave Kate behind. She stayed there, right outside the window.

He would like to have talked to her but he knew that was not possible; if he tried to say anything to her she would disappear. He could only look.

She was just as beautiful as on the day they had met. Then he noticed someone else, another woman almost her age, standing next to her and talking with her. It was Moni. He had never thought about the fact that they might know each other. He wondered how they would get along because they weren't really very much alike. But where they were that probably didn't matter much.

Standing behind them was a young man, tall and slender, with dark hair whom John didn't recognize. Perhaps he was someone whose picture John had seen among the mementos left the family by his great grandmother O'Maury. He wondered what had happened to them. Then the name Krag suddenly popped into his mind but that was all.

He wondered what the two women might be talking about. He guessed it could be that they were talking about him. He thought it was really too bad he wasn't able to hear them. He really would like to have known what they were saying.

THE END

Epilogue

At Indian Lake it is not quite winter, not even December yet; and the water in the lake is not frozen.

Still the waves seem somewhat lethargic. They reach the shore so very slowly. Perhaps they will be frozen soon.

The beach at the end of the path that leads from the campground is invisible. It's covered with an inch or so of early snow so that one can't see it. This new snow sparkles in the sunlight. It would be terrible to walk on it and leave footprints.

The old bench bears a covering of snow too. It looks so different now, all white. The corners, the hard lines, and the cracks, are all hidden by the soft white blanket.

On the bench the snow is not perfect; a bird has walked across it. The small footprints start at one end and stop at the other. The bird that made them is gone and it is not possible to tell where it came from, or where it went. It might have been rather rare. Or it might have been just one of the common birds that are all around the lake. The average observer cannot tell.

Soon something will come and walk on the snow on the beach and alter the surface there too.

It can't be helped.

Anyway, this won't be the last snow.

It will snow again, perhaps tonight.

Things never seem to stop completely.

About the Author

Ted J. McGoron was born in Cincinnati the year before the "great Depression" started. He majored in English at Xavier University. He is an army veteran of the Korean war. He has written two other books, one on the development of computers and the other a humorous account of his own radical prostatectomy.